STEVEN CONTE's debut novel, *The Zookeeper's War*, won the inaugural Australian Prime Minister's Literary Award for Fiction. It was also shortlisted for the 2008 Commonwealth Writers' Prize for Best First Book and for the 2007 Christina Stead Award for Fiction. The novel was published in the UK and Ireland and translated into Spanish.

For more information visit
stevenconte.com

ALSO BY STEVEN CONTE

The Zookeeper's War

The Tolstoy Estate

Steven Conte

FOURTH ESTATE

Fourth Estate
An imprint of HarperCollins*Publishers*

HarperCollins*Publishers*
Australia • Brazil • Canada • France • Germany • Holland • Hungary
India • Italy • Japan • Mexico • New Zealand • Poland • Spain • Sweden
Switzerland • United Kingdom • United States of America

First published in Australia in 2020
by HarperCollins*Publishers* Australia Pty Limited
Level 13, 201 Elizabeth Street, Sydney NSW 2000
ABN 36 009 913 517
harpercollins.com.au

A catalogue record for this book is available from the National Library of Australia.

ISBN 978 1 4607 5882 3 (paperback)
ISBN 978 1 4607 1257 3 (ebook)
ISBN 978 1 4607 8426 6 (audiobook)

Cover design by Catherine Casalino
Cover image: landscape © Lee Avison / Trevillion Images; soldier © CollaborationJS
/ Trevillion Images
Author photograph by Joanne O'Keefe
Typeset in Bembo Std by Kelli Lonergan
Printed and bound in Australia by McPherson's Printing Group
The papers used by HarperCollins in the manufacture of this book are a natural,
recyclable product made from wood grown in sustainable plantation forests. The fibre
source and manufacturing processes meet recognised international environmental
standards, and carry certification.

For my mother, Rosemary, and my sister, Eira.

ONE

'Captain?' Winkel said. 'You should put on your helmet.'

Paul Bauer, aged forty, an army surgeon, kept his eyes shut. The corporal's concern for him was touching, but after twenty-six hours spent operating under canvas, followed by eleven more of sabotaged sleep — at first near an active artillery battery, then sitting in the cabin of a pitching lorry — he hardly cared whether he lived or died. The lorry heaved and he strained not to give himself away by bracing against the dashboard.

'He's sleeping,' Pflieger said.

'Then wake him,' replied Winkel.

'He wouldn't thank me for that.'

'This forest … you should wake him.'

'You wake him, why don't you?'

'Pflieger, I'm driving,' Winkel said. 'You're sitting beside him.'

The lorry reared again, smacking Bauer's temple on the window frame. It was Pflieger who swore. 'Hey, Sepp, you trying to kill us?'

'*Der Schlamm*,' Winkel said, 'the mud' – oozing loathing and affront.

'Just don't roll the fucker,' Pflieger said. 'Drowning in some Russian ditch, there'd be no glory in that.'

The lorry bucked, halted, then edged onwards again, its speed set by the slowest of the seventeen vehicles in the convoy. Their own was next to last. For a while no one spoke. A sorrowing engine, shifting gears, rain battering the roof. The labouring of wiper blades.

Pflieger said, 'It's getting late.'

'I know,' Winkel said.

'We should have stopped at that village.'

'Says you.'

'Says me. And why not me?'

'The great tactician.'

Sounding wounded, Pflieger said, 'I'm not talking tactics, Sepp, just common sense.'

'Heard of perseverance?'

'I only meant that soon it'll be getting dark.'

A vicious lurch caught Bauer unawares, forcing him to grip the dashboard for support. He could no longer pretend to be asleep.

'Sir, welcome back,' Winkel said. 'Slept well?'

Bauer opened his eyes and made out, between strokes of the wiper blades, the ambulance in front of them, its tail wagging in the mud, though it was travelling barely faster than walking pace. Autumn rains and the passage of more than sixty tanks had churned the road into a striated bog. Beside it there were low embankments sliced up where wagons, lorries and tanks had tried but failed to find firmer ground. Pine forest on both flanks. A gash of sky weeping rain. Three weeks earlier, on the edge of a forest like this one, a Soviet sniper had shot and killed Dieter Clemens, Bauer's closest friend in the battalion and its best anaesthetist.

Winkel said, 'I was just saying you should put on your helmet.'

'But not Pflieger?'

'Sir, Pflieger is an idiot.'

'Hey,' Pflieger said. 'I'm just sick of the weight of it.'

'And there's your hair loss,' Winkel said.

Pflieger patted his head. At twenty-six, and still acne-prone, he was rapidly balding. 'Well, it's possible, isn't it? Sir, what do you think? You're a doctor.'

'I think the corporal is right,' Bauer said, putting his own helmet on. 'We should play it safe.'

Pflieger smirked, which gave him a witless expression, his tongue protruding a little from between his teeth. 'A bit late for that,' he said, but put on his helmet all the same. Another officer might have reprimanded him for the comment, but Bauer was used to making allowances for Pflieger, who in the French campaign had suffered a head wound that hadn't so much changed his personality as denuded it, exposing a simple and essentially good-natured man who was no longer capable of censoring his speech. In this instance Bauer happened to agree with him: it *was* a bit late, five months into Operation Barbarossa, to be fretting about safety, personal or otherwise. Safety was hardly the point. If the Greatest Warlord of All Time had had any regard for human life, he would not have provoked a contest whose savagery made France seem in retrospect like a war of flowers.

Bauer shivered, rewound his scarf and turned up the collar of his greatcoat, reached into it for cigarettes and offered one to Pflieger, who accepted, and another to Winkel, who refused. Winkel was fighting with the steering wheel, a bantam-weight jabbing lefts and rights. 'I could light it for you,' Bauer offered.

'No thank you, sir. I've given them up.'

'Oh?'

'Last week.'

'Your health?'

'Not exactly.'

'He's worried they'll stunt his growth,' Pflieger said.

'Ha, ha,' said Winkel, the smallest man in the battalion. To reach the lorry's pedals with greater ease he drove with a bedroll between his back and the seat.

'So why give them up?' Bauer asked. 'To trade?'

'It was Lieutenant Hirsch who suggested it, sir.'

'The lieutenant?' Bauer asked, aware of the dispiriting effect the dentist's name had on him, an effect more pronounced since Hirsch's appointment as his anaesthetist, filling the gap left by Dieter's death.

'My teeth were staining,' Winkel said. 'Lieutenant Hirsch suggested I give up cigarettes.'

'Good advice, I'm sure,' Bauer said and lit up, unintentionally making Pflieger laugh, a gasping racket that was generally funnier than its cause. Bauer smiled and took a life-giving lungful of smoke.

Still chuckling, Pflieger made a show of nudging Winkel in the ribs. 'Can't let bad teeth spoil your chances with the ladies, eh?'

4

The corporal flung a few more punches with the steering wheel but said nothing. Winkel's vanity about his personal appearance – his hair cream and toothpicks, his ear- and nostril-plucking – was a cherished source of humour among his comrades, an expression of relief at having found a flaw in a man they otherwise held in lofty regard, Bauer as much if not more than the rest. He and Winkel were a similar age and shared a bond, seldom discussed but never far from Bauer's mind, of having both lost a wife less than eighteen months before the war, Bauer's to illness, Winkel's in a traffic accident. Neither had children.

For several minutes all three men were silent. Rain rattled on the roof and Bauer grew drowsy.

'This fucking mud!' Pflieger said.

Bauer muttered, 'Amen.'

Formed from the Russian dust on which they and their engines had choked throughout the summer, the mud weighed on boots and hoofs and wheels, bringing an army of almost four million men to a near standstill along a two-thousand-kilometre front. *Rasputitza* the Russians called the autumn rainy season – the Time of No Roads – a term Bauer had learned three weeks earlier from an elderly peasant woman. His Russian was mediocre, but in a brief conversation with a hostile *babushka* he had grasped what the High Command, with Abwehr spies and Russian linguists at its disposal, had apparently overlooked: in October the roads essential to the German strategy were impassable *by definition*. For half an hour after understanding this he'd been too enraged to speak. From the start of the war he'd been impatient for its end and, because the Wehrmacht had been triumphing on every front, a German victory had seemed like the fastest way to peace. True, the conduct of some of his countrymen in Russia was criminal – at times depraved – but the killing would end when the war did, he'd reasoned, and afterwards it was possible that the gangsters in power in Berlin would moderate their policies or even wither away. That, at least, had been his thinking before his talk with the *babushka*. Since then he had suspected that the Greatest Warlord of All Time was no more than a jumped-up gambler, that the remaining two months of 1941 would not deliver victory, and that defeating the Soviets might in fact take years, assuming it was possible at all. And if it wasn't? In his tiredness he hallucinated the walls of the forest as cliffs of water parted for the Israelites, himself a soldier in the Pharaoh's army squelching across the seabed in pursuit.

They breasted a rise then gently descended, tracking rainwater flowing from one wheel rut to another. Raindrops boiled in the hoofprints of draught horses. From the first it had troubled Bauer that the Soviet forces were apparently better motorised than the Wehrmacht, yet for the most part the horse-drawn supplies of the 3rd Panzer division had kept pace with its tanks, which had been hampered not only by the state of the roads but also by a shortage of fuel – in Bauer's view, another grave operational failing.

Haltingly, a curve brought the whole convoy into view, and shortly afterwards a motorcycle scout appeared at the head of the column and flagged down the lead vehicle, a lorry under the command of Sergeant Major Norbert Ritter, leader of the company's security detail and, for last two months, acting quartermaster. One by one the trailing vehicles drew to a halt.

Pflieger groaned. 'What now?'

As if to mimic the noise of the rain on the roof, Winkel started tapping on the steering wheel, an annoying sound, though to ask him to stop would have been unkind, as it was not in his nature to be still. Bauer had only rarely witnessed the corporal sleeping, and even then Winkel had fidgeted, perhaps dreaming of stripping an engine or staunching a wound.

A minute or two went by and the convoy started moving again, only to halt a few hundred metres further on; in the distance Bauer saw Ritter's security detail piling out of the lead lorry. In an expansive interpretation of Article 8(1) of the Geneva Convention (weapons permitted to medical corpsmen) several were carrying machine pistols, and one man a medium machine gun, experience having shown that red cross insignia on vehicles and armbands offered scant protection in the Soviet Union.

'Fuck it,' Pflieger said, 'it's going to get dark.'

'Karl, language,' Winkel said. 'There's an officer present.'

Pflieger apologised, sucked his cigarette until the tip came close to his lips, dropped the stub and ground it under his heel. 'Oh shit, here comes Ehrlich.'

Corporal Egon Ehrlich was trekking rearwards, pausing at each vehicle to speak with its driver. The mud was forcing him to use a ponderous, high-stepping gait that Bauer associated with neurological injury, and it was a full five minutes before he reached them. Only slightly taller than Winkel, Ehrlich's mud-enlarged boots made him look like a cartoon figure – some sharp-faced relative of Mickey Mouse perhaps, wearing a helmet and a shelter sheet, each dripping with rain. He stepped onto the running board and Winkel wound down his window. 'What's up?'

'A blown culvert. We're laying down some logs. Sepp, get your rifle and report to Ritter. Pflieger —'

'Guard the lorry?'

'Get a shovel and go with Sepp.'

'But I've only just got dry.'

'Don't argue, just do it,' Ehrlich ordered. Hanging off the door with one hand he at last got around to saluting with the other, though in a sloppy style unnatural to him.

'Sir.'

'Corporal.'

Ehrlich stepped off the running board and disappeared towards the rear. Why the man disliked him Bauer was unsure. Not envy of his rank, he thought, though they were about the same age and had similar backgrounds, having both grown up on small farms. No, more likely Ehrlich sensed that he, Bauer, cared too little for the rigmarole of rank. How and when and even if a man saluted didn't bother Bauer, and for Ehrlich this possibly made the business of subordination that much harder to bear.

'Why do I have to dig?' Pflieger asked, pulling his shelter sheet from his kit.

Winkel took his rifle from the rack he'd designed and fitted to the back of the cabin. 'So you don't have to shoot? Perhaps the sergeant wants to save you from moral distress.'

'You think so?'

'Why not? He's thoughtful that way.'

Bauer wished them luck and they clambered out. Pflieger unhooked a shovel from the side of the lorry and the two men started forward, a pair of puppets jerking through the mud, Pflieger lanky and a full head taller than Winkel.

At last, a chance to sleep. A blanket would have been welcome but there were none inside the cabin, and so making do with his greatcoat, Bauer lay across the seat, resting his head on his folded scarf. The rain was easing now, the sound of it on the roof reminding him of rainfall on the slate-tiled farmhouse of his childhood, of lying in bed beneath an eiderdown in the room he had shared with Jürgen, his brother – long dead now, victim of a botched amputation at Verdun.

A rap on the window made him start. 'Hey, Bauer!'

Molineux. Bauer drew an arm across his helmet. 'I'm trying to sleep.'

'Bah! You insomniacs are your own worst enemies.'

'Go away.'

'Exercise! You need exercise!'

'For Christ's sake, it's raining.'

'No longer. Listen.'

It was true, the rain had stopped.

'Open your window.'

Bauer sat up, cursing, and unwound the rain-speckled window, revealing the large and ruddy face of Hermann Molineux. Hooded eyes. A sardonic grin.

'I was almost sleeping,' Bauer said.

'Let's go for a stroll.'

'You're at war with sleep, aren't you?'

'Nonsense, I'm its ally,' Molineux said, cold air making vapour of his breath.

'Some psychological trauma you've sustained from doing anaesthesia.'

'Now, now, let's have none of that Jewish claptrap here. You disappoint me, Bauer. You're too much with your thoughts. Stretch your legs. Get your arteries pumping.'

'I thought you hated exercise,' Bauer said.

'You must be thinking of another, more slovenly man. Fresh air, the scent of pine, bullets ruffling my hair – I'm wild for it.'

'My socks are dry,' Bauer said. 'I don't plan to wet them again.'

'Our billet's not far off and you can change them there. Ehrlich claims we're being put up in style – B Company has found us a stately home no less.'

'Unburned?'

'*Virgo intacta* apparently. The rain perhaps. Some poor Ivan will be getting shot for his carelessness. The point is, before long we'll be drinking vodka by an open fire, admiring some sweet little Galinka or Innushka pegging out our laundered uniforms.'

Bauer sighed and got his shelter sheet.

'So you're coming then?'

'A man as far gone in delusion as you needs supervision.'

'Excellent, excellent,' Molineux said, and stepped off the running board.

Bauer got out and immediately sank boot-deep into the mud. 'A stroll?'

'A slog, a stomp – call it what you will. I couldn't tolerate being stuck in that tin can a moment longer.'

10

'At least, not without an audience,' Bauer said, gesturing at the corpsmen from Molineux's lorry, who had taken up defensive positions by the road.

The first few steps convinced Bauer he'd made a mistake: the mud gave way to his boots easily but then clung on with freakish strength. He pictured corpses clasping him, trying to drag him underground, and to dispel the image strode energetically onwards, so that soon his quadriceps were aching. He was overheating and unbuttoned his greatcoat, though his fingers were cold and water chilled his toes. He felt a fool to have come. Molineux was panting. His face had reddened and in places was starting to go purple. He was a big man, older than Bauer and out of shape, almost portly – proof of his skill at scrounging alcohol and his wife's devotion to sending him calorific foods. At the lead lorry Bauer asked him if he'd like a rest, but in reply he shook his head and pointed to his goal: a stream bisecting the road, alongside it fifty or more of the men felling and trimming pines into logs. Dusk was about an hour away, but beneath the dripping trees twilight had already fallen.

At the blown culvert Sergeant Major Ritter, a big bull-necked man, was overseeing the construction of a rudimentary bridge, delivering orders in a *Berlinisch* accent, his larynx guttural with damage from some long-ago brawl. Nearby stood the battalion's commanding officer and head surgeon, Lieutenant Colonel Julius Metz, one knee jouncing as if to speed up the work. The stream was in full spate and so noisy that at first Metz failed to notice their arrival. Seeing Molineux, he frowned. 'Captain, you're out of condition. Hardly a good example to set for the men, now, is it?'

Molineux nodded, too winded to speak.

Metz continued, 'There are two types of men in this world: those for whom their body is a temple, and those who treat it as a slum. As a medical man, Molineux, you ought to know better.'

Still gasping, Molineux said, 'Sir, what can I say?' He gestured at his boots. 'Feet of clay, sir, feet of clay.'

Metz, who neither drank nor smoked, was at the age of fifty-two in excellent shape, a tall man with a long face that Bauer supposed women of a certain age might find handsome if stern: grey eyebrows, a narrow nose and a cleft chin that Molineux had once pointed out to Bauer resembled buttocks, right down to its bristled crease, an image Bauer had since tried in vain to unremember.

'And where's your helmet?' Metz demanded. 'Didn't I expressly order all officers to wear helmets in the field?'

'Apologies, sir, I forgot.'

'I can't afford to lose another anaesthetist.' He turned to Ehrlich. 'Corporal, give the captain your helmet.'

'Yes, sir,' Ehrlich said, and swiftly obeyed, exposing a head as narrow as his face was sharp. Molineux thanked him, tried on the helmet, took it off again and was loosening its straps when the sound of yelling drew Bauer's attention upstream. Two corpsmen had lost a log in the current, sending it bucking and spearing at the bridge.

'For God's *sake*,' Metz yelled as the log struck home. Swiftly it swung about, forming a dam and then a weir, and although several corpsmen scrambled to retrieve it, they were too late. The bridge gave way.

Metz screamed an obscenity – for him a sign of great rage – only to fall silent, as they all did, at the noise of an engine over-revving in the forest. Bauer pictured a T-34, maybe several, crashing through the trees, but while many of his comrades flung themselves into the muck he stayed standing, curiously unafraid. Norbert Ritter, a brutish man but a brave one, had snatched a rifle and was plodding off towards the danger, palsy-footed with mud, quickly followed by the men of his security detail. Seconds later, a lone Soviet lorry emerged in front of them from the forest. It braked and Ritter and his men closed in, their weapons trained on the cabin. The tarpaulin-sheeted tray was empty, yelled one of the corpsmen. Then the driver's door opened and a young soldier emerged, thrust his hands in the air and stepped down into the mud. He was unarmed. Straight dark hair topped with a brown forage cap. A blanched face. His body quaking. More of Ritter's men arrived and a second Russian, an officer, clambered out of the lorry. He was older, short and paunchy, bare-headed and bald. He frowned at the men pointing rifles at him, gazed skyward, drew a pistol and shot himself above the ear.

TWO

Winkel was shaking him through the half-open passenger door. 'Sir, we're here.'

Nighttime. Wind and rain. The distant thudding of artillery. Bauer groaned. 'What time is it?'

Winkel looked at his watch. '21:05.'

'That late?'

'*Der Schlamm.*'

'Of course, the mud. Why did I ask.'

'I've unloaded your gear, sir. And scouted for rooms.'

'Bless you, Sepp.'

'But the lieutenant colonel …'

'Is asking to see me?'

'Correct.'

Bauer took off his helmet and put on his officer's cap. 'You'd better show me the way.'

He got out of the lorry, his whole body aching – a foretaste of old age, he supposed, if he lived that long. Beneath his boots was the welcome sensation of gravel, on his face a fusillade of sleet. In the beams of ambulance headlights he made out a double-storey building, which though large was not quite the mansion Molineux had led him to expect. A forecourt with an oval drive. Leafless birches flailing in the wind. On the building's front porch he exchanged a salute with a sentry then followed Winkel into a vestibule that was crammed on one side with furniture. Overhead there were lights on – evidently B Company had got a generator running. A pair of corpsmen came in after them carrying one of the unit's trestle tables, followed by the radio operator with his metal suitcases. Directly ahead, beside a pair of glassed internal doors, Molineux was leaning over a wooden cabinet and writing in what appeared to be a visitors' book. He turned and held out a pencil. 'Bauer, be the second to commemorate our arrival. Write something worthy.'

Bauer took the pencil. 'Worthy? Why?'

Molineux cleared his throat and spread his arms. 'Because A Company, medical battalion, 3rd Panzer division is now in possession of a Russian national shrine: the ancestral estate of Count Leo Tolstoy.'

Bauer blinked. Molineux was an incorrigible prankster. 'You're joking, aren't you?'

'Would I debase such a moment with mockery?' He opened the cabinet, revealing shelves stacked with leaflets, and handed one to Bauer. 'Here, proof.' Printed in Russian on poor-quality paper was a guide welcoming visitors to Yasnaya Polyana, the National Memorial and Museum-Estate of Lev Nikolayevich Tolstoy – the 'Leo', Bauer recalled, was a Germanisation – author of the 'immortal works of literature' *War and Peace* (*Voyna i mir*) and *Anna Karenina*, both composed 'in this very house'. On its reverse side was a basic map of the estate.

Molineux grinned. 'And you had the insolence to doubt me.'

Bauer was thunderstruck. In the middle of the last war, as a youth of fifteen, he had read *War and Peace* in translation, a six-week undertaking that had inspired a decade-long fascination not only with the novels of Tolstoy but also with those of Dostoyevsky, Turgenev, Lermontov, Gogol. Hoping to read them in the original, he had tried to learn Russian, an effort ultimately undone by the demands of his surgical training, along with what he had come to recognise as his own wearying of the intensities of the Russian soul – as portrayed, at least, in nineteenth-century fiction – particularly in the wake of his wife Clara's diagnosis.

'Sir, the lieutenant colonel?' Winkel said.

Bauer pocketed the leaflet. 'Of course.'

'First the visitors' book,' Molineux said. 'Your stab at immortality.'

Bauer examined the book. All the entries before Molineux's were written in Russian – the most recent by Red Army soldiers who had recorded their ranks as well as their names, though not the units to which they belonged. Molineux's signature had spilled over the lines designed to contain it. *Veni, vidi, vici*, he'd added in the space assigned for comments.

Molineux said, 'I know what you're thinking: that our own Julius won't approve.'

'Not of us signing before he has, no.'

'Don't be such a coward. The race goes to the swift.'

Bauer raised the pencil but hesitated.

Winkel said, 'Sir, the lieutenant colonel wanted to see you straight away.'

'Hurry up and write,' Molineux said, 'or Metz will have you shot.'

Bauer put down the pencil. 'Later maybe.'

'Oh, come on,' Molineux said, 'that was just my little joke.'

'It's not Metz.'

'Then what?'

'Call it lack of inspiration.'

'In writing, first thoughts are best,' said Molineux. 'The same as in speech.'

In camp at Oryol, days before his death to a sniper, Dieter Clemens had raised the near treasonous topic of whether Operation Barbarossa in any way resembled Napoleon's invasion of Russia, a conversation that had reminded Bauer of his precociously early but, as it turned out, once-only reading of *War and Peace*. To now arrive at the house in which the novel had been written felt deeply uncanny, an emotion that only logic could dispel.

'I should go and see Metz,' he said.

'As should I. Thanks to your dithering he'll have us both court-martialled.'

Winkel led them through a pair of glass-panelled doors into a small reception hall. Polished floorboards, a wooden staircase, off-white walls devoid of decoration. A door on the left led into a drawing room that was empty of furniture apart from a grand piano, around which stood Metz, his orderly Egon Ehrlich and the unit's three subalterns. On the lid of the piano there were maps and papers, logbooks and binoculars. All of the men were muddied, even Metz. 'Where's the major?' Metz asked.

'Settling in upstairs, sir,' Winkel said.

'Bedding down Bertha, I bet,' Molineux said.

'Get him down here immediately,' Metz said.

'Yes, sir,' Winkel replied, and hurried away.

The largest map on the piano was also the most detailed. Molineux asked where they were on it; Metz tapped at the midpoint of a road that ran roughly south to north.

'And the enemy?' Molineux asked.

'At Tula,' Metz said, pointing to the burr of a city on the map's northern edge. 'Population four hundred thousand.'

Before Bauer could draw nearer for a closer view, Volker Hirsch appeared at his side and asked in a whisper if he could have a word.

'Of course,' Bauer said, stepping away from the piano. 'What about?'

Hirsch hesitated. At twenty-four he was a qualified dentist but shyer than the average child. Tall but stooped. Not plump so much as softly muscled. Ginger hair, a freckled face, round spectacles. 'That officer,' he began, 'the Soviet one?'

'Who shot himself?' Bauer asked. He hadn't even noticed Hirsch's presence at the culvert.

'Yes, him.'

'A commissar,' Bauer said, anticipating the question. 'Captured political officers are being executed,' he went on, speaking flatly of the order that he and Dieter Clemens had discussed with so much angst. 'He would have known that.'

'We would have shot him?' Hirsch asked.

'Us? I think not. Though who can say? We wouldn't have lacked for volunteers,' he went on, sounding angrier than he'd meant to. Hirsch hardly seemed like a fanatic, but his generation had been drilled in obedience and it paid to be cautious around them. 'If not us, the next unit along. Failing that, the SS or the Reich Commissariat. I'd like to think that in his position I'd have done the same.'

Hirsch fingered his collar. 'You saw the puff?'

'The puff? From the pistol, you mean?'

'Not the discharge. From his mouth.'

'I don't think so,' said Bauer. 'Vapour?'

'The bullet killed him and the puff left his mouth,' Hirsch said. 'As if ...'

'As if what?'

'Oh, I don't know,' Hirsch said. 'As if his spirit was leaving his body.'

'That would have been vapour,' Bauer said.

At this moment Winkel re-entered the room, followed by Siegfried Weidemann, the battalion's second in command to Metz, as well as its chief physician. He caught sight of the piano and paused.

'Why, Major,' Metz sneered, 'thank you so much for coming.'

Weidemann, sixty, dignified, snowy-haired, greeted Metz with a nod but was still eyeing the piano. He came over, raised the fall board and ran through a scale. 'Lovely,' he said, and stroked the keys. 'A Bechstein. How remarkable.'

'Your attention, Major,' Metz said. Weidemann turned to him, compelled by fused vertebrae in his neck to pivot on his heels, an odd constraint for a man who reminded Bauer of an owl, the effect of winged, white eyebrows. 'I was just explaining that the enemy has withdrawn to Tula,' Metz went

19

on, 'forming a salient there – a protuberance, if you will – that's ripe for excision.'

'Oh very good, sir,' Molineux said.

'In the meantime we have seized a remarkable prize,' Metz said. Here he slapped the piano, leaving Bauer momentarily confused. 'Corporal, those leaflets.'

Ehrlich handed out copies of the guide that Bauer already had in his pocket. On the reverse side the estate's buildings and other features of note were numbered in a legend: an ornamental entrance on the Chern to Tula road; three major and several minor buildings scattered more or less evenly between gardens, orchards and ponds. Across a band of woodland on what appeared to be a ridge at the rear, the dotted line of a trail led to a spot marked as Tolstoy's grave.

'We are here,' Metz said, pointing to a building identified as the Tolstoy House. Bauer looked around the empty drawing room. Leo Tolstoy walked here, he realised, ate and drank and no doubt read. He recalled a photograph he'd seen of the writer in old age, heavily bearded, his eyes piercing, dressed in a peasant's tunic, baggy trousers and high leather boots – the aristocrat turned sage, straying as if by accident into the twentieth century.

Metz said, 'This is not only an ideal site for a field hospital but also, when the front moves on, a base hospital. There's no saying whether Tula will have suitable structures.'

'Or any structures at all,' Molineux said, cocking an ear to the sound of the guns, audible even indoors.

'Quite,' Metz said. 'Accordingly, I've already ordered Sergeant Major Ritter to post guards on all the major buildings.'

'But, sir, surely that's unnecessary,' Bauer said.

'Because?'

'Because the Soviets must have spared this place deliberately.'

'It's a national shrine,' Molineux added.

'Ritter's men could perform other tasks,' Bauer said. Losses from combat, accident and illness, while not as severe as those of a frontline unit, had placed the battalion under pressure, forcing some men into roles for which they were ill-suited, notably their dentist taking over as an anaesthetist. Meanwhile Ritter, a born fighter, had little patience for his duties as quartermaster.

'It's not for me to divine the enemy's motives,' Metz said. 'They've blundered and I won't let them rectify their error by having partisans fire the buildings. Now, may I go on?'

Bauer nodded, feeling intensely weary. Quite possibly Metz was right. In war, who could really distinguish accident from intent?

C Company would remain in Chern, Metz announced, and from there evacuate casualties to Oryol. Meanwhile B Company had gone ahead to establish a dressing station in the village of Malevka, just south of Tula. Divisional headquarters had reported fierce fighting there – the sound of heavy guns was proof enough of that – and tomorrow casualties were sure to arrive. Accordingly, operating theatres would be set up overnight in the building Metz had selected for a hospital. Here he pointed on the map to a long narrow structure about three hundred metres away, the Volkonsky House. Officers would be housed in the Tolstoy House; enlisted men in the third of the estate's main buildings, which the legend identified as the

Kusminsky Wing. Metz spoke briskly and cogently, apparently unaffected by the strains of the past two days. Bauer couldn't say the same for himself, and as Metz moved on to logistical matters his attention strayed. On the walls there were pale rectangular shadows where paintings must have recently hung, though to judge by the piano and the furniture in the vestibule the evacuation of the house's contents was incomplete. *Tolstoy's house*, he reminded himself.

Metz finished his briefing and invited questions. Molineux raised a hand. 'Will there be dinner tonight?'

'Field rations,' Metz said. 'The kitchen can wait.'

Molineux groaned. 'Couldn't Pabst whip us up something special, sir?'

'We eat the same food as the men, Captain. You know that. Show some fortitude, won't you, and if that doesn't work try contemplating the conditions that B Company is likely to be dining in tonight.'

Weidemann asked if there was a usable airfield nearby, and Metz was beginning his reply when a door at the far end of the room swung open and a woman entered, startling all of them, particularly Metz, who drew his P38 and levelled it at her. The intruder looked unperturbed. She was neither young nor old. A small mouth, large eyes. A triangular face. She was wearing spectacles, her auburn hair pulled back in a bun.

'*Ruki vverkh!*' Metz barked at her, making upwards jerking motions with his pistol, but though the woman complied and raised her hands she was lackadaisical about it. She wore a quilted jacket, a knee-length skirt, woollen stockings and a pair of tan-coloured brogues – not a stylish outfit but not that of a manual worker either. In Russian she demanded to know which of them was in charge.

'Isn't it obvious?' Metz said when Bauer translated. 'Corporal, search her for weapons,' he said, and Ehrlich patted her down – avidly, a rat inspecting a cheese.

'I think Egon might need some help, sir,' Molineux said.

'Captain, spare me the humour,' Metz said. 'Now is not the time. Bauer, ask her what she's doing here. And how she got in. Ehrlich, that's enough. She's clearly unarmed.'

Bauer stepped forward. The woman's spectacles gave her a scholarly air, though behind them her large eyes were focused and shrewd. Haltingly, he introduced himself in Russian and asked the woman her name, speaking slowly to avoid errors, aware of his fatigue.

'*Ty perevodchik?*' she asked. 'You're the *interpreter*?'

Metz demanded to know what she'd said.

'I am a surgeon,' Bauer explained to her.

The woman said something too quick for him to catch, saw his puzzled expression and repeated, 'You're a butcher ...'

He stared at her, too tired to think of a riposte.

'Of Russian,' she said.

'Oh,' he said. 'But there is only me. We are doctors,' he went on, 'a field medical unit.'

'Savages,' she said, as if stating a self-evident truth.

'Bauer, she's talking over you,' Metz said. 'Don't listen, command!'

The woman turned to Metz and spoke at him in Russian, so rapidly that Bauer had to ask her to slow down. She complied, her tone satirically plodding. Their men had done something

23

to the buildings, she said. Damaged them, Bauer guessed. He caught the words *doors* and *walls*.

'Where was this?' he asked.

'Many places.'

'Here?'

'My own room.'

'Upstairs?'

'In the Volkonsky House. Are you going to interpret or not?'

Bauer relayed the gist of what she'd said, bringing a look of incredulity to Metz's face.

'She tells *us* not to damage anything? When the Red Army has been burning every house, hut and woodshed between here and Brest-Litovsk? Tell her we've *saved* her precious buildings. She ought to be grateful to us. Who is she anyway? What's she doing here?'

Bauer asked the woman her name.

'Trubetzkaya,' she replied. '*Tovarishch* Trubetzkaya.'

'Don't use "Comrade" with us, please. Not even in Russian. What's your first name and patronymic?'

'I prefer *Tovarishch*,' she insisted.

'Not if you wish to survive the war.'

'*Tovarishch* Trubetzkaya,' she repeated, again speaking directly to Metz. 'Head Custodian – Acting – of Yasnaya Polyana.'

Bauer relayed her answer, leaving out the *comrade*. She seemed young to him for such a senior position, acting or otherwise.

'Tell her she's no longer head of anything,' Metz said.

'Captain,' interrupted Major Weidemann, twisting at the waist. 'I'd like to know if she was violated by any of our men. Ask her this. You said she mentioned damaged doors.'

Metz frowned. 'Major, that's hardly relevant. And besides, no man under my command —'

'Alas, you're wrong, *Herr Oberstleutnant,*' Weidemann said. 'Every day I encounter new cases of venereal disease – some, I regret to say, among men of the battalion.'

Volker Hirsch was colouring – an opportunity too good for Molineux to resist. 'Hirsch, you filthy animal, trust you to get the clap.'

'I … that's …'

'Don't bother to deny it.'

'But I do!'

'Do deny it? Or do have it?'

With a look of pained repugnance Metz turned to Weidemann. 'Aren't the brothels a more likely vector?'

'Still worried about our brothels, *Herr Oberstleutnant?*'

'Not *worried*, Major. It just seems to me that the risks outweigh the benefits.'

'Our brothel workers are rigorously screened for infection. No, I'm convinced that local women are the primary source, and I plan to say as much in a report to Major General Oeding.'

'With respect, sir,' Molineux said, 'that's hardly going to deter a man like Hirsch.'

Ignoring him Weidemann said, 'Bauer, would you put my question to this woman.'

'That won't be necessary,' Trubetzkaya said in flawless German, silencing all of them. 'The answer is no. I wasn't so stupid as to be in my room when you arrived. I've only discovered the damage just now.'

'Well, well, well,' said Molineux.

'You speak German,' Metz said.

'What of it?' she answered.

'You tried to deceive us.'

'Hardly. You deceived yourself.'

'To eavesdrop on us. Gain intelligence.'

'Intelligence? Don't make me laugh.'

Bauer marvelled at her German, which she spoke without a trace of an accent. It was months since he'd heard a woman speaking his native language with such verve, though this pleasure was marred by the realisation that she wouldn't be needing him to interpret for her. He recalled Metz and Weidemann's debate about venereal disease and inwardly cringed.

Metz demanded to know how she came to speak German.

She shrugged. 'Any half-decently educated person can speak the five or six main European dialects.'

Metz, who was monolingual, wisely let this go. 'But you have no accent,' he said.

Actually, this wasn't quite right, decided Bauer. Rather, she spoke a German shorn of regional inflection – the Platonic ideal of the language perhaps. Her voice was deepish for a woman and appealingly hoarse.

'I learned it as a child,' she said.

'Where was this?' Metz asked.

'Leningrad. In those days still St Petersburg.'

'From whom?'

She hesitated. 'A governess.'

'A governess? And yet you're a Bolshevik?'

Bauer said, 'Sir, we should ask the head custodian her first name and patronymic.'

26

'*Former* head custodian. And her surname will do – it's German we're speaking. Your name again?' he asked her.

'Trubetzkaya,' she said, adding, 'Katerina Dmitrievna.'

Mentally Bauer rehearsed the names, a technique he had devised as a youth to keep track of the characters in *War and Peace*.

'Frau Trubetzkaya,' Metz said, 'you will now take us to Leo Tolstoy's study. He had one, I suppose?'

'Of course. But why should I?'

'You needn't concern yourself with why. Those days are past.'

Trubetzkaya laughed. 'No more whys? Remarkable. If I'd known German medicine was so advanced I might have hung out the bunting.'

'The study,' Metz repeated.

'As you wish,' she replied, and led them out of the room, across the entrance hall and down a corridor to a large corner room even emptier than the first.

'This is it?' Metz asked.

'What did you expect?' Trubetzkaya said. 'To find him at his desk?'

'This is where Tolstoy wrote?' Bauer asked. '*Anna Karenina? War and Peace?*'

'Yes, and everything after.'

Metz turned to Ehrlich. 'First thing tomorrow, get a desk in here. And have a telephone set up.'

Trubetzkaya scoffed. 'Hoping a little greatness will rub off on you?'

'Deeds win greatness, *gnädige Frau*, not words. Writers document; great men *do*.'

'Spoken like a soldier.'

'A soldier-surgeon,' he corrected. 'But my point holds: with his rifle our humblest *Landser* shapes the world in a way your Tolstoy never did.'

'How odd. You sound rather like him in *War and Peace* – the dull bits: the little man as mover of Great Events. But you're mistaken. Lev Tolstoy did shape the world. Even now he's tipping the war in our favour.'

'Nonsense.'

'Our troops are reading him: *War and Peace*, abridged. And learning how to win.'

Metz sneered. 'Your Red Army is in headlong retreat.'

'Three days I've been hearing those guns. Whose they are I don't know, but it sounds like resistance.'

'It's only a matter of time until Tula falls, *gnädige Frau,* and when it does the whole Soviet centre will collapse. By Christmas, I assure you, we'll be well ensconced in Moscow.'

It struck Bauer that Metz was giving a good deal of verbal latitude to a woman who only minutes ago he'd wanted to silence.

'Let's say you're right,' she said, 'though I strongly doubt it.' Bauer guessed what was coming and she didn't disappoint. 'In 1812 Napoleon held Moscow for most of September and October, and yet by November his *Grande Armée* was – how shall I put it? – in headlong retreat.'

'Madam, warfare is no longer a matter of rag-tag armies chasing one another about the countryside. It's total, and our strength is the greater.'

'Russia remains large, its winters cold.'

Metz gave her a supercilious smile. 'You seem like an intelligent woman. Don't you know that history never repeats itself?'

'Ah, but there you're wrong, *Herr Oberstleutnant*. 1707, the Swedes. It was in Russia they learned neutrality. If you're smart enough, you Germans will learn the same lesson – though somehow I doubt it.'

Metz's smile had faded. He gestured to the doorway. 'You will now show us the rest of the house.'

Their next destination was a similar-sized room across the corridor, this one lined with bookshelves, all of them empty.

'The library,' Trubetzkaya said. 'Everything in Russian we evacuated, though you'll still find a few things in German.' On the floor were several book-laden crates, and their guide went over to one of them and rummaged inside. 'Here we are,' she said, and held up a hefty green volume. 'For your edification,' she said, presenting it to Metz, who glanced at the title before handing it on to Ehrlich.

'Destroy this,' he said.

'De Sade?' Molineux asked.

'*War and Peace*,' Trubetzkaya said. 'You won't read it?' she asked Metz.

'Of course not.'

'A pity. You might learn something.'

'*I've* read it,' Bauer said.

'The incinerator,' Metz said to Ehrlich, 'just as soon as it's running.'

'By midday tomorrow,' put in Weidemann.

'Thank you, Major,' Metz said, and turned to Trubetzkaya. 'Now if you don't mind, *gnädige Frau* – the rest of the house.'

Following Metz and Trubetzkaya the others departed one by one, Bauer hanging back until only he and Ehrlich remained.

'I'll take that,' Bauer said, holding out a hand for the book.

'The lieutenant colonel just told me to burn it.'

'And I'm ordering you to give it to me,' Bauer said. Let Ehrlich have a proper grievance against him, however small.

Ehrlich hesitated then passed him the book. 'I'll have to tell the lieutenant colonel.'

'Of course you will.'

'I doubt he'll be pleased.'

'That's for me to worry about,' Bauer said, and tucked the book under his arm.

They caught up with the others in a kitchen, and from there followed Trubetzkaya upstairs. A landing. A bathroom. Three or four empty bedrooms.

'Which was Tolstoy's?' Metz asked.

As if to appraise him better, she tilted her head. 'You're really quite a vain man, aren't you?'

'Just show us his room.'

She shrugged and led them to the northern end of the house, where she opened a door into a tiny whitewashed room with a solitary window, little more than a cell. On the floor lay Weidemann's kit and beside it his gramophone, known to Molineux, but nobody else, as Bertha.

'I don't need much space,' Weidemann said, 'and therefore took the liberty of claiming the room for myself.'

30

Ignoring him, Metz asked Trubetzkaya if the room had really been Tolstoy's.

'For his last two decades, yes,' she said.

'I can check, you know. Captain Bauer reads Russian.'

'How reassuring for you. He certainly can't speak it.'

'What about the marital bedroom?' Metz asked.

'Down the hall. Though really that room was Sophia Andreyevna's.'

'The wife?'

'Correct,' Trubetzkaya said. 'That room is grander. Much more your style.'

'There you're wrong, Madam,' Metz said. 'This room will do nicely. Major, take your kit to the wife's room.' To Trubetzkaya he said, 'You Russians call each other comrade, but your system is a sham, a tyranny dressed up as utopia. For true comradeship you need only look at the German army, where command is absolute but hardships are shared.'

'That's lucky because there will be plenty to go around.'

Metz ordered Corporal Ehrlich to bring up his kit.

'The ghost won't unnerve you?' Trubetzkaya asked.

Metz paused. 'There's a ghost?'

Trubetzkaya eyed him as if suspecting a joke, but Bauer feared Metz was sincere. Months ago he had announced the results of his horoscope (a long life, modest fame, disappointment with his children), and around his neck he wore a souvenir from the previous war, a lucky lump of shrapnel that had whirred past his ear and lodged in the door of a dugout.

'There's always a ghost,' Trubetzkaya said.

'Leo Tolstoy's?'

31

'I haven't seen it myself.'

'But others have?'

Trubetzkaya smiled archly at him. 'You can't expect me to answer that, *Herr Oberstleutnant*. The house must have its secrets.'

Metz looked displeased but didn't press for an answer. 'This estate is to be the site of a Wehrmacht field hospital,' he said. 'Soviet citizens, yourself included, are to be gone by tomorrow morning, 09:00 hours.'

'You expect me to leave the old man?' she said.

'Old man?'

'Lev Nikolayevich.'

To hide his incomprehension Metz thrust out his chin.

'She means Tolstoy,' Bauer said.

'Because I won't go,' Trubetzkaya went on. 'And nor will my staff.'

'Suit yourself,' Metz said. 'But don't say you weren't warned.' He turned to his officers. 'You see what scum the Bolsheviks are, leaving their womenfolk behind to face the enemy?'

'We prefer our men at the front, killing Germans,' Trubetzkaya said, then pushed her way to the door, elbowing Bauer in the sternum as she passed. She marched along the corridor to the stairs, and Molineux whistled in admiration. She ignored him and moments later was gone.

THREE

The word *Yasnaya* − bright − Bauer already knew; *polyana* he had to look up in a dictionary − not the scanty phrase book issued by the army, containing expressions like *Hands up* and *Surrender or be killed*, but his own dictionary, the one he'd owned since university. *Glade* or *clearing*, it read. A bright glade or clearing, then. A sunny place.

Though not in late autumn. It was the first day of November and dark outside when Bauer woke in the room he and Molineux had been allocated upstairs. Breakfast was in the drawing room, now the officers' mess. Beyond the curtains and hastily applied blackout paper there was still no hint of light.

At 08:00 hours Bauer joined the other officers and the orderlies in the vestibule. Dawn was coming on at last, but even so the vestibule seemed gloomier than it had the previous night under lights. Metz arrived, greeted them cheerily, then stopped by the door to confer with Sergeant Major Ritter. 'You've secured the perimeter?'

'Around the main buildings, sir, but not between them,' Ritter replied in his pitted voice, which sounded as though it would soon clear but never did.

'But we have an escort?'

'A squad, sir.'

'Excellent. And you've rounded up the staff?'

'Yes, and searched them for weapons. Their quarters too.'

'Good man,' he said, sounding alert and looking immaculate in a freshly pressed uniform. Bauer had slept poorly, kept awake by Molineux's snoring, and despite a change of clothes he felt crumpled and weary.

Metz led them out onto the porch and down the front steps. Drizzle. No wind. The cloud clotted and low. Dead leaves slicked and smothered the grass. On a circle of lawn at the centre of the turning circle a single corpsman stood guard over the estate's Soviet staff: five white-bearded men in peasant smocks and seven women, the youngest looking of them the head custodian, Trubetzkaya.

With the others Bauer followed Metz across the gravel drive, and simultaneously Trubetzkaya advanced towards them, ignoring the guard's shouted warning to stay put.

'You're going to shoot us now?' she asked Metz. 'Is that why we're here?' The corpsman collared her just before she stopped in front of Metz, who motioned him to let her go. 'You'll never kill enough of us, you know,' Trubetzkaya said. 'If every Russian came to the front and threw his hat in your direction, you'd spend three weeks getting over the pile.' She was wearing the quilted brown jacket she'd had on the night before, and a woollen cap from which strands of her auburn hair were spilling. Her nose was ruddy, and in the daylight her eyes and mouth looked a little lined, so that mentally Bauer revised her age upwards, nearer his own, and felt obscurely pleased.

34

'Are you a communist?' Metz asked her.

She considered this. '*Herr Oberstleutnant*,' she said at last, 'I am your enemy. Whether I am also a communist is immaterial.'

'Are you a member of the Soviet Communist Party?'

She stared at him with disdain. 'Yes, I am.'

'And these people here,' Metz said, pointing at the staff, 'are they communists?'

She glanced over her shoulder. 'None of them. I am the sole Party member here.'

Metz said, 'If you're lying, there will be consequences, understand? You could be sent to a camp, or shot. For now I'm inclined towards leniency. Last night I ordered you and your staff to clear out of here by nine.'

'And as I said —'

'*But*,' Metz said, raising a hand, 'if you agree not to interfere with our work, I'm proposing to let you return each day to get on with your duties.'

Bauer allowed himself a little smile of self-congratulation: the estate's staff would have been useful, he'd told Metz the night before, if their leader had been less of a firebrand.

'Return?' she asked. 'Most of us are quartered here.'

'Not from now on. Where you find shelter is your concern. The village, I assume. There will be a curfew from 21:00 to 06:00 hours. Otherwise you will be free to come and go and do your work unhindered – just report to the front sentry post and to the guard at each building.'

Trubetzkaya considered this then said, 'We'll do nothing to help you.'

35

'Your usual duties. If you regard that as helping us, so be it, stay away. You have cleaning staff, I take it?'

'Of course …'

'Then let them clean. Those old men, what do they do?'

'Gardening,' she said. 'Maintenance.'

'Let them garden and maintain,' Metz said. 'Unless otherwise instructed, you will stay out of our way. And be warned: the smallest act of resistance will be punished, and severely.'

'And will you stay out of *our* way?'

'Your meaning?'

'According to your colleague here,' she said, gesturing at Major Weidemann, 'you have rapists in your ranks.'

Metz inhaled so sharply his nostrils flared. Coldly he said, 'He was mistaken. Intimacy between *Wehrmacht* personnel and Slavic females is forbidden.'

Molineux noisily cleared his throat, drawing glances. He gestured an apology and coughed.

'Except in your brothels, evidently,' Trubetzkaya said.

'That I wouldn't know,' Metz said.

'And rules are broken, aren't they?'

'Not by men under my command.'

'Oh? Where do you recruit such paragons?'

'It's not a question of recruitment, *gnädige Frau*, but of leadership. *Führung*,' he repeated, clearly savouring the word. 'Now, kindly brief your staff. You will then join us on a tour of inspection.'

She seemed to bridle at this, and Bauer feared she would refuse, but then she turned to her staff and explained that they were to ignore the 'fascist occupiers' and keep caring for

36

Yasnaya Polyana until the Red Army returned. This wouldn't be long, she said. 'Watch your mouths, though,' she continued, and startled Bauer by pointing at him. 'The one with the big nose is like your pony, Tikhon Vassilyvich: he can't speak Russian but understands it a little.' Her compatriots roared with laughter at this, especially Tikhon Vassilyvich, a big man with a fleecy beard and a forehead as wrinkled as a ram's.

Metz demanded to know what had been said, and Bauer told him it was nothing. The merriment died away. In the silence a crow cawed, and as if in response Trubetzkaya ordered her staff to go about their work. Some dispersed along paths and narrow lanes between the trees, while others entered the main house, which in daylight looked brighter, less manorial than Bauer had expected. Stone walls painted white, a green metal roof, wooden fretwork on the porch.

'You will start by taking us here,' Metz told Trubetzkaya, brandishing the guide to the estate and pointing at one of the buildings.

'The Volkonsky House,' she said.

'Until we find a better name, yes.'

She said nothing to this, only beckoned them to follow, then set off so quickly they had to trot to catch up. For about a hundred metres they strode after her along what Bauer took to be the main drive, before turning right onto a footpath through a narrow orchard. This led to the Volkonsky House, a long but mostly single-storey building, painted white like the Tolstoy House and with the same metal roofing in green. From upstairs windows in the central two-storey section, a pair of corpsmen were roping a red cross banner over the entrance.

Metz gestured at the building. 'Gentleman, our hospital.'

The entrance hall was polished and echoing, and like the vestibule of the Tolstoy House it contained a stack of furniture. Metz pointed at it. 'Caught napping?' he asked Trubetzkaya.

She shrugged. 'All the important objects are gone.'

Metz chuckled. 'There's nothing here of value?'

'Not especially.'

'The great man's chattels aren't all sacred?'

'He was a man and, as you say, a great one. Not a god.'

'Then if I were to take out my pistol, like so,' he said, 'and aim it at this armoire, you wouldn't be concerned?'

'Only for your sanity.'

Bauer glanced at Siegfried Weidemann, trying to assess what their second in command was making of Metz's behaviour. Weidemann's winged, owlish eyebrows were perhaps a little raised, but otherwise his expression was neutral.

'But I forgot,' Metz said, still threatening the armoire with his P38, 'you Bolsheviks only believe in the material realm. To you this is merely wood and glue, not an object of veneration.'

'It's Soviet government property and I'd thank you not to damage it.'

'Ha!' Metz cried, as if she'd conceded some essential point. He reholstered his weapon and, still smirking, proceeded into the entrance hall. Directly ahead of them was a large double doorway and through it a high-ceilinged room that Bauer guessed must have once been a ballroom and which Metz announced was to function as a reception room for the wounded. A linking doorway led into a smaller but still spacious room that overnight had been turned into an operating theatre,

38

with a trestle table running the length of one wall, arrayed with instruments, dressing canisters, plaster of Paris, bottles of saline and plasma, stethoscopes, a sphygmomanometer, two paraffin stoves. Four pairs of sawhorses stood ready to take patients' stretchers, two of them topped with operating lamps, beside them cylinders of oxygen and ether. Bauer gazed in amazement at the wide doorways, polished floorboards, off-white plaster walls and towering windows.

'Optimal,' Metz murmured, 'optimal.'

'A step up from the hovels we've had to work in,' Molineux agreed.

It was as if the Volkonsky House had been purpose-built as a hospital. Down its central axis ran a corridor that led to a series of large rooms, ideal for wards. Already the first of these contained rows of camp beds, fully made, while in a room across the corridor two corpsmen were setting up an X-ray machine.

'Katerina Dmitrievna,' said Molineux, clasping an estate guide like a conscientious tourist, 'what was this place?'

'Childhood home of Tolstoy's mother and her father, Count Volkonsky. The estate's oldest building.'

A memory of *War and Peace* came to Bauer – more of an impression, really – of an old count and his daughter in a country house.

'How fascinating,' said Molineux, who Bauer noted had his own knack for remembering Russian names. 'Why didn't Tolstoy live here? It's so much grander than the other place.'

'There's your answer,' she replied. 'He wanted a home. In his day this building housed servants and guests.'

39

And latterly its acting head custodian, Bauer thought.

They went upstairs, which was less extensive than the ground floor but big enough for Metz to have assigned rooms for Weidemann's clerical staff, the pharmacy and Hirsch's dental surgery.

'Talk about luxury,' Molineux said. 'When the time comes, we won't want to leave.'

'When the time comes, you won't have a choice,' Trubetzkaya said.

Molineux sighed. 'How true, Katerina Dmitrievna, how true! The life of a military man is never his own. Go here, go there, they say. We take our pleasures where we can.'

'Where are your nurses?' she asked Metz.

Metz looked puzzled by the question, and Bauer explained on his behalf: 'Female nurses aren't permitted this close to the front.'

Trubetzkaya looked contemptuous. 'Your German girls can't take the sound of guns?'

'The front is no place for a woman,' Metz said.

'Men of fighting age deployed as nurses – my God, you will certainly lose this war. The front is no place for anyone, *Herr Oberstleutnant*, but Soviet women do their duty on or near it every day.'

'Katerina Dmitrievna,' Molineux said, 'is it true the Soviet airforce has lady pilots?'

'Several of them aces, yes.'

'I can well believe it. God in heaven. That's how I'd like to go if I could choose: caught in the cross-hairs of a lipsticked fly girl.'

'Captain, enough,' Metz said, turning back to Trubetzkaya. 'Next, the barracks,' he said, pointing on the map at the Kusminsky Wing, which was situated near the Tolstoy House but approached along a separate drive.

On the way there they caught glimpses of the ridge behind the estate, not especially high but close and densely wooded – the site of Tolstoy's grave, remembered Bauer. When the opportunity arose he would visit the great man, who would perhaps overlook the circumstances and regard him less as an invader than a reader.

'Why "wing"?' Molineux asked Trubetzkaya as they approached the barracks. Like the main house it had two storeys, and though less broad it was built in an identical style. Outside it there were corpsmen assembling for what was sure to be a long and arduous day.

'Both it and the main house were once wings of one building,' Trubetzkaya said.

'Which burned?' Metz asked.

'Which Tolstoy lost at cards,' she said.

From Molineux came a hoot of joy.

Bauer said, 'I wouldn't haven't guessed he was a gambler. Not from his work. Dostoyevsky yes, but not Tolstoy.'

'He was young at the time,' Trubetzkaya said. 'On campaign in the Crimea. Seeing off the French and the English.'

'A difficult debt to collect,' Molineux said.

'Stone by stone, I suppose,' Metz said. He climbed the front steps. 'These people like to take wealth not make it.'

Molineux nodded at Trubetzkaya. 'I bet this one's speciality is stealing hearts.'

'Captain, I won't have any more tomfoolery,' Metz said. To Trubetzkaya he went on, 'We will now look inside.'

They entered the Kusminsky Wing, which resembled the Tolstoy House inside as well as out, though with their enlisted men in residence the central staircase was busier, its mess hall raucous with talk and scraping chairs. At some washing-up tubs by the door Karl Pflieger and another of Bauer's theatre assistants, Yuri Demchak, a Ukrainian volunteer, were cheerfully trading vile insults.

Perhaps noticing his accent, Trubetzkaya pointed at Demchak and demanded to know who he was, just as the room fell quiet and the men came to attention.

'One of our Hiwis,' Metz said into the silence.

'Meaning?'

'*Hilfswilliger*. A countryman of yours who's been wise enough to join us. A clever fellow, isn't that right, Bauer?'

'That's right, sir. He is.'

Demchak was still standing at attention, his face expressionless. Young, blond, with matinee-idol looks only partially marred by a crude cleft-lip repair. Trubetzkaya turned to him and hissed a single word at him in Russian, to which he reacted with a furious look.

'*Ismennik*,' she repeated.

Demchak looked wildly to Metz.

'German!' the lieutenant colonel snapped at Trubetzkaya. 'You will speak to us in German.'

'Who's *she*?' Demchak asked.

Bauer had never seen the young Ukrainian so heated. 'We'll deal with this, Private. In fact, you may go now.'

42

'He goes nowhere,' Metz said, then turned to Trubetzkaya. 'Listen here, *Frau*, I don't know what any of that was about, but if you interfere with one of my men again I'll have you sent to a camp, understood?'

'I understand you perfectly,' she said.

'Good. Then we can continue.'

The inspection party left the mess and followed Metz up the stairs.

'My God,' Molineux whispered stagily to Trubetzkaya, 'what on earth did you just call our Hiwi?'

'A traitor.'

'How very tactless of you.'

'I was stating a fact.'

'Good Lord, we can't have you lobbing facts about – our defences are stretched enough as it is.'

Metz entered a room converted into a dormitory and immediately demanded that the windows be opened.

'So tell me, Katerina Dmitrievna,' Molineux went on, 'how did you get to be so fearsome?'

'Breeding. The same way you came by your manners.'

Molineux clutched his heart as if shot. 'You wound me, madam, most grievously you wound me.'

'Not grievously enough.'

Molineux chortled, slapped his hands together and turned to Bauer. 'Hear that? "Not grievously enough." Sensational! We're going to have so much fun here, I'm certain of it.'

★ ★ ★

43

The first casualties arrived shortly after midday, ferried by ambulance and lorry to the Volkonsky House. Those able to walk were helped inside by drivers and nursing attendants, while the badly wounded were brought in on stretchers. Soon the reception room was crammed with pale and muddy men: the walking wounded on bench seats along the walls; stretcher cases on the floor, so that Bauer was forced to tread gingerly between rows of bloodied and bandaged men, some with jagged entry wounds, others badly burned or with bones protruding from lacerated skin. Though the room's windows were ajar, the air inside already stank of vomit and faeces and sweat, as well as cordite from spent munitions.

In tandem with Metz, and with the help of their respective operating assistants, Bauer set about identifying which men to transfuse, which to X-ray and which to operate on without delay. In the scramble Pflieger collided with one of Metz's men and swore, and swiftly Winkel stepped between them. 'Take it easy, lads. There's plenty for all.'

Some of the wounded were moaning but most of them were silent, either from stoicism, unconsciousness or the approach of death. Several were past medical help, and in order to spare others from having to watch them die, Bauer ordered Pflieger and Yuri Demchak, the Hiwi, to take them to a curtained-off corner of the room. Men were gazing at Bauer, some expectantly, others imploringly, and two or three with something like accusation in their eyes, as if he were personally responsible for all this mayhem and pain. In response he donned a mask of doctorly calm, inwardly registering sights and smells and sounds that he had never grown used to, only learned to set aside. Every casualty had received first aid of some kind, either on the front line or at the dressing station in Malevka, and on a string around his neck each wore a field medical card that recorded not only the nature of his wounds but also, with the aid of two perforated strips, their severity: both strips retained for a light wound, one detached for something serious, both removed if the risk of death was high. On the floor there were many men whose cards lacked both strips.

By the doorway that led into the operating room the transfusions officer, Lieutenant Hans Zöllner, was infusing several patients with saline and blood. The anti-vampire, Molineux called him. Excessively nice. Zöllner was twenty-three, sandy-haired, athletically built, open-faced and by nature optimistic, the type of officer you wanted at your side when casualties came in. Bauer turned to him now for a report on the condition of his patients. Most were ready for surgery, Zöllner said. Among them Bauer found a grenadier with mortar wounds to the abdomen. His record showed he was eighteen years old, but he looked closer to sixteen, a fair-haired boy who appeared never to have shaved. He was conscious, staring up from his stretcher with grey-blue eyes. Bauer examined his abdomen and found two separate wounds, one leaking faeces, the other a mixture of oatmeal and lentils. There were no exit wounds. Involuntarily he glanced at Winkel, who imperceptibly shrugged and looked away. Bauer re-examined the boy's card, frowning to himself. Occasionally Metz would chide him for selecting a patient who probably couldn't be saved, and in all likelihood this boy would be one of them.

45

'Doctor, am I going to die?' the boy asked, his accent Low German, educated. It was a common question, one to which Bauer usually answered no, or on rare occasions dodged, but this time before he could reply the boy said, 'I only ask because I'm thirsty, you see, very, very thirsty, and the medics say I can't take any water.'

'It's true you can't have water before surgery.'

'But if I'm going to die anyway? It's all right, doctor, I understand – so many have to die. It's just that I want water so badly.'

'We're operating,' he said, then in a gentler tone added, 'You're going to survive.'

'You're in good hands,' Pflieger reassured him. 'You're going home! Just think of all those pretty nurses at your beck and call.'

The boy turned from them and stared instead at the ceiling. 'I've never made love to a woman.'

There was a brief pause, then Bauer said grimly, 'You will.' He motioned Pflieger and Demchak to pick up the patient's stretcher, then followed them into the operating room. There he introduced the boy to Hirsch and explained that the lieutenant would anaesthetise him. The boy said nothing, and to reassure him Bauer pressed his hand and told him he was going to be fine, the placebo of optimism better than truth – for Bauer's own sake as much as the patient's.

Metz appeared, handed over his first patient to Molineux, and, as Bauer had expected, raised an eyebrow at the severity of the boy's wounds. While Metz might quibble about individual cases, he too selected patients *in extremis*, even if this meant

46

operating for hours on men who either succumbed on the table or died not long afterwards.

At the preoperative table Hirsch was botching the insertion of the boy's cannula, spattering blood on the floor. His hands were visibly shaking. Presumably he was more assured doing dental work, Bauer thought, while praying he would never have to discover this for himself. The boy was luckily in no state to notice what was happening to him.

Bauer turned away, put on his scrubs and soaped his hands. Of course, from a military point of view it would have been more logical to operate first on men with moderate wounds, since the length of time these patients had to wait for surgery often led to complications that hampered their recovery, delaying their eventual redeployment to the front; yet there was a deeper, psychological reason for operating first on patients like the young grenadier, since men fought more courageously if they knew beforehand that every effort would be made to save their lives if they were wounded. And sometimes there was a miracle – the patient who survived when ninety-nine others would have died – and then Bauer experienced a kind of thrill, free of ego, or almost, since his own role was often secondary: in fact it was luck or the patient's will to survive that had allowed him to save a life that to people at home might mean everything.

Finally Hirsch succeeded in getting the cannula in, and with a small dose of Pentothal put the boy under. Swiftly Pflieger and Demchak cut off what remained of his uniform then proceeded to clean and shave around the wounds. Bauer took the opportunity to return to the reception room and select a second patient and, by the time he returned, the boy was under drapes on the operating table, his abdomen bare and illuminated, an ether mask cupping his face. Pflieger and Demchak were standing by, and at the head of the stretcher sat Hirsch. Bauer glanced enviously at the other operating table, where Molineux occupied the corresponding seat. It wasn't Hirsch's fault he had to do a job for which he was untrained, but it was hard not to resent his apparent inability to learn. The cannula was the least of it. Too often Bauer had found himself probing muscles that twitched from too light an anaesthetic or, alternatively, dealing with a patient whose vital signs were suppressed by too much ether. Supposedly Metz had asked the medical command for a proper anaesthetist, but Bauer suspected him of not pressing hard enough, or even of boasting that they could do without.

From the sideboard on which their equipment was arrayed Bauer took a pair of latex gloves and put them on, then from the instrument tray he selected a scalpel. He approached the patient. Of the two wounds, the one to the colon was more dangerous, and it was here he would begin. He breathed deeply, not only to steady himself but also to take a moment to recall that the material he was about to work on was an individual, irreplaceable to himself and almost certainly to others. That was the point of all this equipment, this activity. Of the roughly two hundred and fifty men in the battalion, nearly half were tasked in one way or another with getting the wounded onto an operating table, so that he and Metz could save their lives. This was his instant, his moment to act. He positioned his scalpel. And cut.

FOUR

On their fourth night at the estate Bauer slept even worse than usual, half aware he was cold but never quite cold enough to put clothes on over his underwear or to shut the window at the foot of his bed, which by agreement with Molineux he had left ajar. When he did sleep he dreamed – mazy epics of hiding and running and eventually of being buried alive. He woke early and sensed a weight on his legs, reached over his blankets and felt a layer of snow.

At breakfast Molineux had to describe the incident to each new arrival. The first snowfall had excited him immensely. 'Minus sixteen degrees Celsius!' he cried when Winkel told him the temperature. 'And it's only the fourth of November! My God, that's cold. My wife will hear of this, you can count on it. She won't believe it.'

'For Christ's sake, Hermann, shut up about it,' Bauer said. 'Spare a thought for the men at the front.'

'What about them?'

'You could sound less cheery, that's all.'

'Why? You think it'll keep them warm?'

49

'You needn't celebrate is my point.'

'I'm just discussing the weather, Paul, not making it. You needn't be so touchy.'

It was true he was feeling irritable. To compensate he said, 'At least there'll be fewer casualties.'

Metz, who was getting up from the table, paused and said, 'What gives you that idea?'

'Only that the snow will hamper combat operations,' Bauer said.

'On the contrary, Captain. The frost will solidify the mud, improving the manoeuvrability of our tanks. Never underestimate the toughness of the German fighting man. I won't have it. It smacks of defeatism and sets a bad example to the men. Do I make myself clear?'

'Yes, sir,' Bauer said, suppressing his annoyance.

'That goes for all of you,' Metz said, gazing round the table. 'And the men under your command. I won't have any talk of lulls or a slackening of effort.'

Breakfast continued in silence. Bauer breathed deeply and reminded himself how many operations he and Metz had performed the day before – twenty-seven and twenty-nine respectively. It was hardly surprising they were both feeling tetchy.

He needed a cigarette. He *deserved* one, he decided. Even after all the intervening surgeries, he remained troubled by the death of his first patient at Yasnaya Polyana, the young grenadier, who had survived the removal of his spleen, a haemorrhaging liver, repairs to rents in his small intestine and colon, plus the creation of a temporary stoma, only to die as the final bandages were being applied. Bauer had begun to believe that the boy might be one of his miracles, and mentally he had cursed him for holding on so long. None of his assistants had spoken. They hadn't needed to, since all of them were experiencing the same sense of letdown. The boy had touched them somehow, bypassing their normal defences, their acceptance that a portion of their patients would die. In particular Bauer regretted refusing the boy a drink of water. True, having decided to operate he'd had no choice, but had he been right to operate? A zeal to save lives could tip into surgical vainglory, and in this case ego had perhaps affected his judgement. Though who could really tell? Unlike, say, engineering, where preparation and diligence more or less guaranteed success, surgery was an unpredictable trade. Patients died, or indeed survived, inexplicably, regardless of how skilfully he performed, and in this sense surgery resembled other operations on human beings: the arts, for example, or politics. Even so, there were days when he grew exasperated by the gap between the abstract and the real, between the anatomical illustration of a human being and the strange flesh and soul hybrid it was his job to cut open.

It had been Hirsch, of all people, who had tried consoling him about the boy – no surgeon could have done more; the patient would have died in any case. They were well-meaning words but the correct response would have been silence, something their acting anaesthetist might have understood had he been with them longer.

Given the harsh weather, two lorries were arranged for those wanting to ride the short distance to the hospital, and by 07:15 hours officers and orderlies were gathered in the vestibule, knowing that Metz would insist on leaving on

51

time. Like the others, Bauer was wearing almost all of his clothing, and yet even indoors he was cold. His comrades were subdued, all except Molineux, who was marvelling at the blizzard outside. Bauer thought of the soldiers – on both sides – under canvas or in foxholes; of their having to rise and feed themselves, visit latrines, tend to horses and vehicles, see to their weapons and to dozens of other mundane duties in order to prepare themselves for combat.

When Metz arrived, Ehrlich held open the door and the lieutenant colonel led them outside. On the porch a duty sentry was taking shelter from the wind, his head so bundled in scarves and hoods it seemed doubtful he could see anything at all. Beyond the porch the wind was arctic – hard to imagine a human being surviving it for long. Faster men were already leaping into the cabins of the lorries, questions of seniority thrust aside, so that Bauer had to join the others piling into the back. Two bench seats. A tarpaulin cover buffeting its stays. Someone – Zöllner – pulled up the tailgate and mercifully the lorry got underway, its slipstream a vortex of snow. The air was biting but the tarpaulin was fending off the wind, and luckily the distance they had to travel was short.

Directly opposite Bauer was Egon Ehrlich, watching him intently with close-set eyes. 'Sir, do you really think we should go on the defensive?' Ehrlich asked, swaying like a cobra as the lorry shifted gears. The concern on his thin face was laughably false, the malice behind it unsettling, since technically defeatism was a capital crime. In his peripheral vision Bauer sensed Hans Zöllner turning away, either unnerved or too innocent to grasp Ehrlich's intent.

'The lieutenant colonel is no doubt right,' Bauer said, speaking to Ehrlich coolly, as if from a communiqué. 'Our fighting men are more than capable of overcoming whatever challenges they might face.'

★   ★   ★

When Bauer and the others from his lorry reached the hospital they found Trubetzkaya berating Metz in the entrance hall. 'I protest,' she was saying, 'and in the strongest terms.'

'Protest all you like,' Metz replied. 'It won't do you any good.'

'It's desecration,' Trubetzkaya said.

Corpsmen, drawn by the noise of raised voices, were appearing at the edges of the hall. Metz drew back his shoulders and thrust out his dimpled chin. 'The presence of our fallen can hardly constitute desecration.'

The cause of the woman's anger became clear soon enough: the designation of the Tolstoy burial glade as a German military cemetery. This was news to Bauer. The first batch of dead was already in the ground.

'I'd rather see your troops in Soviet soil than on it,' Trubetzkaya said, 'just not anywhere near Tolstoy. I want them disinterred.'

'Must I point out to you again who's in charge here?' Metz asked.

'In charge temporarily,' Trubetzkaya said.

'I'm not listening to any more of your ignorant prophecies, *gnädige Frau*. From now on if you have anything else to say, you may say it to Captain Bauer here.'

'You think you can palm me off onto a flunky?'

'She's right, sir,' Molineux said. 'Palm her off onto me.'

'German swine,' Trubetzkaya said. 'There'll be plenty more burials, you can rely on that.'

'See, sir?' Molineux said. 'She's too much for Bauer. Sorry, Paul, but you know it's true.'

'Bauer speaks Russian,' Metz said.

'Not according to Frau Trubetzkaya,' Molineux replied. 'And besides, she speaks such lovely German.'

'I'm appointing Bauer,' Metz said, 'and that's the end of the matter.' He turned, saw the spectators, bawled at them to go back to work, then strode into the reception room. Trubetzkaya stared after him, her face so full of hatred that for a moment Bauer wondered if he'd been wrong to advise Metz to let her stay on at the estate. Each time she entered a building she would be searched for weapons, but in that stare he thought he glimpsed a woman ready to sacrifice herself for a chance to crush a skull with a poker or plunge a fork into a throat. The sniper who killed Dieter Clemens had died for the privilege. *You'll never kill enough of us*, Trubetzkaya had said.

Molineux clapped him on the shoulder. 'Well played, friend.' To Trubetzkaya he added, 'Now, don't go thinking you can push our Bauer around. He might seem like a poodle but the man's a lion.'

From the reception room doorway Metz called out, 'That includes you, Molineux.'

'Just coming, sir,' Molineux yelled over his shoulder. 'Quickly, tell us, Katerina Dmitrievna, how cold will it get?'

'Much colder.'

'*How* cold?'

'Too cold for you.'

'Molineux!'

'Yes, sir,' he yelled, then beamed at them and left.

Bauer turned to Trubetzkaya.

'The *reader*,' she sneered.

'When I'm able,' he replied, wishing he'd never mentioned his reading.

'You think I'll hate you less?'

'I suppose the answer must be no.'

She peered at him. 'You know what I think?'

'I can't say I do.'

'I think your commanding officer expects you to placate me with polished manners and talk of books.'

'If I did, would that be so bad?'

'Yes, if those graves aren't relocated.'

He considered this and said, 'Metz is less unreasonable than he seems.'

'Your Metz is unstable. Drawing his gun. And now this.'

It was true that Metz had been behaving erratically of late. 'You have to understand that he's fearful,' Bauer said, then realised how disloyal this sounded. 'Of course, in our own way we all are. It would be strange if we weren't.'

'True, since most of you won't see Germany again.'

So much for conceding that he and his comrades were human. He was annoyed with himself. 'I should check on my patients,' he said. 'But later this morning would you show me the grave?'

'You haven't been there?'

'I've been working.'

'Good,' she said. 'But if it helps, certainly; I'll show you the grave.'

Ninety minutes later they met by the large entry doors. 'That's all you have for your head?' she asked him, gesturing at his forage cap.

'I'm afraid so.'

'And you think you'll be able to stand it out there?' On her own head she wore an *ushanka*.

Bauer gazed out the windows flanking the large entry doors. The snow had stopped but there was still a powerful wind. 'You told Molineux the weather would only get colder.'

'True enough. Now or never.'

If anything the wind felt harsher than before, an ice-spiked gale all the way from the tundra. Big clouds flew fast and low overhead, their edges frayed, wild and unstable. Trubetzkaya led him into the wind, and enviously he glanced at her clothes: a grey cape over her quilted jacket, fur-lined boots and mittens and her *ushanka*, the flaps of which she'd tied beneath her chin. His own cloth cap did little to fend off the wind and left his earlobes cruelly exposed. His wrists stung where his gloves didn't reach. Already his face was stiffening.

'Cold?' Trubetzkaya asked him.

'A little,' he mumbled, his lips no longer quite under his control.

They passed the delousing station, a raw-looking cabin that contained the hospital's sauna, built by Weidemann's men in a single day.

'You know what I find odd?' Trubetzkaya said. 'That in the whole of recorded history only two men, Hitler and Napoleon,

56

have failed to realise that in winter Russia gets cold. Don't you find that odd?'

Bauer replied with a grunt, and Trubetzkaya didn't press the matter, perhaps because she too was finding it difficult to speak. On the right Bauer glimpsed the roof of the Kusminsky Wing; above it scudding clouds, before it thrashing trees. The cold was bad, the wind intolerable, so he was glad to reach the rise at the rear of the estate and in its lee get some warmth back into his clothes. From the bottom of the rise a track rose diagonally through a forest, most of it made up of birch, its silvery bark scarred and banded in black. The snow underfoot was deep and new, and as a courtesy Bauer took the lead.

'And the Swedes,' he said, looking back over his shoulder.

'True, the Swedes,' she replied, immediately grasping the conversational thread. 'But they learned. Your Führer is a fool.'

He hesitated, aware this was treacherous territory. 'That's not for me to say,' he replied. 'I'm just a surgeon.'

'"Just a surgeon",' she mocked, making him wish he hadn't spoken. Since joining the army the only person with whom he'd discussed politics had been Dieter, and only then after they had worked together for months, sounding out each other's views and by stages coming to trust one another. The desire to confide in this woman felt fiercer, more reckless.

'So tell me, *Herr* Surgeon,' Trubetzkaya asked, 'when will the Führer equip you with winter uniforms?'

'I don't know,' he admitted. 'And of course frontline troops will receive them first.'

'They haven't already?'

'Not in every case,' he said, though in fact he knew of none.

Trubetzkaya smiled at him. 'Oh, how you're going to *suffer*.'

He and Dieter had co-operated to build trust, he reflected. From Frau Trubetzkaya he would get no such help.

'How did you come to have a governess?' he asked.

'Who wants to know? You or Metz?'

'Me,' he replied.

'But you're reporting to Metz.'

'As a matter of fact, I doubt he wants to hear from you again.'

She laughed. 'Then he'll be disappointed.'

'Very well, but are you evading my question?'

'Not at all. I've nothing to hide. My father was a count. We had a governess.'

'Yet you're a communist.'

'As I said, my father was a count.'

'That's your answer?'

'It's one answer.'

From further up the slope, among the birches, there came a resounding crack; Bauer ducked and unclipped his holster. Behind him, Trubetzkaya chuckled. 'Why, Captain, you're so nervous.'

'A branch?' he asked.

'Freezing sap.'

'Yet the trees survive?' he asked.

'Of course. These are sturdy Soviet trees. With ice in their veins,' she added, laughing. They continued up the trail.

'You never hear the shot that kills you,' Bauer said. 'Or so they say. I find that comforting.'

'But the one that wounds?'

'There's that,' he admitted.

They reached the top of the trail and entered a clearing, the burial glade, in which five Wehrmacht graves stood opposite a snow-covered mound that Bauer took to be the grave of Leo Tolstoy, as if a firing squad had shot the great man, only to be gunned down themselves and buried where they fell.

'No monument?' Bauer asked.

'His tastes were simple. At least, they were by the end.'

As he could afford them to be, Bauer thought. Each of the German graves was marked with a birchwood cross and a wooden plaque on which the fallen man's name and service number were inscribed – those snippets of biography with which ordinary mortals strove to ward off oblivion. Bauer went over and read each man's name in turn and, as he reached the last grave, the young grenadier's, a gap in the clouds strafed the clearing with light. He turned to Trubetzkaya. 'Are we in it, the Bright Glade?'

'Quite possibly,' she said. 'You should see it in summer.'

Already the light had zoomed away. 'I'd like that,' he replied. He imagined the forest in full leaf, the burial mound covered in grass. He turned back to her. 'If you're so sure the Red Army will drive us out, why not wait and exhume the bodies later?'

'Because there'll be more of them by then. Naturally. And because the memory of them will linger – unnaturally – long after their corpses are gone.'

He sniffed. The hairs in his nostrils, he noticed, were spiny with frost. 'Shall we go?' he asked, making a move to leave. Even out of the wind his face was in pain.

'Not before you promise to have these men disinterred.'

'I can't promise you that.'

'Then what good are you?'

He surveyed the clearing. Quite apart from its cultural significance for the Soviet people, the site was impractically small. In weeks it was likely to be full.

'It'll be up to Metz,' he said.

She scoffed. 'I was right. You're the shapeless pillow shoved between me and him. I'm meant to punch you till I'm out of breath.'

'At least you'll be warm,' he said, pretending the insult hadn't hurt. Again he looked enviously at her winter clothes. 'Is this your way of killing me, Katerina Dmitrievna? Exposure?'

She smirked at him. 'You know what this is, don't you, this situation?'

'No, what is it?'

'A portent. You arrive and learn that you're not dressed for the conditions, then have to abandon your dead and scurry back home.'

He was shuddering from the cold now. 'You win. I have to scurry.'

She chuckled at this but relented, and they returned to the trail, Bauer relieved but also sad to cut the excursion short. It was so long since he'd spoken at length with a woman, let alone one as smart as Katerina Dmitrievna. 'So when did you become communist?' he asked.

'Why do you want to know?'

'I don't,' he said. 'I'm just being polite.'

She laughed at this but tried to disguise it as a cough. 'Officially?' she said, clearing her throat. 'April 1919. Shortly after the Revolution. By conviction, a few months beforehand.'

'You were how old?'

'Seventeen.'

'That young?'

'Isn't seventeen the perfect age to cast off one life for another?' she asked.

'Some would leave it till later. Or not do it at all.' He calculated that she must be thirty-eight or thirty-nine and felt a frisson of slight seniority.

'It was then or never,' she said. 'The Civil War had begun and my father had taken us – my mother and sisters and me – from St Petersburg to the Crimea, to Yekaterinodar, where he was high up in the White government. He was sending us to Paris.'

'High up how?'

'A minister. Justice. They must have been desperate; he wasn't even a lawyer and in his home life was something of a bully. An anti-Semite too. That alone I couldn't forgive him for. Such a vulgar prejudice. You know, you're the first foreigners I've encountered in years. Imagine, then, my disappointment.'

'You were due to go to Paris,' Bauer prompted.

'And so I slipped away.'

'Just like that?'

'And never saw them again.' Her tone was neutral, and because she was ahead of him he couldn't read her face.

'Did you miss them?'

'Not at first. I thought the whole world was about to go communist, and that my family and I would reunite – that even my father would realise his mistake. I'd read Proudhon, I'd read Engels. I'd read *Das Kapital* from cover to cover and thought

I understood it. My task, I believed, was to fan the flames of revolution until the whole globe caught fire.'

'Quite an ambition for a seventeen-year-old.'

'I was in a hurry. History was happening and I had to help.'

'So you slipped away,' he said.

'Quite easily in the end. I got plainer clothes, caught a train, hitched a ride on a cart and then walked through the night. In the morning I reached the Red Army.'

'You weren't afraid?' he asked.

'No. Why would I have been?'

'You were seventeen. A girl, alone.'

She stopped and turned around. 'Afraid I'd be raped? Tell me, what is it about you Germans – pleased to do it, shy to give it a name?' Fortunately she didn't wait for answer. 'The truth is I didn't believe that Bolsheviks could be rapists. Oh, I'd heard otherwise – from my father, for starters – but I'd dismissed it as propaganda. Of course, now I see the risks I was running.'

'Did they identify you?'

'I didn't hide who I was. I assumed the Revolution was for everyone, and my sincerity must have told in my favour. A spy would have been more circumspect. Imagine the idealism streaming out of me, a protective glow, imperceptible to the eye.'

'Like Joan of Arc.'

'Ha! But less holy. More like a forcefield, as the science fiction writers say, a shimmer of ignorance. Or maybe I was just lucky. Certainly I chanced on a unit whose commander was welcoming and intelligent.'

'Oh yes?' he said.

They had arrived at the bottom of the hill. She peered back at him and said, 'If I were you, I'd pick up a handful of snow.'

'Why?'

'Your nose, it's gone white. The start of frostbite.'

He touched his nose, felt nothing and scooped up a handful of snow.

'Now rub your face with it,' she said.

'Really? This isn't another allegory?'

'It's first aid, but what do I care? You can listen or not.'

He pressed the snow against his nose, half convinced she was trying to humiliate him but alarmed enough to do as she said. Treating frostbite with cold felt plausibly counterintuitive, a vaccination of sorts.

'That's right,' she said, 'but harder. *Harder*. Till it hurts.'

He rubbed but still felt nothing in his nose, rubbed until his lips and cheeks were aflame and the snow on his palm fell apart.

'Get more,' she ordered.

He picked up another handful and mashed it on his face until he began to feel a burning sensation on his nose. 'I think it's working,' he said.

'Keep going.'

For another half-minute he kept rubbing, his face feeling more and more aflame. 'It's starting to hurt,' he said.

'Let me see.'

He lowered his hand and presented his nose for inspection. His face must be scarlet, he thought, which he supposed was the point.

'Now dry it,' she said. 'You have a handkerchief?'

He did, and again did as he was told.

'Now let's keep moving,' she said. 'You should get indoors.'

They continued back the way they had come, with the welcome difference that the wind was at their backs. Even so he began to shudder again. If he'd been at risk of losing his nose, he thought, how must it be for the men at the front?

'Thank you,' he said. 'I didn't say thank you.'

'Don't mention it.'

'You could have said nothing.'

'It's my duty to kill you, Captain, not to ruin your looks.'

They turned right near the Kusminsky Wing, from where Bauer could make out the hospital's small second storey.

'And would you?' he asked, trying to sound light-hearted.

'Would I what?'

'Kill me?'

She appeared to think the matter over then said, 'Reluctantly I'll have to say no. How many of my staff would be shot if I killed a German officer. Ten? Twenty? Frankly, you're not worth it.'

'But if there were no consequences,' he persisted, 'for you or anyone else?'

'Fishing for compliments, Captain? Nice enough not to kill? You're setting the bar exceedingly low.'

'All right, leave me out of it. Hypothetically, if you could get away with it, would you kill a German for your country?'

'If I could get away with it, most certainly.'

'I don't believe that for a moment.'

'So much the better for me.'

'Faced with the reality, you'd hesitate.'

'Why? Because I'm a woman?'

'Because you're a human being,' he said. Seeing her sardonic expression, he added, 'A civilised one, I mean.'

'Well, I'm sorry to disappoint you, Captain, but as it happens I've already killed for my country.'

He looked sideways at her and the wind slapped his cheek. Her expression was solemn. 'Not recently,' she said. 'And at a distance, which I daresay made it easier.'

'In the Civil War?' he guessed.

'I operated a machine gun for a time.'

'Where was this?' he asked, hoping to catch her out.

'Along the Don. September 1919. They were Cossacks I killed. At the time they were on foot.'

'How many?' he asked.

'Five went down, that I counted. Two slithered away. Three of them stayed where they were.'

The strangeness of others, their alienness, he thought. The hospital was coming into view.

'Have I shocked you?' she asked.

'Not at all,' he lied.

'I've shocked you. Good.' She made a pistol of her right glove and aimed it at his belly. 'Those graves, I want them stopped.'

'As I said, I'll do my best.'

'I'm serious.'

'I can see that,' he said, nodding at her phantom gun.

'Good,' she said, and fired, a gesture slightly blunted by the lazy recoil of her hand.

FIVE

'I'm the ping-pong king of Bavaria,' Pflieger said, batting a table-tennis ball against the wall. 'None of you stand a chance against me.'

'Oh yes?' said Norbert Ritter. 'I'm fairly handy myself.'

Bauer paused at the door of the quartermaster's store, a large room at the hospital's northern end. Standing at a trestle table that served as a counter were Pflieger and Molineux; on chairs behind it, Ehrlich and Ritter, the latter lounging in an unquartermasterly way, reminding Bauer of a silverback gorilla that he had once seen with Clara at the zoological gardens in Berlin.

'Bauer!' cried Molineux. 'You're not still working, are you? You've been at it all afternoon. Give it up. Come and see our spoils.'

'I'm looking for Metz,' Bauer said. 'Any of you know where he is?'

'His office?' Molineux said.

'No, I checked there.'

'He's in the motor pool,' Ehrlich said. 'Went with Winkel.'

This was odd. Despite a let-up in casualties there was plenty of work to do at the hospital.

'Actually, I'm out of practice,' Pflieger continued. 'I gave up the game. Lost a match to a Jew boy, a typical Yid. I said to myself, "This isn't really a sport."'

'We found all this in the cellar,' Molineux announced. 'Bats, balls, a net, a table. Who would have thought? No vodka, alas.'

Bauer tried to picture the author of *War and Peace* and *Anna Karenina* playing table tennis. No, it was impossible. Nor did it seem likely that such equipment had been brought here by a Bolshevik, especially one as serious as Acting Head Custodian Trubetzkaya. No, it must have belonged to Tolstoy's children or, more likely, to his grandchildren, either towards the end of his life or in the seven years between his death and the Revolution.

He asked Ehrlich what had taken Metz to the motor pool.

'You'll have to ask him yourself. Sir.'

'I'm asking you.'

'The lieutenant colonel didn't say,' Ehrlich said.

'And wait till you see this,' Molineux said, unknotting a calico bundle on the table before him and revealing a large mortar and pestle – brass or bronze, tarnished, the mortar hardly smaller than a dinner plate. 'A real beauty,' he went on, taking up the pestle and grinding an imaginary substance in the bowl. He turned the mortar upside down and cupped a hand over its underside 'Just needs a little polish, that's all.'

'You're aware of the standing orders against looting?' Bauer said.

'Steady on,' Molineux said, looking hurt. 'The Bolsheviks don't believe in private property. This isn't looting but requisitioning enemy assets.'

'For Pabst?'

'Why Pabst?'

'Our cook,' he said.

'Oh, *that*,' Molineux replied. 'Pabst be damned. Pabst has cooking utensils coming out of his arse. Flavour enough for anyone. No, this will do nicely for my wife – she's all for private property.'

'I'm relieved to hear it,' Bauer said. 'Now, if you'll excuse me, I need to find Metz.'

The gravel road to the motor pool had been reduced to two tracks of ice through the snow. The motor pool itself, a former coach house, was a long, low building situated near the gates, with three sets of carriage-sized wooden doors. Outside it were several lorries and a sentry stamping on ice, his head wreathed in the steam of his breathing. Bauer saluted and went inside. An ambulance. A military-brown Soviet limousine. Winkel and Metz were bent over the limousine's engine, while beside them stood Fabian Drexel, the battalion's pharmacist. Had someone declared a day off? Bauer wondered. Winkel was a gifted motor mechanic, but Drexel's presence here was puzzling. Bauer coughed a little and all three men looked around.

'Ah, Bauer, how good to see you,' Metz said. 'What do you think of the …' He turned to Winkel. 'What is it again?'

'A ZIS-101,' Winkel said, clearly enthused.

'A ZIS. That's it. The Soviets have kindly left it for us. What do you think? A beauty, isn't she?'

'Did they also leave fuel?' Bauer asked.

'Now, now, there's no call for sarcasm. Compared with a lorry or a tank this won't be thirsty at all.' To Winkel he said, 'Can you get her running?'

'I think so, sir, but it might take a few days.' Catching Bauer's eye, he added, 'Not full time, just off and on.'

'Excellent,' Metz said. 'Then I'll leave you to it. Now, Captain, to what do I owe the pleasure?'

'I was hoping to speak with you, sir.'

'Then feel free to join us. Lieutenant Drexel and I are on our way back to the house.'

Bauer glanced at Drexel. Thirty years old. Stocky. Dark hair on the back of his neck. Spectacles. A wide mouth and – by cruel coincidence – overactive salivary glands.

'All right,' Bauer said. He had planned to speak with Metz in private, but why shouldn't Drexel hear what he had to say? They left the motor pool and Bauer got straight to the point. 'Yesterday I visited the cemetery. It's too small for our purposes. If we stay for more than a few weeks it's going to overflow.'

'You forget that in a few weeks' time we'll be in or near Moscow,' Metz said.

'And if Yasnaya Polyana becomes a base hospital?'

'Good God, Bauer, try to be an optimist for once. Our job is to keep the cemetery small.'

'There are also propaganda implications,' Bauer said. 'As Frau Trubetzkaya pointed out, even in death Tolstoy remains a major figure for the Soviets.'

'What of it?'

'We'll be goading them unnecessarily.'

'More than we already have?'

'I take your point, sir, but why magnify their hatred? They'll only fight us that much harder.'

'I can't agree with you,' Metz said. 'The propaganda advantage is ours. *We* control this place, and by asserting our authority here we strike a blow against the enemy. If we're to call ourselves the master race we must act like it. "German swine" that woman calls us, and do you know why? Because we Germans are too humane. Look at our great men: Wagner, Beethoven, Goethe, Schiller – and yet she calls us "German swine". She exploits our fundamental decency to mock and abuse us. Watch her, Bauer. See she doesn't get the better of you.'

They were drawing near to the main house, where in addition to a sentry there were corpsmen about, and although it was starting to snow Metz stopped to emphasise his point. 'We won't secure our position here by showing weakness, Captain. Lieutenant Drexel, don't you agree?'

'Yes, I do, sir,' Drexel said, then sucked back on surplus saliva.

Bauer glanced at the pharmacist's large square face. A bulbous nose. Wet, rubbery lips. Quite possibly he genuinely agreed with Metz. 'Sir, humiliating the enemy isn't a sign of strength,' Bauer said. 'If anything it's the opposite. One day we'll have to live with them —'

'Who says?'

'Well, isn't it inevitable?'

'You know, Bauer, your problem is that you lack imagination, and do you know why that is? It's because you're backwards looking. Oh, I don't mean as a surgeon – professionally you're sharp enough, and I commend you for it. But you suffer from a sickly attachment to the past. That book, for example.'

Bauer guessed at once which book he was referring to. '*War and Peace?*'

'Corporal Ehrlich tells me you made him surrender it to you.'

That Metz was raising this in the presence of a junior officer was annoying. Had he planned it this way?

'I thought it might be a first edition, sir. Of the translation, that is. And I was right about that.'

'I don't care what edition it is. I ordered it destroyed.'

'I thought if you knew of the book's true significance you might change your mind, sir.'

'Yet you failed to tell me about it.'

'To be frank, sir, I forgot about it. There's a lot going on.'

'Indeed there is. In the *present*, Bauer. The present. To forge a better future. And yet here you are mired in the past. Worse – the enemy's past!'

'Sir, this is a work in German,' Bauer said, 'a translation by the great Ernst Strenge.' In fact before opening the book he had never heard of Strenge, and he had no idea whether or not his work was esteemed.

'A translation of a *Slavic* book. A book, moreover, about a Slavic victory.'

'Permission to speak, sir?' Drexel said. Bauer and Metz both looked at him.

'Go ahead,' Metz said.

'I think it's possible that, apart from ignoring your orders, the captain has done the right thing.'

'Oh? How so?'

'By securing a trophy of war. If this book is as significant to the Bolsheviks as the captain makes out, it perhaps belongs in a museum. As a historical relic. A curiosity. Otherwise people might forget someday that the Slavs once thought themselves unconquerable.'

'Interesting,' Metz said. 'I do seem to recall reading years ago about an exhibition in Munich of degenerate art. You mean something like that?'

'Something like that,' Drexel said, then visibly swallowed some more spit.

'A Reich Museum of Superseded Cultures,' Metz said. 'You might be onto something, Lieutenant.'

'And if this estate has such special significance for the Soviets, our occupation of it is likewise significant. Possibly deserving of commemoration.'

An unfocused expression had entered Metz's eye, giving him the chiselled look of a Roman emperor in marble. 'Very well,' he said at last, 'I'm persuaded. Bauer ...'

'Yes, sir?'

'Secure the book. Perhaps hand it over to Quartermaster Ritter for safekeeping.'

'Very good, sir.'

'But be warned: subvert my orders again and I won't be so tolerant.'

'Yes, sir. And the graves? Shall we relocate them?'

'Good God, Bauer, were you listening to anything I said? Not one step backwards! Come on now, let's get out of this infernal snow.'

★   ★   ★

The casualty rate continued to be manageable, and because the following day it was Metz's turn to do surgery, Bauer lingered at the main house in the hope of seeing Katerina Dmitrievna. Outside there was another gale blowing, making it possible she wouldn't come, but after writing letters in his room for half an hour he was rewarded by the sight of her coming up the drive, accompanied by the head housekeeper, a woman of similar height but much larger girth. The wind was at the women's backs, bullying them forward, forcing Katerina to keep braking with short, jarring steps. A coil of her auburn hair, escaped from her *ushanka*, was frantically whipping her face.

Quickly Bauer put away his notes, tucked the estate's German copy of *War and Peace* into his greatcoat and went downstairs, arriving in the vestibule just as the women opened the door. With them came a blast of wind, causing the tasselled floor runner to rear like a snake and strike at their knees. Bauer sprang forward and stomped on its neck, then shouldered the door shut behind them. Katerina was laughing – not in the sardonic way he'd become used to, but joyfully, without reserve. Her hat and her coat were spangled with ice. 'It's freezing out there,' she cried in Russian. 'Even for me it's freezing! Much more of this and I'll have to start pitying you,' she added in a more familiar vein. Bauer bowed a little. The housekeeper bobbed, and in response Katerina tapped her on the arm. 'None of that, Comrade. He's a trespasser, not a guest.'

'Could you introduce me?' Bauer asked. Katerina Dmitrievna narrowed her eyes. 'We keep seeing one another,' he explained. 'I'd like to greet her by name.'

Katerina contemplated this then said, 'All right, if that's all. Your name's Paul, correct?'

'Yes, that's right.'

'Then, Paul Bauer, meet Daria Grigorievna, our housekeeper,' she said in Russian. 'Daria Grigorievna, meet Captain Paul Bauer, fascist beast.'

'Pleased to meet you,' Bauer said, deciding not to press for her surname, since Daria Grigorievna looked far from at ease. She was a stout woman, round-shouldered. Middle height, middle-aged. A doughy face with burst capillaries on her cheeks and nose. Frizzled brown hair pressed down with a calico scarf, which, if he was reading the Cyrillic correctly, was fashioned from a sack of flour.

'Goodbye, then,' Katerina Dmitrievna said abruptly, and both women turned to leave.

'But I have something for you,' he said. She turned around and he tapped his chest where *War and Peace* was wedged beneath his greatcoat.

'The Wehrmacht order of battle?'

'Hardly.'

'Then what is it?' she asked, signalling Daria Grigorievna to go.

'Could we go somewhere private?' he asked. 'The library perhaps?'

'All right, the library. I was going there anyway.'

From the vestibule they went into the small entrance hall, along the corridor and into the library. Bauer shut the door.

'Should I be worried?' Katerina asked. Her tone was derisive, but with something like horror Bauer realised there was apprehension in her eyes.

'No, no, no, I'm just returning your book,' he said, drawing it out of his greatcoat.

Katerina glanced at the book with indifference. 'I thought Metz was going to have it destroyed.'

'I intervened.'

'And you expect me to be grateful?'

'I thought you might have had second thoughts.'

'When you're gone, everything in German will likely be expunged.'

Ausgelöscht – how pleasurable to hear such a polished turn of phrase. It was hard to believe she was not a native speaker. 'Very well then. But the book. Will you take it back?'

'If Metz won't read it, why not an underling? Go ahead, since you're such a big reader.'

'I've already read it,' he replied.

'That's right, you said.'

So she'd noticed his little boast. 'A long time ago,' he said. 'I was fifteen.'

'And how old are you now? Fifty?'

'I'm forty,' he replied.

'Really?' she said. 'Your hair loss, I suppose.' Involuntarily he palmed his hair. It felt no thinner than normal.

She smiled. 'So it's been – what? – twenty-five years since you've read it. Time for a reread, I'd say, this time as a cautionary tale.'

'I'll return it to the shelves,' he said.

75

'That would be a pity. A Wehrmacht officer following in Napoleon's footsteps – now that I think about it, you and this volume could have been made for one another. Keep it. Read.'

'Only if you're sure.'

'I'm sure. But first there's a passage I want to find for you,' she said, putting out her hand for the book.

'You know it that well?' he asked, passing it to her.

'I've read it four times,' she said, riffling through the pages. 'Never in German, mind. Though I must admit, *Krieg und Frieden* sounds more euphonious than *Voyna i mir* – that partial rhyme, I suppose, the reason you Germans slip so readily from *Frieden* to *Krieg*, perhaps.'

'I should go,' he said. This was true. At the hospital they'd be wondering where he was.

'This won't take long,' she said. 'Keep talking. Start by telling me why you read *War and Peace* at fifteen.'

'My house was in mourning. A brother. Verdun. My escape was reading. *War and Peace* was long.'

Had he spoken of this to anyone before? He couldn't remember discussing it with Clara. Perhaps it helped that Katerina Dmitrievna was looking not at him but at the book. 'Before I studied medicine I wanted to be a writer,' he went on. 'Even afterwards, for a while.'

Now she did look up at him. 'Really? What sort of writer?'

'A novelist, I suppose. At least that was the idea. I even started a novel. Never finished it, of course.'

'Why "of course"?'

'The usual reasons: work, friends, love. Life,' he said, then trailed off, suddenly aware how pitiful his old ambitions sounded in this of all places.

'Ah, here it is,' Katerina Dmitrievna said. From her jacket she took a pencil, marked the passage and with a scrap of paper bookmarked the page.

'You won't read it to me?' he asked.

'Read it yourself,' she said, and flung the book at him straight and hard.

'*Ouf*,' he said, taking it on the chest. 'I'll return it when I'm done. But more gently.'

'As you wish,' she said. 'Frankly, by then I expect you'll be gone. And I don't mean to Tula.'

'But to Chern?'

'I was thinking of Berlin.'

'Well, if that happens you'll be able to have those graves removed. Apologies – I couldn't talk Metz into relocating them.'

'You're too timid.'

'He outranks me, that's all.'

'Too *ängstlich*,' she repeated, compounding the insult with a smile. 'But don't worry, we can't all be heroes.'

★ ★ ★

All day he kept the bookmarked page of *War and Peace* closed, a task made easier by the demands of the operating room. It was not until midnight, sitting propped up in his camp bed, as Molineux snored on the other side of the room, that Bauer opened the book and, by the light of a Hindenburg candle, read the passage that Katerina Dmitrievna had marked.

Bonaparte was born lucky. He has excellent soldiers. And the Germans were the first he attacked. You'd have to be a do-nothing not to beat the Germans. Ever since the world began, everybody's beaten the Germans. And they've beaten nobody. Except each other. It was on them he earned his glory.

Bauer chuckled. He liked her impudence. The passage was from relatively early in the book, and the speaker, he saw, was old Prince Bolkonsky – one of the novel's patriarchs, he recalled, the knowledge shooting like a cork from the depths of his mind. Bolkonsky was addressing his son Andrei on the eve of his departure to fight the French, his fatherly anxiety wrapped in badinage.

Bauer closed the book, wondering if Metz's hostility to it was in some sense justified. *Everybody's beaten the Germans.* The old prince was partly a comical figure, his pronouncements often foolish, yet somehow Bauer was stirred by the thought that German principalities that had once been the playthings of Russia and France were now, as a single state, capable of dominating both; even if, in another part of his mind, he loathed nationalism and all its works. He'd felt similar ambivalence during the Berlin Olympics, an event he'd first dismissed as propaganda, a distraction from the regime's crimes against workers' unions and the Jews, only to find himself surreptitiously pleased as one German athlete after another won gold.

He glanced again at the book. It was a massive tome, well over a thousand pages. In the last three years he had read very little fiction, Clara's death having sapped his desire – no, his capacity – to be moved by a story on a page. It had taken him by surprise, this impairment, as he'd had years to anticipate losing his wife. Clara had even spoken beforehand of how liberating for both of them her death would be: for her, from physical suffering; for him, from the anguish of having to witness it. But no. When she had died his only relief had been on her account, and far from experiencing her death as a liberation it had blighted everything that had given him pleasure, not only fiction but also art, cinema, friendship, talk of politics and ideas, travel, sexual desire and even immersion in water, be it a bath, a lake, or, on rare occasions, the sea. Cigarettes, too, had lost their savour for him, though he still smoked two packets a day. In fact, the only source of satisfaction to escape this great winnowing had been surgery, which demanded so little of his heart but so much from his hands and brain.

He opened the book. Yes, it was monumental, but he had insomnia on his side. He found the first page, settled down and started to read.

SIX

One week into their stay at Yasnaya Polyana the flow of casualties from the front was if anything lighter than at first, contradicting Metz's claim that the frost would intensify combat operations. From what Bauer could tell, the division was spent, the attack on Tula having faltered against defences far stronger than any the 3rd Panzer had encountered before, not only conventional trenches and barbed wire but also anti-tank ditches, scrap-metal hedgehogs and concrete dragons' teeth, designed to funnel attackers into minefields or zones of concentrated artillery and machine-gun fire. Into these shooting galleries the already exhausted division had poured men, machines, munitions and fuel. And then fallen back. Tula remained hemmed in from the west, south and east, but according to aircraft reconnaissance reports the city was still receiving supplies and reinforcements from the north.

A kind of crazed humour convulsed the unit. Before dinner one night Molineux performed an imitation – all the funnier for its unsparing realism – of a gibbering, shell-shocked man who'd lost control of his limbs. In the barracks practical jokes became cruel: two corpsmen reading a letter to an illiterate comrade pretended his fiancée had married someone else; others convinced an eighteen-year-old recruit that his tinea cruris was syphilis.

The first frostbite cases began to arrive. Bauer had never seen frostbite, let alone treated it, and had cause to be thankful again for Metz's experience of the previous war. The key was patience, Metz explained to a gathering of doctors and nursing attendants. In the right conditions frostbitten tissue could regenerate, either partially or in some cases altogether. To encourage healing, patients were to be put in a warm but well-ventilated ward, their bedclothes pulled aside to allow blackened limbs and digits to dry. Amputation would only be considered if and when a clear line of demarcation had formed.

At this time a *Landser* arrived in theatre with a mortar wound to his leg. He was conscious and admitted to 'bad enough' pain, and to take his mind off it during the examination Bauer asked him what his occupation had been before the war. Stonemason, he replied. His accent was Swabian. He gestured at the wound, a brutal gash to the thigh. 'Do you think I'll get back to it?'

'It depends on what I find in there. But based on what I'm seeing so far I don't see why not. The bone's unbroken. We'll do our utmost with the muscle.'

'Thanks, doctor,' the Swabian said. 'I know you'll look after me.'

Bauer pressed the man's arm, knowing that a well-timed touch could do more to reassure a patient than any number of reassuring words. He handed the Swabian over to Hirsch, went to the basin and scrubbed and soaped his hands, rinsing with the aid of a pair of elbow taps made by Winkel from the gearsticks of shot-up lorries.

'Jesus *Christ*,' he heard behind him and turned around to see Winkel ripping the ether mask from the Swabian's face and replacing it with oxygen.

'A problem?' Bauer asked, striding over to the stretcher.

'Heart's stopped,' Winkel said, then with the heels of his palms began pumping rhythmically on the Swabian's chest. Bauer seized the patient's wrist, probing for a pulse. Nothing, nothing, nothing. After half a minute Winkel ceased his thrusting, tore off the drapes, called for silence and put an ear to the man's chest. 'I think he's gone, sir.'

'Try more compressions.'

Winkel obeyed as Bauer held on to the patient's wrist. Demchak and Pflieger were standing by in silence, while Hirsch ... Hirsch remained seated by the head of the stretcher, his expression stunned. This was an anaesthetic death, pure and simple. Again Winkel checked for a heartbeat. He straightened up. 'He's dead, sir.'

Around the stretcher the others were immobile, as if in imitation of the corpse. Bauer himself couldn't move, felt weak and empty, a roaring noise inside like wind in a tunnel.

It was Winkel who reacted first, nodding at the body and telling Pflieger and Demchak to take it away. They obeyed. Bauer felt stupefied. He had lost plenty of patients on the table before; it was to be expected, part of the job. But not like this.

Winkel was tugging him by the sleeve, by his medical patch, the staff of Asclepius with its helical snake. 'Sir?'

'I'm taking a break,' Bauer said, and peeled off his scrubs. He said nothing to Hirsch, couldn't bring himself to look at him, though God knows he had to be in a bad way himself. 'I'll be having a smoke,' he announced to nobody in particular. He fetched his coat from the reception room and went outside into a punishing wind. Turning his back to it he lit up, drew the smoke into his lungs and began walking, just walking, allowing himself to be driven along by the wind, knowing that the return journey would be arduous, even painful, and not caring a jot. He had to get away. It was mid-afternoon but already the light was dim. To the south-west, beyond the main drive, the sun was a pale disc crashing at an angle through the trees.

He thought of the Swabian, the stonemason, Hans Jürgen Voigt, who had trusted him to do his best; a man whose existence had been as rich, as vivid and involving as that of anyone who had lived. Such a *stupid* death, and one for which Bauer felt responsible, since twice before he had pushed away the suspicion that Hirsch's ineptitude had cost a patient his life. Well, no more. He would never work with Hirsch again.

★ ★ ★

Dinner was tense, or Bauer found it so, rage rising in him each time he glanced at Hirsch, who for his part avoided his eye.

So far Metz didn't know of the Swabian's death, but after dinner Bauer meant to remedy that. As if sensing what was coming to him Metz looked irritable. The others, too, seemed out of sorts. Molineux's conversation was cutting and mean, a reliable sign he'd run out of booze, while the situation at Tula probably explained the glumness of the rest. Strategically, the stalemate there was disastrous, further delaying the capture of Moscow. The latest aim was to take the capital by Christmas, though if Tula kept resisting even this looked unachievable.

'Quartet?' Molineux suggested as two of Pabst's men cleared up the plates.

Drexel adjusted his spectacles, slurped on his saliva and said, 'Give me twenty minutes.'

'Bauer, what about you?' Molineux asked.

'The same,' he replied. When he was done with Metz, a game of cards might be calming.

'You won't slink off to that damn book of yours, will you?'

It had been impossible to hide the book he was reading from Molineux, and just as hard to get him not to mention it in the mess. Bauer flashed him a warning look and he appeared to get the message, turning instead to Zöllner. 'Hans?'

'Sure, I'll play,' Zöllner said, smiling his agreeable smile. 'But not for too long. I have to write to my fiancée.'

'Christ alive, you write to her every night.'

'Every second night.'

'Either way she'll get the impression you love her, and then where will you be?'

'In love with each other?' Zöllner ventured.

'Ha! Have you had her yet?'

'For the love of God,' Metz said from the head of the table, 'some *decorum*, Captain. This is an officer's mess, not a bawdy house.'

'Sorry, sir,' Molineux said. 'I got carried away.'

There was silence for a while, then Zöllner said, 'I'm a practising Christian, if that answers your question. And so is she.'

'I'm glad to hear it,' Molineux said piously. 'As long as you're up for cards. In fact, put some cash down and you could be Zoroastrian for all I care.' He swung about. 'Hirsch, what about you, you retrograde microbe? Are you in?'

'I don't think so. Not if you're playing for money.'

'Come on, just a few pfennigs. To keep things interesting.'

'I'd better not.'

'Oh, come on, don't be such a pansy.'

'You took six marks off me last time.'

'So your luck is due to change.'

'My luck never changes. Not at cards.'

'Hear that, sir?' Molineux said, appealing to Metz. 'Defeatism. And look, he's not even ashamed of it.'

In fact Hirsch was blushing, more overtly unsettled by Molineux's teasing than by accidentally killing a patient.

'If the lieutenant is unlucky at cards,' Metz said, 'he shouldn't have to play.'

'But, sir, he's not unlucky, just cowardly.'

'If the stars are against him,' Metz said, 'he'd be a fool to play.'

'Stars?' Weidemann said, drawing everyone's attention; it was rare for the major to speak at table. 'You mean that figuratively, I take it.'

'Both figuratively and literally, Major,' Metz said.

'You think the stars could influence – *literally* – the lieutenant's luck at cards?'

'I don't say they do – at least, not with any certainty. How could I? But Major, let me ask you this: can you prove that they don't?'

Weidemann swatted away this idea. 'I can't prove a negative, *Herr Oberstleutnant*. But what you're saying is superstitious rot. Astrology belongs in the Dark Ages.'

Bauer suppressed an urge to applaud.

'You're assuming science knows everything,' Metz said, 'our ancestors nothing at all. Has it crossed your mind that the traditions you deride as superstitious might contain insights into the workings of the cosmos?'

'Such as a tendency to make Hirsch lose at cards?'

'Scoff if you wish, Major, but consider the fact that our bodies are more than fifty percent water. The brain, as we know too well here, is viscous. Now, contemplate the gravitational pull of the moon on the oceans, the tides, and tell me that a heavenly body can't alter our behaviour.'

'It's true,' Molineux said. 'A heavenly body invariably alters my behaviour.'

Weidemann said, 'All right, let's pretend you're correct about the moon —'

'And the planets,' Metz said. 'Don't overlook the planets.'

'All right, the planets too. Shouldn't their effect on human behaviour be uniform?'

'Not at all,' Metz replied in the weary drawl of a professor addressing a slow-witted undergraduate. 'Not only do human bodies differ from one another, they routinely respond differently to identical stimuli.'

'Very well, but you were talking about the stars,' Weidemann said. 'Surely you're not suggesting that their gravity reaches us from so far away?'

'Again, Major, why not?'

'You claim that stars … no, constellations, composed of stars arrayed in depth and so not even near one another, can affect individuals here on Earth?'

'Major, as I said, I'm just speculating. Science doesn't hold the answers to such questions. It can't even tell us whether the effects stars have on human behaviour – if such effects exist – are gravitational in nature or the consequence of some undiscovered force. Time will tell, I suppose.'

'Unless it doesn't.'

'Major, there are two types of men in this world,' Metz said, 'those whose minds are open and those whose minds are closed.'

There was a brief pause, then Hirsch said, 'I do keep losing at quartet.' All eyes turned on him and he violently blushed.

'There you have it,' Metz said without a trace of irony. Looking suddenly exhausted he rose from the table, wished all of them goodnight and excused himself. Bauer would have liked to go after him straight away, but even allowing for his anger at Hirsch he preferred to spare him anxiety about a situation that was fundamentally of Metz's making.

In fact the next to leave was Drexel. Bauer then had to reassure Molineux that he really did intend to turn up later for cards, and by the time he reached the entrance hall Metz had been gone for some time. The lieutenant colonel was an early sleeper and was possibly already preparing for bed, but, opting first to try his study, Bauer went down the corridor and rapped twice on the door. How often had Sophia Andreyevna stood here after dinner, he wondered, and knocked on the door of her world-famous husband? How many times had she been angry enough to barge in?

'Go away,' Metz called from inside. 'I'm busy.'

'It's me: Bauer.'

'Later.'

'Sir, this is urgent.' He would not be put off. 'Sir?'

'Later, dammit.'

Bauer grasped the doorknob. A man had died and there had to be consequences. He opened the door, stepped inside but immediately stopped. At his desk Metz was sitting with his tunic half off, exposing the pallid underside of one arm to Drexel, who was piercing it with a large syringe. Metz turned, swinging the lucky shrapnel on its chain around his neck. 'I'm busy,' he snarled. 'Get out of here.'

Bauer reversed and closed the door. His first instinct was to leave, but leaving wouldn't lessen Metz's fury, and what he'd just seen had no bearing on the business with Hirsch. From behind the door there was murmured conversation, then about two minutes later Drexel emerged, greeted him coolly and strolled away, carrying a book-sized wooden box inlaid with ivory or nacre.

Bauer knocked on the half-open door.

'Yes?' Metz called, his voice much milder than before. Bauer stepped inside and closed the door behind him. Metz was sitting behind his desk, his uniform rebuttoned. 'Captain, what can I do for you?'

Bauer blinked. If Metz wanted to pretend nothing unusual had happened, then so be it, Bauer thought, and in measured tones he described the Swabian's death.

'That's all?' Metz said when he was done. 'We lose patients all the time.'

Bauer was stupefied. 'Sir, this wasn't a normal death.'

'Well? What do you want me to do about it?'

'Reassign Hirsch. Get a new anaesthetist. A trained one.'

'We've already been through this. I've written to Major General Oeding. There are no anaesthetists to spare.'

'Write again. Surely Oeding can't approve of patients dying for no reason.'

'Oeding has bigger concerns.'

'And what about you, sir? Do you have bigger concerns?'

'Meaning?'

'Promotion, say? Not rocking the boat?' This was reckless but he didn't give a damn.

'Captain, you're overwrought,' Metz said, his voice preternaturally calm. 'Accordingly, I'm going to overlook your remarks.'

'Do as you please, sir, but I can't overlook the lieutenant's incompetence.'

'Incompetence? Isn't that putting it too strongly? The man's a trained dentist.'

'He has no feel for anaesthetics.'

'He needs more training, that's all. Ask Hermann to help.'

'Sir, Molineux might be good at what he does but he's no teacher. And he dislikes Hirsch.'

'Dislikes him? What makes you say that?'

'Sir, it's obvious. Surely you've noticed?'

'Captain, I have two hundred and fifty men under my command. I can't be expected to know all their petty goings-on.'

Bauer paused, consciously collecting himself. 'Sir, what about the other solution we've discussed: giving the job to Corporal Winkel?'

'No and no again. Anaesthesia is the preserve of officers.'

'That's all very well; you're not the one who's lost a patient.'

'Captain, I'm warning you: don't push your luck. In case you haven't noticed you're on active service in the field. The standard of care here won't always match what you were used to in a civilian hospital.'

'A year ago you would have said that constraints in the field are the very reason we should strive for perfection.'

'A year ago we were in France. A year ago my officers weren't getting killed.'

In his voice there was a hint of real distress, and while it was unclear whether this was for himself or for Dieter, Bauer was touched – previously the loss had apparently only irritated Metz. Encouraged, he said, 'Sir, what I just saw in here with Drexel —'

'Is no concern of yours.'

'As a fellow surgeon I believe it is. Your judgement —'

'Listen, there's nothing wrong with my judgement, Captain. On the contrary, I've never felt such clarity of purpose.'

'I can only comment on what I've noticed, sir. Your volatility. Your anger.'

'Volatility? Nonsense.'

'In recent weeks you haven't seemed yourself.'

'If I'm angry at times, that's natural. These are testing times. And a little anger, rightly directed, can spur men on. Yourself included, Bauer.'

'Sir, what was in that syringe?'

'That's a private matter between me and Lieutenant Drexel.'

'Weidemann didn't prescribe it?'

'Weidemann has nothing to do with it.'

'Shouldn't he, though?'

'I'm making myself hardier, not treating an illness.'

'But how?'

'I prefer not to say, at least not at this stage. Though I can reveal that one of the components is Pervatin.'

'Good God, sir, and you expect me not to be concerned? What about the side effects?'

'Captain, calm yourself. Drexel and I are conducting an experiment whose results we will report to the authorities at the proper time. For now all you need to know is that the formulation both magnifies the benefits of Pervatin and eliminates its risks.'

'Including the risk of addiction?'

'As a smoker you dare to lecture me on the topic of addiction?'

'The consequences of smoking are quite different, sir.'

'Yes, wholly deleterious,' Metz said.

'Sir, why not get Major Weidemann's opinion? He's the most experienced of us. If he concurs with you, good. If not, reconsider.'

'Oh, Weidemann,' Metz said dismissively. 'An arch conservative —'

'All the better —'

'Whose time has passed. The Reich's future depends on young men of action and imagination. Men like Drexel.'

'Maybe. But what about the long-term damage to your health? Have you considered that?'

'Captain, we all face long-term damage to our health. It's called death. Life is damage. War is damage. We must be bold enough to take risks. Boldness is all if we're to beat the Bolsheviks, who though inferior to us are far more numerous. Luckily boldness is an Aryan trait, a trait Drexel can enhance.'

'He's bottling Germanness?'

'You say that satirically, but why not? Taking the native strengths of an ordinary German like myself – intelligence, daring, resolution, rigour – and enhancing them, that's precisely what we're doing. To shrink from the attempt would be cowardly, a dereliction of duty.'

Bauer hesitated. He was getting nowhere, that was clear. 'Sir, I can't work with Hirsch any longer,' he said, returning to the purpose of his visit. 'Not after this.'

'Captain, you can and you will. You're a fine officer, I know you can.'

Bauer grimaced, incensed but also swayed a little by the praise. 'Besides,' Metz went on, 'it's an order.'

SEVEN

The following morning, Tuesday, 11 November, Bauer asked Molineux if he would give Hirsch some more training in anaesthetics.

'Waste of time,' Molineux said, straining to pull on a boot.

'What makes you say that?' Bauer asked.

'Anaesthesia is an art – you either have a gift for it or you don't.'

'I'm not suggesting he'll reach your level,' Bauer said, 'just that you'll drag him up a bit.'

'Drag him up a lot,' Molineux said. His second boot was giving him even more trouble than the first. 'I trained for years.'

'I'm only asking you to do your best.'

'Under the hands of a skilled anaesthetist the patient is an instrument to be plucked and played,' Molineux said, finally getting his second boot on.

'Rubbish. Musicians bring their instruments to life.'

'As do I!' Molineux said. He stood up and reached for his tunic. 'Wakefulness depletes; unconsciousness restores.'

'Whatever you say, Hermann. The point is, will you do it?'

'What's in it for me?'

Bauer had anticipated this question, or something like it. 'The first bottle of vodka I can find.'

'You have a deal,' Molineux said. 'But don't expect a miracle.'

'I won't. Just stop him killing any more of my patients.'

Molineux went to the mirror he'd hung by his bed and began flicking a comb through his thinning hair. Bauer waited by the door, resisting an urge to share the information that Metz was injecting amphetamines, knowing Molineux would treat it less as a cause for concern than as a choice bit of gossip.

But was it a concern? Bauer wondered. Pervatin, in tablet form, had been in widespread use throughout the army since the French campaign, particularly among tank crews, who took it to stay awake for the vital two or three days after breaking through an enemy's line. To Bauer's knowledge there was no one studying the consequences for health, no doubt because there were more pressing threats than Pervatin to the wellbeing of the average panzerman. Taking it intravenously, as Metz was doing, would no doubt concentrate its effect. It would be necessary to keep an eye on Metz, though assessing his behaviour wasn't going to be easy when, as Metz himself had pointed out, certain side effects of amphetamine use – determination, dynamism, grandiosity, aggression – were established aspects of his character.

'Ready?' Molineux asked.

'For the last fifteen minutes.'

'Unprecedented. This Hirsch thing has really shaken you up.'

They left the room and went downstairs, where they found Winkel trying to speak with the housekeeper.

'Oh, *hello*,' Molineux said. 'What's going on here?'

'I'm asking her name,' Winkel said.

Bauer turned to her. 'Daria Grigorievna, *da*?' She nodded but wouldn't meet his eye.

Molineux said, 'Planning to have it off with one of the local ladies, Corporal? Slav females are strictly forbidden, don't you know?'

'It's not like that,' Winkel said. 'Our duties overlap.'

'I'll bet they do. Lucky you. Just watch yourself, though, she's quite a heifer. You don't want to get crushed.'

'Sir, you'll embarrass her.'

'She can't understand us, Corporal. Can you, Milk Cow?'

'But you're staring,' Winkel said. 'It's not nice.'

'Good God, man, what's the point of being the master race if we can't ogle a lady subhuman?'

Bauer seized him by the elbow and began steering him towards the mess.

'Steady on,' Molineux said, 'I'm not finished here.'

'All right, but hurry up. Breakfast calls.'

'A favour, Sepp?' asked Molineux.

'What is it?' Winkel said, uncharacteristically abrupt.

'The temperature?'

'I'm not sure. I haven't checked.'

'Could you now, though, before it rises? My chattering teeth are saying it's a record low.'

*　　*　　*

Bauer found Katerina Dmitrievna in the library, on a ladder, returning books to the shelves. 'Restocking?' he asked.

95

'Making it harder for you to carry them off when you go.'

The room was icy, their breaths vaporous, though for what seemed like the first time in weeks there was sunshine outside, making the frost on the window panes glitter.

'You needn't worry. Our top priority if we have to retreat won't be books.'

'And burning's more your style with literature, I've heard.'

It would take decades, he supposed, for Germans to live down the barbarities of National Socialism. To make a beginning he said, 'I'm enjoying *War and Peace.*'

'Good for you.'

'But there's something you should know about the copy you lent me.'

'Gave you,' she corrected.

'There are annotations.'

She peered down at him, making him think of his allegedly thinning hair. 'What sort of annotations?'

'They're in pencil, just a handful in the opening chapters. Comments on the translation. Did Tolstoy know German?'

'Of course.'

'Then you'd better check,' he said, and held out the book. 'I've marked them all.'

She descended the ladder, accepted the book and examined the first of the pages he'd marked.

'What do you think?' he asked.

She looked at a second page, a third, then smiled. 'I think you've made a small discovery, Captain. Congratulations.'

'You think it's Tolstoy?'

'Undoubtedly. The handwriting. The irascibility, come to that.'

'There are nine of them,' he said.

She began to read and Bauer took the opportunity to admire her. Her neck was slender and elegant, her pulled-back hair revealing a small brown mole on her nape. After three or four minutes she closed the book, her expression thoughtful.

'I suppose you'll be needing it back now,' he said.

She considered this for a moment then shook her head. 'No, a book needs a reader and, as I said the other day, you are this one's. Its one and only, probably, since I doubt Lev Nikolayevich would have read very far beyond this point.' From a pocket of her quilted jacket she took out a pencil. 'I'll just transcribe what he's written.'

'Of course. And don't worry, I'll return it when I've finished.'

'If you wish. But as you know, I doubt you'll still be here.'

'I'll read quickly.'

'You'll need to,' she said.

Using an empty shelf as a desk she began transcribing Tolstoy's annotations into a notebook. Bauer wandered over to one of the room's two windows, intending to look outside, only to be dazzled by sunlight in the frost on the glass. Instead he turned around, as if to warm his back, and gazed again on Katerina. Her expression was serious, which in combination with her glasses emphasised her teacherly look; she was peering downwards, compressing her smallish chin. Bauer's heart rate was escalating. She looked lovely to him – radiant – and in alarm he shook his head. Such feelings were futile, absurd.

'Done,' she said, and handed back the book.

'The original manuscript,' he said. 'Is it here somewhere?'

'Don't be ridiculous,' Katerina said. 'It's in Moscow.'

'Of course,' he replied, feeling foolish. He made to go.

'So, Captain,' she said, ascending her ladder, 'which parts do you prefer: the war or the peace?'

'I couldn't say,' he replied, turning to face her again.

'Don't be a coward. Choose.'

'If I say war, do I incriminate myself?'

'Just answer truthfully.'

'All right. The war parts.'

'Why?'

He hesitated, assembling an answer. 'Because the novel's drawing room scenes are all alike, while each war scene is warlike in its own way. I'm generalising, of course.'

'Of course,' she said. If he had managed to amuse her she wasn't showing it. She had no more books in her arms but seemed in no hurry to come down.

'For example, the first time the French appear,' he said, 'at a distance, lobbing cannon balls at the Russians on a bridge. This is Austria somewhere. I forget the river.'

'The Enns,' she said.

'You *remember* it?'

'I told you, I've read the book four times,' she said. 'Go on.'

'Then you'll know what I mean,' he said, aware she might find his observations banal. 'The bottleneck on the bridge, the suspense – will they get across or won't they? The various ways the Russians repress their fright – with humour, annoyance, bravado. And then they *get away with it*. No casualties. That's the surprise. But as a reader you've been warned. There's going to be blood.'

'Something rather hinted at by the title, wouldn't you say?'

'But even when blood *is* spilled, Tolstoy startles you. The first battle …?'

'Schöngraben.'

'Yes, Schöngraben,' he said, reassured she knew what he was talking about but also keen to prove that his interest wasn't boyish or, worse, militaristic. 'The Russian rearguard is saved by a junior officer, an artillery captain who's homosexual.'

Trubetzkaya laughed. 'Now *that* I don't remember.'

'I'm inferring,' he admitted. 'Tolstoy depicts him as gentle and fey. You get the impression he's a military ignoramus who chooses targets on instinct, as an artist dabs paint onto canvas. And yet with only four cannon he holds the Russian centre together and stops the French deploying their reserves. I've never read a war scene like it.'

'I'll have to reread it,' she said.

'To tell me I'm wrong?'

'Not necessarily. Your interpretation might have offended Tolstoy, but what of it? He was only the author. Good novels always outflank their authors, and *War and Peace* is better than good. Had poor Lev tried to resist, it would have put him to flight.'

What a pleasure it was to talk literature with her. A similar conversation might be had with Molineux, but only in an ironical mode. With Katerina Dmitrievna sincerity appeared to be an option, and suddenly it struck him she might be in need of a friend as much as he was.

'Tell me, what made you notice that particular detail? The artillery captain. Are you homosexual?'

'No,' he said, taken aback but determined not to show it. 'It just struck me as a sign of Tolstoy's ... capaciousness. The range of his curiosity, his empathy. Mind you, he's clearly writing for Russians. He uses phrases like "our army", "our flank", "our cavalry". That startled me a little, I must say.'

'To be excluded.'

'Exactly. And of course I'm not reading him in Russian.'

'Oh, I wouldn't worry about that,' she said. 'You're not missing much. As a stylist he's no match for, say, Turgenev. Or Flaubert.'

He laughed. 'Now I'm scandalised.'

'I'm not saying he's not a great writer. The greatest, even. Just that he's not especially concerned with mellifluence. Flaubert would be in agony if he had to use the same word twice on one page, whereas if a word suits Tolstoy he'll flog it to death.'

'I think you're trying to shock me, Katerina Dmitrievna.'

'Trust me, Captain, however much my words might shock you, you shock me more by being here.'

He let this comment pass, and luckily so did she. 'The drawing room scenes,' she said, 'what about them? All those women. Are you in love with Natasha?'

'When I read the book at fifteen I was. Besotted.'

'But now?'

'When the novel begins, Natasha is thirteen – I'd forgotten that – so it makes sense I loved her when I was much the same age. This time I'm not so sure.'

'By Volume Two she's a young woman.'

'I'm no longer a young man.'

She laughed. 'That's true.'

'And she doesn't mature much, does she?' Bauer said. 'Yes, there's heartbreak in store – I'm up to Book Two and she's confronting it already – but she's girlish to the end, or almost to the end. That's what makes the epilogue so shocking – I still remember *that*: how Natasha turns into a portly matron.'

'Girlish girls are by nature conventional, don't you find? Personally, I don't care for Natasha. If I were to meet her I doubt we'd be friends – though of course by putting it that way I'm praising Tolstoy, since even when I'm cross with his female characters they engross me. Take Anna Karenina.'

'You're cross with Anna?' Bauer asked, pleased the conversation was expanding.

'Enraged. She's so implacably bent on self-destruction – as if she weren't a woman but a force of nature, a daemon of desire. She's tragic, in the Greek sense, and tragedy of that kind has no place in the novel.'

'Oh, why not?'

'Because the novel is about little people, not gods and heroes.'

Bauer pondered this for a while then said, 'A woman bent on self-destruction – sounds like you when you first met Metz.'

'Oh, Metz is more a figure from farce, don't you think? He'd fit into a novel just fine.'

Somehow he'd brought them back to the present. To return to literature he said, 'So Tolstoy can't write women?'

'Oh, he can write them all right – just when I'm most annoyed with him, he'll astound me by turning the soul of a woman inside out.'

101

'For instance?'

'Countess Rostova,' she said, without hesitation, 'receiving a letter from her son Nikolai, who's off soldiering, and marvelling at the man he's become.' She was gazing into space, her expression abstracted, and in a rush Bauer understood why.

'You're a mother,' he said.

Katerina looked down at him. 'Am I so transparent?'

'A lucky guess,' he said. 'You have a son?'

'Now a man, off killing or trying to kill as many of your countrymen as possible.'

'You must have been young when you had him.'

'Are you trying to flatter me, Captain?'

'Just stating the truth.'

'Because, if so, you're wasting your time.'

'What's your son's name?' he asked, pressing on. She hesitated, and he said, 'I can hardly arrange to have him hurt.'

'I don't suppose it matters,' she said. 'We called him Marlen.'

'Is that a Russian name?' he asked, though what interested him more was the other half of that 'we'. Why hadn't it occurred to him that she might have a husband? A senior Red Army officer, for example. Or maybe a civilian doing vital work for the Soviet war effort. A scientist. A politician. An engineer.

'Yes and no,' she said. 'It's a portmanteau name, a splicing of "Marx" and "Lenin".'

'How ingenious.'

'Please, you needn't pretend. Marlen was born in 1921, when his father and I were young and very zealous revolutionaries. It's a ridiculous name, but quite a few boys his age had it foisted on them, so he's not alone.'

'He's twenty?'

'Nineteen. He turns twenty next month.' She shelved the last of the books in her arms, descended the ladder and opened a new crate.

'You must be worried about him.'

'Of course.'

Bauer hesitated. 'And his father?'

'Dead. Four years ago.'

'I'm sorry to hear it,' he lied, and immediately felt ashamed of himself.

'We were divorced. But thank you anyway. His name was Viktor. In many ways a very fine man. And a funny one. I miss him. His replacement makes me laugh far less often.'

'You remarried?'

'I haven't gone that far.'

'This replacement, where is he?'

'In this room, I suppose. If anywhere.'

Bauer glanced around, idiotically, though he knew they were alone. He turned back to her in confusion.

'Lev Nikolayevich,' she explained, gesturing at the shelves, 'is the only man in my life these days.'

'Oh, I see.'

'A dead man is easier to get on with than a live one, I find. With Tolstoy I get genius, compassion and searing love without the unpleasantness of an actual marriage. He was an awful husband to Sophia Andreyevna: evidently raped her when it suited him, especially later in life, after he'd sworn himself to celibacy. Thirteen children she bore him – all of them, at his insistence, on the *chaise longue* his mother had used to give birth to him.'

'It sounds as if you don't like him at all.'

'Oh, I don't. But I also adore him. It's like any good marriage.'

'You have a bleak view of marriage, Katerina Dmitrievna.'

'Are you married?' she asked.

'I was. My wife died. Three years ago.'

'That recently, eh. You're still grieving, I take it?'

'I suppose so, yes.'

'And how angry does she make you?'

'Angry? Like I said, she's dead.'

'You don't believe the living can resent the dead?'

'Well, yes. Just not in this case.'

'If you say so,' she said. 'And when she was alive? How angry did she make you then?'

'She was an invalid,' he said. 'Disseminated sclerosis.'

'When you married her?'

'No, but shortly afterwards.'

'Well, that must have been aggravating, surely?'

'I wouldn't say aggravating. In the beginning we were newly in love and didn't really argue; then she fell sick and, well, she was so brave about it, so stoical, I could only admire her.'

'Poor you. Did you have any children together?'

'We didn't, no. Clara's illness ...'

'Or with anyone else?'

'No.'

'But you wanted to be a father?'

'When she fell ill I was still a student and hadn't given it much thought. Probably I assumed we'd have children one day. But that didn't happen.'

'Yet you still haven't let yourself hate her.'

'For falling ill? I have to say, Katerina Dmitrievna, I'm beginning to see why your own marriage failed.'

'I don't mean she was objectively to blame,' Katerina said. 'I'm speaking here not of the head but the gut. Viscerally you must have hated her at times but been unable to express it – even to yourself, apparently.'

He considered this, unsure if it was true but certain there was nobody else to whom he had spoken so candidly about his marriage. 'Well, you have me there,' he said. 'I can't deny having feelings you claim I've repressed.'

'There's no need to be ashamed,' Katerina said. 'No marriage would be complete without some murderous rage. Of course, one tries not to act on it ...'

'Is that what happened to your ex-husband?' he said, attempting a joke. 'You killed him?'

'Not me, no,' she said, and made to come down the ladder.

'Here,' he said, 'let me pass them up to you.'

She accepted the books and, as if the topic flowed naturally from the last, said, 'What I find so compelling about Lev Nikolayevich are the contradictions. A love–hate attitude to women, fictional and real. The obsession with celibacy while fathering all those children, the legitimate ones – how many he had with maids or peasants is anyone's guess. Also his attraction to what he saw as the simplicity of the peasants – no small part of his attraction to peasant women, by the way – which in later years he tried to emulate; for example, by making his own shoes, badly, and by wearing peasant smocks. This from a nobleman who could trace his ancestry even further back than the Tsar could, to Ryurik the Viking himself.'

105

'For a communist you sound impressed,' Bauer said.

'I'm just noting, not admiring.'

'Not your blue blood coming out?'

'None of us chooses our family, Captain. It's where we end up that counts.'

'And where have you ended up, Comrade Countess? If I'm not mistaken this is the only surviving manorial estate in the entire Soviet Union.'

'What do you know about it?' she said, smiling.

'You're right. I'm just a peasant.'

She came down the ladder and advanced on him. 'Show me your palms.' Obediently, he turned up his hands and without warning she seized the left one and brushed her thumbs across it. 'Soft – as I thought,' she said, and went over to one of the open crates.

'That's all you have to say?' he asked. 'What about my future?'

'I only tell the past. Which in your case is clearly bourgeois.'

'It's been a while since I've worked the land,' he said, the tracks of her thumbs still pulsating on his palm. 'But since we're speaking about class, how is it you communists so admire an aristocratic writer like Tolstoy?'

'Easy,' Katerina said. 'His championing of the peasants. His feud with the Orthodox Church.'

'But his writing – no proletarian could have done those drawing room scenes.'

'Your point being what? That Lenin should have stayed on his train at the Finland Station so that aristocrats could go on writing novels? There are modern writers of Russian, you know. And poets. Also a Union of Soviet Writers which provides its members with the time and space to write.' She carried another armful of books to the shelves. 'I myself was once a member.'

'As a *writer*?' he asked.

'What else? A chimney sweep?'

'A writer of what?' he asked.

'Novels.'

'Which were published?'

'Of course. Only two of them, mind.'

'Well, that's … I'm lost for words.'

'You needn't sound so amazed.'

'Sorry, I didn't mean … Oh my God, and there was I the other day boasting about my literary aspirations. You must have thought me such an idiot.'

'You needn't worry – women are used to dealing with men with inordinately high opinions of themselves.'

'Please stop,' he said, making a shield of one arm. 'Tell me about your books.'

'There were only two, as I said, and they were a long time ago. I was young.'

'You seem to have done a lot when you were young.'

'Yes, but so did most of my generation. Anyone who survived those times has an epic or two in them.'

'Your books are epics?'

'Hardly.'

'Then what are they?'

'You really want to know?'

'Of course.'

'Well, the first was about three women friends, all Party members, coming of age during the Revolution and the Civil War.'

'The title?'

'*Three Women.*'

'*Tri Zhenshchiny*,' he said. 'Direct. Straightforward.'

'That was the idea. I saw myself as writing for the workers. Ordinary men and women on the factory floor.'

'And did the workers read it?'

'Not at first, no. But then the book was praised in *The Young Guard,* the Party's youth magazine, and immediately afterwards bitterly denounced in *Izvestia*. After that a lot of people read it, including some highly influential Party men who, as it turned out, weren't really lovers of literature.'

'Denounced for what?'

'Sexual themes, mainly. Not sexual *scenes*, mind – apart from a little kissing. But the women characters *talk* about sex, and that was enough. None of my critics seemed to notice that they also talk about romance, revolution, family. It's one of the book's main failings, actually: too much talk.'

'Why? In life people talk about ideas. Young people especially.'

'That's true, I suppose. Certainly it was true of us. In a novel, though, conversations about ideas invariably sound forced, no matter how true to life they might be.'

'So now I'm intrigued: what kind of scandalous conversations were your characters having?'

'Oh, it was formulaic stuff really. One of the women was a sentimental romantic who was constantly being exploited by men. The second had a baby daughter and a straying husband and was questioning how best to go on working for the Revolution. The third was a tireless Party activist, and while the other two characters came in for criticism, it was Zhenya, the Party worker, who got me into the biggest trouble, since in order to dedicate herself more fully to the cause she rejects romance and only has sexual encounters as the need arises, "like drinking a glass of water", as she says at one point. You can't imagine what a storm that phrase caused. In the papers all kinds of critics and Party men lined up to condemn my "glass of water" theory of sex, without stopping to consider whether or not I shared my character's views.'

'You were the young mother, I take it.'

'Yes, but it would be truer to say I was all three women. And none of them.'

'And you really had no polemical intent?'

'I had observations. For instance, that bourgeois romance was corrupt, but that new ways of loving had yet to be found. That the Revolution had complicated but not yet transformed the lives of young women. I had observations, I had questions, and I honestly believed that the Party would come up with the answers.'

'But it didn't?'

'It did not. The Revolution had changed how we worked, how we talked, how we dressed – how we undressed, come to that – but it didn't change men's assumption that their work was more important than ours, and that whatever else a woman might do, her first responsibility was looking after children and keeping house. Zhenya, my activist character, threatened that view. Behaving sexually like a man – in the critics' opinion, that is – was only part it.'

'What I'd like to know,' he said, 'is how this incendiary work got past the censors.'

She smiled at him. 'Quite easily. There were none. Not in those early years. This was revolution, Captain. This was tumult and freedom. A contest of ideas. We were upending the world – the entire world, we believed – and were out of our minds with excitement.' She shook her head a little and made a rueful face, though her eyes, Bauer noticed, were gleaming.

'I'd like to read your book. Your books.'

'You can't, I'm afraid. For one thing, I don't have any copies.'

'What? I don't believe that.'

'For another, I doubt your Russian is up to reading fiction.'

'Even fiction written for the proletariat? I do read Russian slightly better than I speak it, you know.'

'Even if I had a copy I wouldn't give it to you now. Not while you're reading *War and Peace*. The letdown would be grotesque.'

'I don't know Tolstoy personally.'

'Knowing the author only leads to disappointment.'

'In the author or the book?'

'In my case, both.'

'Mmm,' he said noncommittally. 'What about your second novel?'

In the open doorway Hirsch appeared and tentatively knocked.

'Yes, what is it?' Bauer asked, sounding snappish, he noticed, even Metz-like, a recognition that only worsened his annoyance.

'I was just passing,' Hirsch said, 'and saw you in here, and thought ...'

Katerina had returned to sorting books, the spell of their conversation broken.

'These books ...' Hirsch said to Katerina, who pretended not to notice him. He tried again, 'Excuse me, *gnädige Frau*, but are there any more books like the one you offered the lieutenant colonel? In German, I mean?'

'Some,' she admitted.

'It's just that I've been looking for something to read. And so ...'

Katerina pointed to a neighbouring bookcase where the German language volumes were arranged on the lower shelves. Bauer made for the doorway.

'Sir?' Hirsch called to him. 'Do you have any advice? You know, about which ...?'

'You ought to read? That would depend on your interests,' he said.

'My interests?'

From Katerina came a noise that might have been a snigger.

'What have you tended to read in the past?' Bauer asked.

'Textbooks. Some magazines.'

Bauer went over to him, squatted and perused the books' spines. Goethe, Hoffman, Hölderlin, von Kleist, Mörike, Novalis, Schiller. Hegel, Herder, Kant, Marx, Nietzsche, Schlegel, Schopenhauer, Weber. There was a German translation of another of Tolstoy's novels, *The Death of Ivan Ilyich*, which Bauer had read as a medical student for its portrayal of terminal illness. 'From the pen of our host,' he said, passing the book to Hirsch. 'The dead one,' he added in Katerina's direction, hoping to draw her into the conversation.

Hirsch looked doubtfully at it. 'Is there a more German one?'

'There are books *by* Germans, if that's what you mean.'

'I'll be reading in my room, that's all. In front of Hans.'

'And you think a Russian novel will offend him? Good God, Zöllner reads the Bible and that was written by Jews.'

From Katerina there came a stifled laugh. Bauer put *Ivan Ilyich* back on the shelf and handed Hirsch *The Sorrows of Young Werther*. 'Here, have this one instead. You should be safe with Goethe.'

'I've heard of him,' Hirsch said, examining the book. 'He's important, isn't he?'

'There's no doubt of that.'

'Then I'll read him,' Hirsch said.

'Very good. Now come on, we should leave Katerina Dmitrievna in peace.'

EIGHT

The generator, normally only distantly audible, was thunderous in the shack in which it was housed.

'Well?' Bauer shouted at Molineux, still unclear why they were here.

Molineux shone his torch past the generator, revealing in the corner a zinc or steel tank the size of a barrel, linked by copper tubes to a pair of smaller copper canisters. A still. 'Beautiful, isn't she,' Molineux yelled. 'Two Red Army laundry tubs. Riveted, soldered.'

'Clever,' Bauer yelled back. 'By whom?'

'Our Sepp. The da Vinci of improvisation.'

How Winkel had found time to build Molineux a still, or for that matter to recondition a limousine for Metz, struck Bauer as so remarkable that finding fault with either project seemed beside the point. It wasn't as if the corporal's regular duties had suffered. The man was propellor-driven, a conscientious machine.

'Where's your product?' Bauer asked.

'Somewhere safe. Want a sample?'

'What I want is to get away from this racket.'

Outside, the noise and the temperature dropped. The sky was inky, the snow dark blue only metres from their feet.

'Look sharp,' Molineux said to the guard on duty, the company cook Waldo Pabst. 'You haven't moved from that spot since we got here.'

'It's more sheltered on this side, sir,' said Pabst, who was huddling on the leeward side of the shack, his helmet, neck and shoulders wrapped in a blanket, his boots trussed and bundled in cloth.

'That won't do you any good, Waldo, if the partisans come. They'll fillet you faster than you would a fish. Then see how cold you get.'

'Yes, sir,' Pabst said.

'It's for your own good.'

'Yes, sir.'

'And for mine. How could I possibly survive without your goulash?'

Pabst brightened at this. About his cooking he was touchingly vain, a weakness ruthlessly exploited by Molineux, who now clapped him on the back. 'Good man.'

'Thank you, sir.'

'When do you get off duty?'

'At midnight.'

'Excellent. In the men's common room you'll find a glass of something waiting for you. A little fire to go in that belly of yours.'

'Why, thank you, sir,' Pabst said. He saluted them and shuffled off around the shack.

They were safely out of earshot when Molineux said, 'Always stay on the right side of the cook, I say. Your cook is the most important man in the unit. Upset him and he'll spit in your food, or worse.'

They reached the lane that led back to the Tolstoy House, but instead of heading towards it Molineux went to the right in the direction of the Kusminsky Wing.

'Organising a drink for Pabst?' Bauer asked.

'Organising a drink for you,' Molineux said. 'Come along or we'll freeze to death.'

This was literally true, a drowsy phrase jerked awake by the cold. Bauer considered returning to his room to read, but even a good routine could grow stale, and so instead he followed Molineux, a man-shaped blot in the jolting light of the torch, until they arrived at the Kusminsky Wing. There they went directly into the common room, where as many as fifty corpsmen – a good half of the company – were talking and carousing around the captured ping-pong table. There was a match in progress, and from the noise Bauer guessed there was money at stake, though as men noticed their arrival they came to attention, the players included, and the noise fell away. Unparried, the ball bounced onto then over the floor.

'As you were, gentlemen,' Molineux said. 'This is an informal visit.'

Most knew Molineux knew well enough to take him at his word, and before long the room was as loud as it had been when they entered. Norbert Ritter appeared with clusters of enamel mugs in each hand and, like some beefy barman at Oktoberfest, began handing them round.

'Over here!' Molineux yelled, and Ritter made his way towards them. '*Dankeschön*,' said Molineux, seizing the last two mugs and handing one of them to Bauer. He frowned. 'But this is no good,' he said to Ritter. 'You've none for yourself.'

'I'm up next,' Ritter said in his corroded voice, and thumbed backwards at the ping-pong table. 'There's a helmet full of Reichsmarks on offer.'

'My God,' Molineux said, 'don't let that hold you back. Drink anyway! Add some oomph to your swing.'

Ritter smiled but excused himself and went over to the table. He was a man who knew what he wanted, Bauer thought, and also how to get it – a trait that in someone else he might have admired.

Bauer took a sip from his mug.

'So what do you think of the schnapps?' Molineux asked.

'Is that what you call it?'

'You can call it what you like. What matters is the taste.'

'I taste Red Army underwear.'

'Splendid. Drink up. There's plenty more.'

At the ping-pong table the spectators were two or three deep, though above their heads Bauer could make out the gangling figure of Karl Pflieger performing star jumps, limbering up to play. 'Shall we watch?' Bauer suggested, and Molineux agreed, and together they found a vantage point in the crowd.

Pflieger's opponent was Joachim Knoll, Metz's chief operating assistant, a strikingly redheaded man of medium height, though in comparison to Pflieger he looked short. Waiting for Knoll to serve, Pflieger dropped into a half-crouch and swayed from side to side, a praying mantis observing its

116

prey. He had bragged of being good at the game, and from the first ball it was clear he hadn't been exaggerating; along with his extraordinary reach he was a magician of spin, curving the ball in flight and wildly skewing its bounce.

Quickly Knoll began to lose and, growing bored, Bauer turned away. It was then that he noticed the presence of a third officer, Fabian Drexel, seated at a table in the corner. The pharmacist was watching a game of chess, his fingers interlaced behind his squarish head. Since seeing him with a syringe plunged into Metz's arm, Bauer had been waiting for a chance to ask him what the hell he believed he was up to, and though there were others at the table he went over and sat down. All the seated men rose, and when Bauer waved them down again Drexel stayed standing. It was time he watched some table tennis, he announced, and immediately slunk away – a sign of shame, Bauer supposed, or at the very least discomfort.

The chess players were Corporal Ehrlich and Yuri Demchak, Bauer's operating assistant. Demchak, playing black, had captured most of Ehrlich's pieces and corralled the rest into one corner of the board. Ehrlich was twiddling his king by its crown, muttering as he rehearsed the few available moves.

'You could concede,' Demchak said, his voice accented and grave.

'Go to hell. I might still force a stalemate.'

'In theory, yes.'

As sometimes happened, Bauer found himself staring at Demchak's cleft-lip and wishing that the surgeon responsible for repairing it had done a better job, as the scar was not only wide but tugged Demchak's philtrum into a permanent sneer. Ordinarily the aesthetics of surgery didn't bother him very much – he was too busy saving lives – but Demchak's otherwise classical countenance made the scar annoying, though it occurred to Bauer this possibly reflected badly on him. Like everyone else in Germany he had for years been subjected to images of the regime's Nordic human ideal, in both its male and female forms, and now it struck him that he might have absorbed not only an association of blondness with perfection but also the fantasy of human perfection itself.

'Checkmate,' announced Demchak.

'What?' Ehrlich said. 'Are you sure? Oh, screw it, yes.'

'Play again?'

'No fear,' Ehrlich said, then looked to the other end of the table where Winkel was sitting alone with a pencil in one hand and, in front of him, an army guide to Russian. 'Hey, Sepp, you up for chess? We need someone to beat Zip Face here for the sake of Aryan pride.'

'I'm busy,' Winkel answered, keeping his eyes on his books.

'Sepp's learning Russian to sweet-talk the housekeeper,' Ehrlich explained, his usual hostility gone, his tone in fact affectionate and warm. The Sepp effect, Bauer thought. Not only was it impossible to dislike Sepp Winkel, around him even a man as spiteful as Ehrlich was ambushed by goodwill for all.

'Is that true?' Bauer called out to Winkel. 'About you and Daria Grigorievna?' Winkel gazed at him like Caesar at Brutus. Feeling abashed, Bauer went on, 'Because if so you should forget about that phrase book. She'll think you want to take her prisoner.'

'He does,' Ehrlich said. 'A prisoner of *love*.'

'Borrow my dictionary instead,' Bauer said.

'Could I?' Winkel asked, sounding touchingly pleased.

'Of course. I'll give it to you tomorrow.'

From the ping-pong table there were cheers – Pflieger defeating Knoll. Ehrlich excused himself to go and watch the next match.

'What about you, sir?' Demchak asked, indicating the chess board. 'Would you like a game?'

'Why not,' he replied, though it was months since he'd played. Against occasional players like himself, chess was a game he could win, but quickly it became apparent that Demchak was an expert, and too late Bauer wondered how wise it had been to go into mental battle with a subordinate whose obedience he relied on in theatre. To excuse the likely loss, he thought of feigning distraction, perhaps by striking up another conversation with Winkel, but this would be ignoble, he decided, and so he gave the game his full attention, aiming to stave off defeat for as long as possible. Forty-five minutes later he was still alive, but only just, when Molineux brought news from the ping-pong table that Pflieger was about to take on Ritter in the final. Bauer toppled his own king. 'Time to concede, I think. Well played,' he told Demchak. 'We ought to go and cheer on Pflieger.'

Demchak thanked him. Possibly he was pleased, but as usual his face gave nothing away. It was good to know that his competence in theatre was backed by a keen intelligence, something also hinted at by his excellent German. For that matter, it was good to be reminded of the talents of the young, who in time would run the world and, one hoped, make a better fist of it than those who were currently in charge.

The table-tennis final was a contest of strength versus guile: Ritter repeatedly smashing the ball at speed, Pflieger returning it with spin. Both styles were in their own way unplayable, making for speedy rallies and, though the match was close, a fast result, with Ritter victorious. From those who'd bet on the outcome, curses or cheers. With a thin smile Ritter collected the Reichsmark-laden helmet, while for his part Pflieger looked far from downcast, making Bauer wonder if he'd thrown the match, or alternatively was just enjoying the attention. Molineux was handing out more drinks, and as corpsmen rushed to refill their mugs Bauer spotted Drexel in the corner, rolling a cigarette. Bauer strode straight over to him. 'What are you administering to Metz?'

Calmly Drexel sealed his cigarette with his tongue, leaving a shred of tobacco on his wet lower lip. 'You must know I can't tell you that, Captain.'

'Why not?'

'Patient confidentiality.'

'Rubbish. You're not a doctor.'

'All the same, it wouldn't be ethical,' Drexel said, the fleck of tobacco bobbing as he spoke.

'Don't lecture me about ethics, Lieutenant. You're on very weak ground.'

Drexel gestured at the cigarette he'd made. 'Mind if I smoke?'

'I do,' Bauer said, annoyed by an instant need for nicotine. 'Mostly Pervatin, Metz told me.'

'He told you that? Actually, Pervatin is a fairly minor ingredient.'

'So what are the major ones?'

120

'I can't say.'

Bauer regarded him steadily. Drexel straightened his spectacles. 'Is that all?' he asked, feigning boredom, and looked away. Involuntarily Bauer followed his gaze to where Molineux was cheerfully dispensing schnapps.

'Lieutenant, when did you join the battalion?' Bauer said, making Drexel look at him again.

'May last year, the French campaign.'

'Shortly after me, then. We've both known Metz for eighteen months – long enough to realise that he's not himself, not the same Metz who went into France.'

'Of course he's changed; we all have,' Drexel said – a version, Bauer realised, of something he'd said to Katerina.

'Yes, but the lieutenant colonel has deteriorated. You must know that. At the very least your concoction isn't doing him any good. More likely it's doing him harm.'

'Look, with respect, sir, can I go now?'

'No, you cannot.'

'You should raise this with him, not me.'

'I have done,' he admitted.

'And what did he say?'

'That it was none of my business,' Bauer said, conscious that here was the vulnerable point in his position.

'There you are then.'

'He was wrong. Impair Metz's leadership and you undermine us all. Not to mention the safety of the patients.'

'As far as I can see, sir, you're the underminer here. Of Metz. The battalion. The Reich, come to that.'

'The *Reich*?'

121

'You think I'm exaggerating?' Drexel asked, and thrust out his chest and chin, which along with his swarthy complexion made him faintly resemble Mussolini. 'For more than six months I have been working on various compounds designed to sharpen soldierly performance. If they prove successful – and already it looks as though they are – I believe these drugs could deliver us absolute victory, not just over the Soviets but also the English. In due course, the Americans.'

'We're not at war with the Americans.'

'Oh, but we will be. And I mean to ensure that we win.'

'All this by drugging Metz?'

'Not only Metz.'

'Jesus Christ, who else are you doping?'

'Not *doping*.'

'Who else?'

'The Sergeant Major. Indeed, we may have just witnessed some encouraging results.'

'The table tennis? You see Ritter batting back enemy grenades?'

'Not exactly.'

'Anyone else?'

'Just myself, at this stage.'

'You're taking this stuff while experimenting on others?'

'Naturally I began with myself. To do otherwise would have been unethical.'

On a sudden hunch Bauer said, 'Hence the salivation?'

Drexel swiped a floret of little bubbles from the corner of his mouth and at last dislodged the stray bit of tobacco. 'That's nothing.'

'You don't find it inconvenient?'

'There's no such thing as a drug without side effects, Captain.'

'Metz believes otherwise. You've circumvented them, he says.'

'Mostly, yes.'

'Come to think of it, I don't believe I've noticed Metz or Ritter having problems with their spit. Just you then?'

'The formula I'm taking differs from theirs. And theirs from each other's, for that matter.'

'Because? Pardon me, none of this seems particularly scientific.'

'Bigger trials will follow. As for the need for different formulas, I would have thought that was obvious: it takes more than one type of man to win a war. Metz, for example, is a leader. I'm merely boosting his existing attributes.'

'So he said. An *ÜberMetz*.'

'If you like, yes.'

'And Ritter? What are you doing to him?'

'Ritter – how shall I put this? Ritter is a quintessential warrior.'

'A brute?'

'Maybe. But a useful brute, wouldn't you say?' Here he took off his spectacles and started jabbing them for emphasis. 'Captain, we Germans must be harder, more ruthless than the other races. To that end we require a substrate of men who are tougher and more remorseless than the norm. If there were centuries to spare we could breed males of Ritter's type with aggressive females. Your estate custodian, for instance,' he said, and smirked. 'Then in several generations we'd have the ultimate soldier. Only we don't have the luxury of waiting that long.'

Bauer observed him steadily for a while then said, 'So what sort of man are you, Lieutenant? A visionary? Is that what you think?'

'That's for others to decide,' Drexel said modestly. He put his spectacles back on. 'But I do think I see further than most. I recognise problems, analyse and solve them.'

'And there's a drug to help you do that?'

'There is now.'

'Well, frankly, Lieutenant, I think you're unhinged – a danger to yourself, to Ritter, to Metz, and to anyone else foolhardy enough to let you near them with a hypodermic.'

'You won't be a subject, then?' He seemed to be in earnest.

'You're enterprising, I'll give you that. But no.'

'Metz says you're a good surgeon.'

'That's kind of him.'

'With my help you could be better.'

Bauer couldn't help but smile. 'You're not a visionary, Lieutenant, you're a salesman.'

'I'm not interested in money.'

'What a pity, you'd make a fortune.'

'You won't help me, then?'

'Of course not.'

'Will you at least not stand in my way?'

'I'll do whatever's necessary to protect the patients. If that means standing between you and Metz, I will.'

Drexel inhaled and visibly steadied himself. 'Captain, please remember we're talking about the future of the Reich. Very well, I understand you might be sceptical. I also admit that what I'm doing is not without risk – what worthwhile endeavour is? Don't you see, though, that doing nothing is also full of risk? Let's say Metz kills —'

'Hey, you two,' Molineux said, appearing at their sides bearing more mugs of the so-called schnapps, 'why so grave?'

'Drexel is telling me his prescription for winning the war.'

'Élan!' said Molineux. 'What's needed is élan.'

'I agree,' Drexel said. 'Certainly that's one ingredient.'

'Ingredient be damned! Élan is all. Here, have a mugful and we'll take on the world.'

So much for his conversation with Drexel. Not that it had been going anywhere useful, Bauer supposed. He accepted the mug that Molineux was offering and took a swig big enough to quell thought.

NINE

'How cold will it get, Katerina Dmitrievna?'

'Much colder.'

'How cold?'

'Too cold for you.'

When they crossed paths, Katerina and Molineux's exchange never varied, and while Katerina's tone was reliably frosty it bothered Bauer that she went along with a comedy that his comrades had noticed and started to relish. The expression *much colder – viel kälter –* became a catch-cry among them, then in the modified form *Kälter* and, before long, *Frau Kälter,* a nickname for Katerina herself. Katerina hadn't objected to the name, which even Metz had taken to using, and Bauer suspected her of liking it. Soon he and Molineux were the only ones addressing her by name.

'Frau Kälter is looking for you,' Pflieger told him halfway through his morning rounds. 'I didn't let on where you were.'

'Oh? Why not?'

'Didn't dare to. She looked even colder than normal. I said to myself, "Better check with the captain whether he wants to be found."'

'And where is she now?'

'In the outer office upstairs.'

'Tell her I'll be there as soon as I can.'

'Take your time, sir. That'll teach her.'

'Thank you, Private. Just pass on my message.'

Completing his rounds took longer than he'd hoped. In the post-operative ward he was forced to argue with a patient, a hardened Nazi who had lost a spleen but not the will to fight and who was demanding to go back to the front. Then in the amputations ward he spoke for longer than was strictly necessary with an eighteen-year-old who had gone through basic training, taken a week to reach the front and within a day of arriving had lost an arm to a shell. He seemed not at all despondent, just proud to have served, though it occurred to Bauer that exposure to combat might have convinced him he was getting off lightly.

The burns ward was the last he visited. It contained a panzerman on whom he and Weidemann had tried every treatment they could think of, from powdered sulphanilamide, saline baths and now aniline dye, so far without stemming the oozing of plasma from his skin. The patient was unconscious and almost certainly dying, and the inevitability of this death both enraged Bauer and depressed him. Here was failure of the most demoralising kind.

Finding Katerina in the office startled him, so absorbed had he been by the cases on the wards. He apologised for making her wait, unhooked his stethoscope and asked what he could do for her.

'Is there somewhere private we could speak?' she asked.

127

The two clerks on duty exchanged a rapid glance. Bauer scowled at them and asked if there was an office free. Metz and Weidemann were both in theirs, the senior clerk replied, though Hirsch was out and the dental surgery was free. Bauer thanked him and ushered Katerina into Hirsch's surgery, a narrow room with a single sash-window on the short northern wall. A stool and a wooden dental chair, both silhouetted in the wintery light. A tray of instruments on a trolley. A pedal-powered drill with a fly-wheel and wires. Switching on the room's only lightbulb hardly lessened the gloom, so Bauer resorted to the examination lamp, all but blinding them.

'Good grief,' Katerina said, shielding her eyes, 'I think I preferred it before.'

'I'll turn it off,' Bauer said.

'No, no, I'll get used to it.'

'Can I offer you the chair?'

'Ugh. Is this where you torture people? No thank you. The stool.'

'I'll get us some chairs from the office.'

A minute later they were seated opposite one another, half in and half out of the cone of light from the lamp.

'So how can I help?' Bauer asked.

'Medical supplies,' Katerina replied. 'Swabs, bandages, forceps, syringes, iodine, morphine, Novalgin. Oh, and two or three scalpels.'

'That's all?'

'Yes, for now.'

'And what do you plan to do with these supplies?'

'Use them in the village as required.'

'You have a doctor there?' he asked, ashamed at not having asked this before.

'Our doctor went into the army.'

'Any nurses?'

'No. But the people are resourceful. They're used to making do.'

Bauer recalled how during the French campaign the impracticality of treating civilians had so tormented him that he'd nearly come apart. In the Soviet Union he had by and large managed to ignore the issue.

'Metz would never agree,' he said. 'He'd think you were handing it on to partisans.'

'I don't know any.'

'I doubt he'll take your word for that,' Bauer said, unsure if he entirely believed her himself.

'So don't involve him,' she said. 'I'm not asking for much. No food, for example.'

'Because you have enough?' he asked.

'No, we don't, as it happens.'

Lamely, he said, 'I've been meaning to check.'

'It's one of the reasons there's sickness.'

'What about your new sleeping quarters? You're reasonably comfortable?'

'I wouldn't say comfortable, no. But it could be worse. The estate's steward and his wife have taken me in.'

'Tikhon Vassilyvich?' he asked.

She tilted her head to one side. 'That's right. I'm surprised you remember.'

'With your help he was memorably rude.'

'He was? I don't remember. I'm sure you deserved it.'

He examined her face – the slim, triangular chin; her cherubic lips; her large knowing eyes – and wondered how she got away with such antagonism.

'The supplies,' he said. 'I wish I could say yes. But the Wehrmacht doesn't take kindly to thieves.'

'Then don't get caught,' she replied. 'You're a doctor. Just spirit things away. A little here, a little there – no one would notice.'

He made a show of considering this, bitterly aware he would have to say no. 'I'm sorry. The kind of items you mentioned, we're running low on them ourselves. I just can't help you. I wish I could, but I can't.'

'Because you're low on supplies or afraid of getting caught? Which is it?' Seeing him hesitate, she went on, 'Or is it neither? Oh God, don't tell me – it's your honour, isn't it? Your German sense of rectitude. You people make me sick – helping yourselves to most of Europe but baulking at pilfering a few of your own supplies.'

'I'm sorry. In time there ought to be a ration system for civilians. Some kind of medical care.'

'Excuse me if I'm sceptical, Captain. You can't clothe yourselves adequately, that's obvious, and now you tell me you're running low on medical supplies. Personally I think you're deliberately trying to starve us, but even if you're not I doubt we can rely on you for food, let alone medical care.'

'Look,' he said quietly, 'let me see what I can do.'

'Not good enough, Captain. Should I tell Metz you called him a coward?'

So this was how things stood, he thought. 'I'll do what I can,' he repeated. He was fairly sure he hadn't described Metz as a coward, but even if Metz disbelieved it the accusation would cause trouble.

'And there's another thing,' she said.

'God, who's torturing whom? Should I get in the chair?'

'It's your Corporal Winkel.'

'What about him?' Bauer asked, taken aback, the name Winkel not one he normally associated with trouble.

'He's been making a nuisance of himself with one of my housekeepers.'

'Ah, I see. Daria Grigorievna.'

'You know about it then.'

'I know he's become fond of her, yes.'

'I can't have it.'

'Why? Because Daria doesn't like it?'

'On the contrary. That's the problem. Your stay here is limited, as I keep trying to explain, and any woman who's gone with a German … well, she'll likely face retribution.'

Bauer thought of saying something cutting about Soviet justice, but if the situation were somehow reversed he had no doubt his own people would be vengeful in just the same way. 'You seem very sure we'll lose this war.'

'I'm certain of it. But even if I weren't, the risk to Daria would be unacceptable.'

'It sounds as though she disagrees with you.'

'I'm sorry to say that Daria isn't particularly bright. She's unmarried. Has never married. So she's vulnerable. Also, she has a drinking habit.'

Bauer couldn't help laughing. 'You want me to tell all this to Winkel?'

'Tell him what you like, just make him desist. Metz vowed that his men would leave my female staff alone. Harassing them was forbidden, he said.'

'For racial reasons, yes.'

'If your ludicrous prejudices protect my staff, then I'm all in favour of them.'

'Winkel is a good man – have you thought about that? Daria Grigorievna would be lucky to have him. Aren't you novelists meant to see things from other points of view?'

'For a start, I'm no longer a novelist. As for your corporal, his goodness won't matter a damn if he's in Germany and Daria is on the end of a rope.'

'Maybe he could take her with him.'

'Captain, don't be ridiculous. In the midst of a retreat? If you had Stalin on the run I might have gone along with this sweet little romance – endorsed it, even. But you haven't, so I have to be sensible, for Daria's sake. You should do the same for your corporal.'

'All right then,' he muttered. 'I'll do my best. Though in my experience the heart is a tricky organ to police.'

'I would have thought you Germans were experts at it.'

'You'd be surprised, Katerina Dmitrievna. Occasionally even our hearts rebel.'

★ ★ ★

Bauer ligatured the ulnar artery, half attending as he did so to his assistants' conversation. Metz's limousine was fixed, Winkel said. To get it running again he'd had to machine a new carburettor out of scrap.

Pflieger gestured at their unconscious patient. 'Could you do the same for this poor sod?'

'A prosthesis?' Winkel asked.

'I meant knock something up in flesh and blood.'

'Don't be an idiot, Pflieger.'

Bauer asked for the bone saw. Demchak passed it to him, and immediately Bauer set to work on the bone.

'In fact, that's not so absurd,' Hirsch said from his seat at the top of the table. 'It could happen one day.'

Even focused as he was on the task at hand, Bauer was aware of the others turning their attention to Hirsch, who normally said little during surgery, especially since the Swabian's death. Hirsch blushed scarlet and pressed the bridge of his spectacles to his nose. 'A knocked-out tooth can survive if reattached. Why couldn't an arm?'

'Maybe,' Winkel said, sounding sceptical. 'But Pflieger's talking about a replacement limb. That will never happen.'

Bauer got through the bone, leaving just tricep and skin.

'Why not?' Hirsch replied. 'The first step is to imagine it. Then, when techniques are more advanced, someone is bound to make it happen.'

Bauer finished the cut and Pflieger picked up the severed limb, but instead of binning it straight away he held it up and, by slapping his spare hand against the amputated one, gave

Hirsch a limp round of applause. 'Thank you, Lieutenant, for your generous support. See, Sepp: I'm a genius.'

'Put it down,' Bauer ordered him. 'Jokes, yes, but no maltreatment of body parts. That could be you lying there.'

'That's right,' Winkel said. 'Then we'd have to build you a brain.'

★　★　★

That evening they finished operating late. Bauer felt tired but elated, adrenaline-sluiced, and to calm down he lit a cigarette before settling in to review his notes. Next the wards; then, knowing that sleep was out of the question, he hurried through the snow to the delousing station, meaning to take a sauna. On the hooks inside the door hung a corporal's uniform, which from its size and tidiness was obviously Winkel's. This was disappointing; he'd hoped to have the place to himself. Evidently Sepp had come here straight from their shift, no doubt also seeking solitude, and since NCOs were entitled to use the sauna during morning hours he was within his rights, as it was now after midnight. Bauer considered retreating, not only because he preferred to be alone but also on account of his obligation, if obligation was the correct term, to caution Sepp about his friendship with Daria Grigorievna. However, the idea of lying in bed listening to Molineux snoring was unappealing, and so he undressed, hurrying to escape the icy air, making plenty of noise to warn Winkel of his presence.

The sauna, when he entered, not only felt hot but looked it, firelight shining through a sooty glass panel in the stove. Sepp was seated on the upper bench furthest from the door, arms slung about his knees, his slight but muscled frame somehow birdlike and vulnerable. Immediately he leaned forward and offered to leave, but Bauer motioned him to stay. 'It's morning, Sepp. I'm the one who's intruding.'

'You're sure you don't want me to go, sir?'

'Certain. You've saved me the trouble of lighting the fire. I can hardly turn you out into the snow now, can I?'

'I don't mind,' he insisted.

'No, stay. You deserve it. You worked hard tonight.'

'I should see to the fire,' Winkel said but didn't move, such passivity so unlike him Bauer sensed something must be wrong – illness, or even an insubordinate erection. Wordlessly he refuelled the stove himself, ladled water onto the stones, then, averting his eyes, sat lengthways on the bench seat opposite Winkel, resting his back on the warm timber wall. The under-ceiling air was scorching, which felt heavenly, and consciously he relaxed. It had been a hard day. A hard week. A hard campaign. A hard few years, come to that. If feeling cold half the time made heat more rewarding, it followed that life's hardships ought to intensify its joys; though this presumed there were joys available, which on the eastern front was doubtful. He should be satisfied, he supposed, with the gift of this super-heated air, which at this instant possibly made him if not the happiest then at least the warmest man in the war.

Winkel, on the other hand, was looking awkward and tense, his arms still clasped about his knees. Bauer would never have picked him as a physically bashful man – in fact he recalled that in July, when they had reached the Dnieper River, Winkel had been one of the first men to strip off and wade in. Bauer sat up. 'You look uneasy, Sepp.'

'I do?'

'My fault,' Bauer said. 'I shouldn't have disturbed you.' He began to get up then noticed a nodule at the front of Winkel's armpit, a dark, strangely bristled lump in his underarm hair. Winkel noticed him noticing and covered up, revealing a similar protrusion at the back of his armpit, on the fleshy edge of the teres major. 'Sepp, what *is* that?' Bauer asked.

'What is what?'

'That thing in your armpit. Those things, I should say.'

'Nothing. It's nothing.'

'Then why cover up?'

At this point Winkel dropped his head between his arms, and if possible seemed to shrink further into himself. He didn't want to answer, that was obvious, but on the other hand he looked so distraught that Bauer felt duty-bound to persist. 'Well?'

Winkel groaned, raised his head and dragged downwards on his face, giving it a rubbery expression of pop-eyed resignation. 'You won't tell the others?' he asked, letting the skin recoil.

'If you don't want me to, no.'

'Then I suppose take a look,' he said, swung his legs off the bench and raised his left elbow, exposing his armpit.

Bauer went closer. There were four lumps in total – skin tags, he was relieved to see, each trussed at the base with suture thread. 'You did this?' he asked, straining not to laugh. Winkel nodded, looking miserable. Along with the ones he was garrotting there were some smaller tags he'd left alone, presumably because he'd been unable to lasso them. 'Well, I must say I admire your dexterity,' Bauer said, 'you could have been a surgeon. And there's nothing wrong with your thinking either – these are starting to shrivel.'

Winkel lowered his arm. 'So you think they'll fall off, sir?'

'Yes, in time. But, Sepp, you should have come to me. I can get rid of these for you in a minute or two. It'll sting a bit, but not for long. And there'll be less chance of infection.'

'Sir, it's embarrassing. You've better things to do.'

'As I said, it won't take long. Any others?'

Winkel raised his right arm, revealing another two knotted tags, each with a little ruff of hair.

'I'll do it tomorrow when I get a spare moment,' Bauer said. 'Some of the smaller ones too.'

'You really won't tell anyone?'

'Of course not. I'm a doctor.'

'Because – this is hard to say, sir – that's not all of them,' Winkel said, glancing downwards.

'Ah, I see. Never mind. We'll deal with those too.'

Winkel thanked him and Bauer returned to the opposite bench. 'But Sepp, I'm curious,' he asked. 'Why now? Is it Daria Grigorievna?' he asked, unable to think of a more tactful way to introduce the topic.

'*Sir*,' Winkel said.

Hurriedly, Bauer said, 'God knows it's understandable, we're all lonely here. It's just I'm not sure that Daria Grigorievna is the answer.' Winkel's expression was rigid, defensive. Bauer went on, 'I should be clear, this isn't about the race laws. As far as I'm concerned they're nonsense.'

'What is it about then?' Winkel asked.

'It's that sooner or later we'll be leaving here, and that could place Daria Grigorievna in a difficult position.'

'I've already thought of that, sir. I'll arrange to send her money.'

'Right. I see. So you're serious about her. But Sepp, if you don't mind me saying, isn't this all a bit sudden? You've only known her for – what is it? – less than two weeks. You can't have been in her company for more than two hours altogether.'

'Sir, that's true but trust me, that's long enough. Long enough to know. My wife and I, we grew up in the same tenement. Played in the same courtyard. This is a different thing. When I saw Daria for the first time I thought, "Here is someone special. Here is someone I need to know."'

Bauer pictured Daria Grigorievna, a stout woman with coarse and mottled skin, and caught himself wondering uncharitably what Winkel found so tantalising about her. 'You say you need to know her. Are you sure this isn't more about the death of your wife? A reaction to it? How long has it been?'

'Two years. Or more like three. Sir, I loved my wife. Loved her dearly. But this feels different – as if fate itself has brought me and Daria together.'

'But you don't even share a common language!'

'I'm working on that, sir. And anyway, what we share is deeper than language. We love one another. We're going to get married. I don't know how yet, but we will. I'll make sure of it.'

Bauer hesitated, rather alarmed for him but also a little awed. 'Good for you,' he said at last.

'Thank you, sir, I knew you'd understand.'

'I'm not sure I do, to be honest. But I admire your tenacity. Just bear in mind though, since you love her, that if the war turns against us her countrymen won't look kindly on her relationship with you.'

'Sir?'

'She could be imprisoned, Sepp. Even killed.'

He looked troubled by this; clearly it hadn't occurred to him before. Bauer said, 'Just be discreet, that's all. Particularly around her own people. Katerina Dmitrievna, for example – she's a good woman but if we're forced to retreat she might feel it's her duty to report any fraternisation between us and her staff. I'm not saying that's likely, mind, just a possibility.'

'Of course, sir. I see what you mean. But do you really think we might have to retreat?'

'I don't know. We seem to be winning but are we winning *hard* enough? Now that I just don't know.'

★   ★   ★

Friday, 14 November. They had been at Yasnaya Polyana for little more than two weeks, and yet as Bauer stood waiting for Metz by the stairs their stay felt longer, both for good and ill, a time of recuperation of sorts, but also of forced introspection, the newsreel motion and clamour of their advance from Brest-Litovsk having abruptly come unspooled.

It would be good to get out, he decided. Metz had promised him a drive today in the ZIS, the repaired limousine, a mobile meeting in which Bauer planned to point out the advantages of supplying the villagers with medicines and food.

Metz emerged from his office at the other end of the corridor, threw back his shoulders and strutted the ten metres to the entrance hall. 'Ready?' he said. Bauer answered by snapping his heels together, surprising himself with his enthusiasm.

Outside, the day was calm and, by recent standards, luminous, the snow bright beneath a pale-blue sky. The temperature had risen to a remarkable minus three degrees, so that the walk to the motor pool was almost pleasurable. They arrived to find the ZIS parked outside, its engine idling. Nearby in one of the coach-house doorways stood Egon Ehrlich, who saluted their approach. Metz returned the salute then turned his attention to the car, now painted Wehrmacht grey, with red cross insignia on its roof and front doors. 'What do you think?' he asked.

'It's a nice car, sir,' Bauer said, 'if that's what you mean.'

Metz chuckled. 'Captain, there are two types of men in this world: those who can recognise the beauty of machinery and those who can't. You, I see, are of the latter kind.'

'I must say, sir, I'm surprised that you're so impressed by a Soviet vehicle.'

'Well, naturally the engine is rubbish,' Metz said equably. 'That's why it broke down. But Winkel assures me he's fixed its hereditary flaws, as it were. No, it's the *body* I admire. Just look at those lines! That sweep. Those curves. I can acknowledge good design when I see it.' In apparent seriousness he went on, 'Perhaps they stole it from a German. Anyway, get in,' Metz said. 'Egon will drive.'

Bauer disliked the idea of Ehrlich listening to what he had to say, but if more wounded arrived he and Metz might not be able to meet again for days. He went around the car and got in alongside Metz in the back. Ehrlich took his place at the wheel, revved the engine then gently steered onto the estate's main drive. 'Easy does it,' Metz said, 'there's likely to be ice. I don't want her going back to the workshop, Corporal.'

Regular use was keeping the driveway open to traffic, and as they reached the front gates Bauer saw that the main road, too, remained driveable – though winter, he reminded himself, had a long way to run. Strictly speaking, it hadn't even started.

'Stop here, Corporal, and turn around,' Metz said.

Bauer glanced at him. 'Forgotten something, sir?'

'Not at all.'

On the open ground before the gates Ehrlich turned around then drove the car back the way they'd come, but instead of returning to the motor pool they continued on to the main house. There Metz instructed Ehrlich to circle the forecourt and to Bauer's astonishment they went back down the drive. Metz turned to him. 'So, Captain, what did you want to discuss?'

'Let me see,' Bauer said, trying to collect his thoughts. Whenever he began to think of Metz as normal – the Metz he'd known in France: an able, predictable man – along came evidence of some new peculiarity. 'It's about the local people, sir. Frau Trubetzkaya has asked us for a donation of medical supplies. Just a small amount. I believe we should agree, sir. It will be in our own long-term interests.'

'How so?'

'Because the locals are useful to us. Certainly they haven't been causing us any trouble. We should aim to keep it that way.'

'Bauer, Bauer – what did I say about Frau Kälter? *Watch her!* I said. And now she has you on a string. You fancy yourself

141

in love with her, I suppose.' He leaned forward. 'Another turn about, Corporal, if you please.' They were back at the front gates, Bauer realised; as instructed, Ehrlich turned the car around. Metz slid back onto the seat. 'Well, Captain, what do you have to say for yourself?'

'That I'm curious why we're driving in circles.'

'We aren't circling, Captain, we're oscillating on a line.'

'All right, oscillating. Why?'

'Because beyond those gates there are units of active partisans. It will take us time to entirely pacify the place.'

'Sir, wouldn't that happen faster if the local people didn't hate us? We need to give them reasons not to help the partisans.'

'That's what reprisals are for. Kill one of us and they'll have twenty reasons not to do it again.'

'Positive reasons, I mean. I'm no historian, but it seems to me that the Ancient Romans, as well as being excellent soldiers, were clever assimilators of conquered peoples. They were wise enough to reward compliance.'

'The Romans, ha! And where did that get them? Racial degeneration, that's where. Lacking a proper theory of race, they bred willy-nilly with subject peoples. The results were catastrophic.'

'In the end. Arguably. Though their empire did last a thousand years – two thousand, counting the Byzantines. Even the Führer is only promising us a thousand.'

'A prudent man, the Führer.'

Bauer wondered if this was a joke. Surely not, since if he knew one thing about Metz it was that he lacked a sense of humour.

They had reached the main house again, and Metz signalled Ehrlich to return to the gate.

Bauer said, 'Isn't this rather a waste of fuel?'

'We need to run her in, Captain. And anyway, if you'd had your way we'd be God knows where by now – halfway to Oryol.'

'If you let me out here, sir, I can walk over to the hospital.'

'Let me drive you,' Metz said.

'Thank you, sir. And please give more thought to sending medical supplies to the village. Yes, I know we're running low, but I'm convinced a small outlay now will save us problems later on.'

'Absolutely not, Captain. Don't you realise we're among savages here? Generosity would be interpreted as weakness.'

They pulled up at the front of the hospital. The discussion, if not their route, had been circular and Bauer was glad to be out of it. He stepped from the car and was reaching for the door when Metz twirled a finger at Ehrlich. 'Once more for luck, I think, Corporal.'

Bauer pushed the door shut.

TEN

After the comparatively balmy conditions the day before, the temperature dropped overnight to minus eighteen degrees. The morning was windy, worsening the cold, and setting out for the hospital with Winkel and Molineux, Bauer almost slipped several times on the ice, forcing him to walk in the style of a skater, knees slightly bent, legs a little apart.

As they approached the turnoff for the Volkonsky House, Katerina appeared coming the other way, her footing seemingly secure. Molineux made a bullhorn of his hands, yelled his customary greeting but got no reply. 'Time of the month,' he said sideways. In fact it was clear that Katerina hadn't heard him; the wind was against her and her head was lowered, her *ushanka* a fur-lined battering ram. She was close before she noticed them, and then barely reacted. Bauer asked her if anything was wrong.

'Apart from the war?' she said, without slowing down.

'Irina Petrovna?' Winkel asked, a name that meant nothing to Bauer but instantly made Katerina halt.

'Who's she, then?' Molineux said. 'And why don't I know?'

'The baby's come?' persisted Winkel.

'Not yet,' Katerina answered.

'You're worried?'

'I am. She's weakening.'

Irina Petrovna, Winkel explained, was Daria Grigorievna's daughter, who at twenty-one was due to give birth to her first child. Bauer asked Katerina if the village had a midwife.

'It did, but she died. Only weeks ago. Daria is there with her mother and sister.'

A minute later it was settled that if Daria's daughter was still in labour when Bauer completed his rounds he and Winkel would go to the village and see what could be done. Katerina thanked him, lightly touching his sleeve.

'You're sure about this?' asked Molineux when they had parted from her. 'Metz'll have a seizure.'

'I'll deal with that afterwards.'

'He needn't hear about it,' put in Winkel. 'I know a back way out.'

Molineux guffawed. 'A back way to your lady love? Winkel, you depraved little man, I salute you.'

'We'll go the front way,' said Bauer firmly. 'If there are consequences I'll deal with them. If necessary, Sepp, I'll tell Metz you were acting on my orders.'

'The truth?' Molineux asked, sounding doubtful. 'Are you sure that's wise? And what if you run into partisans?'

'My guess is that partisans are leaving Yasnaya Polyana alone,' Bauer said.

'The village too?'

'The village was once part of the estate.'

145

Molineux gave a low whistle of admiration. 'That's one gutsy guess, Bauer. Hell, if this doesn't get both of you heaps of Bolshevik pussy there's no justice in the world.'

At the hospital Bauer was intercepted by Zöllner asking for help with a patient, another man who had lost his eyelids to frostbite. Bauer was unsure what Zöllner expected of him, as the damage couldn't be repaired in a field hospital and the patient would have to be evacuated, but nevertheless he agreed to go. At the patient's bedside Zöllner looked uneasy, apparently more troubled by the swivelling eyes of a man forced to see than by more commonplace cases of blinding. Gently Bauer briefed the patient about what a maxillofacial surgeon might be able to do for him in Germany, emphasising the chances of a favourable outcome, though in truth he was guessing. The patient thanked him warmly, a tone at odds with his skittish gaze. Zöllner instructed a nursing attendant to regularly bathe the man's eyes and between times to cover them with patches – less a physiological than a psychological treatment, suspected Bauer, and quite possibly more for Zöllner's benefit than the patient's.

As the morning wore on and no message arrived from the village, Bauer thought frequently of his offer to help Daria Grigorievna's daughter. Were partisans really avoiding the district, he wondered, or simply readying themselves for action? Could this, in fact, be their first operation? Winkel had astonished Bauer by admitting to having already slipped away at night to visit Daria Grigorievna in the hut she shared with her family, though apparently her pregnant daughter had been absent at the time. What if this daughter, this Irina Petrovna, was a fiction, Bauer wondered, a way of drawing a German

146

officer into a trap initially prepared for the corporal? There was no way of knowing, but he had committed himself and couldn't back out now.

He finished his rounds before midday and, having heard nothing from Katerina, sent Winkel to fetch a vehicle from the motor pool. Shortly afterwards Winkel pulled up outside the hospital in the unit's Kübelwagen. 'There was nothing else?' Bauer asked, lowering two bags of equipment into the storage well.

'I'm afraid not, sir. Not counting the ZIS, that is. Should I get some blankets?'

'No, best get away while we can,' he said, and climbed into the passenger seat.

At the front gate a sentry asked where they were going, looked perplexed by the answer but waved them through all the same. Across the road a newly erected signpost bristled with planks inscribed with the names of cities and their distance from Yasnaya Polyana.

'*Victoria*?' Winkel asked. 'Where's *Victoria*?'

'It's Latin,' Bauer said, 'for "victory".'

'Oh yeah? It doesn't say how far, though, does it.'

'Just the direction,' agreed Bauer. 'Tula and Moscow.'

'And we're going the other way,' Winkel said, turning in the direction of the village. A light snow was falling, and as they picked up speed the windscreen did less and less to block the wind, but Bauer was pleased to be in open countryside again. A quicksilver cloudscape. The buffeting cold. Frozen ruts as tangled as railway switches. Low distant ridges that bracketed the plain, paradoxically making it look wider.

147

Yes, it was good to be out, but in a short time they were entering the village, a string of huts on either side of the Chern to Tula road. Left and right a few side roads terminating in snow. There was no one about. Presumably those who hadn't fled the German advance were taking shelter from the weather. The emptiness of the place felt eerie.

It was only when the huts began to thin out that Bauer realised they had already passed whatever counted as the centre. If there was a store of any kind he had missed it. A few hundred metres further on Winkel turned left onto a snowy track that led up to a hut and a cluster of small outbuildings. Bauer tugged off his gloves and unbuttoned his holster, fingers clumsy with cold.

'Stop here,' he told Winkel as they drew nearer the hut. Winkel obeyed and Bauer stepped out onto the snow. 'Keep the engine running. I'll let you know when it's safe to come in.'

'It'll be all right, sir. I've been here before.'

A dog was barking at them – a Samoyed chained to a snow-capped kennel. 'Just do as I say, Corporal,' Bauer said, then to soften the rebuke slapped the vehicle's front mudguard. He set off for the hut. A bitter cross-wind was blowing, stripping smoke from the flue of a squat brick chimney, as the Samoyed barked at him in a patriotic frenzy, lunging on its chain. The hut's door twitched open and in the entrance Katerina appeared.

'Thank you for coming,' she said. 'Nothing's changed. Come inside.' She gestured at the Kübelwagen. 'The corporal, too.'

'He's waiting.'

'For what?'

148

'For you to kill me. Or not.'

'Oh, that. Then you'd better hurry up and find out. Quickly now, you're letting in the cold.'

He stepped past her into the comparative gloom of the hut, its only sources of light one small window and a feeble fire. A little table and beside it two chairs. Smells of woodsmoke, damp wool, boiled cabbage. In front of the fire a small woman with pronounced kyphosis of the spine was adjusting a pot on a hook above the flames.

'This is Agrafena Viktorovna,' Katerina said, 'Daria's mother.' Bauer greeted the old woman in Russian and she responded with a nod, then Daria herself emerged from a curtained-off area at one end of the hut, tearfully thanked him and pressed both his hands.

'*Kto tam?*' a woman cried behind a curtain.

'A doctor,' Katerina answered in Russian, the kind of simple exchange Bauer was equipped to understand. 'That's Irina Petrovna,' Katerina said to him in German. 'As you see, you're in no danger here. Better get your corporal before he freezes to death.'

'A *German?*' yelled the patient.

'Here to help,' called Katerina.

'I'd prefer to *die*.'

'What about your baby?'

'Fuck off and go away.'

'She'll come around,' Katerina said, switching back to German. Bauer asked who else was behind the curtain.

'Good grief, how suspicious you are,' Katerina said. 'The girl's aunt, Daria's sister. Here,' she said, and reached out and drew back the curtain, revealing a small alcove almost entirely filled by a bed. Irina Petrovna was kneeling on the floor with her arms flung over the bed, her fists twisting the sheets. Holding her was her aunt, a thinner woman than Daria but unmistakably related to her. The labouring girl looked exhausted, shivering and pale. She caught sight of him and snarled abuse of some kind.

'Pay no attention to her,' Katerina said. 'It's the labour talking.'

'Not only the labour, I think.'

'Her husband was killed in the first week of the war. But the labour's not helping.'

At this moment Irina clawed the bedding to her chest and emitted a long, unearthly groan. Her aunt pulled her close, as if to relieve the pain, while with his watch Bauer timed the length of the contraction. Thirty-nine seconds. When it was over Irina let go of the bedding but stayed slumped across the mattress, shoulders heaving, head lolling, her hair sweat-darkened on the sheets.

'She's a good girl, strong,' Katerina went on. 'And though you wouldn't know it from that foul mouth of hers, educated. A university student.'

'I'll bear it in mind as she gouges my eyes.'

'Just do what you can. I'll hold her down if it comes to that.'

'Have her waters broken?' he asked.

'*Nyet!*' Irina wailed.

'She understands German?' he asked.

'No, just doesn't like hearing it,' Katerina said. 'Her waters *have* broken. Hours ago.'

'I'll need to examine her.'

'Of course. I'll speak to her. Call your man in.'

Bauer went outside and beckoned Winkel, who jumped out of the Kübelwagen and lugged their equipment over. 'Ether?' he asked, lifting the heaviest of the bags.

'Just in case,' Bauer said, and led him inside.

'Shouldn't we have brought Lieutenant Hirsch along, sir?'

'It wasn't his affair.'

'But if we need to do an anaesthetic?'

'It might not come to that.'

'But if it does?'

'Then I'm sure you'll do an expert job.'

'But, sir!'

'Don't worry, Sepp. At least not yet. As things stand she won't even let me examine her.'

In the alcove Irina Petrovna was abusing Katerina, her mother and even her aunt. They were traitors, fascist lackeys; they deserved to be shot. Wisely Winkel refrained from greeting Daria and instead busied himself with unpacking their equipment. Bauer gazed about, taking stock of their surroundings: a dingy hovel, a humpbacked crone by a steaming pot, an infuriated woman in labour. It was as if he'd stumbled into a Dostoyevsky novel, the only character missing a despairing, tubercular youth playing Russian roulette with a flintlock pistol.

'This is pointless,' Katerina said, coming away from the bed. 'We'll have to force her.'

'Ideally she'd be calm.'

'Tranquillity has failed. Thirty hours she's been at it.'

'And if she doesn't want my help?'

'She's in no state to judge. And there's her baby to consider.'

'True,' he said, still hesitating. He'd had soldiers resist examination, crazed by pain and sometimes fear of how it might be relieved, yet he had never had to treat a woman against her will.

'Look, if it's your conscience bothering you,' Katerina said, 'I absolve you. It's my decision.'

'All right then. Let me wash my hands.'

With his usual efficiency Winkel had prepared a basin of hot water and beside it placed soap and a hand towel. By the bed Katerina and the aunt were trying to haul a screeching Irina Petrovna onto the mattress, her mother pleading with her in rapid Russian. Bauer hooked his stethoscope around his neck, washed and dried his hands.

'*Nyet*,' the young woman yelled, '*nyet*.' Though fighting hard she was weakened by her labour, and soon they had her on her back.

'Let me speak with her,' he said.

'*Nyet*,' cried Irina Petrovna, as between them the women wrenched up her nightdress and prised her thighs apart. Bauer glimpsed pubic hair, dark and dense, and registered an undoctorly shock that was part sexual, part childlike, a jolt of primal surprise.

'Let me speak with her,' he repeated, this time getting Katerina's attention, which in turn allowed Irina to wrench down her nightdress. Katerina yelped with annoyance.

Bauer went to the bed and in his stilted Russian told the young woman his name. 'I'm a doctor,' he added, and because in the search for sincerity the only tense he could muster was the present he went on, 'I am sorry your husband is dead. This trouble, I am sorry. This war.'

She had an arm flung over her face, and with her other hand was clenching her nightdress by the hem.

'I'm a doctor,' he repeated lamely. 'I can help you.'

Irina screwed up her face, as if angry again, but then shuddered as the next contraction took hold, forcing another long moan from her throat. Six minutes had passed since the previous one, Bauer noted. Too long. Its duration was much the same. Throughout it her aunt massaged Irina's belly, and then, cooing endearments, released the young woman's grip on her nightdress.

'Could you describe to her what I'll need to do?' he said in a hushed voice to Katerina. 'Check her abdomen first, then her cervix.'

Katerina relayed this message, and though Irina said nothing she did not resist when Bauer placed a hand upon her, slid back her nightdress and gently palpated her belly, his mental probity fully restored. '*Khorosho*,' he said, 'good', though in fact he was not reassured. Methodically he repeated his examination, this time with his eyes on the ceiling, the better to see with his hands.

'You've done this before, I take it?' Katerina said.

'Of course. Though not often,' he admitted. 'And not recently. There's not much call for it in the Wehrmacht.'

'Only in its wake,' said Katerina.

Ignoring this jibe he leaned forward and addressed Irina. 'Now inside?' This made her tense and he pressed for an answer. '*Da?*'

'*Da*,' she said irritably, her face still turned away.

'Good,' he said, 'good.'

As gently as possible he examined her internally, probing with his middle finger for the cervix, thinking that contrary to the innuendo of certain poets a woman's genitals were quite unlike a wound, which was typically macerated and weak and not at all like this muscular tube. He found the cervix and assessed its dilation as no more than five centimetres, which was disappointing but at least clarified what had to happen next. He went to the basin, removed his gloves and washed his hands. Katerina appeared at his side. 'Well?'

'I'll have to operate,' he said. Poor Winkel froze.

'You're sure?' Katerina asked. He nodded. 'You're not biased towards surgery? Doing what comes naturally?'

'It's a breech presentation, plus the cervix hasn't dilated enough. If we don't operate she'll die. The baby too.'

'I see. Then you'd better operate.' As if on cue Irina Petrovna groaned at the onset of another contraction, drawing her aunt and mother to her in a flurry of support. Katerina went on, 'What can we do to help?'

'Explain to her what's going to happen and why.'

'And?'

'Have someone shave the upper portion of her pubic hair.' He peered around the hut. 'God knows we need to do all we can against infection.'

'You have a razor?'

'Winkel will give you one.'

From their equipment Winkel handed her a razor, and with the soap and warm water she took it to the bedside, drawing the

154

curtain behind her. Winkel, a veteran of countless gruesome operations, was staring at him in obvious fright. 'Sir, I can't deliver an anaesthetic, I'm not qualified.'

'Sepp, in the land of the blind the one-eyed man is king. You've seen it done a thousand times. I have every confidence in you.'

'God in heaven.'

'Good man. Now clear and swab down this table for me. If you can, find a way to extend it a little.'

Bauer knew how to look more composed than he felt, in this case not only for Winkel's sake but also his own, years having passed since he had last done a caesarean, though before leaving the hospital this afternoon he had taken the precaution of reading up on the procedure. Behind the curtain Katerina was explaining what was going to happen. Daria Grigorievna started sobbing again, as her daughter continued to gasp and groan, either resigned to the news or too exhausted to object.

'She's agreed,' said Katerina, emerging from behind the curtain.

'Good,' he said. 'Now, how squeamish are you?'

'Not very. Not since the Civil War.'

Somehow this part of her biography had slipped his mind. 'How would you feel about acting as my operating assistant? Swabbing blood, passing instruments? At times I'll need you to hold the incision apart. Can you do that?'

'Of course.'

Good girl, he almost said but didn't. He would have hesitated, he suspected, had she been twenty years his junior, her age in the Civil War.

Ten minutes later, with the women's help, the patient was lying on clean hospital drapes, washed and shaved and her abdomen painted with antiseptic. Bauer told her that all would be well, that they were putting her to sleep and that when she woke up she would be a mother. Another contraction began. When it was over, Winkel put a cannula in her arm, then, as if to overcome his misgivings, swiftly injected her with Pentothal. Three minutes later she was under.

'That wasn't so bad now, was it,' Bauer said to him. In reply Winkel grunted; they both knew that the harder part would be monitoring the ether: too much of it and both the mother's and baby's lives would be endangered, too little and Irina Petrovna might wake up mid-procedure, with or without the capacity to signal she was conscious. Accordingly, Winkel placed the mask on her with exceptional care and then grew absorbed in her respiration and the release of the ether, making Bauer aware of how heavily he would be relying on Katerina. Dressed in scrubs she certainly looked the part.

'Ready?' he asked her, and she nodded. A little behind him and to one side stood Daria's sister, whose job it would be to shine an electric torch wherever he asked her to. Daria had retreated into the room, where her mother remained on hand with her pot of heated water.

Bauer took up his scalpel and commenced a transverse incision above the pubic bone, only to realise immediately that the patient's muscles were too tense. 'More ether please, Corporal. We have to get her deeper.'

Poor Winkel – having witnessed Hirsch accidentally kill a patient, he was rightly terrified of overdoing the gas, but when Bauer tried again the incision was easier, a runnel of blood a reassuring sign they were underway. Having parted the skin he cut through the peritoneum, releasing more blood, which Katerina quickly swabbed. In Russian he checked if the aunt was feeling all right. She nodded. He put the same question to Katerina.

'Fine thanks. And you?'

Smiling, he said, 'No impertinence in theatre. I need you to part the incision.'

'Like this?'

'Exactly.'

Between the dilated lips of the wound was the uterus, visibly flexing.

'She's keen to get out,' Katerina said. 'Poor thing.'

'She?'

'I'm guessing.'

'Can you be ready to take her when she's out?'

'Of course.'

'Good,' he said, and checked again on the aunt, who assured him she was fine.

'They're bred tough around here,' Katerina said.

'And born that way,' he said, repositioning his scalpel. With exceptional care he cut through the uterine wall, spilling amniotic fluid and blood, making an incision approximately eight centimetres long. Ordinarily this would have revealed the baby's head, but here it was the legs that appeared. Bauer seized them and, in one controlled movement, delivered the baby and with it the umbilical cord in a mess of amniotic fluid, vernix and blood.

'A boy!' the aunt marvelled. '*Mal'chik! Mal'chik!*'

'*Oh,*' cried Daria from behind the curtain. '*Oh.*'

Bauer cut the cord and handed the boy to Katerina, who in seconds had him swaddled. He was black-haired, bawling.

'So much for my powers of divination,' Katerina said, laughing and to Bauer's surprise shedding tears.

Behind the curtain Daria was weeping uncontrollably, while the aunt, too, was crying. By God, even Winkel's cheeks were wet, though his eyes stayed riveted on the ether dial.

'Makes a change from digging out shrapnel, eh, corporal?'

'That it does, sir, that it does.'

Only himself, the old lady and the unconscious mother were dry-eyed, yet even as he noted this his emotions welled, so that with a finger he had to clear the corner of one eye.

Katerina smiled at him. 'Are you all right?'

'Yes, thank you,' he said, and motioned at the baby. 'Sorry to spoil the moment but it's time to hand him on. We've more to do here.'

'Of course,' she said, and passed the baby to the aunt, who in turn delivered him to Daria. Bauer asked Katerina to wash her hands again, rewashed his own, took the end of the umbilical cord and, like some surgical Theseus, traced it through the incision and into the wound until he reached the placenta. This he also removed, taking care not leave behind any tissue that might subsequently fester. In the background Daria was walking to and fro, softly singing to the now placid newborn.

'Now we tidy up,' Bauer said, and with a suture needle began stitching the breach in the uterus.

'Will she be able to have more children?' Katerina asked.

'If all goes well, yes.'

'Including naturally?'

'Certainly, if luck is with her. Though there ought to be a surgeon on call.'

'And those stitches?'

'Catgut. Her body will absorb them.'

With a second layer of sutures he repaired the peritoneum; with a third he closed the skin. He sluiced the wound with antiseptic and then demonstrated to Katerina and the aunt how to inject it with sulphonamide. He applied a dressing. Finally he explained to the women in Russian the importance of keeping Irina Petrovna's wound clean. 'If you have to touch her, wash your hands. And make sure she washes hers. Keep the baby clean. I will leave you some soap. This is ...' He turned to Katerina. 'Crucial,' he said in German, 'I want to say it's crucial. Can you tell them that? It could save her life.'

Katerina relayed this message, sounding suitably severe, getting each woman in turn to confirm she understood.

Bauer turned to Winkel. 'How's our patient doing?'

'So far so good, sir.'

'Excellent. You've done well, Sepp. If it were up to me I'd give you the job permanently.'

'Thank you, sir, but my heart would give out.'

'I doubt that. Yours isn't the type to fail. Still whirring like a dynamo at a hundred, I bet.'

'Not the best way to circulate blood, sir, your dynamo.'

'Pedant. Now pack up while I go and check on the baby.'

'Will do, sir.'

The newborn looked healthy, had a full set of fingers and toes and no obvious abnormalities. His heart and lungs sounded normal. Bauer removed his stethoscope and turned to the new grandmother. 'Congratulations, Daria Grigorievna. You have a perfect grandson.'

Promptly she began crying again. The old woman, whose name he had forgotten, patted her daughter on the back, then she went and fetched hot water in earthen mugs and handed them around; she was sorry, she muttered, she had nothing else to offer him. Bauer thanked her; it was just what he needed, he said. Was this her first great-grandchild? he asked. She replied that it was. Her face was enthralling: thin and beaked and extraordinarily furrowed. On her chin were strands of white wiry hair, filling Bauer with what he supposed was a German impulse to retrieve a pair of tweezers from his instruments bag.

'Tired?' Katerina asked him.

'A little,' he admitted.

'I'm exhausted,' she said. 'Shall we sit down for a while?' He agreed and they sat on a wooden chest by the wall. 'I've never watched a surgery before,' Katerina said, 'or seen a birth. Except my son's. Not that I saw much of *that*.' Irina Petrovna's baby was crying again, ignoring the women's efforts to soothe him. 'He's hungry,' Katerina said.

'It won't be long before the anaesthetic wears off. How's the mother's diet?'

'Before your occupation, adequate; after it, poor. We've given her whatever we have had to spare, but that can't go on much longer.'

160

'I'll see what I can do about supplementary food.'

She turned to him, smiling. 'Getting sentimental, Captain?'

'Perhaps,' he said. 'By rights I should be at war with every one of you, I suppose.'

'Men, women, children, babies.'

'Without distinction, yes. That would be more logical.'

Winkel came over to them and reported that the equipment was packed. Were there any further orders? Bauer told him he could stand down for a while; they would stay put until Irina Petrovna came to.

'Permission to … you know, talk?' Winkel said, gesturing towards Daria, her mother and sister, all three of whom were doting on the baby.

Bauer sent Katerina a questioning glance and she shrugged. 'Go on then,' he told Winkel, 'but be ready to leave.'

'Yes, sir, I will, sir,' Winkel said, and went to Daria's side.

'Changed your mind about them?' Bauer asked Katerina, keeping his voice low, though only Winkel understood German, and his attention was fixed on Daria.

'I've just given up standing in their way,' Katerina said. 'At least for today.'

'Like I've said, he's a good man.'

'And if his goodness could make Daria happy and safe I would marry them myself.'

Winkel, he noticed, was busy talking with the women in Russian, his syntax mangled but his meaning clear enough. 'Listen to that,' Bauer said, 'already he speaks better Russian than I do.'

161

'Less hampered by correctness,' Katerina said. 'And of course love is an excellent motivator.'

'Is that how you learned your five or six main European dialects?' he asked. 'Love affairs?'

'If only,' she said. 'No, it was governesses mainly, though now you mention it I *was* devoted to Signorina Pasquale. Nothing came of it,' she said, noticing his eyebrows rise. 'Alas. But my Italian certainly came along in leaps and bounds – *molto velocemente*, you could say.'

'Poor Metz speaks only German, and so you had him outgunned that day. Certainly you made *me* feel inadequate.'

'Why? Is Russian your only other language?'

'Kind of you to include Russian. I speak French reasonably well. Also a smattering of English. But that's it, unless you count Franconian.'

'Franconian, eh? And what does that sound like?'

'More guttural than Low German. That is, even more guttural.'

'Say something in it.'

He searched his mind for some characteristic sentence or phrase. 'There is this little nonsense thing,' he said, 'a tongue-twister. It sounds like Arabic, or in any case what a German imagines Arabic sounds like.'

'Go on.'

'All right,' he said, paused to recall it then recited: '*A Hammala hamma daham, a Mamalad'n-Amala hamma a daham.*'

Katerina clapped her hands a single time. 'That *does* sound Arabic. What on earth does it mean?'

162

'*We have a little hammer at home, a little jam bucket we also have at home.* Like I said, a bit of nonsense.'

'Say it again,' she demanded, and he did so, only this time when he finished she immediately repeated it, coming impressively close to the original. 'And again,' she said.

In less than two minutes she had it word for word, and it was Bauer's turn to applaud, though discreetly, not wanting to draw the attention of the others. 'So your method is remorselessness?'

'Yes, and not only in language.'

For a time they said nothing to one another. Instead they watched Winkel, Daria, her mother and sister marvelling at the new baby boy, as Bauer grew more and more aware of how close to him Katerina was sitting. Wind keened in the chimney, and in the fireplace a log collapsed, spraying sparks. 'I should check on Irina Petrovna,' he said, got up and went over to the alcove. The patient was still unconscious but seemed fine. He went back to Katerina.

'Are you a good man, Paul Bauer?' she said to him when he sat down again. 'Is that why you're here?' He glanced at her sideways to see if she was mocking him. 'I have to say, I like you better as a saviour of civilians than as a cog in the German war machine.'

'You're most welcome.'

'Is that why you became a surgeon – to do good?'

'Something like that.'

'Were you an earnest young man? I picture you as terribly earnest.'

'You weren't? What about your revolutionary zeal?'

'That's different. I was *impassioned*. I went into battle; you sat in lecture halls.'

'That's true,' he admitted, and explained how after his brother's death he had vowed to become a surgeon. 'If I saved a single life, I told myself, my own life would be worthwhile.'

'And here you are saving two.'

'We hope.'

'All right, no guarantees. But in half a day you have probably achieved your life's ambition twice over.'

'I suppose that's right. Lately much of my work has seemed futile – like trying to catch falling water. The men whose lives I save are often permanently maimed. Or if not, they go back into that war machine you mentioned.'

'And yet for all that you love it, don't you? I could tell from watching you working on Irina.'

'It was a rather special operation.'

'Perhaps, but that's not what I was seeing. Irina could have been anyone, I thought: one of yours, one of ours, Adolf Hitler, Joseph Stalin – it would have been the same. You were so absorbed, so immersed in what you were doing. Here is a man in his element, I thought, doing what he loves and doing it well.' With mock severity she added, 'At least I hope you were doing it well.'

'I do enjoy it,' he said, 'though I can hardly claim credit for that, can I? Especially lately. A war for the likes of me is a bonanza.'

'You monster.'

'War is filthy, of course. It hurts and it hardens. But the fact is that for surgeons it's also an opportunity. Every month we're making medical advances: honing old techniques, inventing new ones, even upending a dogma or two.'

'You're a seeker after truth.'

'Is that irony I detect?'

'Yes, but go on.'

'Truth be told, professional satisfaction is the least of it, because as well as seeking truth I'm also revelling in mystery. I delve *into* people, and you've just seen how strange, how wondrous that can be. What I'm trying to express,' he said, 'earnestly ...'

'No matter. Go on.'

'... is that surgery is more of an art than a science. There's an imprecision to it – a fuzziness, if you will – that's maddening but also compelling.'

Katerina said, 'Well, I confess I envy you. To apply a Marxist analysis, it's hard to imagine a worker less alienated from his labour.'

'But I envy *you!*' Bauer said. 'All right, my work is important. For the individual it's vital. But the body is transient, we all know that. It's stuff. You writers, you forge culture – and culture is eternal. Or as good as.'

She pulled a sour expression. 'Well, firstly, I'm no longer a writer. Secondly, I fear you're exaggerating literature's influence on the world.'

'You more or less told Metz that Lev Tolstoy was going to win the war for you.'

'I was trying to provoke him. If literature exerts any influence at all it's subtle and slow. Possibly not even beneficial, at least not always.'

'I believe it *is* beneficial,' he said. 'And enduring. Even the worst of it survives its author, and the best outlives the language it's composed in. I can't imagine what it must be like to be you and know that in fifty, one hundred, two hundred years there will be someone, somewhere reading your books.'

'Not my books.'

'You can't know that.'

'My books are already obscure.'

'But is that true?'

'Most definitely.'

He searched her face for signs of false modesty, but she only shrugged. 'Anyway, you've written,' he said. 'That's something. More than something: it's marvellous.'

'I have dabbled, that's all.'

'Compared to whom? Tolstoy? By that yardstick almost every writer is a dabbler. You've published. You've earned the right to call yourself a writer.'

She made a scoffing noise but otherwise didn't try to defend herself.

'I still don't know anything about your second book,' Bauer said.

'Oh, that.'

'Yes, that.'

'It was nothing, a failure.'

'According to whom?'

'To critics, to readers, to *me*. It sank without a trace, and rightly so.'

He asked her what it was called and she screwed up her face. '*Europa, 1975*. It was awful, truly awful.'

'It was science fiction?'

'Of a kind. Social-science fiction, maybe. The setting was a neat fifty years into the future, which rather emphasises what a product it was of its time.'

'And so – assuming you're right – what was so bad about it?'

'In short? Too little strife. The setting is utopian, a world in which sexuality is regarded as natural and love of all kinds is esteemed.'

Attempting gallantry, he said, 'That doesn't sound too bad.'

'It was execrable. I'd been so shaken, you see, by the reaction to *Three Women* that I forgot to make my second book interesting – was too busy trying to prove my revolutionary credentials: under communism the sexes would be reconciled; all citizens would work for the common good. That sort of thing.'

'And they weren't? You don't?'

'Being invaded has done wonders for national unity. But unity of the sexes? That's not decades away but centuries. Certainly you and I won't live to see it.'

'Can you be so sure of that?'

'Very.'

'I'll tell you what: in 1975 let's reconvene and check. If by then there's harmony between the sexes, you can – I don't know – buy me a drink or something.'

'And if there's not?'

'I'll mop your floors and iron your clothes.'

She laughed. 'All right, Captain. We have a wager.'

My God, how he loved hearing that laugh. He knew better, though, than to attempt more humour. He was no comedian.

167

'You know, your story surprises me a little – that you allowed the criticism to affect you. You don't seem like the type to fold under pressure.'

'It's kind of you to say so, but remember I was only twenty-three. Also, much of the criticism was coming from men I had previously idolised. The book – I mean the first book – was pornographic, they said. Perverted. Sexually nihilistic. One reviewer pointed out there were no obscenities in *War and Peace*, whereas *Three Women* had four or five, and because *War and Peace* is the pinnacle of realism, it followed that my book had to be "unrealistic". I was a philistine.'

'A literary hooligan.'

'Exactly. And that wasn't the end of it. While some were calling me a barbarian, there were others denouncing me as decadent and *Three Women* as bourgeois – an unkind cut, let me tell you, for the daughter of a count.'

'I can imagine. How did they justify such a calumny?'

'The book's portrayal of Anastasia, the romantic one. Bothering herself with the trivialities of love was criminal, they claimed, since love was a cult of the parasitical classes. I was dumbfounded. Lenin had urged us to rework morals to serve the Revolution, and that's exactly what I thought I'd done, showing young women loving in ways old and new.'

'Marrying Marx and Freud.'

She laughed so loudly at this that the others stopped talking and looked over at them, Daria and her sister with questioning little smiles on their faces. Katerina waved to them apologetically and resumed speaking, her voice hushed. 'At the time I hadn't read any Freud, but now that you've put it that way, that's *exactly* what I wanted to do: show the Revolution its id. I suppose repression was the only possible reaction.'

'So if Anastasia was your romantic and … Zhenya, was it?'

'That's right.'

'Zhenya was your good-time girl —'

'No, that's wrong. In fact Zhenya was the most politically ardent of the three. She only had sex as necessary, to meet her physical needs, the better to devote herself to the cause.'

Bauer dropped a forearm into his lap. 'That leaves the young mother,' he said, 'your autobiographical character.'

'Semi-autobiographical,' she corrected. 'Dominika.'

'I see. And how did she enrage the critics?'

'Well, among other things, Dominika develops a weakness for fashion. At first she dresses drably, as befits a revolutionary, she thinks; but when she has a baby her husband takes a series of lovers who Dominika notices are always glamorously dressed. Secretly she's always enjoyed nice clothes, and so she begins to dress fashionably herself.'

'Rather than leave her husband?'

'From the start he's advocated free love. Made no secret of it. He quotes Engels: "Bourgeois domesticity is a sham, in which artificial sentimentality disguises exasperation and malice." And she agrees with him.'

'But only in theory?'

'Why "only"? Naturally there's a gap between what she thinks and what she feels. It doesn't follow that what she thinks is wrong.'

'I stand corrected. Maybe it would be better to ask whether by dressing differently she gets to keep her husband.'

'Her husband goes on loving her like he's always done, only more so now that she's borne him a child and got a better wardrobe. And so she goes on loving him in return, all the while tortured by his liaisons with other women.'

'So there's no resolution?'

'Not unless you count self-knowledge.'

'Like life, then.'

'Like life,' she agreed.

He wondered when he'd last had a conversation like this one. Years? Never? No, that wasn't right: he'd had one recently. With Katerina. How pleasurable this was, and how pleasurable to learn about her life in this way, by refraction, as it were, through this Dominika. 'So the critics didn't like her taste in clothes?'

'A doll-parasite, one female critic called her. Worse, she claimed that as a former aristocrat Dominika was tainted, her marriage to a proletarian akin to bestiality.'

'*No*. She wrote that?'

'In *Pravda* no less.'

'I can see why you might have been shaken.'

'In hindsight I should have been amused. Some of the time I was, but as I said, I was young and overawed by these people. Not Viktor, though. He was superb. He was a handy writer himself and sent a counter-blast to *Pravda*, which they were good enough to publish. If cross-class marriage resembled bestiality, he asked, how were we to regard Marx's marriage to a woman of the minor nobility? And besides, didn't the same hot blood run in the veins of communists as that of other people?' She was smiling at the memory, a faraway expression on her face. 'Around the same time a notorious killjoy on the Central Committee published a "Regimen for Youth" in *The Young Guard*, and Viktor sent in a parody, which amazingly they also published. I can paraphrase if you like.'

'Go ahead,' Bauer said, wondering if it were possible to feel jealous of a dead man.

Katerina looked inwards, visibly collecting her thoughts, then looked up and began to recite:

> *Wake up*
> *Don't think about women*
> *Clean your teeth*
> *Go to the factory*
> *Work hard*
> *Don't swear*
> *Go home*
> *Bathe*
> *Attend Komsomol meeting*
> *Avoid touching women*
> *Don't think about women*
> *Go home*
> *Find a rope*
> *Time to hang yourself.*

Again she smiled. 'Or something like that.'

'He sounds like a character.'

'He was. Funny, combative. Throughout the twenties he wore a knee-length leather coat and had the swagger to match. He was more Italian in temperament than Russian, really. But a

Tartar in war. Viktor wasn't his real name but a *nom de guerre*: Viktor Krasny.'

'Red Victor. Clever.'

'I'd say blunt rather than clever. A lot of the ambitious men gave themselves *noms de guerre* – Lenin, of course, and Stalin. Viktor's real name was Gennardy. Oh, they were grand days,' she said, smiling, '*thrilling* days. You've no idea. We were poor, of course. Everyone was. But there was a feeling of extraordinary possibility in the air: factories would end want, mechanised agriculture would abolish hunger, science would conquer disease. People would be free to work as they pleased, play as they pleased, love as they pleased. Some of this we even accomplished. Homosexuality was made legal, though that was later reversed. And literacy – there's one achievement that's endured.'

Her eyes were shining and it occurred to Bauer there was no period in his own life that he looked back on with such passion.

'I don't know why I'm telling you all this,' Katerina said. 'You're probably a Nazi. *Are* you a Nazi?'

'No, I'm not,' he said. 'In the election that brought Adolf Hitler to power I voted for the Social Democrats.'

She pretended to recoil at this. 'Oh, good grief, one of *those*. If it gets out I've talked with a petit-bourgeois socialist I'll be shot when our forces come back. And here I was worrying about Daria Grigorievna.'

Simultaneously they looked over at Daria, who was still nursing her grandson, Winkel hovering solicitously at her side.

'Then you'd better hope we're not driven back,' Bauer said.

'Oh, you'll be driven back all right.'

He should have grown used to her patriotic certitude, he thought, but the more plausible her predictions, the more wounding they were. 'You should write about the twenties,' he said. 'You're so eloquent about them.'

'No, no. My writing days are over.'

'That seems a pity. A waste.'

'My genre now is silence.'

'Well, *that's* untrue,' he said.

Ignoring the dig she went on, 'I lack the drive, the egotistic conviction that the world needs my voice in its ear. Tolstoy, of course, had oceans of that.'

'There you go again, comparing yourself to Lev Nikolayevich. If you're to write again you'll have to break free from his clutches.'

Before Katerina could reply, the other conversation stopped. Irina Petrovna was stirring. Bauer half stood but Katerina drew him back down.

'You should wait,' she said.

'I need to check she's well.'

'Yes, but first let her meet her son.'

★   ★   ★

When next morning Metz asked him to report to his study after breakfast, Bauer was unsurprised. 'Bring Frau Kälter with you,' Metz said.

'If she's here, sir. But really that won't be necessary.'

'I'm the one who decides what's necessary, Captain.'

'Frau Trubetzkaya's role in the affair was minor.'

'What affair?'

'The birth. Frau Trubetzkaya only told me about it; I was the one who decided to respond.'

'And you were wrong to do so without consulting me,' Metz said. 'Don't do it again. But this is more important than that. Report with Frau Kälter to my study at 08:00 hours.'

Mystified, and on balance not relieved, Bauer ate breakfast, waited for Katerina to arrive and, when she did, explained what Metz had said.

'It's like school,' she replied, sounding amused. Irina Petrovna was doing well, she added, and so far seemed free of infection. Her baby was feeding well.

'I'm glad to hear it,' Bauer said, gazing at her to assess whether anything had changed between them. A new ease, he hoped. Greater cordiality.

Ehrlich was waiting for them outside Metz's office. He showed them in and then withdrew, pulling the door shut behind him. Metz at his desk. Two empty chairs in front of it. A fire burning in the grate. Metz directed them to sit, then without preamble began speaking to Katerina: 'The night we arrived you mentioned haunting, that the ghost of Leo Tolstoy might appear.' Katerina raised an eyebrow, said nothing, and Metz went on. 'Were you telling the truth?'

Bauer glanced sideways at her, but neither she nor Metz noticed.

'Come, come,' Metz said to her, 'you weren't shy about it then.'

'What would you like to know?'

174

'Whatever you can tell me,' Metz said. 'How often the apparition appears; what form it takes; whether it speaks, and, if so, what it says.'

'Why? Are you being haunted?'

Metz hesitated. 'I'm curious, that's all.'

'As I told you before, I'm not prepared to reveal the house's secrets to an enemy occupier.'

Metz smiled tightly, got up and went over to the fire, took a poker and started prodding at the flames. Bauer wondered if the Wehrmacht had protocols for dealing with a superior who had lost his mind. Fortunately Metz returned the poker to its hook and sat down again. 'The captain tells me you want medical supplies for your village.'

'Yes,' said Katerina swiftly. 'And food.'

Metz chuckled. 'Madam, we are doctors not greengrocers.'

'Maybe, but I'm only asking for the partial return of what your countrymen have stolen.'

Metz huffed at this then said, 'Bauer, what do you think? A goodwill gesture to the natives?'

'An astute move, sir. A clever move.'

Metz turned back to Katerina. 'Very well. I'll take up the matter with our quartermaster.'

'And the medical supplies.'

'A small quantity of those as well. You drive a hard bargain, Frau Kälter.'

She acknowledged the compliment with a nod.

Metz said, 'So, go on, tell me: what do you know about this ghost?'

'Sir, I'm all in favour of helping the villagers,' Bauer interrupted, 'but this business of a ghost is plainly … well, ludicrous.' He glanced at Katerina and saw she was looking serene. He could hardly blame her for exploiting Metz's credulity – might even have found it amusing if Metz had not been a compatriot and a colleague.

Metz was smiling good-naturedly. 'Why so narrow-minded, Captain? The universe is mysterious, its possibilities infinite.'

'Not infinite, surely.'

'Bauer, if science were left to you and your ilk – the dreary so-called realists, the humdrum thinkers in prose – human progress would cease. Yes, the spirit realm may be largely opaque to us at present, but I have not the slightest doubt that scientists will one day uncover its laws and learn how to monitor what goes on there.'

'You say that with such confidence, sir.'

'And why not? Frau Trubetzkaya has evidence.'

'Well, I can't say I've seen the ghost personally,' Katerina said. 'But I've spoken with several who have. Former servants of his.'

'And how long ago were these sightings?' Metz asked.

'The first was seven years after the count's death. This was only months before the Revolution. In fact he foretold it.'

'He did?'

'Remarkable, isn't it.'

What seemed remarkable to Bauer was that Katerina had spoken personally with former servants of Tolstoy.

'But how did he appear?' Metz asked. 'As himself?'

'As he had been in the year or two before his death. An elderly man.'

'Indistinguishable from his appearance in life?'

'The witnesses say he appeared to be made not of matter but of light, less like a man than a man's image on a cinema screen.'

'Transparent?'

'Not transparent, but strangely unstable. The edges of him trembled, they claimed.'

They claimed – as if Katerina herself wasn't wholly convinced. A cunning touch, Bauer thought. What she was up to, he had no idea.

'There was more than one witness, then?' Metz asked.

'Of course. But only those who had known him in life could perceive the ghost.'

'My God,' Metz said. 'I've never heard of that.'

'Though there were others,' she went on hastily, 'who hadn't known the count but who nevertheless heard him talking or moving about.'

'And did any of them try to approach this apparition?' Metz asked. 'To touch it?'

'No. No, they didn't. Not because they were afraid. They weren't. It's just that Tolstoy's people, servants and peasants alike, were – indeed, still are – much closer to the spirit world than we are. We moderns, if you see what I mean. No, it was deference that held them back, their habitual respect for the count.'

'Are any of these people still alive?' Bauer asked.

'Yes, two or three.'

'Including any still here?'

'I'd prefer not to say. It's a private matter really, between them and Count Tolstoy.'

Bauer fixed her with a penetrating stare, which she answered with a winning smile.

'All that can wait,' Metz said. 'What I'd like to know is how this ghost of yours foretold the Bolshevik uprising. Prediction or prophecy? Informed opinion or an insight gained from the beyond?'

'Or a lucky guess,' Bauer said.

'Captain, if you're not going to take this seriously you can leave,' Metz said. 'In fact, consider yourself dismissed. Frau Kälter and I have much to discuss and can do without your puerile interventions.'

'Yes, sir,' Bauer said and got up, surprised by how disappointed he felt. If the realm of the occult held little interest for him, the woman pretending to know about it certainly did.

★ ★ ★

At the hospital Bauer went to see Weidemann in his office. He felt furtive, and this annoyed him. He disliked subterfuge. One of the clerks knocked on Weidemann's office door, paused for a moment then entered, releasing the sound of opera from inside. Evidently Weidemann had brought his gramophone to work. Seconds later the clerk reappeared and said that, yes, the major was willing to see him. Bauer entered the office, a smallish room with a pair of tall south-facing windows, which even at this time of year let in plenty of light. A desk, two chairs, a small filing cabinet. An ammunition case on which the gramophone was sitting, its metal larynx stretched open in song. Weidemann was reaching for its dials, but instead of switching it off he lowered the volume a little, leaving the voice of a soprano wafting from the horn. Bauer didn't recognise the tune.

'You don't mind?' Weidemann asked, swivelling around in his stiff-necked, mechanical way.

Bauer told him he didn't, they both sat down and Bauer got directly to the point: Metz's behaviour was becoming erratic; Drexel was injecting him with drugs.

'What kind of drugs?' Weidemann asked.

'Some concoction of Drexel's,' Bauer said, and explained what he knew, including that Drexel was dosing not only Metz but also himself and Norbert Ritter, supposedly with formulas tailored to each man.

Beneath his flared white eyebrows Weidemann's gaze was unfriendly. 'And what do you want me to do about any of this? Relieve Metz of his command? You're aware he outranks me, I suppose?'

'Of course, sir. I wasn't thinking of anything as drastic as that.'

'Then what?'

'I was rather hoping you might have thoughts about the situation. Ideas I haven't considered.'

'Is his performance in surgery affected?'

'Not that I've noticed.'

'Then I recommend you forget about it. Half the Wehrmacht is on amphetamines, Captain. Half the country probably. That's why we're winning the war. For all I know the Führer himself is a dope fiend.'

Bauer looked at him, startled. Such a statement could get a man into serious trouble. Since Dieter Clemens's death Bauer had resigned himself to being the only man in the company who was critical of the regime. Had he been mistaken about that? 'There's something else,' he added.

'Go on,' replied Weidemann.

'As you know, the lieutenant colonel is superstitious.'

'Yes, I'm all too aware of that.'

'And when we arrived, do you remember how Katerina – Frau Trubetzkaya – tried to tell him that his bedroom was haunted?'

'Some nonsense of that kind went on, I recall.'

'Well, it's still going on,' Bauer said, and described how Metz had summoned Katerina that morning to ask about the presence of Tolstoy's ghost in the house. 'And he was serious, utterly serious.'

The gramophone had begun to play an aria that Bauer did recognise, though he couldn't name it, his knowledge of opera being minimal.

'"Nessun dorma",' Weidemann said, following his gaze. 'This is *Turandot*.'

'I thought I'd heard it before.'

Weidemann looked at him pityingly then said, 'Does Frau Kälter believe in this ghost?'

'Of course not. At least I have no reason to think she does.'

'Then why indulge Metz with it?'

'I've been asking myself the same question. It amuses her, I think. She enjoys demeaning him. It's a form of retaliation – against him, against all of us, I suppose. Though I'm not blaming her,' he said hurriedly. 'Metz is begging to be humiliated.'

'And therein lies your answer,' Weidemann said. 'There is no law, civil or military, against a man being a fool. Indeed, in the army it's often an advantage. Forget about it, Bauer, that's my advice. Let Metz be Metz.'

'You weren't doing that the night you criticised his astrological beliefs.'

'And look where that got me. Nowhere. No, there are enough ills in the world without taking on other people's. Keep your head down, Captain. It's the only way to stay sane.'

'Even if Metz is going crazy?'

'To lose his command Metz would have to be drooling and soiling his pants, and only then in the presence of a superior officer. You know what the army is like. Focus on your own job, Bauer, that's all you can do. Don't look left or right. Obey orders and let someone else fret about the rest.'

Weidemann rose from his desk. Clearly the interview was over. Bauer stood up and thanked him for his time. *You know what the army is like.* But did he? Did Weidemann? Belonging body and soul to the military was bad enough; shedding concern for its personnel felt like one sacrifice too many.

As he left the office the opera swelled, and in the doorway he turned and caught a glimpse of Siegfried Weidemann by the gramophone. In one hand he was wielding an imaginary baton; his eyes were closed, his expression beatific.

ELEVEN

He was woken the following morning by the dazzle of an electric lamp that Molineux had set up beside his bed.

'For Christ's sake, Hermann, show some consideration.'

Molineux groaned. 'My God, what a headache.'

'Turn off the damn lamp.'

'I need a glass of water.'

Bauer checked his watch. 'It's four in the morning. Get your water and go back to sleep.'

'As if. Hear that barrage? Someone's getting it in the neck.'

'All the more reason to sleep while we can.'

Molineux fetched some water, returned to his bed and switched off the light. But Bauer was awake, the damage done. Soon Molineux was asleep again, snoring in concert with the guns around Tula, whose shock waves were perceptible through fifteen kilometres of earth, the foundations of the house and the frame of Bauer's bed.

At 05:00 hours Winkel knocked on the door and announced that there were casualties arriving in less than an hour, and by 06:00 hours Bauer was at the Volkonsky House amid all-too-familiar scenes of pierced and torn and dismembered flesh, groans and pleas and imprecations, the stink of faeces and sweat. His first patient was a grenadier with a gunshot wound to the lung. Though conscious, the grenadier's breathing was laboured and he was coughing blood. He was severely shocked. Zöllner set to work to transfuse him, and when the line was established Pflieger and Demchak stretchered him into the operating theatre. There Bauer bent over and, addressing him by name, told him his prospects of recovery were good. His was a *Heimatschuss*, a home-wound, Bauer told him, the sort of harm that a man might welcome. The grenadier nodded forcefully – a promising sign – then wheezed, exhaling misty blood. Bauer squeezed him lightly on the shoulder, stepped back to make way for Lieutenant Hirsch and, with his usual sense of foreboding, let him administer the anaesthetic. Pflieger and Demchak scissored off the unconscious man's uniform and Bauer returned to the reception room to choose a follow-up patient, which as usual meant confirming the selection already made by Winkel, whose decisions about triage were rarely wrong. The reception room was rapidly filling. Metz and Molineux were examining their own first patients, and young Zöllner was busy setting up more transfusions. Weidemann was there, and in the curtained-off corner a visiting pastor was ministering to a panzerman whose wounds had been judged unsurvivable.

Back in the operating theatre Bauer found the grenadier readied for surgery, masked and draped, his chest shaved and radiantly lit. The entry wound was four centimetres below his left nipple, which it slightly resembled. There was no exit wound. Bauer washed his hands, took up a scalpel and began excising the damaged tissue around the wound. The bullet had struck the seventh rib, breaking it cleanly before continuing into the chest, piercing the pleura and penetrating the left lung's inferior lobe. Fortunately Hirsch had administered a good anaesthetic. With Pflieger swabbing the wound as required, Bauer followed the bullet's path, excising blood clots and damaged tissue which if left undisturbed could precipitate a stroke. In the background Metz's first patient had begun to shriek, a distraction Bauer was able quickly to ignore, having all but forgotten the calm of peacetime operating theatres. The grenadier's bullet had gone deep into the lung and come to rest in the dorsal side of the pleura. Exchanging his scalpel for forceps he extracted the bullet and, knowing he was going to be too busy to reunite patients with their missiles, tossed it onto the floor. With catgut he repaired the damaged walls of the lung but left the rib to set by itself. He closed the wound and dressed it then checked his watch. Operating time, thirty-seven minutes. Demchak and Pflieger picked up the grenadier's stretcher and carried him away, and in the gap between operations Bauer wrote up his notes, aiming for the precision and economy essential to the patient's future care.

When he re-entered the reception room most of the wounded who were conscious turned and stared at him intently. Doing his best to assume an air of confidence he selected a third patient before returning to his second, a *Landser* with mortar wounds to one arm, his pelvis and chest. The man was grossly shocked, a result of the toxins spreading from dead and disorganised tissue which, if not speedily excised, would destroy his kidneys. Two of the wounds were huge and all were contaminated not only with soil but also with fabric from the *Landser*'s uniform. Automatically Bauer went to the sink and washed his hands, then with the aid of X-rays he located and extracted each projectile. Next he debrided dead tissue, scooping it like crabmeat from a tin, creating surgical wounds where before there had been only chaos and dirt. From Metz he had learned not to suture unless absolutely necessary, since the tension it caused often resulted in infection. Instead he injected each wound with sulphonamide and dressed it, trusting the flesh to granulate naturally. Operating time, forty-eight minutes.

The third patient was another grenadier, younger than the first, with a shrapnel wound to the groin. His genitals had been spared but he had severe abdominal pain and the muscles of his abdomen were rigid, and when Bauer lowered an ear to his belly there was no sound of peristalsis. The decision to open the abdomen was a grim one, since the forty percent survival rate he and Metz achieved with this surgery was considered high, infection too often undoing their good work. The risk of doing nothing, however, was usually greater. This time Bauer was relieved to discover that the missile, a steel fragment the size and shape of a thumbnail, had severed a vein but narrowly missed the bladder and bowels. Retrieving it was easy. He tied off the vein and closed the wound.

When he returned to the reception room the assurance he projected was more or less real. Zöllner, a non-smoker, lit and handed him a cigarette; Bauer thanked him and took a series of quick, restorative puffs, gave the rest back and then selected another patient. Returning to the theatre he felt he was part of a well-functioning machine, each man knowing his role and, with the exception of Hirsch, performing it to perfection – though to be fair to Hirsch, so far today he'd done well. At the

185

other table Metz was admonishing Molineux for some ribald remark, a soothingly familiar exchange.

Bauer's next patient was a panzerman, the victim of an anti-tank mine that had mangled his lower right leg. Transfusion had failed to improve his condition, making the decision to amputate an easy one, since nothing killed a patient faster than attempting to save an unviable limb. The panzerman would have to lose his leg above the knee, and so Bauer began by making two vertical incisions in the lower thigh, creating a pair of cuffs which he then folded upwards. The muscle of the thigh he severed with a scalpel, clamping and ligaturing arteries as he went. The femur he sawed. More muscle, a final strip of skin, then the knee and lower leg came away. Pflieger carried off the amputated limb and Bauer turned his attention to the stump, aiming to minimise the risk of painful complications by severing nerve endings as far as possible inside the muscle, and then by bevelling the bone. He then let the skin flaps he'd created fall into place, dressed the stump and protected it further with a plaster cap. In Oryol the unsecured flaps could be sutured into place in a less hurried and more reliably aseptic theatre. Already the patient's heart rate and blood pressure had stabilised. There was colour in his cheeks.

Bauer had planned to operate next on another burned panzerman, but in the reception room an even more desperate case had appeared, a *Landser* who had lost his right leg below the knee to a shell and whose thigh had taken on the telltale blackish-green hue of gas gangrene. Bauer selected a site on the thigh for amputation, the highest possible, then noticed swelling in the abdomen, put his ear to it and heard gas crepitating underneath the skin. Immediately he instructed

Zöllner to set up a transfusion and hurried back to the theatre to wash his hands, but before he could explain to Hirsch the change of plan Zöllner appeared at the door and told them the *Landser* had just died.

It was the burned panzerman's turn, after all. About thirty percent of his body was affected, chiefly his chest and neck and arms, making his prospects for survival better than those of the man Bauer had failed to save the week before, though his neck, in particular, was in a bad way. Zöllner had set up transfusions of both plasma and blood, and Bauer began the grisly task of cleaning the scorched and contaminated skin. When this was done he dressed the affected areas with Vaseline nets and saline compresses. Only time would tell whether these measures would succeed.

As he wrote up his notes he lit a cigarette, then in the reception he devoured a plate of biscuits and knocked back a cup of real coffee – a treat that Winkel reserved for lengthy shifts. The floor was crowded now with the wounded and the stench was bad. Zöllner was as usual tireless, here cradling a man vomiting into a dish, there replacing a blood-sodden bandage, before washing his hands and returning to the transfusions bay.

In the operating room Metz was performing abdominal surgery, and along with the odour of ether the air stank of faeces. Bauer's next case was also abdominal, a gunshot wound to the upper left of the patient's midriff. Part of the colon was protruding, and in the wound there was a great deal of faecal matter, which Winkel swabbed away. This in turn exposed a rent in the splenic flexure, too large to close, and so instead Bauer excised the damaged area and mobilised the ends,

187

bringing them to the surface and stitching their sides together to form a double stoma. Later, if the patient survived, this could be repaired and closed, either in Chern or at the base hospital in Oryol. The essence here was speed.

Next was a landmine wound to a lower leg, the foot so severely pulped there was no question of saving it, though he thought the knee could be preserved. Accordingly he amputated at the ankle, closed the artery but otherwise left the stump unsutured, protecting it for travel with a plaster cap. In his notes he recommended a revised amputation below the knee.

The following case was a shell wound to a thigh. The femur was broken, its fractured ends protruding from the back of the leg, so that at some point during the evacuation one of the shattered points had pierced the canvas of the patient's stretcher and snagged. Bauer's first thought was to amputate, since a fractured femur was a perilous wound, prone to both haemorrhage and infection. This particular wound was grossly contaminated; however, the break was simple and so he decided to repair it, resigning himself to the painstaking task of debriding the dead and dirt-riddled flesh. When finally the wound was clean he set the bone and encased the thigh in a plaster splint, another technique he had learned from Metz, who had himself discovered it in a paper by Trueta, who had been with the Republicans in Spain – proof that when it came to honing his surgical skills Metz was smart enough to set ideology aside.

In the reception room Bauer ate a sandwich, gulped down a coffee and smoked a cigarette before scrubbing up again and returning to the fray. He resumed with a nephrectomy of a kidney too damaged to save. Followed it with another shotgun wound to a lung. He had to amputate both legs of a *Landser* who had been machine-gunned in the thighs, causing Pflieger some dismay, as the entry and exit wounds looked positively tidy, the real damage being maceration from the pressure waves of the transiting bullets. He sutured multiple rents in a small intestine, and one large tear in a liver. He plucked spicules of skull from a brain. He stabilised a panzerman whose field medical card had both of its side-strips torn off, rhyming grimly with his torso, which was deprived of arms. He excised shrapnel from a shoulder. Drained fluid from a knee the size of a football and injected it with sulphonamide. Plastered a second fractured femur. Amputated a hand. Inserted a catheter through the abdomen of a *Landser* in great agony from urine retention caused by a paralysing gunshot wound to his spine. Looked up and in amazement saw that night had come, thought of stopping for a meal but kept working. Alongside him Metz seemed indefatigable, and there were casualties still coming in, the reception room as crowded as it had been at the start.

Another *Landser* arrived, this one with gas gangrene in an arm; Bauer amputated and the patient rapidly improved, only to deteriorate again forty minutes later and die of renal failure caused by protracted shock. 'Another one gone to Valhalla,' Pflieger said – an allowable blasphemy, Bauer decided, as he worked on clearing the airways of a red-headed grenadier with a gunshot wound to the face. He followed this with exploratory surgery on an officer who was showing signs of intra-abdominal injury from a shell wound to his back, and to his relief discovered only bruising to the posterior wall of the belly. He sutured another liver. Reassembled a shattered forearm. Selected, with deep foreboding, a third gas gangrene case, this time in a knee, amputated at thigh level and then an hour later experienced a surge of elation at the news that the patient had woken, was speaking and looked likely to live. *This* was the reason for his being, he thought: a life saved, a soul plucked bodily from the flood.

'A break, sir?' Winkel asked.

'Why? Are you tired?'

'I thought you were, sir. You didn't answer when I spoke.'

'I didn't?' He checked his watch and saw that midnight was approaching, looked at his men and saw they were exhausted. 'Very well, gentlemen, let's break for a meal.'

In spite of fitful attempts to keep it clean, the floor was a shambles of dirty bandages, scraps of uniform, spent ordnance, body tissue and poorly mopped-up blood. Bloody footprints formed paths around the tables, from the tables to the instruments and autoclaves and towards the door. Bauer removed his mask and scrubs and instantly felt poleaxed by fatigue. He could scarcely stand, and yet Pflieger and Demchak were getting a broom and a mop. How he loved these men, he thought. Loved them like brothers. Even Hirsch, he realised. Hirsch, who had laboured alongside him for eighteen hours at a task for which he wasn't trained, mostly performing well enough and certainly without deadly consequences.

Metz looked up from his patient. 'Leaving already?'

'For a bite to eat,' Bauer said. 'The men, you know.' Immediately he felt ashamed of this evasion, though if it made

190

Metz think of his own team it would be no bad thing. They looked exhausted, even Molineux, whose wisecracks had long since petered out. Clearly Metz's men weren't benefiting from whatever boost Drexel was administering to their boss.

When twenty minutes later Bauer returned, Metz relented and gave himself and his men a break. Without them the operating room seemed tranquil, an effect also of the hour, the dead of night – a time of lowered vitality for all, not least the wounded, further endangering their lives.

The next patient had a gangrenous knee, not the gaseous kind but if left untreated just as deadly in the end. However tired he was, Bauer reminded himself, he had to give this man the same care and attention as the first. *Loves or is loved*, he thought constantly as he amputated, concerned less about the truth of the incantation than its usefulness in keeping him alert.

The next patient, a gnarled looking sergeant in his forties, had had the left side of his chest punched in by shrapnel, his efforts to breathe causing a triangle of skin to flap on the wound. He was heavily sedated, presumably because some medic had thought he would die before reaching a surgeon. This was a desperate case. The morphine, the eleven hours that had elapsed since his wounding – everything counted against him; but having made it this far, concluded Bauer, the man deserved a chance to live.

'Look there,' Winkel said, gesturing at a scar on the patient's chest, right beside the sternum, faded evidence of an old gunshot wound. 'The last war?'

Bauer nodded. 'So it seems.'

'Poor sod,' Pflieger said.

'Or born lucky,' Bauer countered, taking up his scalpel and entering the wound. From the thorax the shrapnel had travelled diagonally into the abdomen. Using a series of incisions, Bauer found and methodically repaired the lacerated lung, the left kidney, the liver and the small intestines, choosing thoroughness over speed, the dangers of a lengthy operation outweighed in his mind by doubts that the patient could survive a second surgery.

When Metz returned he paused to watch what was happening, and when the patient died, at the forty-four minute mark, he left his own patient to come over and put a hand on Bauer's shoulder, an unprecedented act. 'Bad luck, Captain. You did your best. You did well to get him as far as you did.'

Bauer mumbled his thanks, close to coming undone. To pull himself together he went and washed his hands, wondering if he'd been wrong to draw out the surgery. Could he have packed the liver to contain the bleeding instead of painstakingly under-running each haemorrhaging vessel? Rather than suturing the small intestine, should he have excised the damaged portions and created stomas? He could only put the failure behind him and press on, though what he yearned to do was rush outside and bellow into the darkness for this to stop, for someone to take pity and in the name of everything true and good bring this slaughter to an end.

The next patient's injury was if anything worse than the dead sergeant's. At least, this was Bauer's instinctive reaction to the sight of a bloodied pubis, the genitals shorn off by shrapnel. The 23-year-old victim, like the sergeant, had been heavily dosed with morphine, and though his life was in no immediate danger there was presumably a distinct risk of suicide, men preferring, as a rule, to lose both legs rather than their genitals. Bauer felt that way himself, proof of the strangeness of the human condition. Hirsch administered the anaesthetic, while Molineux, noticing the wound, came over to the stretcher and swore. 'Thought I'd seen everything,' he said. 'Bits shot off, destroyed. But pussified? That's something else.'

Unwillingly Bauer saw that the resemblance was real: a ruff of pubic hair, lips of remnant flesh. 'Hermann, of all the vile, abhorrent things to come out of your mouth, that is by far the worst.'

Molineux guffawed, and suddenly all of them were laughing, Bauer too, so violently that he doubled over, tears streaming from his eyes. Metz was yelling at them, demanding quiet, but though appalled with himself Bauer couldn't stop. For more than a minute he laughed, and when finally it was over he felt abashed but relieved, wrung out, exhausted but calm. He gathered his thoughts, did what he could for the patient then called for the next.

For the rest of the night he operated in a kind of trance, fuelled by cigarettes, coffee and the knowledge that he had no choice but to press on, that he and Metz were it, there was no one else, and that to stop would cost men their lives. His hands were sore, his neck was sore, his feet and legs were in pain, and increasingly he envied Hirsch's seated position and fantasised about changing places with him. Between procedures he forced himself to take detailed notes, knowing that the moment he put down the pencil the last surgery would vanish from his mind.

Towards daybreak, in a gloomy corner of the reception room, he encountered a patient he was in no danger of

193

forgetting, a supply sergeant with an enormous furrow across his abdomen. Where previously there must have been organs, all that remained were tags of fat that Bauer guessed were mesentery or omentum. Amazingly the man was conscious. Carefully Bauer put the field dressings back in place then surreptitiously shook his head to the medics who had brought him in, prescribed morphine and had them carry him off behind the curtain.

They had learned the day before that a major offensive was underway, but it was only when daylight arrived and the flow of casualties increased that Bauer became preoccupied with its progress. Reports varied, but as the day went on it became clear to him that regardless of the outcome, the division was being destroyed. No city could be worth such a sacrifice. By late morning even these thoughts fell away, his world narrowed to the patient in front of him, until this too was beyond him and he could only cope with acts. Now I am ligaturing, he told himself. Now I am picking up these forceps. Now I must open my mouth and ask Hirsch to titrate the ether. Twice Winkel had to prompt him when he forgot what he was doing, and so when Hirsch fell asleep in his chair Bauer let him doze, completed the operation then lay down under the instruments table and let himself sleep. Fifteen minutes later, as instructed, Demchak shook him awake and he went back to work, feeling partly restored, though by the time the others had each taken a nap he felt just as exhausted as before. It was like operating drunk, and he was terrified of killing someone. But there was no one else, he thought. No one else.

Night was falling for a second time and the wards and the corridors were choked with post-operative cases when at last the reception room began to clear. Bauer felt like an automaton, halting, slow. He spoke little. Dreamed of sleep. Of home. He commenced his final surgery. Finished it. Stepped away. He had operated for thirty-six, almost thirty-seven hours. Winkel too. Demchak, Pflieger. They had performed magnificently and he thanked them for it, then because words seemed insufficient he shook each of them by the hand, felt a rush of emotion and had to turn away. Luckily Metz then called him over and, sounding irritable, asked for help with some suturing. His hands were trembling, Bauer saw. Fortunately it was a simple task, and quickly he was able to hand the patient back. He wrote up the notes from his last operation and then took the precaution of checking the reception room. Zöllner was still there, tidying up with an attendant. Bauer thanked him, told him he'd done a fine job, and was turning away when a beefy face appeared at floor level between the curtains in the corner.

'Oi, doctor! What about me?'

Bauer walked over and pulled the curtains aside, revealing a big man on a stretcher.

'Since you saw me last night they ain't done nothing for me,' he said.

Bauer was about to deny having seen him at all, but hesitated, lifted the man's blanket and instantly recognised the field dressing on his abdomen. The supply sergeant, he recalled. With some difficulty he peeled off the dressing and re-examined the enormous transverse wound, first with dread and then incredulity, followed by mortification and suppressed hilarity. The sergeant was immensely fat, and what in poor light and deep fatigue the night before Bauer had seen as an evisceration was in reality a deep trench through the adipose layers of the belly, the tissue he had mistaken as mesentery and omentum no more than shreds of fat. This was a flesh wound, albeit a gigantic one, not the mortal injury he had taken it to be. Immediately he called for Winkel and the others to help him get the fellow into surgery, and there he cleaned up and tidied the wound. A delayed primary suture in Chern or Oryol would not only restore the sergeant to health but also to a trimmer version of himself.

All that remained to be done was to finalise his notes. Swiftly he wrote up the supply sergeant's operation, mentioned the long delay between his wounding and the surgery and, after a moment of reflection, the reason why. Let his colleagues have a chuckle at his expense, he thought; he wasn't perfect, and if it helped them comprehend how much pressure the unit was working under, so much the better. He leafed back through the patient notes he had made during the shift, pages and pages of them, certainly too many to review, went to close them but instead took up his pencil and below the final paragraph wrote a final phrase: *Otherwise quiet.*

★ ★ ★

'A drink?' suggested Metz.

Bauer eyed him with surprise. They had operated for nearly forty hours, and having just eaten supper Bauer was desperate for sleep. 'That's unlike you, sir. I've not known you to take a drink.'

196

'There are plenty of things you don't know about me, Captain. I don't often drink, that's true, but on rare occasions I make an exception. I do believe this is one of them.'

Bauer nodded and, too exhausted to object, followed Metz down the corridor to his office. He was tired beyond tired, his vision hazy, the floor unstable, the transmission from his brain to his tongue intermittent. Yet Metz was right: the shift they had just finished had been so interminable, so extreme, that going to bed without marking it would have seemed wrong, obscurely improper.

In the office Metz unbuttoned his collar, revealing his gold chain but not the lucky shrapnel shard. He sat down, invited Bauer to pull up a chair beside his desk, and from one of its drawers produced a pair of tumblers and some cognac. 'For God's sake don't tell Molineux,' he said, indicating the bottle. 'I've had this since Paris.'

'Thank you, sir, I'm honoured.'

Metz poured a centimetre of liquor into each of the tumblers, handed one over and raised his own. 'To the Führer.'

'To the Führer,' Bauer repeated, too tired to think of an evasion. He took a polite sip, reached for a cigarette then remembered Metz's prohibition on smoking in his presence. How much more he would enjoy this with nicotine, he thought. Metz's hands, he noticed, were trembling slightly, as they had been towards the end of the shift, a symptom of the drugs he had taken to endure it, perhaps, or an effect of them wearing off. Still, Bauer thought, who was he to judge? Every officer in the unit, and probably every enlisted man too, had a crutch of some kind to help them get by: alcohol for

Molineux, for Weidemann Bach, for Zöllner faith, and for Drexel messianic pharmacology. And for himself ... what was he leaning on? Cigarettes, certainly. Also books, he supposed. Tolstoy currently. And Tolstoy's fierce protector.

'... a lofty place,' Metz was saying, 'and thus a lonely one. Do you see what I'm saying?'

'Sorry, sir, I'm not sure I follow you.'

'At the Olympian heights occupied by the Führer, the pressure must be immense, the loneliness by definition absolute.'

'No doubt,' Bauer said. Briefly he grappled with the problem of altitude and pressure, gave up and took another sip of booze.

'I believe in my own small way I understand how he must feel: the burden of responsibility, the isolation of command.'

'Is that so?' Bauer said, striving to attend to what Metz was saying. Was he sharing a confidence? Such a thing had never happened before.

'You know, I've not received a letter from my wife in over a month. No parcels. Not so much as a single note.'

'The post, I daresay. What with resupply there must be limited space for mail.'

'It's kind of you to say so, Paul, but you're wrong. The post is working perfectly well.'

'Are you concerned about her, sir? Is that what you're saying?' Three months earlier a corpsman had gone home on compassionate leave after his daughter was killed in a British air attack. Metz was from Breslau, and Bauer asked him if the city had been bombed.

'No, it's too far east for that. I'm not worried about her safety. She's perfectly well. I know because I've received two letters from my sister, who lives only blocks away. No, my wife is safe and well. She and I have grown apart, that's all. The war hasn't helped, of course, but even before it there were difficulties between us. You know what the life of a surgeon is. The hours. The call-outs. In my case I was also frequently away on manoeuvres.'

For some reason – nervousness, fatigue-induced hysteria – this last detail struck Bauer as terribly funny, so that he had to strain to keep his face neutral.

'More cognac?' Metz asked, offering him the bottle.

'No thank you, sir. I haven't finished this one. In fact I really ought to be getting to bed. Can barely keep my head up.'

'Allow me to top you up just a little,' Metz insisted. He recharged both tumblers then raised his own. '*Prost.*'

'*Prost,*' Bauer replied and sipped. They said nothing for a while, Bauer gazing into the lens of his cognac, his mind oddly limpid and serene. He heard men talking in the vestibule, some traffic on the stairs. It was still early evening, he recalled, not yet 20:00 hours.

'You know,' Metz declared, 'for twelve years my marriage has been sexless.'

'Oh?' he replied, unable to think of anything else to say.

'Yes.'

'That sounds ... difficult for you, sir.'

'Is that what you think?'

What Bauer thought was that this was not a conversation he had ever envisaged having with Julius Metz. 'Yes,' he said, 'though if I may say so, sir, not particularly unusual.'

'What do you know about it?'

199

'From what I've gathered – from hints, the disclosures of one or two friends – desire in marriage often fades, if not for both parties then for one.'

'And of course your wife was mortally ill, wasn't she.'

'Well, that's true,' Bauer said, taken aback by the bluntness of this statement, though Metz's tone was factual, even friendly.

'In my case I confess it was not my wife but myself who lost interest in the sexual act.' Again Bauer felt an urge to laugh, even as he tried to judge what depths of sadness might have prompted these unlooked-for disclosures. 'Of course,' Metz continued, 'unlike you I am the father of children. Three in total.'

'I know that, sir.'

'Not a large number, true, and admittedly all daughters, but even so. The last was born in the twenties. Later, when the Mother's Cross was introduced my wife wanted a fourth child to qualify for Bronze. I told her no. We had already done our duty, I said. Exceeded the replacement rate.'

'Though not to the extent of, say, Tolstoy.'

'I've done my duty,' Metz repeated. 'By my wife, by Nature, by the Reich, and having done so I am under no obligation to continue. People fail to appreciate the physiological costs imposed by sexual congress, the high demands of the reproductive system.'

From habit Bauer tried to answer logically. 'Doesn't the system make those demands whether or not it's being used?'

Metz sniffed. 'Not at all. It's the *dissipation* of bodily resources that's dangerous.'

'It sounds complicated,' Bauer said, hoping to leave the matter there.

'On the contrary, it's straightforward.'

'To apply in ordinary life, I mean. In a marriage.'

'All that's required is discipline,' Metz said. 'More cognac?'

'No thank you, sir. In fact, do you mind if I go now? I'm really very tired.'

'One moment. Just let me finish my point.'

'Oh yes?'

'This is no ordinary war we're engaged in, Paul, but a struggle for national survival. Indeed, racial survival.' Was this topic new, Bauer wondered, or somehow related to Metz's marital life? 'Militarily, industrially, spiritually, ideologically,' Metz continued, 'we and the Slavs are in a fight to the death. It's us or the Slavs, Paul, us or the Slavs.'

'Some of the Slavs are our allies, sir. Our comrades, even. My *Hilfswilliger* Yuri Demchak, for example.'

'Some could be spared. Those who accept the yoke.'

'*Spared?*'

'Why not? As long as the overall numbers are regulated.'

Bauer thought of Katerina Dmitrievna, one Slav who would never accept the yoke, as Metz put it. Who would not be spared. But that was unthinkable. He would protect her, thought Bauer – marry her, if that's what it took, as Winkel meant to marry Daria Grigorievna. My God, he thought, he would marry Katerina *anyway*. Abruptly everything was clear. Regardless of how the war turned out, he and Katerina would marry. It was simple, settled. He felt an astonishing sense of joy.

'To find a historical moment of equal import,' Metz said, 'one would have to go back to the annihilation of Varus's legions in the Teutoburg Forest, by which Germanness itself was preserved.'

'But here we are the aggressors,' Bauer pointed out, the Soviet Union appearing for the first time in his mind as the homeland of his future wife.

'A war with Bolshevism and Jewry was inevitable. By attacking first we showed greater foresight and resolve.'

'Presumably Varus thought the same.'

Metz smiled at him and shook his head. 'Paul, Paul, what a prophet of doom you are. I used to believe you'd fallen prey to defeatism, but I now see that your pessimism is congenital.'

'Why, thank you, sir.'

Metz chuckled and drained his glass. 'No more of this tonight,' he said, returning the bottle to its drawer. 'God knows we've plenty of work ahead of us tomorrow. Do you think you'll sleep?'

'Tonight I know I will,' Bauer said, putting his own glass down and nudging back his chair, preparing to stand.

'Good for you. I wish I could say the same. For some nights now I've been receiving visitations.'

Bauer inwardly groaned. What new folly was this? Metz was looking expectantly at him. 'What visitations?' he asked.

'From Count Leo Tolstoy.'

'You've dreamed of him?' he asked.

'Not dreamed. Seen. He comes at night, an apparition, just as Frau Kälter described it.'

'Sir, I can't believe that. Surely you can't either. Frau Trubetzkaya was making mischief,' he said, the mildest term he could think of. 'Whatever you've experienced, it must have been a dream.'

'There you go again, Paul. More knee-jerk scepticism. It's unscientific, close-minded.'

Ignoring this, Bauer continued, 'Or an effect of the drugs you're taking.'

'That's irrelevant, not your concern. As I've said before. I'm describing this phenomenon to you because you're a man of science, a fellow surgeon.'

'Which is why you should take my opinion seriously.'

'Are you giving *me* that courtesy? Answer truthfully.'

Bauer sighed, too tired for tactfulness, and crossed his arms.

Metz continued, 'You're not even curious? Your entire worldview might be mistaken, Paul. This could change your life.'

'All right,' he said, 'let me take you at your word. How do you know it's Tolstoy?'

'From his photo, the one in the brochure. I assume he died in the room I'm occupying? You seem informed about the man.'

'He died a long way from here. In a railway station. He had argued with his wife.'

'Well, even so, he appears in my room.'

'But why would he do that?' he asked, listening to himself in disbelief – *observing* himself, as if from the ceiling, the suggestion of a bald patch on his crown.

'Because he's angry with me,' Metz said. 'For planting our dead around him.'

'Then exhume them, sir. It was always a bad idea.'

'*Never,*' Metz said with a startling vehemence.

'It's a difficult site to reach. It's too small. Need I go on?'

'We can't give way, not now – whatever the practicalities might be. He's issuing a challenge. We can't be found wanting.'

'He's dead, sir. Tolstoy is dead.'

'But returned.'

Bauer threw up his hands. 'Then I don't know. Move out of the bedroom.'

'And let him win? Are you mad? He'd only pursue me anyway. No, this is a contest I can't avoid. And can't afford to lose. If I hesitate, if I prove myself unworthy, the consequences would be grave – and I don't only mean for the battalion. If we don't prevail here, if we fail to vanquish Tolstoy, what hope do we have of winning the war? It is here, Paul, *here,*' he said, bringing his fist down on the table, 'that we have to assert our dominance.'

Bauer stared at him aghast, yet at the same time he felt … what? Not persuaded, certainly, but *stirred*. Metz believed that Tolstoy was back from the dead, and hadn't Bauer himself sensed the great writer's presence here?

Abruptly, somewhere in the house a woman started yelling. Metz leaped from his chair. 'What in God's name is that?' he asked, drawing his pistol.

Bauer sprang up and followed Metz into the corridor, where the shouting grew louder. Katerina. Upstairs. In two or three strides he reached the bannister.

'Stop!' Metz screamed at him. 'It might be a trap.' He was wild-eyed, his collar askew. 'Where's the sentry, the *goddamned* sentry?' he cried. Hans Zöllner sauntered in from the officers' mess, looking puzzled and half-asleep. Metz yelled at him, 'What's wrong with you? For God's sake draw your weapon!'

'But, sir, it's only Katerina Dmitrievna,' Bauer said. The yelling upstairs was if anything getting louder, and now included the voice of at least one man.

'She could have brought others!'

'Others?'

'There might be tunnels!' Metz shrieked. From the vestibule the sentry appeared with his rifle unslung. 'How'd she get in here?' Metz yelled at him. 'Through the *walls*?'

Before the sentry could react Bauer stepped past him, bounded up the stairs and, following the noise, rushed to his and Molineux's room. Inside it were Katerina, Molineux and Daria Grigorievna, the last two naked, though Molineux had flung a sheet about him and reversed into a corner, brandishing a half-empty bottle of schnapps in self-defence. Katerina was in fact aiming her fury at Daria, who was pawing the wall while trying to unknot her underpants from her ankles. Clearly drunk, she tottered and fell face down on the floor.

'*Pozor vam!* Shame on you,' Katerina shouted. 'Look at you. A mother. A grandmother now. Thank Christ your daughter can't see this.'

Daria tried to get up but only managed to roll over, floundering and splayed. At Bauer's shoulder Metz appeared, still waving his pistol. 'My God,' he cried, 'what's going on? Molineux?'

'I can explain, sir.'

'Sir, it's not eight o'clock yet,' Bauer said, interposing himself between Metz and the room. 'They're permitted to be here.'

'Permitted?' Metz screeched.

'Not like this, obviously,' he said, gesturing at Daria. 'But they're not violating curfew.'

'I ought to shoot them now,' Metz yelled, thrusting his pistol between Bauer and the doorjamb. 'Cover that woman up! Cover her up or by God I'll put a bullet through her.'

'Sir, please,' Bauer said, pressing down on Metz's wrist. 'The weapon could misfire.'

Katerina crouched over Daria and bundled her into a blanket. 'Get out, get out, the lot of you,' she raged. 'Have none of you any decency?'

'You tell *us* to leave?' Metz yelled back at her. Behind him several spectators had appeared: Weidemann, Ehrlich, Drexel and Hirsch, and, worst of all, Sepp Winkel, his face rigid and pale.

'Why not?' Katerina said. 'You're the intruders. Rapists and bullies, all of you.' She pointed an accusing finger at Molineux: 'Rutting her in her *sleep*, he was, when I came looking for her.'

Molineux straightened his back, made a toga of his sheet and replied with the gravitas of a man unjustly accused. 'At first she was awake.'

'You, I'll deal with later,' Metz said.

Katerina stood up. 'Not a threat to my people, you said.'

'You call that a person? Look at the state of her.'

'He plied her with alcohol!'

'We don't have any alcohol,' Metz replied.

'What's that then?' she demanded, pointing at the bottle in Molineux's hand. Metz glanced at the bottle, as did Molineux, who looked genuinely startled to find it there.

'She must have brought it in,' Metz said. 'For all I know she's a poisoner. I could have her shot.'

'Sir, you're short of sleep,' Bauer said. 'We all are. Let's turn in for the night and deal with this in the morning.'

'You Germans are pathetic,' Katerina said. 'Booze, cards, licentiousness, and why? You're nervous wrecks. The war's turning against you, that's why. You're like actors: you can't bear a flop.'

'So help me God, I'll do it!' Metz roared, aiming his pistol at her. 'I'll shoot her where she stands.'

In Russian Bauer said to her, 'Please go now. He's unstable. He might do as he says.'

'Not without Daria Grigorievna.'

'What are you saying?' Metz demanded. 'I won't have it. Speak German.'

Katerina said, 'He's saying you're unstable. Barking mad.'

'That's it!' Metz screamed.

'More baboon than man.'

'Sir, she's *lying*,' Bauer said, stepping between her and the pistol.

'Lying?'

'To provoke you. For God's sake be reasonable.'

The pistol was pointing directly at his chest, the barrel trembling, though Metz had both hands on the grip. Bauer's chest contracted. How complex and compact were the organs there.

'Whatever's going on,' Metz said, his voice as shaky as the gun, 'I won't put up with it.'

'Feeling vulnerable, *Herr Oberstleutnant*? You should be,' Katerina said.

207

The sense of detachment he had felt in Metz's study unexpectedly returned. 'Don't,' he told Katerina, risking Russian again. 'Don't. I'm trying to save your life.'

'I don't care about my life.'

'In *German*,' Metz yelled.

Obliging him, she said, 'You're monsters, all monsters.'

Bauer seized her by the upper arm and managed to haul her through the doorway, her free arm flailing. Metz and the others backed away.

'Keep that Bolshevik slut away from me,' Metz said. 'Do you understand? If I so much as see her again, I swear I'll shoot her on the spot.'

'*Bastards*,' she yelled.

'She's just going, sir.'

In fact he was finding her hard to control. Their legs became tangled and he almost lost his balance, and with her free hand she started punching the side of his head.

'Need any help, Captain?' Ehrlich said maliciously.

'I'll handle it,' Bauer said. Between punches he seized her free wrist, pinned her arms behind her back and then marched her to the landing.

'If any of you touch her, I'll kill you,' she yelled. 'Is that clear? I'll kill you.'

From behind her he whispered, 'Please, Katerina, please,' only for her to ram her skull backwards into his face, the blow hard, bone on bone, his left orbit and cheek. Somehow he managed to hang on to her wrists, and like a trout on a line she began to writhe. 'Please,' he repeated stupidly, 'please.' She twisted around, her lips pursed, and warm spittle hit his face.

TWELVE

Helsinki
7 May 1967

Dear Paul,
How extraordinary it was to hear from you, and from such
an unexpected source. I had thought you were probably
dead. It was last September that Irina Petrovna came to me
in Moscow and passed on news of your visit to Yasnaya
Polyana. She had to work hard to convince me she had
met you and not your ghost. Had I been able to, believe
me, I would have written to you straight away, but as I will
explain, it is something of a miracle I can write to you at all.

Paul Bauer. How often I've thought of you these last –
my God! – two and a half decades. Time has mass, don't
you find, as well as duration, and those six weeks we knew
each other in 1941 are among the most densely experienced
of my life. Even before Irina's visit not a month would pass
without a memory of that time arising in my mind, and
since September I've thought of it every day. Of course

the war was a vivid period for all of us who lived through it, and I suppose it's only natural that I'm haunted, as it were, by that brief time under enemy occupation. And yet I sense the same might be true for you – why else, I ask myself, would a West German citizen opt for an Intourist-supervised excursion to the Soviet Union, when presumably the Bahamas was an option, or Finland?

Not that I'm entirely surprised. Whatever else may have befallen you later in the war, you can have scarcely forgotten the maddening of Julius Metz (how exceedingly strange it is to write that name) or the deaths of your three comrades. (*Their* names, I regret to say, I no longer recall – so much for my supposedly excellent memory.) Was it to pay your respects that you returned to Yasnaya Polyana? 'To the scene of the crime', I was tempted to write, but that would be inaccurate, wouldn't it, as I recall you behaved rather nobly there, or tried to. Do good Samaritans return to the scenes of their benignities? Perhaps you are like my late husband who once likened his compulsion to revisit Tula, his hometown, which he professed to hate, with a dog's urge to eat its own vomit – a crude analogy, I know, but one I can't help remembering when, under the cover of professional obligation, I sometimes go back to Yasnaya Polyana.

So how did the estate seem to you after such a long absence? Essentially unchanged, I hope, if I did my job properly when you and your comrades left, though visiting in summer is a different proposition from staying in winter, as you are in a position to know better than most.

Irina confessed she didn't recognise you, even after you introduced yourself, so I presume that, like me, you are *not* unchanged. Distinguished looking, is how she described you, which if I remember correctly you were already on the way to becoming in 1941.

Irina mentioned, too, that there were fingers missing from your right hand. Frostbite, I take it? Or wounding? I was desperately sorry to hear of it and immediately thought of your surgical career, which I can recall meant so much to you.

Learning of your injury made me wonder what your war was like. In the Soviet Union we haven't put much effort into imagining the German experience of the war, but in your case I wish to make an exception. Where did you serve? How did you survive? I know that by the end the Wehrmacht was badly beaten up, and even without Irina's report about your hand I would have guessed you had suffered.

And after the war? You've returned to Nuremberg, I see, but what else? Did you remarry, and if so did you have children after all? Please write back and tell me all. (I will explain to you how.) Any letters between us are likely to be infrequent, so I warn you I won't tolerate platitudes or evasion.

In my vanity I'm assuming that my curiosity about you will be reciprocated, so what follows is a summary of my life since 1941. After you and your comrades' forced eviction from Yasnaya Polyana I continued working there until 1953, the year of Stalin's death. The timing was not a coincidence. Do you remember me once telling you that my ex-husband Viktor had been murdered? What made me disclose this I don't recall – at the time I was more than a little crazy. What I meant was that Viktor had been one of thousands of Party veterans who in the late thirties had fallen victim to Stalin's Great Purge. Indeed, it was his arrest which drove me to Yasnaya Polyana in the first place, since I still had enemies on account of my first novel and, despite divorcing Viktor, felt vulnerable in Moscow. So I rusticated myself – went with Marlen to Tula and lay low there with Viktor's relatives. From there I managed to land the job at the estate. Sixteen years later Stalin's death reversed that process. I sent out feelers about returning to Moscow and ultimately secured a lectureship at the State University (an easier task, it turned out, than resurrecting my Moscow residency permit). I have been with the university ever since. My speciality? Tolstoy studies, with a focus on narratology – a dry and technical subject, but one on which Marxism rarely intrudes. Furthermore, after more than a decade of blameless service I have discovered to my amazement that I have acquired some *blat* – influence, pull – and for several years I have been permitted to travel internationally to speak about Tolstoy at academic conferences. Thus the postmark on this letter.

There isn't a great deal more to tell. Needless to say, I have never remarried, but live happily by myself in a minuscule but comfortable flat in the Khamovniki District. I catch a bus to the university. I walk beside the river. If the need arises I shop at GUM, Moscow's main department store. I attend the Bolshoi as often as possible. My income stretches to books. In short, I live a privileged life and couldn't ask for more.

Irina told me that her supervisory duties made talking with you difficult, particularly since your Intourist guide might have asked awkward questions had he realised you'd once known each other. That and her surprise prevented her – again! – from thanking you for saving her and her baby's lives all those years ago, and she has made me swear to put this right. She *is* profoundly grateful. That baby is now an Aeroflot pilot – Time the Conjurer working his usual miracles. Daria Grigorievna, sadly, didn't live to see her grandson grow up, as she died in 1949. Drink, you won't be surprised to learn. Her self-destruction was heart-rending to witness, because Daria was a kind soul who had a lot to live for: useful work, friends who overlooked her failings, a wonderful daughter and an adorable grandson who as a child was already handsome and smart. Even after the events of your stay I had hoped to save her, but I failed. You once told me of your feelings of powerlessness whenever a patient of yours died on the operating table, and after Daria's death I believe I felt something similar. *Her* mother, you might be interested to know, lived well into her eighties, outliving Daria by several years. Agrafena Viktorovna – remember her? I'm smiling because I know you can't have forgotten her part in your lieutenant colonel's undoing.

Irina mentioned your discretion in handing over your address, which suggests you have some understanding of the constraints we continue to operate under in the Soviet Union. I am therefore hoping you will appreciate the need for the convoluted method I have devised for sending and receiving letters from you, assuming you decide to write back. In comparison to Stalin's day the Party has become downright vegetarian, and as a Party elder (a better term might be 'relic') I probably wouldn't be imprisoned, let alone executed, if this letter were intercepted. I would, however, lose my travel privileges, and this would be a pity, in particular for certain others who have come to depend on the blue jeans, contraceptive pills and other little luxuries I bring them from the West. I say this not in order to make you anxious on my account but simply to ask for your discretion.

Of course it would be more prudent of me not to write to you at all, since among other things I've wondered whether you might be acting on behalf of a Western intelligence agency. Does that seem paranoid? In my defence I should point out I've been approached before. Rome 1962. My first conference abroad. I can't imagine what the spooks thought I might divulge, since my knowledge of the Russian military is one and a half centuries out of date, and in any case freely available in translation. I rejected that advance, needless to say. Needless to say, that is, unless you're working not for the West but for the KGB – in which case, greetings comrades! May I keep my apartment?

After decades of conditioning, this is how my mind runs. I tell my friends it's our era that's deranged not ourselves, but the sane ones think I'm a little mad. I can see their point. Though normally cautious, I seem to be compelled, every decade or so, to behave really recklessly. Hardly surprising, I suppose; one doesn't need to be dear old Dr Freud to see how lengthy periods of repression – in both senses of that term – might account for these eruptions of unreason of mine, but most of my friends have managed to behave rationally, or at least warily, throughout their lives, so clearly there's something amiss with me. And here I go again, losing my mind, pushing my luck and deciding to trust you, Paul Bauer, as I did once before. The cost that time (this will sound mawkish, but it can't be helped) was a disconcerting sense of sadness when you left; but sadness, I tell myself whenever it threatens to overwhelm me, is the coinage of a richly lived life.

As you may know, with the exception of diplomatic mail, the KGB monitors all letters in and out of the Soviet Union. By 'monitors' I mean 'reads'. Every single word. Sadly, my *blat* doesn't reach into diplomatic circles, so I must ask you to address any reply you wish to make to a Canadian friend of mine, Professor Simon Fleet, whom I believe I can trust and whose address I will append to this letter. Professor Fleet regularly attends the same conferences I do (including one last year at Yasnaya Polyana), and he is willing to help by passing on any mail in person when he and I meet at our next conference, which will be in March next year, in Sydney, Australia. That's a terribly long time to wait, I know, but really there is no safe alternative. Even this method is not without its risks, as I am generally shadowed when abroad by 'cultural attachés' from the closest Soviet consulate or embassy. To save me skulking

around postboxes, Professor Fleet has also agreed to post
this and any future letters I might write to you.

Let me end by again requesting your discretion. If
you dispose of this letter, I'd be grateful if you burned it;
if you decide to keep it, please do so securely. Apologies
again if these precautions and warnings seem ridiculous.
I do hope they don't deter you from writing back, since
frankly I'm fascinated to learn what's become of you.
Until then, Paul, farewell.

Yours,
Katerina

★ ★ ★

28 Jonah Strasse
Nuremberg
1 February 1968

Dear Katerina,
How good to be writing to you at last. I had hoped but not
expected to find you at Yasnaya Polyana, and with mixed
feelings learned from Irina Petrovna of your long-ago move
to Moscow. I was pleased for you. Am pleased. Despite
some restrictions, you do appear to be living an enviable
life. That this is due to your devotion to the 'old man', as
you once called Tolstoy, strikes me as wonderful. What an
excellent match you and Lev have turned out to be. Sophia
Andreyevna will be enviously writhing in her grave.

I chuckled at you picturing me at Yasnaya Polyana as a ghost, since I felt just like one as I wafted up the driveway and into the main house. From poor Irina's perspective I might as well have returned from the dead, what with the veil of all those years between us, not to mention the Iron Curtain my guide drew around me. Ivan, his name was, which I noted because 'Ivan' was our generic nickname in the Wehrmacht for the Russian fighting man. Fortunately for him, this Ivan was too young to have seen combat – had he done so he might have been friendlier towards me, as I've noticed that old soldiers tend to grow fond of former enemies in proportion to how bitterly they once tried to kill one another. My Ivan knew I had been a surgeon in the Wehrmacht (I had admitted as much, and more, in my application for a visa), and perhaps as a result he seemed to think it his duty to make my stay in the Soviet Union as unpleasant as possible. And who could blame him? He'd lost an uncle at Kursk. Naturally I didn't tell him I'd been stationed at Yasnaya Polyana, though it is possible he guessed this from my demeanour there, which was hardly that of the casual tourist.

Yes, my compliments – I did find the estate essentially unchanged, though with all the furniture returned the buildings felt homelier than they had during our occupation. And of course the grounds were indescribably lush in comparison to how they were in the winter of 1941. I experienced the visit as a series of recognitions of the strange in the familiar, and the familiar in the strange.

Why did I go back? you ask. Well, for a start let me assure you that I am *not* working for an intelligence agency, Western or otherwise, though I can see why you might have wondered. No, my reasons were entirely personal. As you suggest, I was thinking of the men of my unit who had died there or thereabouts. But by the end of the war I had lost more comrades in Russian fields and barns and forests and swamps than I could possibly recall, and so there was more to it than that. You asked me to write candidly, and so I will. The overwhelming reason I returned was my hope of seeing you. In your letter you write of how frequently you recall the time we knew one another in 1941, and this gladdened me because as time passes I think of it more and more often myself. Indeed, looking back, I have come to regard those six weeks as something like the fulcrum of my life – because, while events occurred after it which affected my fate more drastically, at Yasnaya Polyana I turned from the past to the future, from mourning my wife to imagining some kind of life with you. Not that I was naive about this; I was forty, not twenty, and understood the obstacles. I also had my reading of *War and Peace* to remind me not only that love doesn't always conquer but that, arguably, *it's better that way* – that thwarted love is stronger, more enduring than the domesticated kind, which as you once pointed out often descends into bickering, as happened between Lev Nikolayevich and Sophia Andreyevna. *War and Peace* also had the effect of restoring my faith in doing good in the world; because if, as Tolstoy argued, we are all specks in a vast world-historical drama, including those who think they're in charge, it follows that everyone's actions are potentially significant, that the humblest person can influence events as much as any general, emperor or tsar. When I became a killer I had to accept the full implications of this: that the young man I shot (or his unborn descendants) might have – I don't know – written great symphonies, cured cancer, or in some more subtle way made the world a better place. But even then I found self-serving comfort in the thought that I was neither good nor bad but simply human, an atom in the claw of a beast intent on flaying itself.

No doubt that last sentence shows how wise I was not to pursue a career as a writer. You, Katerina, have no such excuse. Is it too late for you to go back to fiction? I have a memory of a conversation of ours at Yasnaya Polyana in which you unfavourably compared your writing with Tolstoy's. Since then I've encountered a quote of Isaac Newton's, which he borrowed from elsewhere, I believe, about his seeing further by standing on the shoulders of giants; and it seems to me that, likewise, modern writers might aspire to see further than Tolstoy by mounting *his* shoulders. If I'm wrong about this, set me right. If not, you may send me a draft of your *next* novel – or for that matter, copies of your previous ones, since you'll be pleased to know I can now read reasonably complex Russian. I'm rather proud of this skill, a small compensation for the loss of three fingers and six years of my life, and lately I have been putting it to use by re-reading Russian novels which as a youth I read in translation.

219

You asked how I spent the remainder of the war. After
retreating from Tula and abandoning Yasnaya Polyana,
the 3rd Panzer withdrew to the neighbourhood of Chern,
though the term 'withdraw' in no way captures the chaos,
panic and despair of our flight, particularly during its early
stages. What happened later at Stalingrad is so well known
that it tends to obscure the cataclysm we experienced in
the winter of 1941, when we lost hundreds of thousands of
men and, I am convinced, effectively lost the war. When
the 3rd Panzer went back on the offensive the following
spring – bypassing Yasnaya Polyana and the tough nut of
Tula – we did so without the sense of invincibility we
had carried into previous campaigns; and even after our
subsequent capture of Voronezh the dominant emotion in
the division was anxiety, an anxiety which of course turned
out to be well founded. From 1943 onwards I experienced
the war as a sequence of retreats, each more catastrophic
than the last, until in October 1944, in the vicinity of
Lvov, a Soviet armoured brigade overran the tent hospital
in which we were operating. I wish I could report to you
that I stayed with my patients that day, but those who did
so were killed, without exception, and their patients too.
I can't even pretend I made a conscious choice, because
the truth is I simply started to run and kept running, like
a hunted animal, a cliché that aptly describes what I had
become: a pop-eyed, panting, sweating beast. And so I saved
myself. For the next several days I attempted with a handful
of others to get back to our lines, huddling around a fire at
night like Neolithic survivors of a slaughtered tribe, then on

220

12 November 1944 we were duly captured and marched directly into Lvov. Years later I learned that in 1943 the SS had rounded up the Jews of Lvov and sent them to their deaths at Auschwitz and Treblinka, so there was some crude justice in what happened to us next: transportation, by stages, from Lvov to a place I came to know as Gulag Hozzi, near Borovichi, roughly halfway between Leningrad and Moscow – the first of several prisoner-of-war camps in which I was interned until May of 1950.

Gulag Hozzi was a hard place, as all the camps were. We cut peat, retrieved logs from the Msta River, and when the river was frozen we processed those logs at the local paper mill. Many of us died. That first year I caught typhus and nearly died myself, and it was during my time at Gulag Hozzi that I lost those fingers – not to frostbite but to an accident on the river, when my hand was crushed between logs. As Irina noticed, it was my right hand, and I have never held a scalpel again. At first I despaired about this, though not for long, since in the gulag my medical skills were in high demand. In reality I was more like an apothecary than a doctor, dispensing medications such as lichen and charcoal, caraway and yarrow, and in this I was helped by a fellow officer you might remember: Fabian Drexel, our pharmacist. At Yasnaya Polyana I disliked Drexel, and while I can't say we became friendly at Gulag Hozzi, I certainly came to see him in a new light. Being younger than me, Drexel had been exposed to Nazi propaganda earlier in his life, and as a result he experienced Germany's defeat as a profoundly personal (indeed, metaphysical) crisis, demanding nothing less than a reformation of the soul. In his case this took the form of a conversion to Christianity, a creed he'd previously reviled for its pacifism (however notional), and probably also for its association with Jewishness. In Gulag Hozzi he became a vocal anti-Nazi, and on one occasion had his nose broken by a former SS man who was still in possession of an Iron Cross presented to him in person by Heinrich Himmler. Drexel dreamed of returning to Germany and becoming a pastor, but after Gulag Hozzi we were sent to different camps and I never heard from him again.

I should concede that Stalin made two contributions to my welfare: the first by encouraging me to give up smoking, cigarettes being a form of currency in the gulag which I couldn't see the logic of burning; and the second by curing me of insomnia, which vanished – overnight, you might say – around the time of my capture, one of those developments that I dare say your 'dear old Dr Freud' could explain.

The final point I would like to make about my captivity is that you helped me through it. Again, this wasn't due to some romantic delusion that I would somehow walk free into your arms, but rather to my then recent reading of *War and Peace*. The copy you gave me I had wisely left in Nuremberg on what turned out to be my final furlough home, but in the camps I made a mental project of recalling as much as I could of the novel, which turned out to be a surprisingly large amount, no doubt thanks to the intensity with which I had read the book at Yasnaya Polyana (with the additional benefit that events in the novel in turn reminded me of interactions with you). In particular I often thought of Pierre's ordeal as a prisoner during Napoleon's retreat from Moscow, and whenever I was gnawing some revolting morsel which in the gulag counted as a treat – the leg of a nutria, say – I would think of Pierre reflecting on how deprivation sharpens pleasure as he devours horse meat seasoned with gunpowder. This consoled me; I was the sort of fellow who knew what style of rat he was eating and who, furthermore, was able to philosophise about it.

It was in the camps that I learned to speak fluent Russian, albeit of a very slangy kind, and in Gulag Gagri, near Gagrilovo, my final camp, I convinced the commandant to let me read *Das Kapital* in Russian. For all I know this may have hastened my release, though I didn't plan it that way and the opposite might just as easily have happened, as POWs were granted freedom in a very haphazard fashion until as late as 1955. I was lucky. On 23 May 1950 I left Gulag Gagri with about a hundred others and was taken by train on a journey of several days to Leipzig, where those with homes in what had become East Germany were released (and where, incidentally, guards discovered the Iron Cross of the SS man who'd punched Fabian Drexel, and sent him straight back to the camps). From Leipzig the train continued to Fulda in West Germany, where the authorities gave us food and coffee, and there it began to dawn on us that we had not only travelled in space but in time, a thousand changes, stupendous to small, having turned us into foreigners

223

in the country of our birth. We stood in line and took orders like awed little boys, and although grateful to be fed we gradually realised that strenuous efforts were being made to keep us apart from other travellers, our rag-tag group being an embarrassment, a troubling reminder of the war. When we were transferred onto a passenger train for Frankfurt the stationmaster insisted on cramming all 'homecomers', as he called us, into the rear carriage, though the train was half empty and its seats unticketed. It was at this point I committed what I later came to see as my first overtly political act, leading a contingent of the men into the other carriages, where we proceeded to sit where we liked. This earned us a good deal of hectoring from the conductors, but apart from a few furloughs during the war, I had been out of the country for over fifteen years and had lost certain habits of obedience, and when we refused to budge, the conductors were forced to back down.

This is already a long letter, I see, and so you will be pleased to know that the eighteen years since 1950 have been less eventful than the preceding nine. Yes, I did go home to Nuremberg, and while my hand prevented me from practising as a surgeon, I was able to return to medicine as a hospital physician. This involved a great deal of administration, and early on I realised that the only way to reform inefficient or outmoded procedures was to engage in some practical politicking. This in turn led to an invitation from the Social Democratic Party to stand as a candidate in local government elections, and in 1954

I became a councillor for the City of Nuremberg. Four years later I was elected mayor, a post I held until two years ago, when I opted to stand down, making way for my deputy.

You asked about children, and the answer is no, I have none. I was forty-nine when I returned to Germany but looked and frequently felt much older, and certainly no women of child-bearing age expressed an interest in me. Perhaps I could have tried harder (or married a woman my own age), but my professional life was exceptionally busy, because even when I entered politics I continued to work at the hospital, though in a part-time capacity. Of course now that I have retired from both medicine and politics I occasionally wish I had a family of my own, but at these times I remind myself that the war deprived millions of people of their lives, while I merely lost a few years and some fingers.

Having personally experienced some of the 'constraints' of the Soviet system I do understand your caution in writing to me, yet the prospect of having to wait such a long time for a letter from you is, I confess, rather dismal. Are you sure we couldn't write openly to one another? What about that *blat* of yours? A few minutes' research at the Nuremberg city library showed me that you have acquired a considerable international reputation as a scholar – might that grant you a type of immunity? Also, when you are abroad, could we speak by telephone, or even meet in person? I have considered travelling to Australia in the hope of meeting you there, but being unable to consult you about it I've reluctantly given up on this idea. Do you know when and where your subsequent conference will be? By definition, it can't be as far away as Australia!

One last question. How is Marlen? In your letter you don't mention him, and this omission makes me uneasy, as I know very well what horrendous losses the Red Army suffered during the war. Perhaps the 'certain others' for whom you bring gifts from abroad are relatives of his, a sign he survived the war? I hope so. Please write back and tell me your son is safe and flourishing. Tell me everything, in fact – including, if you wish, more about Viktor. At Yasnaya Polyana national loyalties drove a wedge between us, but having both suffered from Nazism *and* Stalinism, it occurs to me we now have much in common. So hold nothing back. Like you I find myself craving openness and truth (which the young, especially, seem to think I can't handle – by far the worst indignity inflicted on the aged).

Yours candidly,
Paul

P.S. Please send me copies of your novels. I mean this. Don't let me down!
P.P.S. Can you be entirely sure that this Professor Fleet of yours is trustworthy? As our only way of communicating with one another I certainly hope so, but for your sake I thought I should ask.

THIRTEEN

Two days later, Thursday, 20 November, Bauer and his team left Yasnaya Polyana in a pair of lorries, himself and Demchak in the lead vehicle, Winkel and Pflieger behind. Bauer's mood was dark, much like his eye where Katerina had struck it with her head.

He had not expected praise for working the lengthiest shift of his life, but neither had he anticipated being sent to the front. Even allowing for the normal arbitrariness of military life, the redeployment made little sense. Operational reasons, Metz had said when Bauer had asked for an explanation. It was time to 'revitalise' the battalion. Whatever the real reason, Bauer felt for his men. In his operating team the only man spared had been Hirsch, retained at the hospital as the unit's only dentist.

Privately he wondered if Metz was punishing him, but if so for what? It was Molineux who had violated the race laws, to say nothing of what he'd done to Daria Grigorievna. Of course Molineux was Metz's anaesthetist, as well as a rogue with a knack for a making a crime look like misconduct, and misconduct a character quirk. Liking him was probably a personal failing, Bauer

227

thought. A better man would have preferred the company of Hans Zöllner; but Zöllner's style of goodness was irredeemably dull, his character a whitewashed room in comparison to Molineux's dim and damasked persona, the shadowy corners of which were best ignored but whose surfaces were choked with curios and books and evocative droppings of wax.

Not that he would be seeing either man for some time, he supposed, as he gazed through the windscreen at the snowy plain. Or Katerina, for that matter, who he might never meet again, and who in any case now clearly despised him. The region of impact around his eye still pulsated, a nasty reminder of their parting. Better not to look back, he thought. This was a mobile war, and he would do better to focus on what lay ahead.

The afternoon was clear, or what passed for it in the Soviet Union at this time of year, the sky a duck-egg blue that faded lower down into folds of mist on broad, snowy fields, stands of pine appearing in the distance like formations of Napoleonic soldiery. The temperature was minus eighteen degrees. Ever since the arrival of the frost he had wondered how fighting could be sustained in such weather, and the prospect of returning to the field brought home the lunacy of it. *Combat*? What about eating, shitting, sleeping? How was it possible for men to go on fighting in temperatures that made the basic functions of life if not impossible then prodigiously difficult? The prospect of winning the war and going home might have helped, but the recent offensive against Tula had by all accounts failed, and Bauer's despondency about this revealed to him that he had become as hooked as anyone on the stimulant of victory. He glanced at Demchak, wondering how the Hiwi regarded their changed circumstances, but as usual the young man's chiselled face was unreadable, his eyebrows too blond, apparently, to register lesser fluctuations of emotion. Was Demchak sorry to have thrown in his lot with the Wehrmacht? To ask him directly was out of the question, but it was rare for them to be alone together and so, seizing the moment, Bauer asked why he had chosen to join them in the first place. The Ukrainian's expression didn't alter. 'To crush the Reds.'

'I see. And to what end? An independent Ukraine?'

'No end. To destroy them. To scrub them off the face of the earth.'

'You hate them, then.'

'Of course. Don't you?'

The question sounded sincere, unpremeditated, and yet Bauer hesitated, unsure if his loyalty was being tested. 'By the sound of it, not as strongly as you.'

'Stalin starved Ukraine,' Demchak said. 'This was 1933. My mother died, and my younger brother. I was fourteen years old. I boiled and ate my belt. Not all at once, understand. I rationed it out. Ate slowly. You can't imagine.'

As a widower Bauer sometimes felt sorry for himself, and yet he kept finding people whom life had treated more harshly. 'I don't suppose I can,' he said.

'The famine killed millions,' Demchak said, '*millions*. Stalin wanted to kill us off and make way for Russian settlers.'

'And you think it was a policy, not a policy failure?'

'It was deliberate. The Bolsheviks stole our land, our crops. Imposed grain quotas they knew we couldn't meet. There were even laws against gleaning. So now I hate them, their system,

229

their leader, their language. Want to know how to tell if you're free or unfree?'

'Go ahead, tell me.'

'When you're unfree you can't take your goods to market. Can't negotiate a price. At least not in public.'

Bauer mulled this over then said, 'That seems true to me. But incomplete? I can think of other symptoms.'

'That's the fundamental one. If you can't buy or sell you're no better than a slave.'

It occurred to Bauer that, except in the case of the Jews, National Socialism had largely left commerce alone. In fact to Demchak this was probably part of its attraction.

'May I speak plainly, Captain?'

'I'd say you have already.'

'These losses we're taking. Do you think the army will let us take on Ivan – we Hiwis, I mean? Give us weapons, training?'

'It's not something I've thought about,' Bauer said.

'But with such heavy losses. Someone like me who really hates the Reds, it can't be long before they let me go to the front.'

'We're going there now.'

'Sir, I don't want to seem ungrateful. To you, to the battalion. But I joined up to fight the Bolsheviks, to really hurt them, not to patch up the damage they're doing to us.'

'I'd be sorry to lose you.'

'You won't let me go?'

'I'd have to discuss it with Metz.'

'It's not as if the work is difficult,' Demchak said. 'There are others who could do it.'

'Probably. But don't underestimate yourself. You're more intelligent than most.'

'All the more reason to be in combat.'

Bauer glanced at him, at his outlandishly Aryan looks, the scarred upper lip. His fighting spirit was in some ways commendable. In fact it was not so different from Katerina's, and it hardly made sense to admire *her* zeal while finding fault with Demchak's. They both believed, and with a strength Bauer himself had never mustered.

Ahead the road fell gently down to a causeway that ran about two hundred metres across a frozen lake. The ice was windswept, blue. To either side marshland, stubbled under snow. The causeway was narrow, not much wider than a lorry, and crossing it from the opposite side was a column of troops – prisoners of war, Bauer realised, a great brown millipede of men escorted by a handful of guards on motorcycles. Demchak pulled over beside a burned-out panzer, and behind them Winkel did the same. With both lorries' engines off, the silence seemed profound, all the deeper for the distant buzzing of the motorcycles. Snow lay on the marsh, on the fields, on the slopes and on the ravaged tank, bandaging its burns. There was snow on its turret and its cannon, which were pointed to one side. 'We probably treated some of the crew,' Bauer said.

'Probably,' Demchak said.

Perched on the cannon's muzzle was a solitary crow, an avatar of blackness in the white. It cawed and Demchak seized the handle of his door. 'Permission to get out, sir?'

'Granted. Just shut the door.'

231

Demchak got out – to urinate, Bauer presumed, but in the driver's side mirror he glimpsed him pivot on his heel and methodically spit three times across his shoulder. 'Troublemaker,' Bauer said to the crow, which can't have heard him through the glass but nonetheless tilted its head. A lip-reader perhaps.

Demchak clambered back into the cabin, and Bauer offered him a cigarette. They both lit up. Four of the advance motorcyclists were coming off the causeway. Two immediately peeled off on either side, while the other pair roared further up the slope. Both of the riders who had stopped were wearing bits of Soviet kit: boots and gloves, an *ushanka*, the risk of being shot by a comrade regarded as lower, evidently, than that of freezing to death.

The cabin was filling with cigarette smoke, making Bauer's eyes sting, though this was marginally preferable to opening a window and getting flayed by the cold. How he hated cigarettes really – the stink, the cough, the staining of his fingers – and yet, Christ, how he adored the silken hit of nicotine. On no account, he decided, could he let himself be captured and, like these poor devils on the causeway, have to go without.

The column was about five or six men wide, the faces at the front of it now near enough to read. Some looked resentful, others indifferent or resigned. This wasn't a body of men but a shambling mass, each man responsible now for his own salvation. Demchak pointed at a group with Asiatic features. 'Fucking Tartars,' he said. 'Sorry for my language, sir, but I can't stand their slanty eyes. Millions of them, the Reds have – an endless supply.'

Bauer had heard rumours of so-called 'Siberian' troops arriving from the east: well armed, well clothed and better organised than the Soviet soldiers they had faced in the first phase of the invasion. The men so violently reviled by Demchak looked to Bauer as pitiful as the rest, but he could see Demchak's point about numbers. As individuals the prisoners looked beaten and demoralised, but as they came off the causeway and began to stream past the lorry they became, by dint of numbers, an impressive, even intimidating sight. Yes, their capture represented a triumph of German arms, but the ongoing resistance at Tula rather supported Demchak's claim that the Soviet Union's supply of manpower was effectively endless. Bauer recalled Katerina's taunt the day she'd shown them around the estate: that hurled hats alone could halt the German advance. Hyperbole, yes, but by a similar logic was it possible for the Soviet troops to give up in such numbers that the Wehrmacht would run short of men to escort them to the rear? And how were they to be fed? Could an army surrender its way to victory? Bauer smiled at the notion – one for Molineux – then grew pensive again at the sight of a wounded prisoner limping past with the aid of a stick. Would there be medics among them, or doctors? He hoped so. In fact hoping was all he could do. Hope as evasion. As neglect. Hope as cowardice.

★ ★ ★

The village of Malevka, or what was left of it – the retreating Soviets had burned it to the ground – lay on a rise a few hundred metres behind the front lines, in range of the enemy's artillery and mortars but safe from small-arms fire. To the right was a pine forest, and it was here Bauer was directed when at a guard post he asked the way to the divisional dressing station. The road in was rough but serviceable, enclosed on either side by drifts of snow and pines that were densely canopied but branchless lower down, making the forest a dim, vastly pillared cathedral. Here and there shells had punched gaps through the branches, though in comparison to other battlefields they had passed through, the damage here was slight, the defenders of Tula and its inhabitants having no doubt come off worse in an artillery duel that had gone on now for a month. Even so, between the trees Bauer spotted log-cabin bunkers, widely dispersed to minimise the damage of direct hits on command posts, barracks and divisional stores.

The dressing station occupied what appeared to be the only surviving original building in the forest, a barn that stood beside the burned ruins of a farmhouse. Demchak and Winkel parked the lorries in the space between the buildings and all four men got out. Bauer scrutinised the barn. It was waist-deep in snow but on the sheltered side bore the scorch marks of a failed attempt to set it on fire. A red cross flag hung above a pair of timber doors big enough for a tractor or a cart. Set into the right-hand door was a man-sized hatch.

'Not quite the standard we've become used to,' Bauer said.

'We've had worse,' Winkel said, but halfheartedly, his mood morose after Molineux's bedding of Daria Grigorievna. Bauer had tried that morning to console him but failed, though the wound was still fresh, he reflected. With time it would presumably heal.

The barn was gloomy inside, an effect worsened by vertical

slits of daylight in the walls. Behind them the door swung shut with a bang; Bauer heard himself greeted by name, and at the furthest end of the barn, in the glow of a pair of paraffin lamps, he recognised Erich Pilcz, the lieutenant he had come to replace. Pilcz was putting stitches in the scalp of a patient who was seated on a chair. 'Come in, Captain, come in,' Pilcz called. 'Make yourselves at home. My hands are full, as you can see.'

'I can't see anything much,' Bauer said, edging further into the barn. 'Where's your operating lamp?'

'Ah, our lamp. Yes, it is rather gloomy in here.'

Pilcz had two of his men with him, one assisting, the other trying to spirit away some pages that looked like a letter. Against the back wall a wounded man was sitting on a bench while another lay on a stretcher on the earthen floor, loosely covered by a blanket, his boots exposed.

'The lamp never arrived,' Pilcz said.

'But you've been here three weeks!' Bauer said.

'That long?'

Bauer stopped in front of him. Pilcz was young, still in his twenties, a delicately built young man wearing so many clothes that he looked rotund. His black hair was parted exactly like the Führer's, but there the resemblance ended, since by temperament he was sunny and eager to please. Possibly too garrulous at times, but no more than Molineux was, and he had proven his worth as a surgeon.

'You could have ordered another,' Bauer said.

'Well, yes, I meant to. I certainly did. But then we were busy, as you know. And I suppose I got used to making do with less light.'

With satisfaction Bauer noticed his own men deploying either side of him to attend to the wounded.

'You could have mentioned it over the radio this morning,' he said. 'We would've brought one with us.'

'Sorry, sir, I didn't think of it.'

'Well, it can't be helped now.'

'Sir, am I in trouble? Is that why Metz wants to see me?'

'Lieutenant, you have a patient to attend to.'

Pilcz peered down and seemed startled to find himself holding a needle. 'Of course, of course.'

'We'll talk later, in private.'

'Yes, sir, but first, your black eye – did the lieutenant colonel do that to you?'

'Don't talk nonsense, Lieutenant. Just get on with it, will you.'

Pilcz did as he was told, and Bauer gazed about the barn. The lieutenant's operating table was a sled that had been raised on wooden blocks. It looked precarious. Come to that, it was uncomfortably crammed into a corner, which, given the size of the barn, was mystifying. More seriously, there appeared to be no screen between it and the reception area, suggesting that men waiting for treatment had been obliged to watch others going under the knife. Finally, there was the general disorder of the place, something to be expected during a battle or in its immediate aftermath, but not two days later. And at no time was it admissible to leave dirty bandages touching an instruments tray. Clearly Pilcz was not himself; yet even more disturbing in a way was the negligence of his men, implying there was a wider collapse in morale.

236

'Mind if I check on those two?' Bauer said, gesturing at the wounded men.

'Go ahead, be my guest,' Pilcz said, airily waving the needle.

The man on the ground was unconscious. 'Where's he wounded?' Bauer asked Winkel, only to be answered by the unoccupied man, a sergeant, who sounded keen to make amends. 'In the calf, sir.'

'What sort of wound is it?'

The sergeant admitted he wasn't sure.

'Let's see then, shall we,' Bauer said, kneeling down. Pilcz's sergeant fetched scissors and cut away the wounded man's trouser leg, revealing a shotgun wound to the calf. Fortunately neither bone was damaged, and there were clearly delineated entry and exit wounds. Both, however, were already blackening with frostbite, suggesting that the wounded man had lain for some time in the snow.

'Excuse me, sir,' Pilcz said, 'would you mind giving me a hand?' Bauer stood up and went over to him; Pilcz passed him the needle. 'Much obliged,' he said with a winning smile, then before Bauer could answer turned and left the barn. Bauer finished stitching the patient's scalp then got to work on the others. An hour later Pilcz had still not returned.

★　★　★

It was dark by the time Bauer finished treating Pilcz's patients and was able to go looking for him. According to his men, the lieutenant no longer dossed down at the dressing station but instead shared a bunker with some fellow officers. Pilcz's

237

sergeant showed him the way, for which Bauer was grateful, as the sky was clear but moonless and the starlight too weak to penetrate the trees. The night air was incomprehensibly cold. A first deep breath through his nose set his septum stinging, a lingering, eye-watering pain. He blinked and tears crystallised in his lashes.

Luckily the bunker wasn't far, and in a few minutes Bauer was standing at its half-sunken door. He thanked his guide and went inside, swapping the icy purity outside for the foetid warmth of men living crammed together half underground. There were about a dozen or so, most of them seated around a trestle table at the centre of a long and shallow room, its ceiling not much higher than a tallish man. Log walls, the wood still encrusted in bark. Bedding and kit bags at the rear. A diminutive cast-iron stove to one side, and around it several men in their underwear plucking lice from the lining of their uniforms. About half of those present glanced up as he entered; he wiped snow off his boots and shut the door. Some of the men he didn't know, others he knew by sight, and there were a few he knew by name, including, yes, Pilcz, who immediately sprang up, greeted him cheerily and began a round of introductions.

'You've come at the right time!' he brayed when the introductions were over. 'Dinner's almost served.' He wasn't normally so frenzied, and Bauer resolved not to reprimand him for abandoning the barn.

Dinner was a beef stew simmering on the stove, its fragrance reconciling him to the stink of unwashed socks, cigarette smoke, unclean armpits and feet. He hadn't realised how hungry he was. Someone made space for him at the table and he sat down on an empty ammunition case, his back to the stove. To his left sat Pilcz, incessantly talking; to his right a captain from the neighbouring Grossdeutschland division who was as taciturn as Pilcz was loud and whose name Bauer had already forgotten.

The stew arrived, and though Pilcz kept talking Bauer fell silent with most of the others. The stew was good, very good. No doubt the beef had come from a local farm. Bauer thought of Katerina and her staff and how they would find enough to eat now that the Reich Commissariat was requisitioning food.

One by one the men around the table finished their meals and began lighting cigarettes. They had just survived a major battle and looked spent, not only physically but mentally. Their hands were chafed, their faces reddened and cracked. Bauer coughed. Even for a smoker like himself the atmosphere in the bunker was insufferable. The nearby stove was baking his back, while his hands and feet were cold.

To his right the captain whose name he had forgotten finished eating, pushed aside his mess tin and surreptitiously scratched an armpit. Bauer turned to him and, under cover of Pilcz's chatter, quietly asked him if the lice were very bad. The captain gave him a guarded look. 'No worse than you'd expect.'

'I want to know what I'm in for,' Bauer said, 'and to work out whether to build a delousing sauna.'

'Rather than waiting until we take Tula?' the captain asked, his accent Prussian and distinctly privileged. He looked to be about thirty-five years old but was so careworn and weary that it was hard to know for sure.

Bauer hesitated. 'I had assumed we'd be wintering here.'

'Based on what?'

Bauer gestured around them, at the ceiling and the walls. 'This. Someone has gone to a lot of trouble.'

'Someone wanted not to die of exposure. We will of course be taking Tula any day now. Moscow shortly after that.'

The irony was unmistakable. No Nazi, then. Or at least not the ardent, brainwashed type. At his neck an Iron Cross. A wound badge on his breast.

'You're quartered with your division?' Bauer asked.

'About two kilometres away. This is just a visit.'

'I've forgotten your name,' Bauer admitted, proffering his hand. 'Paul Bauer.'

They shook hands. 'Gerd von Rauschenberg.'

'Where were you wounded?' Bauer asked, nodding at the badge.

'Geographically?'

'I meant anatomically, but why not: tell me where you were.'

'Poland. In the arse. Thanks be to God nothing serious. A flesh wound, on the second day of the war. Chronologically speaking. You weren't my surgeon by any chance?' he asked, drawing back and squinting in a mock effort of recall. 'I was face down the whole time, you see.'

'No, not one of mine. I didn't start until France.'

'Ah,' said von Rauschenberg. 'I suppose it's for the best. And what about your wound?' he asked, pointing to Bauer's black eye. 'I must say I don't think of you surgeons as brawlers.'

Bauer was about to answer when on his left Pilcz seized him by the arm. 'You're going to need boots, sir, proper boots, and we've just the thing.'

'Oh?'

240

'There, by the stove. Soviet issue, felt–lined.'

Bauer turned around and saw three pairs of boots lined up beside the stove, their leather damp, their openings stuffed with what looked like brown fabric but which he recognised an instant later as human flesh, six legs sawn off at the shins, tibias and fibulas sprouting as if attempting to regrow.

'No thank you,' he said, and turned back to the table.

'Don't be too hasty, sir. It won't be long till they're thawed.'

'I said no thanks.'

'But, sir, they're splendid boots, I assure you, and God knows you're going to need them.' He seemed not mocking but genuinely concerned.

Von Rauschenberg said, 'Surely you're not squeamish, Captain. How many legs have you amputated? Scores, I imagine.'

'It's not squeamishness.'

'What then?'

'Anger, to be frank. Where are our own winter boots? It's like something from *War and Peace*,' he said, gesturing behind him, 'the retreat from Moscow.'

'Though of course in our case we are *advancing* on Moscow,' von Rauschenberg said, 'and that makes all the difference.'

'Sir, you'll see,' Pilcz said, 'felt-lined boots are essential here. It's practical, not unpatriotic. You'll see. Spend a day at that dressing station and you'll see.'

The conversation shifted to the merits of fur versus wool, but before Bauer could join it Pilcz was back on the topic of why he was being transferred to Yasnaya Polyana. Had he done something wrong? No, Bauer explained, it wasn't a disciplinary matter. *At least not in your case*, he thought.

241

'Then why?' Pilcz asked.

'I don't know. I'm just following orders, but if I had to guess I would say that Metz wants us to experience every aspect of the battalion's work.'

'That's what I'm afraid of,' Pilcz said, his tongue probing about his teeth as if searching for trapped shreds of food. 'I'm not sure I'm up to it. At any rate, not with the lieutenant colonel breathing down my neck.'

'Try to regard it as an opportunity,' Bauer said, grimly amused to find himself consoling Pilcz for the neat reversal of their fortunes. 'The lieutenant colonel can seem a bit harsh but he's an excellent surgeon. You'll learn a lot.'

Pilcz bared his teeth in a show of mock fright that was nonetheless disturbing.

'Oh, come on,' Bauer said, 'think how you'll benefit later, after the war. You'll have more experience than a civilian surgeon accrues in a lifetime.'

Pilcz looked away, his expression despairing. 'I don't know, sir. I just don't know.' Again he began searching his teeth with his tongue, though as far as Bauer could tell his teeth were pristine. Or were his own teeth clogged, he wondered, and driving Pilcz to distraction? Surreptitiously he tongued his own teeth in search of detritus, felt nothing and with a conscious effort forced himself to stop. That way madness lay.

'You'll be fine,' he said. 'You need more experience, that's all, and the lieutenant colonel is ensuring you get it. And don't forget the comforts. Living conditions are much easier at Yasnaya Polyana.'

'I suppose,' Pilcz said, then shook his head. 'I just don't know.'

Clearly he wasn't quite right in the head. The proper thing to do would be to radio Metz and explain the situation, but why should he bother? Let Metz sort it out. It was his decision; let him cope with the consequences. 'I should be getting back to the men,' he said.

'You won't stay here, sir?' Pilcz asked. 'Believe me, it's warmer. You should. You really should. I can send for your kit.'

'No thank you, Lieutenant,' he said, and pushed the ammunition case away from the table. 'I'll stay at the dressing station, at least at first.'

'I should go too,' said von Rauschenberg, also rising.

Bauer thanked his fellow officers for their hospitality and again noticed their muted mood. The usual camaraderie of mealtimes had been mostly missing. Apart from Pilcz, nobody had bothered to say goodbye.

'They're tired,' von Rauschenberg said when Bauer mentioned this outside. 'All of us are.' He stamped his feet in the snow. '*Fuck*, it's cold,' he went on, his accent adding polish to the phrase. His officer's cap had had its wire stiffener removed, giving its wearer a kind of louche, crumpled glamour.

'I'm going that way,' Bauer said, pointing. 'What about you?'

'The opposite,' said von Rauschenberg. 'We're dug in at Malevka.'

'Then I'll say goodbye.'

In the far distance he could hear rifle fire; somewhat closer a burst from a heavy machine gun.

'Before you go, though,' said von Rauschenberg, 'let me ask you something. You mentioned *War and Peace*. Have you read it?'

'Once, as a youth. But I'm re-reading it now, and so it's on my mind.'

'I read it in my twenties. Stupendous. Superb. I will again one day, if I get a chance.'

'You can borrow my copy when I'm finished,' Bauer offered, then wished he hadn't.

Von Rauschenberg shook his head. 'No, you keep it. We're sure to be redeployed, or our units will, or one of us will get killed, and then you'll never get it back.'

'If I get killed I won't need it back.'

'Very well, but your relatives might want it as a keepsake. Are you married?'

'No,' he answered, feeling too cold to elaborate.

'Lucky you.'

'You think?'

'No one at home waiting for you, extracting promises from you to stay alive.'

'Yes, I can see that might be difficult. Though for every married soldier who wishes he was single there must be at least ten bachelors yearning for a wife.'

Von Rauschenberg chuckled. 'That's true. We all just want to go home.'

Was he another Dieter, Bauer wondered, a possible friend? Though initially guarded, he now seemed willing to talk. There was more gunfire and a red streak of tracer some way off above the trees.

'I should get back,' said von Rauschenberg. 'If you'd like a tour of our sector sometime, just radio. *War and Peace* it isn't, but it's not without interest.'

'I'll do that,' he said. 'That is, once I've whipped the dressing station into shape.'

They said farewell and went their separate ways, Bauer retracing his steps to the dressing station in the most literal way, reusing the boot holes he'd punched into the snow ninety minutes earlier. Even so, it was heavy work and soon he was puffing like a locomotive. Then from somewhere in the direction of Malevka he heard the hiss of a flare, then turned and watched it pass its zenith, extinguishing stars, before sizzling earthwards, spilling light between the trees.

FOURTEEN

The next day dawned like the last one: windless and misty, exceptionally cold. Smoke from cooking fires in the bunkers rose vertically through the trees, the ethereality of the mist only partly offset by the sound of artillery fire. The shells were falling far away. Bauer ordered his and Pilcz's men to unload the lorries, and shortly afterwards Pilcz himself arrived, still looking and sounding jittery about having to face Metz. Bauer offered him more encouragement, then sent him and his men on their way.

For the next few days casualties were light, allowing for the reorganisation of the dressing station along more sensible lines. From Yasnaya Polyana they took delivery of a field operating lamp, to which Winkel added a cone of aluminium foil, substantially increasing its brightness. They gathered timber for building a delousing sauna, only for Metz to order them by radio not to proceed with its construction, as the fall of Tula, he said, was 'imminent'. Bauer stockpiled the timber. Winkel got wind of a damaged T-34 nearby, went to inspect it and returned saying he believed he could fix it. They could use it as a tractor, he argued, or even as an ambulance in rough terrain, and because things were in hand at the dressing station Bauer agreed to let him try, relieved to see him behaving more like himself.

His own morale was up and down. In effect, Metz had demoted him, and though there was satisfaction to be had in speeding up the transfer of wounded men to Yasnaya Polyana, already he missed the complexity of the surgeries he had done there. His skills were being wasted, and by coincidence or otherwise he began to feel homesick for the first time in the war, not just fed up with being in the Soviet Union but missing Germany: the hilly woodlands of Franconia, his childhood farm, his village, the city of Nuremberg – not the Nuremberg of National Socialist rallies but the city as it had been in the early twenties, his student days, when he had frequented its bars and cafés, not only with fellow students but also with writers and artists, some of them good, as well as would-be or genuine intellectuals, reproducing in a provincial form the ferment going on in Munich, Hamburg and Berlin.

The physical hardships at the dressing station were acute. The barn was perpetually freezing, and they rarely changed clothes. The latrine was in a tent about fifty paces away, its canvas frozen stiff as Bakelite. Reaching it felt like an Arctic expedition, baring his buttocks an ordeal. Even worse, though, were the lice. Within forty-eight hours of arriving he was scratching himself, and had the barn been less cold he might have been tempted to strip down and spend all day picking at his hide.

He noticed compensations. Discomfort had a way of intensifying pleasures that in civilian life he might barely have registered. The taste of hot chicory was bliss, and even a good scratch, properly viewed, felt like ecstasy. Yes, objectively his life might be miserable, but it was *his* misery, his struggle, and if some genie had wobbled out of his paraffin lamp and granted him three wishes, becoming someone else would not have been one of them. He had invested too much in his own existence, his stubborn fondness for it something akin to what he guessed a soldier might feel for a filthy trench he had occupied and defended for months. It was his trench, his filth, and he'd hold on to it till the last, since the one thing worse than tribulation was meaninglessness.

The same applied to Katerina, he decided. At times knowing her had been painful, like being dunked in icy water, but by God the shock of it had been invigorating. Expecting warmth from her had been ridiculous, he now saw, the fantasy of marrying her exactly that, a fantasy. Katerina wasn't *wifely*. Her forte wasn't tenderness but strength. She was *admirable*. He missed her, missed her badly, but he wasn't going to worsen the pain by sentimentalising his memories of her.

One distraction was reading, and in spare moments and at night he took to lying in his bedroll and blankets, engrossing himself in *War and Peace*. As usual he found it consoling. Whatever the fate of individuals might be, Tolstoy seemed to say, the rhythms of life would remain the same. The young would be foolish, hopeful and wild, would fall in love and out of it, become sadder, maybe wise. Some would meet their deaths sooner than others, yet there would come a day when everyone engaged in the struggles of their age would without exception die, bequeathing the world they had made to those strangers, their children, who would struggle to change it again.

* ★ *

With its turret reversed and swastika flags on its hull, the T-34 grumbled up to the dressing station, squealed through a ninety-degree turn and braked. Its engine fell quiet and seconds later Winkel wriggled out onto the turret. He looked pleased with himself. Bauer led Demchak and Pflieger in a round of applause and Winkel grinned and took a bow.

'Well done, Sepp,' Bauer said.

'Why, thanks, sir,' Winkel said. He hopped onto the hull, and from there into the snow. 'All we need now is fuel.'

From overhead there came the sound of an aircraft and they all looked up.

'Reconnaissance,' Demchak said. 'One of theirs.'

They stepped away from the barn to get a clearer view. The aircraft was small and heading against the wind, its engine straining. Its course was westerly, tracking the front lines, though high enough to stay clear of ground fire.

'Where's the Luftwaffe?' Winkel asked, voicing the question that Bauer had just put to himself. In France they had operated with air superiority, especially in the second half of the campaign.

'Buzzing Moscow,' Pflieger said. 'Giving Stalin hell.'

'How would you know?' Winkel said.

'They're not here so they must be elsewhere, right? I bet it's Moscow. Concentrate your forces where they're needed the most.'

'They're needed here,' Winkel said.

'The main prize is Moscow. Tula is a sideshow.'

'Some sideshow.'

'It's all a matter of perspective, Sepp. In war not everyone gets to fight the big battles. Some of us have to play supporting roles.'

'Oh, good grief,' Winkel said. 'Leave the thinking to the horses.'

'Very funny.'

'They have bigger heads.'

'Oh, you got me one there, Sepp. Got me good, you did.'

Where the front lines turned northwards at Malevka the plane did the same, and a short time later it disappeared behind the trees, its engine noise trailing like a glider under tow.

'That's it, gentlemen,' Bauer said. 'Show's over.'

'Not much of a show, sir,' Pflieger said.

'Let's just hope we don't get a better one.'

★ ★ ★

Six days passed before he could take up von Rauschenberg's offer of a tour of his sector of the front. Bauer radioed, they made the necessary arrangements and met early that afternoon in front of von Rauschenberg's company headquarters, a log bunker in the forest near Malevka. There had been a snowstorm overnight but the wind had since dropped. The sky was dark and overcast. Somewhere to the west a howitzer battery was in action, though without much intensity.

'Softening them up?' Bauer asked.

'Hardly,' said von Rauschenberg. 'There's a shortage of shells. Disturbing their afternoon nap, that's all.'

Machine-gun fire sounded in the distance, its timbre unfamiliar, unfriendly, and Bauer felt his heart begin to thump.

'I'll get you one of our helmets,' von Rauschenberg said. 'We've painted them white.'

'Sounds sensible.'

From the bunker von Rauschenberg returned carrying a machine pistol and a pair of white helmets. He put on one of the helmets and handed over the other. 'Ready?'

Bauer buckled his chinstrap. 'Ready. How far?'

'Six hundred metres, give or take. But first a social call.'

They set out on a well-trodden track through the snow, not towards the front, Bauer calculated, but in parallel. Von Rauschenberg pointed at another bunker about a hundred metres away among the trees. 'Our casualty collection point. It doubles as a barracks.'

The second bunker contained ten or so men who stood to attention as Bauer followed von Rauschenberg inside. The place stank, of course, but when the men learned he was a surgeon they offered him hot chicory, chocolate and schnapps, which Bauer regretfully refused. Instead he asked to see the company's medical supplies, found them in good order and said so. A sergeant explained that during a battle the room's main table was pushed aside to make way for the wounded, who were then evacuated in groups to the dressing station.

The next stop was well forward, though still inside the forest: a machine-gun nest protected by a berm and a roof made of slim, bark-covered logs. 'This isn't like the last war,' von Rauschenberg explained as they approached. 'There are no trenches as such. We're deployed in depth, and most of our strength is to the rear.'

The machine-gun nest contained three men, two of whom were trying to warm their hands over a paraffin stove. All three men looked perished with cold, but when they saw Bauer's medical patch they welcomed him with the same warmth he had met with in the bunker. Von Rauschenberg chatted with them a little, addressing all three by name. When they moved on he said, 'You know, to these fellows a surgeon is as good as divine. The medics they regard as angels, you surgeons as gods.'

'You make it sound like we're despatching them to the afterlife.'

'It's the *before*-life they're longing for, that place of splendour, home. Never mind that home was a hovel or an overcrowded tenement, to some of my men your operating table is beginning to seem like a flying carpet that will take them where they want to go.'

'You're exaggerating, surely.'

'Only a little. They've seen too many frostbitten wounds to truly welcome being wounded, but I can imagine some of them half-consciously putting themselves in harm's way.'

'It's going badly here, then?' Bauer asked in a neutral tone, not wanting to sound like an Ehrlich sniffing out sedition.

'That last attack knocked the stuffing out of us,' von Rauschenberg replied. 'And we'd already lost plenty before it began.'

'So we're not about to capture Tula?'

'Still wondering whether or not to build your delousing station?'

'Well, yes. Among other things.'

252

The path they were on began to slope subtly downwards, and up ahead an opening in the forest appeared, a V-shaped clearing littered with tree stumps, beyond it snowy fields.

Von Rauschenberg gestured at the clearing. 'I'd take you over to meet your divisional comrades but Ivan's snipers might take a potshot at you.'

Bauer peered again in the direction of the clearing and saw, less than fifty metres away, a panzer dug in at the crook of the V, its hull draped with sheets and further camouflaged by the background brightness of the fields. Of the things he'd witnessed in the last six days the sight of a tank behind earthworks was the most ominous, since if he had learned one thing about armoured tactics since joining the 3rd Panzer it was that mobility was all. Digging in was an admission of defeat.

'This way,' von Rauschenberg said, taking a path to the left.

Bauer started to follow him then paused. 'Wait,' he said and pointed at the tank. 'Are they *hit*?' From the undercarriage, black threads of smoke.

Von Rauschenberg looked over his shoulder. 'Burning diesel,' he said. 'A pan underneath. Apparently it stops the engine freezing.'

'You're telling me they have to burn diesel to stand still?'

'Not ideal, is it.'

They were walking uphill now, staying within the forest but in sight of its edge. Von Rauschenberg pointed towards a hollow between the trees. 'Nest for the wounded,' he said. Bauer pictured wounded men, including some he had no doubt treated, being brought to this and scores of similar spots, a network of extraction, the capillaries and veins of a system pumping casualties all the way back to Germany.

'In answer to your earlier question,' von Rauschenberg said, 'no, I don't expect us to take Tula soon. We're short of fuel, short of ammunition, short of warm clothes – the other night one of my sentries froze to death. We're short of paper. Short of boot grease. Tools. Nails. We are *not* short of food, thank Christ, at least not yet, and as you saw we still have some medical supplies. And we don't lack heart. I honestly believe that were we properly supplied we could take Tula tomorrow, in spite of everything.'

They reached a dugout with a shelter sheet drawn across its entrance, beside it a sentry pacing to and fro. Bauer returned his salute and von Rauschenberg engaged with him in the same easy manner he had displayed with the others under his command. The soldier was wearing a quilted Soviet jacket and, for added warmth and proof of nationality, a field-grey Wehrmacht blanket.

Von Rauschenberg slapped the sentry on the shoulder and came away. 'Excuse me while I stop to piss,' he said, and went over to a nearby tree. He glanced over his shoulder. 'Better do the same if you need to – further forward there's nowhere to stand.'

Though his need wasn't pressing Bauer went to the closest tree, turned his back to the breeze and urinated, wondering if agreeing to this excursion had been wise. It was one thing to be killed or wounded in the line of duty, quite another as a result of curiosity. He pictured himself as a casualty making a return journey through the forest, leaving his blood at each evacuation point, looking like a fool to the men he had met on the way in. Next would come the dressing station, and then – Christ almighty – Yasnaya Polyana. Was that his motive here? Was he one of those von Rauschenberg suspected of wanting to go home via the operating table? Surely not, since nothing short of dying would be worse than having Metz or, God forbid, Erich Pilcz rummaging about in his entrails. Along with the pain and humiliation involved, Metz would regard his getting wounded as a dereliction of duty, even a personal affront. Still, backing out now was not an option, and surely the danger was minimal, especially compared to what the men of the Grossdeutschland division were exposed to every day.

At the extreme edge of the forest von Rauschenberg stopped and pointed to their destination: an observation post on a rise another fifty metres further forward. 'We'll run hunched over till we reach that wooden marker,' he said. 'From that point onwards you have to crawl. Do as I do and you won't come to any harm.'

Bauer crouched a little, a sprinter taking his mark. His heart was hammering and it occurred to him that this was a good thing, this was normal – that between arriving at Yasnaya Polyana and now he had relearned a fear of death. Then von Rauschenberg set off running, bent over, holding his machine pistol low to the ground. Bauer scuttled after him in the same ungainly style, listening for gunshots but hearing only his breathing, shallow and fast, the flapping of his greatcoat, his boots squeaking on the snow. At the wooden marker von Rauschenberg dropped into a crawl, Bauer did the same, and in this way they covered the last ten metres, pushed aside a hessian curtain at the rear of the observation post and bellied inside. At first Bauer saw nothing of the interior, only a bar of daylight in the opposite wall, but as his snow-blindness lessened he made out a log-lined space a little larger than the interior of a tank, too low to stand in and too cramped for the five men it now contained. The others, three *Landsers* seated on ammunition cases, greeted von Rauschenberg and shuffled up against the walls to make more room. A medium machine gun stood on a mound of soil, its muzzle thrusting into the light. A two-way radio, a pair of binoculars, open ration packs, discarded cans, three rifles propped in a corner. One of the *Landsers* was wearing a pair of fleece-lined leather gloves, while the knuckles of another were showing through a pair of worn-out socks. Under their helmets all three men had wrapped their heads in rags secured with knots beneath their chins.

Von Rauschenberg invited him forward to the viewing slit and he peered outside. It was a lower vantage point than he'd expected, not much higher than the fields it overlooked, but what seized his attention first was a row of stakes not ten metres away, all sharpened to a point and angling forward. It was an obstacle straight from the Middle Ages, or even earlier – from prehistoric times – and several seconds passed before Bauer could raise his eyes and look across the fields to a low confusion of buildings in the distance: the outskirts of Tula. In front of it were the obstacles he'd heard about: metal burrs and concrete prongs. The latter were uniform and orderly, a cemetery of stone. Columns of smoke were rising over the town, blackening the already dark clouds overhead. Rifle and machine-gun fire sounded sporadically, louder here than it had been inside the forest, though he couldn't tell where it was coming from or where it was directed, or make out any enemy positions. Von Rauschenberg handed him a pair of binoculars, and in their cross hairs he made out the Soviet lines, a suture seam of trenches and barbed wire, stone and concrete buildings. It looked formidable and he almost said so, then remembered that sooner or later the men of the Grossdeutschland would be expected to attack it again. Instead he lowered the binoculars and gestured at the row of tilted stakes. 'Are those really necessary? I thought it was us attacking Ivan, not the reverse.'

'It's both. That is to say, Ivan counterattacks. At least, he's done so once. Look over there, in front of Malevka. You'll need the binoculars. Range, five hundred metres, give or take.'

'Where's Malevka? All I'm seeing is snow.'

'Malevka's further left, behind the trees. It's the snow you should be looking at.'

'What about it?'

'The bumps.'

His hands were juddering with cold, but with some difficulty he managed to steady them enough to see a cluster of human-sized mounds of snow. He set down the binoculars and with the naked eye was able to see what he guessed must be scores, even hundreds, of fallen men. 'My God, I had no idea.'

'Tactically, the Ivans are donkeys. But they're exceptionally brave. After our own attack failed they came at us in waves. We mowed them down, naturally, but that didn't stop them coming. It was a massacre, much worse than what they'd inflicted on us, and utterly pointless. Unless the point was to make us run out of ammunition.'

'Or to demonstrate their bravery?'

'Well, they succeeded there.'

Bauer took up the binoculars and again surveyed the field in front of Malevka. From one mound a foot protruded, from another a hand. '"When the wood is chopped,"' he said, quoting from memory, '"the chips must fly."'

'Oh, and what's that from?'

'*War and Peace*,' he said, lowering the binoculars. 'Do you remember the line?'

'You have to be joking. Not a chance.'

'It's General Katuzov.'

'Him I do remember.'

'I took note because it reminded me of that maxim of Lenin's. You know the one?'

'"You can't make an omelette …"?'

'Exactly.'

'That's all very well but, Christ alive, pelting us with eggs would have hurt us more than a frontal assault.'

Again Bauer took up the binoculars and swept them over Tula, as if to absorb the entire panorama. By chance a shell exploded in his field of view, soundlessly sending up smoke and dust, a billowy puff from a magic act, so that seconds later when the noise arrived it seemed disproportionately loud, reverberant and real.

FIFTEEN

Three days later, orders came from the divisional commander announcing that another offensive was imminent. Bauer read it out to his men. '*At 06:00 hours tomorrow, Sunday, 30 November, we go on the attack again! Army Group Centre will advance on a 500-kilometre front and, by seizing Moscow, rip out the beating heart of the Bolshevik beast! To the 3rd Panzer division has fallen the honour of leading the assault on Tula, thereby securing the southern flank of this momentous operation.*'

Bauer knew it was madness. They were being led by madmen; and for the rest of his life he would recall this as the moment when he knew the war could not be won and as a consequence was lost, as the Soviets would settle for nothing less than total victory.

After making sure that the dressing station was fully prepared for what lay ahead he visited von Rauschenberg, who was at his headquarters making preparations of his own.

'But it's crazy,' Bauer said when they were outside and alone.

'Certifiable,' von Rauschenberg agreed.

'Can't someone tell that to the generals?'

259

'The generals probably already know. The order was issued at the highest level, I heard.'

'It's crazy,' repeated Bauer.

'Agreed,' von Rauschenberg said. He scratched one of his armpits. Frowned. 'Though who knows? We keep achieving the impossible. Maybe we'll do it this time too.'

Bauer said nothing. Wind was soughing through the pines, setting off powdery slippages of snow.

'One thing I do know for sure,' said von Rauschenberg, 'is that you'll be treating some of my men tomorrow. Do your best by them, won't you?'

'Always,' Bauer replied.

They shook hands and wished one another luck.

'Tell your men not to overeat,' Bauer said. 'You know, in the early hours.'

'The anaesthetic? Yes, I'll tell them. Always do. And God knows, we'll all have ample shit on our hands.'

★   ★   ★

Winkel woke him at 05:45 hours and handed him a mug of real coffee. Bauer thanked him and took a sip. He was feeling unwell: lethargic, foggy-brained, his gut aching and clenched; and knowing what lay ahead that day he cursed. Spotted fever was a possibility given the lice bites he'd sustained, but also food poisoning or a viral infection. Whatever the illness was, its timing could not have been worse. Before he could even finish the coffee he was pulling on his boots and stumbling in the dark to the latrine. Once there, he tore down his trousers and

260

blasted shit around the hole, the ice behind it and the uppers of his boots.

At 06:00 hours the artillery opened up, and at 06:48 the first casualty arrived, a young panzerman who had lost an eye. Pflieger, administering a tetanus injection, distracted him with banter. Where was home? Berlin? Too bad, no one's perfect. You'll be there soon, worst luck, you've got your *Heimatschuss*. Not married? Well, you're in luck there – an eyepatch drives the girls crazy. You think *Ivan's* ferocious? On the Ku'damm you'll be fending off women with a stick. No, I'm serious. On furlough I always put on a patch …

Demchak made up the man's field medical card, and on it Bauer recorded what they had done for him, omitting Pflieger's psychological assistance. After a brief hesitation he left both side strips attached, denoting the least serious category of wound.

The second casualty arrived at 07.03, and soon afterwards came the deluge, a flood of damaged, dirty and often hypothermic men. The primary task here was not surgery but triage, and being unable to operate on the worst cases was a constant torment. Adding to his difficulties was the muddled state of his brain, and the diarrhoea that repeatedly drove him from the barn. The day was freezing and blustery, and as he toiled at the latrine the noise of battle thundered overhead.

For hours they worked in a rolling state of crisis, the wounded arriving continually but only leaving in fits and starts, the dead wrapped in shelter sheets and lugged outside into the snow. The barn was chaotic, its earthen floor fouled with bandages, spent ampoules and torn scraps of uniform. In places it was mired in blood. The wounded lay in rows with

261

their cards about their necks, like so many bits of unclaimed baggage, whimpering, groaning or visibly clenching their teeth against the pain. Bauer cut away a man's trousers, smelled the stench of his crotch and thought, as if at random, *And it's the* Jews *who stink?* He had no idea how the battle was progressing but in a dash to the latrine witnessed, about two hundred metres away, a pine tree launching vertically over the forest, roots fluttering. The Soviets were giving as well as receiving, it seemed.

Around midday he was taken aback but also relieved to see two enlisted men bringing in von Rauschenberg seated on a rifle, his arms slung over their necks. He was furious. 'My foot, my fucking foot,' he said when Bauer asked where he'd been hit. 'It's nothing. Fucking shrapnel. Go and treat someone else.'

'That's for me to decide,' Bauer said. 'You're on my turf now.' He gestured at the soldiers to set the patient down on an ammunition case. Von Rauschenberg thanked them and ordered them back to his unit. 'Find Lieutenant Freiburg. Tell him … tell him to do what's necessary but nothing more. No more heroics, understand? Not today.' The men promised to pass on the message, saluted and left the barn. 'The thing is,' said von Rauschenberg, irate again, 'I'm *needed* back there.'

'Why, what's happening?' Bauer asked him, easing off the boot. Winkel arrived and offered to take over. 'I'll do this one,' Bauer said. 'The captain and I know one another.'

The boot came off and von Rauschenberg flinched. In a lower but still furious voice, he said, 'We attacked, and it was more or less what I expected, another fucking shambles, only worse.' His sock was black and sopping with blood. 'We were

weaker than last time, they were stronger. We got half as far.'
Using scissors Bauer cut away the sock, revealing a pulpy gap
in the metatarsals. Von Rauschenberg grimaced. 'Jesus Christ, a
fucking stigmata.'

'Stigma,' Bauer corrected. 'You only have one.'

Von Rauschenberg laughed. 'Pedantic sod. But fuck it, I
think you've cheered me up.'

'The shrapnel's entered here,' Bauer said, 'and exited
underneath.' He showed von Rauschenberg his boot, which
had a rip in its sole. 'Like so.'

'Can you get me back to my men?'

Bauer snorted. 'Gerd, don't be an ass. I was about to say that
with luck we should be able to save it.'

'That bad, eh?'

'We'll repair you, but you're not going back to your men.'

'*Scheisse.*'

'You ought to be grateful,' he said, and began bandaging the
wound. 'From what I've seen, you're well out of it.' Another
possible friendship lost, he thought. Or stillborn. Maybe it was
better to be like Weidemann: detached for the duration.

'But my men. I've got half of them killed.'

'You didn't order the attack.'

'I could've held them back.'

'And got shot for it? You did what you had to. And now
you're out of it.'

'If I *am* out of it. Ivan's counterattacking. Can you evacuate
your patients any faster?'

'We're already at full stretch,' Bauer said, securing the
bandage.

'Then let's hope for the best. Now fuck off and work on someone else.'

Bauer gave him a loose, ironical salute and got back to work. Physically he felt terrible: queasy, dizzy, tired and at least a dozen IQ points below his best. The next hour passed like the previous six, and when he went outside to the latrine again he was greeted by the sound of small-arms fire and the acrid smell of cordite in the air. His insides were producing only liquid now, and the rough toilet paper scraped his anus raw. He pulled up his trousers, desperate to get inside and wash his hands, but as he hurried out of the latrine he was brought up short by the sight of a Soviet soldier in a bulky all-white uniform jogging past not ten paces away, oblivious to his presence and apparently alone; and because of this, and because he could think of nothing else to do, Bauer drew his pistol and in Russian yelled at the man to stop. The soldier skidded, spun about. He was pale, bewildered, helmetless and young.

'*Ruki vverkh!*' Bauer yelled, but instead of putting up his hands the young soldier bellowed and ran straight at him. '*Halt,*' screamed Bauer, shocked into German, '*halt!*' – but the boy kept on coming and Bauer shot him in the chest, knocking him backwards onto the snow. Bauer lowered his weapon. He was breathing fast. Shivering cold, hot. The boy was writhing, his white uniform reddening where the bullet had gone through. He was carrying no weapon. No firearm at all. Had charged at him with empty hands – Bauer could picture it now in photographic detail, yet at the time he hadn't known it, not consciously. He knelt down, still holding his pistol, wary even now. The boy's chest was heaving, and with each breath his

264

wound slurped, a drooling, secondary mouth. He was trying to say something and so Bauer drew nearer, though ready even now to spring away.

'*Zachem?*' the boy asked. 'Why?' His eyes were wide, bewildered.

Bauer said nothing, could only shake his head. From one of his pockets he tugged a handkerchief and pressed it to the wound, hoping to silence it, to make it go quiet, and although he muffled the noise the haemorrhaging continued. There was more blood, he noticed, on the boy's white hood, and when he drew it back he saw a second or, more properly, a primary wound on the young soldier's head. What the boy was – what he had been already, running past – was a casualty, someone needing medical care.

In the doorway of the barn Demchak appeared, and Bauer yelled for a stretcher. Then he turned back to the boy and said urgently in Russian, 'I'm going to help you, understand? I'm a doctor. I'm going to help.'

SIXTEEN

Without saying so outright, his men made it clear they weren't willing to treat an enemy combatant, and for Bauer, sick as he was, still trembling with shock, making them do it felt beyond him. Demchak, in particular, was obdurate, but even Winkel looked dubious, glancing more than once at their compatriots strewn over the floor. Then abruptly Gerd von Rauschenberg was there, wielding a rifle as a crutch and threatening to have any man who disobeyed court-martialled. The men complied, Demchak sullenly, Winkel and Pflieger speedily enough, and because there was no question of sending a Soviet casualty to Yasnaya Polyana, Bauer prepared to operate. A blood transfusion would have helped, but the boy, a private, either didn't know or was too shocked to surely remember his blood type, and in any case it was unclear if anyone would be willing to donate. Sick as he was, Bauer couldn't do it himself. Working quickly then, in the time allowed by a single dose of Pentothal, he opened the boy's lung and retrieved the bullet – *his* bullet, personally loaded six months ago in Brest-Litovsk – staunched the bleeding, mended the lung then sutured the incision. He'd done what he could. Demchak and Pflieger laid the boy down with the other patients. There was other work to do.

Two hours later darkness fell and the sounds of battle died away, but for another six hours Bauer kept working, feeling more and more unwell, until at last he was forced to lie down for the night, leaving Winkel in command. He slept badly, disturbed by the moaning of the wounded, by an aching gut and aching limbs, as well as dreams in which the dead Clara implored him for help which he was too tired, too confused, too frantically busy to give.

At daybreak more casualties started to arrive, bringing news with them that the Soviet counterattack had been stopped. The battle had swung to and fro all day, and several times the division had been forced to plug breaches in the lines. Both sides had been badly mauled, and the front was now quiet. Bauer checked on the young Russian and found him still alive, but only just.

Lorries and ambulances kept arriving to take the casualties away, and in the middle of the morning Metz radioed to say that he wanted Bauer and his team back at Yasnaya Polyana, since Erich Pilcz was unwell and being sent back to Germany. A surgical team from Chern would replace them at the dressing station. There was no need to wait; the replacements were already on their way.

Pflieger whooped when he heard the news, and Winkel also looked pleased, perhaps thinking optimistically about Daria Grigorievna. Bauer himself hardly knew what he thought. He was feeling wretched, and along with the thought of having to put up with Metz again he felt wary about returning to a place that mentally he had already consigned to the past. Still, he would get to do proper surgery again, and the conditions at Yasnaya Polyana were unquestionably better than at the front. And of course there was Katerina. Plus or minus? He didn't know.

It took a couple of hours to prepare for their departure. Bauer and Demchak were to travel in a Kübelwagen, equipment and kit bags piled into its storage well, the wounded Soviet soldier on a stretcher lashed sideways to the bonnet. According to the scroll that the Ivans carried in little cylinders about their necks, the private's name was Kirov, Pyotr Maximovich, aged twenty. The same age as Katerina's son. But not her son, thank Christ. That kind of coincidence – the kind beloved of nineteenth-century fiction – was, if not impossible, then exceptionally rare, and in this instance fate had been merciful.

Winkel and Pflieger were to travel in the salvaged T-34, along with four moderately wounded men inside and nine with lighter wounds on the hull, all heavily blanketed against softly falling snow. One of these was to be von Rauschenberg, who had commandeered a pair of crutches and, though obviously in pain, was hopping about supervising the loading and preparation of the tank, paying particular attention to the flags which, along with the reversed turret, would lessen the risk of being attacked by their own side. When Bauer went to help him onto the tank, von Rauschenberg nodded towards the casualty on the Kübelwagen. 'Are you sure about that? They won't let you keep him, you know.'

'I'm not wanting a pet.'

'And he might die anyway.'

'That's true, he might. But I'm a doctor. It's my job to delay death as long as possible.'

'To keep Death tapping his bony fingers with impatience? A noble aim. Lately all I've done is roll out the red carpet.'

They said goodbye and a short time later got underway, part of a convoy led by an ambulance and two lorries, followed by the tank and lastly the Kübelwagen. Bauer could feel every frozen rut in the road and winced at the thought of the pull and shear forces on the Soviet boy's newly sutured wounds. Stretched out on the vehicle's bonnet he was like an offering of some kind. But an offering to whom? Metz, for one, would not be pleased.

In both directions the road was busy with supply wagons, ambulances and lorries, so that repeatedly they had to stop or slow down to let oncoming traffic get by. At the causeway over the frozen lake a traffic jam had formed, with vehicles on both sides vying to use the single lane. Bauer sighed. So much for the Wehrmacht's celebrated powers of organisation. In normal circumstances he might have got out and taken charge, but today he felt too unwell. Let someone else sort it out. Instead he scanned the sky for Soviet reconnaissance aircraft, conscious that an enemy artillery barrage would make this a very unhealthy place to be.

After a lengthy wait they reached the causeway and began to cross, keeping to the centre on account of the camber on both sides. In this the T-34 had little choice, being so wide it almost spanned the road. It advanced slowly, its exhaust fumes swirling back over the Kübelwagen. Thinking of the patient on the bonnet Bauer asked Demchak to put more space

269

between them, only for the tank to come to a sudden stop. 'Christ, what now?' he said. Not a mechanical problem, he prayed – not here, not now, with thirteen wounded men on board – fourteen counting the Soviet casualty – most of them exposed to the freezing air. The tank's engine was still running, still spewing exhaust in their faces, an encouraging sign, he supposed; then over the noise of the engines – the tank's, their own – there came the sound of raised voices, some kind of heated exchange, in which Bauer could hear the refined but angry voice of Gerd von Rauschenberg. Bauer turned to Demchak and ordered him to go forward and find out what was happening, and in moments the Ukrainian was springing onto the back of the tank, picking his way among the wounded passengers then vaulting the turret. He reappeared a couple of minutes later, leaped down and got back into the Kübelwagen, his expression as usual unreadable. 'We have to go back.'

'Go back? We're more than halfway there.'

'There's a staff car. Some lieutenant general on board. It's urgent. We have to go back.'

'Is that what the captain said?'

'The captain is angry about it,' Demchak said, 'but there's nothing he can do. It's an order.'

'Jesus Christ,' Bauer said. He considered going forward himself and arguing the point as a doctor, but having issued an order this lieutenant general, whoever he was, was unlikely to back down. Hell, it was even possible he was justified: that what he hoped to achieve at the front was more significant, more pressing, than the evacuation of a handful of wounded men.

'All right then,' Bauer said, 'we'd better back up.'

Demchak nodded and changed gears, looked over his shoulder and, with one hand on the back of Bauer's seat, reversed – recklessly, Bauer thought, given the ice on the road – so that they were already a good way off when the T-34 belched exhaust and began trundling backwards. At first the manoeuvre appeared to go well – Bauer could see von Rauschenberg on the turret, yelling instructions through the hatch – but Winkel's line was subtly wrong, bringing the tank's left track to the edge of the road. Someone noticed, thank God, and Winkel braked, then a series of small adjustments followed: a little forward, a little right, a little left again. Demchak had by now reversed the Kübelwagen off the causeway, and at this distance the tank appeared small, a beetle fretting on a twig. Then it swivelled once more and, to Bauer's horror, began skating to one side, the slowness of the motion revealing its true weight and bulk as, shedding men, its engine howling, it tipped and fell, smashed the ice and dropped into the lake.

*　★　*

'Bauer, welcome!' Metz cried from behind his desk. He laughed. 'My God, you look a wreck. What's the matter with you?'

'I'm ill,' he answered then stopped, stunned by the sight of Katerina seated next to Metz's desk, and even more so by presence of the old woman, Daria Grigorievna's mother, who was standing by the fire.

'Captain,' Katerina said, and his heart went haywire.

'Katerina Dmitrievna,' he replied.

271

'You remember Agrafena Viktorovna?' she asked, her voice neutral, controlled.

'Of course,' he said, and greeted the old woman in Russian. Katerina's face, like her voice, was impassive, though when he tried to meet her eye she looked hastily away.

'You should have telephoned me,' Metz cried cheerily, making Bauer suspect that Drexel must have recently visited. 'If I'd known you were sick I wouldn't have left you with those surgeries.'

'I managed,' Bauer said, though in fact several times he had come close to weeping as he and Molineux had operated, first on the survivors from the causeway, then on the two patients Metz had left him, both of whom had required long and intricate procedures.

'In any case, welcome back,' Metz said.

'I should warn you, sir, I'm unwell. I'm going to need some rest.'

'Really? How annoying. Your replacement was useless.'

'I'm sorry to hear that. Will the lieutenant be all right?'

'I doubt it. Not from what I observed.'

Bauer felt a pressure in his gut, a need to vomit that could be deferred but not indefinitely. 'Sir, I have bad news. I ought to brief you about it.'

'Well, as you can see, I have guests.'

'I'm afraid it can't wait,' he replied, and glanced at Katerina, torn between wanting her to stay and the urgency of his need to brief Metz.

'Well, all right then,' Metz said, 'if it's so pressing, go ahead.' Again Bauer glanced at Katerina, and following his gaze Metz added, 'Don't mind Frau Trubetzkaya. We're all friends here now.'

'We are?' Bauer asked, inwardly focused on his gut.

'It looks as though the captain might need to sit down,' Katerina said, looking at him firmly now and with obvious concern, so that yet again that day Bauer felt in danger of crying.

'Really?' Metz said. 'Then go ahead, Bauer, take a seat. Bad news, you said.'

Bauer eased himself onto a chair, took a careful breath and then in a toneless voice gave an account of the accident on the causeway. Of the fifteen men who had been travelling in or on the T–34, only three had survived, Sepp Winkel, Karl Pflieger and Gerd von Rauschenberg not among them.

Metz heard him out with a grave expression, looked up and replied that he was very sorry to hear it. 'Corporal Winkel in particular will be sorely missed. You'll write to their families, I suppose?'

'Yes, as soon as I'm able.'

'Able?'

'Over this sickness.'

'How annoying. What's wrong with you anyway? Typhus?'

'I doubt it. A virus probably. I just need some rest.'

'You don't have to take yourself off to bed straight away, I hope? Frau Trubetzkaya says that the old woman here not only knew Count Tolstoy personally but has seen and even spoken with his ghost. What do you think of that?'

'Incredible.'

'Yes, isn't it.'

Despite his nausea, Bauer felt a twinge of hurt that Katerina had shared with Metz and not himself the revelation that Daria's mother had once known Tolstoy. Though he supposed it was also possible that one or even both of the women were lying.

'Sir, before you go on I should mention something else. I've brought in a casualty I treated at the front for a gunshot wound to the lung.'

'What of it?'

'It's a Soviet casualty, sir. Major Weidemann is refusing to admit him without your approval.'

'An *Ivan*? Who is he? An officer?'

'He's no one. A private.'

'Then why bring him in?'

'He was wounded very near the dressing station, sir. I felt responsible. As a doctor I felt responsible.'

'You felt?'

'And thought, sir. He would have died if I hadn't operated. He *will* die if you don't agree to admit him.'

Metz laughed. 'My God, Bauer, you're as wilful as ever. I thought a trip to the front would teach you a lesson; but no, it seems you haven't learned a thing.'

'I wasn't aware I was meant to be learning a lesson.'

Metz chuckled and turned to Katerina. 'You charge us with cruelty, *gnädige Frau*, and yet look at what humanitarians I have under my command. If Captain Bauer were to have his way he would – I don't know – tenderly see to your countryman's corns. I suppose you're touched.'

'It's no concern of mine.'

274

Metz laughed again. 'There you go, Bauer, she's tougher than you are. No quarter given, that's the spirit. But I suppose I could bend a little, just this once. Exercise some mercy. Frau Trubetzkaya, what do you think?'

'As I said, it's up to you.'

'As a favour to yourself? Do we understand one another?'

'I find that doubtful, *Herr Oberstleutnant.*'

Metz guffawed. He was surely under the influence of something. 'So you'll telephone the major?' Bauer asked.

'Of course, of course.'

'Now?'

'Dear God, Bauer, what a scold you are. All right, all right,' he said, and reached for the field telephone on his desk, 'I'll do it now.'

'Thank you, sir.'

Metz put in a call to the hospital, and while someone at the other end went to fetch Weidemann a silence fell over the room. Bauer gazed at Katerina, and again she met his eye, only this time with a Mona Lisa smile, so that involuntarily he had to clutch his chest, his heart stomping, his grief for Pflieger and Winkel battling with the joy of seeing her again. Then Metz was speaking with Weidemann, instructing him to find the Soviet soldier a bed.

'Happy now?' Metz asked him when he put down the phone.

'Yes, sir,' Bauer said.

'Good. So we can get down to the main business of the evening. Frau Trubetzkaya, how are we to begin?'

'I'm not sure we should. Not with the Captain so unwell.'

'Nonsense. He'll do his duty. Particularly when he comprehends what's at stake.'

'Very well,' Katerina said. 'You've brought a candle?'

'Of course.'

'And something to put it on?'

'An ammunition case, yes,' Metz said.

'Empty, I hope?'

'What sort of fool do you take me for? I want to speak with the dead, not join them.'

'Glad to hear it,' she said.

Metz chuckled. 'I think you'll find the encounter explosive enough. If my adversary shows himself, that is.'

'You're holding a *seance*?' Bauer asked.

'Of sorts,' Metz said. 'Personally I dislike the term. After the last war too many charlatans swindled the bereaved by simulating contact with the dead.'

'But this is different?' Bauer asked, wary of scoffing and getting himself ejected as he had two weeks ago. As it was he would be forced to leave soon enough.

'For several reasons,' Metz replied. 'Firstly, no money will change hands. Secondly, the old woman communicated with Tolstoy's spirit long before we appeared. Thirdly – and this is by far the most significant factor – you and I are here tonight not from need but from a will to conquer.'

Bauer nodded, his face pained in a way that he hoped looked like thoughtfulness. The true mystery, as far as he was concerned, was how he and Metz had emerged from similar medical and scientific training with such wildly divergent understandings of reality.

A minute later they were seated around the ammunition case, their faces lit by a solitary candle. To Bauer's left was Katerina, to his right Agrafena, opposite him Metz. Katerina instructed them to hold hands, and Bauer hesitated. 'I wouldn't want to infect you. I've washed my hands, but —'

'Don't worry. I don't get sick. And Agrafena is as hardy as they come.'

They linked hands, the four of them. Agrafena's palm was callused, the back of her hand papery and dry. Katerina's grip was softer but also cooler than he'd imagined. Even so he felt fiercely moved, as well as indignant that her other hand was being held by Metz.

'Doesn't this one speak Russian?' the old woman asked Katerina, raising Bauer's hand.

'It's all right, he's on our side.'

'He is?'

'We'll know for sure soon enough. Just go ahead as planned.'

All this was said without once meeting his eye, and despite his nausea Bauer was left feeling insubstantial, a mind afloat on a roiling gut.

'Courage, Captain,' Metz said, the candlelight making a cavern of the cleft in his chin. 'Leo Tolstoy might have passed to the other side but there's no need to be afraid.'

'I'm not afraid, I'm sick.'

'Being dead makes a man no more formidable than he was in life, and when he was alive what was Tolstoy? A writer. There are two types of men in this world: those who live an attenuated life of the mind, and those who choose reality and *act*. Tolstoy was one of the former, so we needn't be concerned.'

'Shall we commence?' Katerina asked.

'By all means,' Metz said. 'Should we close our eyes?'

'That's up to you.'

'Good. I'll leave them open.'

For a time no one said anything. The fire crackled and the chimney moaned. To lessen his discomfort Bauer shifted on his chair, loudly creaking its joints, then abruptly the pressure in his stomach rose, so that for a moment he feared he would have to stand up and leave. He resisted, gulped, forced the pressure down; he was determined to stay and witness these proceedings, however bogus they might be. The crisis passed.

Metz and Katerina were both looking at Agrafena, whose own eyes were closed. Then softly she began to hum, a monotone, long and low, pausing from time to time to draw breath. Tolstoy had returned as a bee, Bauer thought to say but didn't. It was a calming sound and Bauer let his own eyes close, until in a voice that was undeniably spooky the old woman cried out, '*Graf Tolstoy? Eto ty?*'

'Count Tolstoy? Is that you?' Katerina translated.

Agrafena cocked an ear and then nodded, as if acknowledging a reply. '*Eto on,*' she said, turning to them.

'It's him,' Katerina told Metz.

'Just as I thought!' Metz cried.

'What would you like to say to him?' Katerina asked.

'I want to know what he's doing here.'

'I dare say he wants to know what *you're* doing here.'

'Just ask the question,' Metz said.

Katerina relayed the question to Agrafena, who in turn spoke to the ceiling in Russian. She made another ostentatious show of listening then said, 'We're his people. He's watching over us.'

'He's guarding us,' Katerina paraphrased in German. 'He's the protector of Yasnaya Polyana.'

Even knowing the whole exchange was a sham, Bauer felt a twinge of awe. He was holding a hand which, for all he knew, had once touched Tolstoy's, even as he sat in the great man's study in a house whose presiding spirit was incontestably the Count's.

'Is that why he's resisting us?' Metz asked.

Again the rigmarole of translation, real and ectoplasmic, before Katerina replied, 'You're trespassing. He'll do all he can to drive you out.'

'I *knew* it,' Metz said. 'Well, tell him he's wasting his time. I'm not afraid of his antics. He's nothing special. We all get to be dead. This land and what's on it now belongs to the Reich. What does he think about *that*?'

As Katerina again went through the motions of consultation, Bauer battled another wave of nausea. His whole body ached. His mind was foggy, confused. He needed to leave but the women's hands locked him in place.

'Like their forebears the Soviet people won't rest until Mother Russia is rid of the invader,' Katerina said.

'Ha!' Metz countered. He assumed a sly expression. 'Isn't he a pacifist? Ask him that.'

'I don't need to,' Katerina said. 'The count hates war, that's understood, but there is a war and Lev Nikolayevich has seen how it ends.'

Metz crossed his arms. 'Oh really? And how does it end?'

'With the annihilation of the German Reich.'

'He's said this to you?'

'To Agrafena Viktorovna.'

For the first time Metz looked unsure of himself. 'I don't believe it,' he said. It's a trick, a typical Slavic ploy. Ask him how he can pretend such confidence when, even as we speak, the Wehrmacht is hammering on the gates of Moscow.'

Katerina conveyed the essence of this to Agrafena, and between them they set about cooking up a reply, the details of which Bauer felt too ill to follow. When they were finished conferring, Katerina said in German, 'Lev Nikolaevich concedes that the Soviet Union is on the edge of a precipice —'

'Hear that, Bauer! They're teetering, they're on the edge. One more push and they're over!'

But this was all Bauer could stand. His thorax was jerking. He lurched to his feet, letting go of the women's hands, ran to the door, wrenched it open and, ignoring Metz's protests, stumbled to the vestibule and onto the porch, and from there vomited into the snow.

SEVENTEEN

Sydney
4 March 1968

Dear Paul,

Mayor of Nuremberg! I had no idea I was corresponding
with such an eminent man. Treating the topic so scantily
counts as evasion, I'm afraid – you must send me news
clippings, photographs and any other information you have
about your political career. In return (and because so far
you haven't set the secret services onto me) I will arrange
for Professor Fleet to post you copies of *Three Women* and
Europa, 1975. Bear in mind that these museum pieces are
the work of a young woman who is long gone – who had
been long gone even when you and I first met. (I'm as sure
as I can be, by the way, that Simon Fleet is not spying for
anyone; he flirts with me too blatantly, in the belief that
I'm too old to take him seriously. The only person he ever
questions me about is Lev Nikolayevich.)

What twists and swerves your life has taken! In
comparison, my own life seems uneventful and, since we

281

parted, considerably easier. You describe Yasnaya Polyana as the fulcrum of your life, and in dramatic terms it strikes me that you and I rather see-sawed at that moment, the big events of my life all occurring before it, while in your case they all came afterwards (in fine academic style I am overlooking the death of your wife, which obstinately refuses to fit this tidy little schema).

Your letter stirred up so many thoughts and feelings, memories and questions. For instance, it has occurred to me that on a trip I made to Leningrad in March 1946 I must have passed within thirty kilometres of your place of internment near Borovichi. I had no idea there was a German POW camp nearby, let alone that you were in it. The thought of your long detention fills me with indignation, so much so that I've even managed to spare a thought for your countrymen who suffered the same fate (though not, of course, for the one who took his Iron Cross into captivity). In turn this makes me wonder what happened to the comrades of yours I knew at Yasnaya Polyana? To Metz, in particular; and to that other fellow, the buffoon – Molineux, wasn't it? – who I confess to thinking of now with amusement. Perhaps I am a little like those veteran soldiers you mentioned who grow fond of their former enemies (though in my case only a very little). If nothing else, we were contemporaries, I suppose – were all children, equally innocent and vicious, before jointly taking our generation's turn on the stage. And now those of us who survived the war are willy-nilly lining up for death.

You asked about Marlen, and with deep gratitude I am able to report that he did survive the war, though not unscathed, as he was badly wounded in 1945 on the outskirts of Berlin. He recovered, though, and has since done very well for himself, rising quite high in the state media, first in production and lately in management; recently he has moved with his wife, Anna, and daughter, Nadia, to a fine apartment in central Moscow. Party membership is a prerequisite for this kind of success, but to the best of my knowledge Marlen hasn't actively harmed anyone in getting where he is. Mind you, he's shockingly conservative. What is it about military service and conservatism, I wonder. Is it because, having sacrificed so much for their country, ex-soldiers can't bear to see time's erosion of what they once fought to defend? If so, it's another reason to outlaw war (if any other reason is needed in the Atomic Age). In Marlen's favour I should point out that his daughter not only tolerates but even loves him – no small thing for a nineteen-year-old who is far from being conservative herself (as you deduced, my little gifts from the West are mostly for her). Even his wife shows signs of loving him a little.

It is generous of you to suggest I could go back to writing fiction, but sadly it's out of the question. For a start, in the Soviet Union any literature worth the name either can't be published or, if it is published, causes the writer no end of bother with the state. I'm thinking here of Alexander Solzhenitsyn. Do you know of his *One Day in the Life of Ivan Denisovich*? An indispensable work. Or even

Pasternak. Personally I find *Dr Zhivago* rather lightweight and overwrought, but there's no denying Pasternak's courage in intermittently standing up to the authorities, including to Stalin himself (being lucky helped, not to mention naive). And then there's Mandelstam, whom naivety couldn't save. And Akhmatova, a brave woman and an extraordinary poet. I met her once, and although she was perfectly courteous towards me I couldn't help thinking, then and afterwards, that compared to her I was a hack and a time-server. She *was* literature, I was its lickspittle; she would have died for it, I used it to get a nicer apartment.

In your kindly way I hear you objecting to this, and since you won't be able to reply to this letter for many months I will raise those objections on your behalf in order to despatch them straight away, saving both of us time. You don't see me as a coward, you say? At Yasnaya Polyana I gave you and Metz hell? Well, yes, I did my best, but as I pointed out to you in my previous letter, my behaviour at Yasnaya Polyana was an aberration, a bout of hysteria, if you will, since for the previous fifteen years I had been an unremitting coward, too scared to write, too afraid to utter a syllable about anything that mattered. When Viktor was arrested I did nothing to defend him, and when he was executed I fled Moscow with Marlen for the comparative safety of Yasnaya Polyana. There I laid low, stayed silent, raised Marlen to manhood and saw him safely off to university. The Secret Service kept away. I wasn't exactly happy, but then again nor was anyone else I knew. And I wasn't dead. Then came your invasion and initially I was thrilled, convinced that the Soviet system was about to collapse; I remained hopeful, even when Marlen was conscripted (to defend the regime that had killed his father, the regime I myself had fought to establish). If only the Germans are sensible, I told myself, half the population will go over to their side and half will stay at home. But as we know now, the Germans weren't sensible. By the time Yasnaya Polyana fell it was amply clear that you had come not to liberate or even to conquer in the customary way but to enslave and exterminate, and, oh, how I hated you for it. Onto you and your comrades I poured all my pent-up rage, and how liberating *that* was. Marlen's life was being imperilled every day, but nothing I said or did could help or harm him, and I revelled in that, because finally, *finally* I was having my say. Shouting the praises of Soviet rule turned out to be a sublime release from having to whisper *under* Soviet rule; and while I knew Metz could have me shot at any time I didn't care, at least not in the beginning. I must admit that I also derived a certain illicit pleasure from suddenly finding myself among foreigners, even foreign invaders, especially when one of them turned out to be a decent man, since under Stalin consorting with foreigners was a shortcut to the gulag.

When the Red Army returned to Yasnaya Polyana, so did my habitual cowardice, but after the war it wasn't fear that prevented me from writing. No, it was simply that I had nothing new to say, let alone a new way of saying it. In your letter you ask whether writers, like scientists, should be able to surpass the work of the giants who precede them by standing on their shoulders. I believe that the answer is no. Literature doesn't work that way; or, rather, it does work that way but only in a narrow, technical and ultimately trivial sense. I could bore you with diagrams of the influence earlier writers have had on later ones (in fact, you may have given me an idea for a paper), but instead let me describe to you a sculpture I came across in 1962 in a small, out-of-the-way chapel in Naples. It was in marble and portrayed the dead Christ laid out on a bier, his body muscular and draped in a diaphanous shroud, both the flesh and the fabric sculpted in extraordinary detail. To my untutored eye the sculptor's technique seemed superior to anything else I'd seen in Italy, including by Bernini or Michelangelo. And yet who was this sculptor? Even now I couldn't tell you; my minder from the embassy was in a hurry to leave and I failed to remember the name. What I *do* recall is that the work dated from the 1750s and was considered so unimportant that it didn't feature in my (admittedly rudimentary) guidebook. Here was a work whose creator had clambered onto the shoulders of giants and, in a technical sense at least, surpassed them. But for what? Nobody cared. It was a derivative work and, by the 1750s, already passé.

So please, no more talk of me returning to writing, which would only end with me producing something second-rate and forgettable. I'm done with it. Instead let me tell you about Sydney, the city I'm in, a subtropical metropolis on the eastern coast of Australia which is seamed with luxuriant vegetation and teeming with parrots and other exotic fowl, all of it clustered around a gigantic harbour comprised of multiple inlets and bays. And the beaches! Golden sand and great breakers rolling in; sharp light and a salt-shot breeze. Coming from Moscow I am struck, as I always am in the West, by the vulgar commercialism of the place, but even so I'm besotted. In the winter of 1941 could we have imagined that such a place existed? And had we done so – feelingly, I mean, as one imagines the setting of a well-written novel – might we have behaved in different ways? Oh, I'm speaking nonsense, I know. I'm rather drunk on this city, which seems to belong to a different century, a different planet, even, than the one we thought we were occupying in 1941. And yes, as you point out, I owe it all to Lev Nikolayevich, who has kept me employed for years and now whisks me around the world. (I have delivered two papers here, one in English and one in Russian, both of which were respectfully received.)

Now for the part of this letter I've been putting off. Paul, I am sorry but we can't write to one another openly, let alone meet in person. I hate to put it like this but I have too much to lose. All international mail into and out of the Soviet Union is opened, as you know; and if you were to appear at an academic conference and speak to me for more than five seconds my minders would make it their business to find out who you were. This would be bad enough if you were an ordinary citizen of West Germany, but far worse given that you're a former politician. Perhaps I have failed to convey to you how suspicious and inflexible our government remains (though I'm sure you will have drawn your own conclusions from the recent events in Prague). Under Khrushchev our situation improved for a time, but his de-Stalinisation program spooked many who had wielded power under Stalin and were thereby implicated in his crimes, and now that Brezhnev is president those people are back in charge. One of my colleagues, who's a poet, claims that the most Russian of all words is 'cement' (no matter it comes from the French), not only because we build with the stuff whenever possible but because invariably our institutions are rigid. Lacking true legitimacy (of the kind your mayoralty no doubt enjoyed) the communist state, like the Tsarist regime before it, will probably fracture and collapse one day, though by then you and I will presumably be dead. The century has sunk its teeth into us, I'm afraid, and even now is mindlessly shaking us about.

When I say that I have too much to lose, please know that corresponding with you is very high on the list of pleasures I aim to keep. Does it matter if our letters continue to be infrequent? Evidently when the British settled Sydney in the late eighteenth century the mail was at best sporadic, so that someone writing home to a loved one had to wait a year or more for a reply. Such a delay must have made letters extremely precious, and I propose we treat our correspondence similarly, as something providential. That way you can picture me as the dauntless if crazy woman I was, rather than the ill-tempered hag I've become. For my own part I suspect that meeting with you in person would only confirm that you're still despicably handsome, still admirable, and one of the kindest men I've known.

Yours,
Katerina

★ ★ ★

28 Jonah Strasse
Nuremberg
19 December 1968

Dear Katerina,
Enclosed, at your request, is a selection of news clippings and articles about my political career – some with photographs that will allay your concerns that I might have retained any vestiges of youthful good looks.

Thank you for asking Professor Fleet to send me copies of your novels. I enjoyed both of them very much, albeit in different ways: *Three Women* for all the usual reasons one values a novel – a compelling plot, well-drawn characters, a powerful sense of a time and place; *Europa, 1975* for a kind of visionary, otherworldly ambience that reminded me a little of Kafka. The young woman who wrote them might be long gone, but you can certainly feel proud of her. Would it be possible to publish one or both of the books in translation in the West? After all, they are fundamentally positive about the Revolution, and in this sense are less like Solzhenitsyn's novels than those of

Mikhail Sholokhov, which appear to be acclaimed equally at home and abroad.

Not only have I read your novels (twice) but also some of your scholarly work, which I was able to track down in various university libraries. The specialist language in the essays and your book about narratology certainly tested the limits of my Russian, but nevertheless I found them thought-provoking. In fact, you inspired me to revisit *The Kreutzer Sonata*, as well as to read for the first time two of Tolstoy's other late works, *The Resurrection* and *The Devil* (as you can see, these days I have plenty of time on my hands). In many ways these are remarkable books, aren't they; but of course they inevitably suffer by comparison to *War and Peace* and *Anna Karenina*. Your narratology book draws attention to how much the late work is propelled by male disgust for women; or, to be more exact, the self-disgust of men who can't prevent themselves desiring women. It seems to me that there's more than a whiff of this in *Anna Karenina* as well, but at least in that novel female desire gets its due (if also its punishment). *War and Peace* is more generous, both to men and to women. It's a book that *cares* about what people want, and this alone goes a long way to explaining its greatness.

You've made it very clear that you plan never to write fiction again, but before I let go of the topic altogether I can't help observing that you seem to have responded rather intensely to that Dead Christ you saw, a work which you claim shows the futility of making art in the shadow of renowned precursors. Surely a sculpture that made you

think about the potency of tradition, the relevance of
virtuosity, and (I'm presuming here) the impermanence
of the body can't be as worthless as you make it out to be.
Indeed, it sounds to me that you remember it just as well or
even better than the Michelangelos and Berninis you saw.

But enough. As promised, I will now put aside the topic.
Not having produced any books myself I'm in no position
to reproach you for ones that you haven't written. Instead
let me turn to the good news (it was news to me!) that
your son Marlen not only survived the war but has gone
on to provide you with a granddaughter. How rewarding
that must be. As a recent retiree I must say I envy you the
friendship you obviously enjoy with your granddaughter,
which will no doubt help you to stay in the current of life
when like me you eventually retire.

In regard to what happened to Julius Metz and
Hermann Molineux, I am able to say that both men not
only survived the war but managed to get themselves
captured by the western Allies, with the result that their
internments were relatively brief. Metz accomplished this
fairly easily, since by the end of the war he was stationed
at a hospital in Munich and was taken captive there by the
Americans. Molineux's path was harder. After avoiding
being captured with me and Drexel near Lvov, he had a
series of other scrapes, including commandeering a staff car
by posing as Albert Speer's personal physician and driving
it thirty kilometres to the British lines. He told me all
this personally in 1952 in a restaurant in his home town
of Würtzburg, where he had returned after the war to be

reunited with his wife. He was fifty-nine and much fatter than when we served together, but as far as I could tell he was fundamentally unchanged, his buffoonery, as you call it, quite unaffected by the war. Not that he had put the experience behind him, exactly. In fact, he was talking about organising a reunion of veterans of the Wehrmacht Medical Corps; and this surprised me because his attitude to the military when he was in it had been sceptical, if not downright contemptuous. In any case, for whatever reason he had become something of an authority on who had died, where, and in what circumstances, as well as who had lived and what they were doing with their lives. It was from Hermann I learned that Major Weidemann, our chief physician at Yasnaya Polyana, had been killed late in 1944 on the day we were overrun near Lvov. Hermann claimed that during the attack Weidemann was seen running to his tent, supposedly to rescue his gramophone, though frankly I suspect Hermann of making this up, as he could never resist doctoring his stories for effect. Hermann himself died (of a heart attack) only months after our meeting, and by the time I heard about it I was too late to attend his funeral. Subsequently, his wife told me he had just turned sixty.

Who else did you know? I've already told you about Fabian Drexel, who according to Hermann perished in the Gulag; and by the sound of it you recall the deaths of my two operating assistants, Karl Pflieger and Sepp Winkel, as well as that of our dentist Volker Hirsch. There was also a young doctor named Zöllner you might remember, who was later killed in the vicinity of Voronezh when he stepped on an anti-personnel mine. There were various others you may or may not remember, such as Metz's orderly Egon Ehrlich, who like Hermann got himself captured by the British, as well as our quartermaster Norbert Ritter, who like me survived the Gulag and who according to Hermann went on to become the manager of a hardware store in Berlin.

Which brings me back to Metz. Before Hermann died he had published my name and address (entirely without my permission) in a newsletter distributed to veterans of the Medical Corp, with the result that a few weeks later I received a letter from Metz. You can imagine how surprised I was, as we had last seen one another in 1941 at Yasnaya Polyana. His letter was friendly, even jaunty, and barely mentioned the war. I already knew from Hermann that after it Metz had set up in Dortmund, not as a surgeon or even a doctor but as the director of a small factory producing prosthetics and other specialised medical equipment; or, as Hermann put it, 'filling a gap he had done his damnedest to create'. Metz's letter added little more. He was prospering and at sixty-three was looking forward to handing over management of the firm to one of his sons-in-law. Apparently all three of his daughters were happily married and between them had given him five or six grandchildren, with another on the way. I replied to him politely, dodging an invitation to visit. He answered with at least one more letter, and there were also a couple of Christmas cards, but by then I was getting very busy at the hospital, and, possibly sensing my ambivalence, he stopped writing to me.

I've been thinking of how you and I came to know one another at Yasnaya Polyana, by fits and starts and in the teeth of your (understandable) hostility. Along the way I seem to recall that we discussed our families a little – your aristocratic one, certainly; your husband and son; also my wife, and the brother I lost in the First World War. The members of my family I don't recall mentioning to you were my mother and father, no doubt because there wasn't much to tell. They were simple, hardworking country people, and I only mention them now because writing to you has reminded me of an incident in my mother's life – perhaps 'development' would be a better term – soon after my father's death in 1928. My mother was younger than my father and only forty-nine when he died, and although she had loved him in her way she was a self-contained woman who, I suspected, half-welcomed her widowhood. Certainly it didn't cross my mind she would ever remarry, and so I was startled six months after my father's death when she told me an 'old admirer' had been in touch, a former schoolmate who long ago had moved to Nuremberg. This admirer, who had also been widowed, had heard of my father's death and had written to my mother expressing his condolences, adding that he would like to meet up with her 'for old times' sake'. As she told me all this, her manner was unlike anything I'd ever seen in her before, a blend of bashfulness, defiance and pride. She wanted my blessing, I assumed – was perhaps even asking my permission – and once I got over my initial shock I gave it to her, declaring with more enthusiasm than I really felt that she should certainly meet this fellow if she wanted to; she was a free woman; she should follow her heart. Her response was scornful. She would write to him, she said, but the past was the past and there was no sense in them meeting. And that's what happened: they wrote but didn't meet – not for several more years, in any case, by which time the admirer had married someone else.

Why am I telling you this? I'm telling you on account of the struggle I'm having accepting your verdict that you and I shouldn't meet. Not that I necessarily think you're wrong, mind you. When my mother opted to keep the past in the past, I remember thinking she had made the right decision, that this admirer, whoever he was, was a bit of a fool to believe he could waltz back into her life after thirty years, knowing nothing of who she had become, and perhaps only a little of who she had been when they knew one another originally. It was embarrassing. What was wrong with old people, I wondered (old people of fifty!) that they wanted to wallow in memory, when clearly the healthier thing to do was to stride into the future?

And yet here I am. Here I am subsisting on memories. Here I am among books I aim to re-read, or have read twice or three times before, opting for the nourishment of repetition over the fizz and flash of the new.

And so I have a proposition for you, Katerina. Let us meet openly. Let's confound the KGB by being exactly who we are: Paul Bauer, former mayor of Nuremberg, formerly a Soviet prisoner of war; and Katerina Trubetzkaya, distinguished scholar and heroic defender of Yasnaya Polyana against fascist aggression. Let Mr Brezhnev have a propaganda victory. Let's invite the press to our meeting, where in front of the cameras I will denounce German militarism. Magnanimously you could then accept my contrition, and we could embrace, symbolically reconciling our once warring peoples. I'm serious. After a performance like that they would surely let us have dinner together, wouldn't they? Will you have dinner with me?

Yours sincerely,
Paul

EIGHTEEN

The night of his return from the front to Yasnaya Polyana he
took to his bed feeling hot and disoriented, the nausea rising in
him until every half an hour he was forced to vomit, first in the
toilet down the hall and then into a pail Hermann put beside
his bed. As the night deepened, so did his confusion – sleep
and wakefulness cartwheeling one into another. He dreamed of
gaping wounds, then of his brother, Jürgen, still with both his
legs, his voice garbled but kind, then sinister and harsh. Then
Jürgen was gone, and on a cliff edge Bauer was clutching the
wrist of Sepp Winkel, who was imploring him to lift, lift him
up, for God's sake *lift*, just as, senselessly, monstrously, Bauer let
go. He wept. He promised his father to be good. Arm in arm
with Clara on a stroll through Ulm he watched the Danube
plaiting currents underneath a bridge, then he sensed daylight,
his pupils flinching under their lids, opened his eyes and saw
that the ceiling had receded, or that his camp bed had shrunk,
and only later understood he was no longer in his room but
in one of the hospital wards. He heard movement, speech –
some of it about him – before sinking again. Then it was night,

297

he was conscious, and in the surrounding beds men were coughing, groaning, labouring to breathe. So much effort. So much misery. He slid again into sleep.

When next he woke, someone was pressing a mug to his lips. He drank. Water. Opened his eyes and saw Zöllner. How was he feeling? Zöllner wanted to know.

'Better,' he replied, though he had rarely felt worse.

'That's good. You've been unconscious for two days.'

Bauer asked him the date. The third, replied Zöllner. Of December, he added.

'My birthday,' Bauer said. 'I've just missed it.'

'I'm sorry to hear that, sir. Happy birthday to you anyway. How old are you?'

'Forty-one. What have I got? Typhus? Influenza?'

'We don't know. Maybe both. Or neither. You're getting better, that's the thing.' There was a pause. 'Terrible news about your men.'

'Agreed,' Bauer said.

'I've been praying for their souls.'

'Thank you, Hans,' Bauer said, feeling moved, his atheist convictions beside the point.

'They'll be hard to replace,' the young man said. 'Especially Sepp.'

'That's true,' Bauer said. He tried to think of something meaningful to add, failed and confined himself to nodding.

The next day his condition was judged no longer contagious, if it ever had been, and he was stretchered to his room to convalesce, hospital beds being in short supply. He was still dizzy, unable to read or even follow conversation.

'I'm thinking of putting Pabst onto it,' Molineux said to him that evening.

'Onto what?' Bauer managed to ask.

'The still. He's tried to poison us before and none of us have died, so I figure we'll be relatively safe.'

As soon as he was able to sit up and think more or less clearly he asked for paper, a bottle of ink and a pen to write to Winkel's and Pflieger's families, a task he wanted behind him as soon as possible. Their men had died trying to save the lives of others, he wrote truthfully. He considered calling them heroes but didn't want to imply they had taken stupid risks. And he definitely wasn't going to describe the true facts of their deaths, which he could hardly bear to think about himself: the tipping metal trap, the freezing water rushing in – a naval death thousands of kilometres from the sea. No, it was out of the question. Truth of that kind was only tolerable at one remove, say in a novel or poem, a mirror of words in which to glimpse the Gorgon's head. Instead he wrote that Winkel and Pflieger had died instantly when a shell hit the tank they were in. They had died 'for the Fatherland', he added, avoiding the phrase 'for the Führer' favoured by Metz in such letters, a formulation that Dieter Clemens's wife, for example, would have felt as a twist of the blade.

Dieter. For the first time in weeks Bauer remembered helping to lower him into the ground, a last favour to a friend, or so he had thought. But Dieter's uniform, as he'd shovelled mud onto it, had jellied and bounced; and when they left that place – the little barrow of mud, the cross on which Dieter's dog tag was slung – Bauer sensed the man under it calling out to him, begging him to stay, not to leave him alone in that dark hole among the trees.

And von Rauschenberg, a man of a different stamp, more hardened than Dieter had been but, Bauer sensed, no less good. Chance traveller with Pflieger and Sepp. This country will consume us, Bauer thought as he sealed the letters to the families of his men. One way or another, sooner or later, it will swallow us all.

'Metz wants to know when you'll be fit again,' Molineux said that evening. 'He's scared of coming in person. Contagion, I suppose. It's a mystery to me why such a fastidious man chose to go into medicine.'

'You can tell him I'll be able to work tomorrow,' Bauer said, thinking that he could do with at least another week.

'Hallelujah,' Molineux said. 'And I mean that sincerely. God knows we need a competent surgeon. Pilcz went down in flames faster than the *Hindenburg*, and now even Metz is going to pieces.'

'To pieces how?'

'Losing his touch. If I'm not mistaken he's getting a tremor, which believe me is unnerving when he's cutting near an artery.'

Bauer remembered how, at the end of their marathon shift, Metz's hands had been trembling. At the time this had seemed understandable. 'Have you discussed it with him?'

'Are you mad? I have to work with the man.'

'All the more reason to speak with him.'

'Bauer, you know it doesn't work that way.'

And he did know. When lives were at stake elsewhere – a gasworks, say, or the railways – procedures were in place to protect against human error. Only surgeons and the Pope were considered to be infallible, and though personally he benefited from the status thus conferred, Bauer doubted it made him a better surgeon, any more than Molineux's tact would help to keep Metz up to the mark.

Through the open doorway drifted the distant sound of a piano – not from Weidemann's gramophone, Bauer realised, but from the Bechstein downstairs. To his inexpert ear the playing sounded flawless. 'My God, who's that?'

'I'm not sure,' Molineux replied. 'Schubert? Brahms? One of their lieder, I'd say.'

'Numbskull. I mean who's playing?'

'Your man Demchak, it must be. Weidemann was threatening to summon him over here this evening. Someone mentioned he could play.'

'Someone wasn't joking.' The music sounded lovely, not only skilful but also, he sensed, infused with melancholy and pathos.

Molineux cocked an ear and said, 'You know, you're right. Certainly an improvement on old Bertha. All Weidemann's records are scratched to shit. Better investigate. Do you mind?'

'Not at all,' Bauer replied, and held up *War and Peace*. 'I have reading to do.'

★　★　★

Even getting out of bed the following morning was arduous, making Bauer wonder how he would get through the day, especially if there were more than the ordinary number of

301

casualties. In the corridor he passed Molineux returning from the bathroom. 'You're up late,' Molineux said.

'Instead of dying,' he replied, went into the lavatory and had to lean over the bowl as a fit of dizziness passed. The porcelain was as finely cracked as a Rembrandt or a Titian, and it occurred to him that Tolstoy himself must have shat here often. Sitting down felt disrespectful. His own output was meagre.

In the bathroom he found Drexel brushing his teeth, his face unnaturally close to the mirror. Bauer greeted him and Drexel grunted in reply, which as a fellow night-owl Bauer could understand and excuse. Despite the cold, Drexel was wearing only a towel, revealing his short but strong and stocky frame. Dense dark hair on his chest and abdomen. An almost shaggy back.

The tub was free and Bauer ran a little hot water, got in and washed himself, his lower half scalding while his upper half froze. Drexel was taking his time with his brushing, arm working hard as if filing his teeth to the nub. A rivulet of dental foam was running down his hand, and with more disgust than as a surgeon he was entitled to feel, Bauer watched the foam snake from his wrist onto his forearm. Hadn't the fellow noticed? The mirror was only starting to mist over, and anyway couldn't he feel his own arm? Or was he aware and didn't care? Bauer kept glancing over at him until finally, with foam dripping off his elbow, Drexel ducked and spat, rinsed his arm and left the room.

Shortly afterwards Bauer got out of the tub and took his own turn at the mirror. He looked terrible, he thought: haggard and gaunt, the lines bracketing his mouth noticeably deeper than before. Half his stubble was white and his hair was greying at his temples and ears. As far as he could tell he wasn't balding, at least not from the front, and though he knew it to be futile he ducked to glimpse the top of his head. Yes, impossible. No doubt there were parts of the soul, he thought, that likewise resisted inspection.

The bathroom door opened and Hirsch appeared, and quickly Bauer took up his razor. Hirsch looked startled then pleased – it was so good to see him, he said. He had visited him in the hospital and then later in his room. Had he noticed?

Bauer admitted he hadn't.

'You would have sensed it,' Hirsch said firmly. 'At some level you would have noticed, and ...'

'Appreciated it?'

'Taken heart.'

Like so much of what Hirsch said, this was irritating, though as usual Bauer found it hard to identify why.

Hirsch pointed at the bath. 'Sir, would you mind if I ...?'

'Go ahead.'

'Even though you're shaving? It won't, you know, fog your mirror too much?'

'I can manage.'

Hirsch thanked him and began to undress. Bauer started to shave. His arms felt heavy, weak. Hirsch had still not mentioned Winkel and Pflieger, and perhaps it was this that was annoying him. Or was ignoring their comrades' deaths understandable, or even necessary? In the mirror Bauer glimpsed Hirsch getting into the tub, his soft, hulking body almost hairless, especially in comparison with Drexel's. His penis, like the rest of him, was flaccid and large.

Bauer returned down the corridor to find Molineux leaning in the doorway to their room. 'Slacker,' Bauer said. 'Short of things to do?'

'I'm waiting for you, aren't I,' Molineux said.

This was touching, or would have been if Molineux had looked less distracted. 'How soon do you think Hirsch will be getting out of the bathroom?'

'Fairly soon, I suppose. Why do you ask?'

'Just wait, you'll see.'

Bauer entered their room and set about getting dressed. 'What are you up to now? You should leave him be.'

'It's just a little fun, that's all. God knows we need it.'

'But does Hirsch?'

'Him too.'

Bauer was buttoning his tunic when Molineux ducked back inside. 'There he goes!' There was a pause and then a shriek, its tone womanly, its loudness the work of a man.

'*Je-sus*,' Molineux said, sounding half amused and half annoyed. 'Now Metz will get involved.'

For a while there was silence in the corridor, Hirsch presumably having recovered from the shock of whatever Hermann had done to him. If shock was the right term – there had been something willed about Hirsch's cry, a suggestion not only of fright but of indignation. There followed the thudding of boots, including from downstairs, and as predicted Metz demanding to know what was going on. Bauer followed Molineux into the corridor, still buttoning his tunic. Not only Metz but Drexel and Weidemann were there, as well as a duty sentry with both hands on his rifle. Seconds later Hirsch emerged in his underwear from his room, his arm outstretched and in his hand a glass of water which contained a sphere, a human eye, its pupil bobbing about in surprise.

'What's the meaning of this?' yelled Metz.

'It was by my bed, sir, when I got back from the bathroom,' Hirsch said, his face noticeably white.

Metz took the glass and held it up. 'Who's responsible for this? It's an outrage. Un-German. I'll have him up on charges, whoever he is.'

'It was me, sir,' Molineux said, much to Bauer's surprise. 'Just a bit of fun.'

Metz bared his teeth in rage. 'I should have known. Captain, this time you've gone too far. I'm a tolerant man, but this I can't countenance. No and no and no. Where's your sense of decency? Your respect for the dead?'

'It's not one of our own, sir. That's a Bolshevik eyeball.'

'Bolshevik? From where?'

'From the Ivan who died, the one Bauer brought in.'

Metz hesitated, then said firmly, 'Even so.'

'How did he die?' Bauer asked.

Metz handed the glass to the sentry and ordered him to get rid of it. 'The incinerator.'

'Yes, sir.'

'How did he die?' repeated Bauer.

'The usual way,' said Weidemann, speaking for the first time. 'Of his wounds.'

'That's enough time wasted here,' Metz said, and turned to go.

'What about me?' Hirsch said.

Metz stopped. 'What about you?'

'Captain Molineux owes me an apology,' he said, his voice tremulous but determined.

'Oh, for what?' Metz asked.

'The intrusion,' Hirsch said, 'the … I would call it humiliation. In my own quarters. It's not … it's improper.'

Metz stared at him then jerked his head in annoyance. 'For goodness sake, man. Get a grip on yourself.'

★ ★ ★

After breakfast, Metz offered to drive Bauer to the hospital in the ZIS, and in his sorry physical condition he was quick to accept. 'It's very kind of you.'

'Kindness has nothing to do with it,' Metz replied. 'I need to brief you on what's been happening while you've been loafing in bed.'

From the porch they stepped into a wind armed with chips of ice. Fortunately the ZIS was parked close to the porch, its engine running. Bauer got into the back and found Ehrlich at the wheel, hardly a surprising discovery but unpleasant all the same, reminding him of the comrades he'd liked more but who now were dead.

'Yes, a lot's changed in your absence,' Metz said when they were underway. 'For a start I've brought Frau Kälter to heel.'

'You have?'

'Ever trained a dog?'

'Not personally, no.'

'Frankly it shows. If you had done, that bitch might have given you less trouble.'

Despite himself Bauer was taken aback; Metz was nothing if not correct. 'The other night you seemed on good terms with each other.'

'I wouldn't say that. Any dog can be petted once you've established dominance over it. You were too trusting, too soft, and look where it got you.' Already they were approaching the hospital. 'Anyway, all you need to know is that from now on Frau Kälter will report directly to me. You needn't communicate with her. In fact, don't – you'll only undo my good work.'

'I'm forbidden to speak with her at all?'

'If you have reason to speak with her in passing, so be it. But for God's sake, do try to remember who's in charge.'

Ehrlich pulled up at the front steps of the hospital and Bauer got out with Metz, saluted the sentry and went inside. They crossed the entrance hall and began to mount the stairs. Metz stopped. 'What are you doing?'

'You wanted to brief me?'

'What do you think I've been doing? Reciting nursery rhymes?'

★   ★   ★

According to Zöllner, the death of the young Soviet soldier really had been routine. Yes, the presence of an enemy patient had raised eyebrows on the wards, but he had received the same standard of care as their own wounded did. Bauer was inclined to believe it. His own assessment of the boy's chances had been pessimistic, though he couldn't shake the feeling that had he not fallen ill he might have saved him, if necessary by willpower alone. But no. He had a victim now. Pyotr Maximovich Kirov, twenty years old, service number TF9674652.

'What happened to the corpse?' he asked.

'Frau Kälter took it away,' Zöllner said.

'*Kälter?*'

'She offered, we agreed.'

'Took it away how?'

'On a sled.'

'By herself?'

'With the help of that old man of hers. White beard. Looks like God.'

'Tikhon Vassilyvich?'

'That's the one.'

'And the missing eye? Did she comment on that?'

'Not while I was there.'

He supposed it was possible that Katerina assumed the young soldier had lost his eye in battle. If she asked about it he would set her right, he decided, but only then. She already had plenty of reasons to detest them.

He had feared a heavy day of surgery but fortunately there were only seven cases, allowing him to get used to his two new assistants. These were worthy men, he supposed, and competent enough, but he doubted he would warm to them as he had to Pflieger and Winkel, though if they went through enough together he supposed this might change. Demchak was still there, of course, taciturn and steady, as well as Hirsch, his nervousness as usual setting Bauer on edge.

All day he looked out for Katerina, his hard-won resignation at the idea of never seeing her again having deserted him utterly. True, Metz had told him to avoid her, but surely there would be ways around that. What bothered him more, though he didn't like to admit it, was Metz's charge that he had treated Katerina too gently. Not that he believed for an instant Metz's boast to have tamed her; no, it wasn't Metz with whom he was comparing himself but Katerina's dead husband, the swashbuckling Viktor, since whatever his own merits were, Bauer knew he wasn't dashing.

In the event it wasn't Katerina but Daria Grigorievna he crossed paths with first − in the officers' mess, the old drawing room, when he returned to the main house at the end of the day. It was dark outside but Daria was still at work, taking mugs and plates off the lid of the piano and wiping its ebony surface. Bauer paused in the doorway and Daria turned around. She looked startled, possibly frightened, her small eyes blinking in her florid, cushiony face. He bowed slightly. 'Daria Grigorievna.'

'*Da?*' she said.

In halting Russian he remarked he hadn't seen her for a while. 'Since the death of Sepp Winkel,' he clarified.

At this she half turned away, clutching her cleaning rag to her chin. Instinctively Bauer moved towards her but she waved him away. He stopped, tried to think of something consoling to say but couldn't shape the words. 'He loves you too,' he blurted at last, botching the tense. Daria moaned and hunched her back to him, as if to a blast. Bauer hesitated, and when her posture didn't change he drew back, softly apologised and left her alone.

NINETEEN

'If you have a moment, sir,' said Joachim Knoll, 'there's a patient in Ward Three I'd like you to look at.'

'Why, is he in danger?' Bauer asked. Knoll was Metz's operating assistant, and today Bauer had no time to deal with anyone else's patient.

'Not exactly, sir, no.'

'Then why …?' he began, only to notice the corporal's pleading expression. 'All right then, lead the way.'

They entered the ward and Knoll showed him to the bed of a patient who was propped up on a couple of pillows, awake and apparently alert. Knoll introduced him as Private Henninger, and Bauer consulted his field medical card, one wing of which was missing. His record stated that a bullet had pierced his right lung and exited his back, all without so much as breaking a rib. Bauer examined the entry and exit wounds, which were healing well. He asked the patient how he was feeling.

'Not too bad, doc,' Henninger replied, noticeably wheezing. 'Suppose I shouldn't … be alive. A bloody idiot … pardon me, sir. No sniper … we thought. Won't make that … mistake again.'

'Well, you're still with us, that's the main thing,' Bauer said. He returned the man's card to its sleeve, met Knoll's eye and understood from his expression he wanted to speak with him in private. Bauer wished the patient well. 'When you're fit to travel you'll be transferred home. Until then you need to rest.'

In the corridor Knoll thanked him and said, 'Perhaps I should have been clearer, sir. It's about the man's surgery.'

'Yes?'

'The lieutenant colonel ...' he said, pausing as a pair of corpsmen hurried by. 'The lieutenant colonel began the operation as normal,' he went on, 'explored the entry and exit wounds ...'

'And?'

'Seemed not to finish, sir. I'm no doctor – I mean, what would I know? – but I've watched the lieutenant colonel do that operation dozens of times and this one was different. He repaired the pleura as normal, and as you saw he dealt with the external wounds. But that's all.'

'No internal repair?'

'Exactly.'

'Did he explain?'

'No, sir. But he never does.'

'No, indeed.'

'There's one more thing, sir,' Knoll said. He looked miserable, his reddish eyebrows expressive against almost lily-white skin.

'Corporal, you're doing the right thing in raising this. Our first duty is to the patients.'

'Yes, sir.'

'But if it helps to put your mind at ease, I can leave you out of it if I take this up with Lieutenant Colonel Metz.'

'But, sir, how? You're getting it from me.'

'I'll think of something, you have my word on that. "One more thing", you were saying?'

Knoll sighed. 'The lieutenant colonel's hands were shaking, sir. It's something I've noticed a few times before, but this was worse. We all saw it.'

'I've noticed it myself a little. You think that's why he opted not to debride the lung?'

'It crossed my mind, sir, yes.'

'And you all saw it, you said. Including Captain Molineux?'

'I'm not sure. I doubt he could have missed it. But I didn't discuss it with him, no.'

'No matter. Thank you, Knoll. As I said, whatever I do I'll leave your name out of it.'

'Thank you, sir. I appreciate that.'

He passed a busy day in surgery, most of it spent amputating blackened fingers and toes, but however absorbing the procedure in front of him, a part of his mind was working on Metz's tremor or, more pressingly, on the state of Private Henninger's lung. After finishing surgery he went looking for Metz upstairs and from the duty clerk learned he was in his office with Drexel. Bauer went to wait by a window with a view over the roof of the northern wing, heaving grey treetops around it like waves. In the middle distance there was a snow squall bearing down, so that the building seemed to be battling through heavy seas, a ship steaming into a storm.

Behind him the door to Metz's office opened. Bauer turned around and in the doorway saw Metz giving Drexel a hearty double handshake. The two men noticed him at the same time. 'Bauer!' Metz cried. 'You're here to see me, I take it? Come in, come in. Fabian is just leaving.'

Drexel acknowledged Bauer with a nod, dabbed a handkerchief to his mouth and then headed for the stairs. Half concealed on the opposite side of his body was the little wooden box with the decorated lid. Bauer went forward and Metz ushered him into the office. 'Come in, come in,' he repeated, then offered him a seat and sat down not behind but next to his desk, so that their knees were almost touching. His breath smelled bad. Imperceptibly Bauer leaned away. 'So what brings you here on this fine snowy day?'

'I've come to discuss one of your patients, sir.'

'One of *my* patients?'

'Yes, sir. A Private Henninger. Gunshot wound to his lung. He's having difficulty breathing.'

'Understandably, wouldn't you say?'

'More difficulty than might be expected,' Bauer said. 'After surgery. I was concerned and took the liberty of checking your operating notes. You don't seem to have debrided the lung.'

'That's true, I didn't.'

'I don't understand why not.'

'It was an unnecessary risk. The patient was in a bad way on the table.'

Knoll had mentioned no such difficulty. 'Was that Molineux's assessment, sir?'

313

'Bauer, as I'm sure you realise, you coming to me about this is a gross impertinence. But since you ask, I formed my own assessment of the man's condition and adjusted my approach accordingly.'

'And what about his condition now? We have no way of knowing what's inside the lung. There are bound to be blood clots. They could even be purulent.'

'That's speculation, Captain.'

'Which is exactly my point: we can't know. Sir, you were the one who taught me that excessive caution in a case can itself be dangerous.'

'Not always,' Metz said.

'The conservative approach was old-fashioned, you said. It risks leaving the patient a pulmonary cripple.'

'You recollect wrongly, or misunderstood me in the first place,' Metz replied. So far he didn't seem especially annoyed, possibly on account of his visit from Drexel. Even so, Bauer thought, he would have to proceed carefully.

'Sir, would you object if I were to perform a follow-up surgery? Just to make sure?'

Metz smiled. 'Good lord, Bauer, what a butcher you've become.'

Even knowing the accusation had no substance, it stung. 'Sir, obviously I wouldn't advocate putting a patient through surgery twice unless I believed it was absolutely necessary. And, of course, I'm conscious that in doing so I'm implicitly criticising your work. For this I apologise. I can only point out that none of us is perfect, and that the next time I make a mistake, as I certainly will, I hope you'll point it out to me.

For the patient's sake. In fact in France I remember several occasions when you did just that.'

'France was different. You were new to war surgery.'

'I'd like to think we could continue to share our expertise.'

'All right, all right,' Metz said, holding up both hands. 'Go ahead if you must. I won't stand in your way.'

'Thank you, sir,' he said, and really meant it. This was a concession. In fact something close to an admission.

'Is that all? I have reports to write, you know.'

'No, sir, it's not.'

'Oh God, what now?'

'Another impertinence. Sorry.'

Metz sighed. 'All right. What is it? Go ahead.'

'Your hands. I've noticed them shaking at times.'

'Oh?'

'You must have noticed it yourself.'

'A little. On occasion. Fatigue. Generally it disappears when I'm underway.'

'That's not what I've observed.'

'Look,' he said, and held out his right hand. 'Steady as a rock.'

'I'm not saying you're always affected.'

'What *are* you saying, then? That I have some dread disease?'

'No, sir, I'm saying —'

'Your wife died of disseminated sclerosis, did she not?'

Bauer paused, momentarily lost for words, surprised not only at the change of subject but also by a spasm of grief. 'That's true, sir, she did. What of it?'

'I'm guessing it's made you over-vigilant. My hands are a mite unsteady and instantly you're fitting me out for a coffin.'

315

'Sir, it's not illness I'm concerned about but the drugs Drexel is giving you.'

Metz scoffed. 'That again.'

'I'm afraid so.'

'Drexel's supplements steady my nerves, not disturb them.'

'In the short-term, maybe. But now you have this tremor, don't you.'

'More speculation. And anyway, as I've pointed out before, none of this is any of your business.'

'There you're wrong, sir. What about Henninger?'

Metz frowned. 'What are you implying? That I would allow a personal infirmity – an imaginary one, I hasten to add – to influence the kind of surgery I perform?'

'Well, didn't you?'

Metz inhaled sharply but his answer was measured. 'No, I did not.' In an injured tone he added, 'I have to say that I'm surprised and saddened that you could have formed such a low opinion of me, Bauer. But I see your mind's made up about this. We will have to disagree.'

Encouraged, Bauer said, 'Sir, whatever it is that's affecting you – even, as you said, just a case of fatigue – might it be time to consider requesting some leave from active service?'

Metz looked scornful. 'Bauer, that's absurd and you know it. The next offensive —'

'It wouldn't have to be immediately. As you say, that would be impossible. Arrangements would have to be made. But as winter draws on I simply cannot believe that combat will continue at the same intensity. Most of my cases this week have been frostbite. January or February, then, might be a suitable time to go on furlough.'

'Bauer, are you trying to get rid of me?'

'Just considering your welfare, sir. And, to be frank with you, the welfare of the patients. It's no slight on you. No one can be expected to maintain indefinitely the standards you set yourself. And you've been in it from the beginning, haven't you? Since Poland. Longer than me.'

'Well, that's true.' For a moment Bauer thought he might be about to relent, then suddenly his tone became unyielding again. 'But of course it's out of the question. I can't abandon my post. Not now.'

'As I said, sir, it wouldn't have to be immediately.'

'Who would stand up to, you know ...?'

'The enemy?'

Metz shook his head. 'To Tolstoy.'

★ ★ ★

On balance the meeting had gone better than expected; Metz had remained fairly calm, and soon afterwards Bauer was able to operate on Henninger, repairing the damage that Metz had neglected.

What surprised him was how sorry he felt for Metz. The tremor, his self-deception and delusions – however unpleasantly he behaved at times, he was, or had been, a first-rate surgeon, and while Bauer had enjoyed closer friendships with colleagues, there was no one who had taught him so much.

But something had to be done.

When Weidemann opened his door he looked disappointed. 'Oh, it's you,' he said.

'Yes, me,' replied Bauer.

'I thought you might be Ehrlich.' For such a stately man he was looking startlingly informal, his tunic unbuttoned, revealing a white spray of chest hair over the collar of his undershirt. 'Do you know anything about gramophones?'

'No, sir, I don't.'

'Then can it wait until tomorrow? Whatever you're here for, that is.'

'It could, yes. But I don't think it should.'

Weidemann gave a little upwards nod of resignation and motioned him to enter. Compared with the other bedrooms this one was enormous; in Tolstoy's day it had been the marital bedroom, Bauer recalled. Weidemann's camp bed looked small in it. A collapsible writing table. A chair. A glass-fronted sideboard, in which most of Weidemann's belongings were arrayed and on top of which stood Bertha the gramophone. Following his gaze Weidemann said, 'Would you take a look anyway? For the life of me I can't work out what the problem is.'

'I could try.'

'I'd be most grateful to you,' said Weidemann, and sat down on the solitary chair.

Bauer tried switching the device on and off, and when this failed examined all its visible parts. 'Maybe it's the wiring?' he said after a decent interval. 'Sorry, sir, not my area of expertise.'

'If only it bled, eh?'

'That's right. I might then know what to do.'

'Thank you anyway for trying. You know who could've helped? Sepp Winkel.'

'That's true.'

'A terrible business, that. I can't get over the fact he's not here.'

For such a reticent man this was strikingly personal. Bauer nodded. 'I feel the same.'

'Tomorrow I'll put one of the radio operators onto it. In the meantime, how can I help you?'

'It's about Metz,' he replied.

'Again?'

'I'm afraid so,' Bauer said, glancing around and realising that apart from Weidemann's bed there was nowhere to sit.

'What's bothering you? The ghost? Corporal Ehrlich tells me Metz is in hot pursuit.'

'Ehrlich told you that?'

'And he's worried. Mind you, I don't think it's the ghost-hunting that bothers him so much as the involvement of Frau Kälter. He doesn't trust her, he says. Probably he's right to be suspicious – we shouldn't forget she's the enemy – but in Ehrlich's case I suspect jealousy is a factor. He wants Metz to himself. Anyway, he thought I ought to know. And now you're here.'

Bauer hesitated, a little irked to be paired with Ehrlich. 'Well, the ghost thing does remain a problem,' he said. 'In fact it's got worse. But that's not what's brought me here.'

'Worse how?'

'Metz seems to believe he's in some kind of battle with Tolstoy,' Bauer said, and gave Weidemann a brief account of the seance with Katerina and Agrafena Viktorovna.

319

'Metz has always indulged in that sort of thing,' Weidemann said.

'Yes, but now it's more than an indulgence. As far as I can tell, he's attributing cosmic significance to his fight against Tolstoy. Nothing less than the war itself depends on it.'

'How curious.'

'Yes, but as I said, that's not why I'm here. I'm here because Metz's drug habit is almost certainly beginning to hamper him in surgery. He's developed a tremor.' Here he outlined the case of Private Henninger, leaving out how he had come to hear of it from Knoll. 'I've confronted him about it and he denies there's a problem, though when I suggested he take leave I got the impression he was tempted.'

'But not convinced?'

'Duty prevents it. He has to stay and win the war.'

'That sounds like that, then,' Weidemann said.

'I was wondering if you could raise it with a more senior officer.'

'As I believe I mentioned last time, resorting to drugs hardly makes him unusual. Likewise his belief in the supernatural.'

'And his problems in the operating room? Surely that counts for something?'

'He'd have to be killing patients by the dozen for a superior officer to take notice. They have more serious concerns. No, Bauer, I'm afraid I can't help you with this.'

'But what about Pilcz? He got sent home.'

'Because he was inconveniencing Metz. Had Pilcz been a lieutenant colonel ... well, that would've been different. Probably he would have served out the war and been decorated for it. From what I've observed, the higher they go the madder they get.'

'And you're exempted from that?' Bauer asked. In response the points of Weidemann's eyebrows rose. 'I'm not trying to insult you, sir,' Bauer went on, 'just raising the possibility that in this instance I might be thinking more clearly than you are. The patients ...'

Weidemann nodded. 'No doubt you're right. About me being mad, that is, or at least madder than you are.' As if to illustrate this point he stood up, distractedly went over to the gramophone, tried to switch it on, and, when this failed, turned around in his ponderous style and went back to his chair. 'I suppose you remember your first day as a qualified doctor?'

'Indelibly,' Bauer replied, puzzled by this turn in the conversation.

'As do I. I was twenty-three years old. The sixth of August 1904. Tübingen University Hospital, the casualty ward. I had been on duty for twelve minutes when my first patient was brought in, a railway worker with a catastrophic eye injury, one that turned out to be even worse than it looked. At the railway yards a crane hook had swung loose from its cargo, piercing the poor fellow's eye socket and proceeding to swing him about – by the skull, as it were. Well, I did what I could, but as you can imagine the trauma to the brain was severe. I kept thinking he ought to be dead. I *wanted* him to die. Here I was with my first patient, on my first day as a doctor, and ardently I was wishing him dead.'

'And did he die?'

'Eventually. Four days it took.'

'That's one tough introduction to medicine.'

'Quite. And I drew two lessons from it: firstly, that I wasn't cut out to be a surgeon; secondly, that in order to function as any kind of doctor I would have to cultivate *detachment*. I couldn't afford to feel for my patients. Not if I wanted to be of any use to them. I would have to treat patients not as people but as matter.'

'There was no middle ground?'

'For me, no. It was either that or admit that my training had been wasted – that I had spent six years pursuing a vocation for which I was unsuited.' He was staring at the floor, frowning now.

'And this is why you won't intervene with Metz?' Bauer asked, reluctant to let the matter rest. 'You're cultivating detachment?'

Weidemann glanced up, his owlish eyebrows raised in surprise, though only briefly. He replied sadly. 'You could say that. Detachment has become something of a habit, I suppose, like any other frequently repeated behaviour.'

'But surely habits can be broken.'

'You're assuming this one is a problem. To me it's a solution. Being what I am. Perhaps I was unsuited for any profession,' he said, turning introspective again. 'Any profession relating to my fellow man, at least. But how was I to know it? In youth we must act, but in ignorance; later comes knowledge, and with it regret.'

Was this a quote, Bauer wondered, something he ought to recognise? 'If you don't mind me saying so, sir, you make it sound like your life is over. But you're only sixty. Our young people have stumbled straight from childhood into war. You, on the other hand, have the advantage of experience and the seniority to act on it.'

'The main thing experience has taught me is caution. I've learned not to interfere. And age is tiring, don't you find – or are you still too young to have found that out? Morally tiring, I mean. Maybe you still think you can alter the world, but I'm past all that. I wish you luck, Bauer, and I mean that sincerely, but eventually you'll reach the same conclusion. I guarantee it.'

'If you say so.'

'There's no need to sound so bitter about it. Save that until you're old. Now, if you'll forgive me, I'd like some time to myself. It's been a long day.'

TWENTY

At breakfast, Monday, 8 December, the officers' mess was alive with news of a surprise attack by Japanese naval aircraft on the American fleet in Hawaii. By all accounts it had been devastating. Based on the little Bauer knew of the Pacific – coconut palms, grass skirts and outrigger canoes – the thought of war there seemed not only tragic but ludicrous. According to Molineux the thermometer in the forecourt showed a temperature of minus twenty-three degrees, making Hawaii seem a long way away. What the attack meant for the war in Europe no one knew.

Having somehow missed her the previous day, and the day before that, Bauer was hoping see Katerina, but when he reached the hospital he was intercepted by Demchak asking to speak with him in private. The operating room was empty, and they went inside.

'I have a crime to report,' Demchak said.

'What sort of crime?'

'Lieutenant Hirsch, he tried to touch me. This happened in the sauna.'

Bauer frowned. 'Touch?'

'He put his hand on my thigh. But it was my dick he was going for.'

Bauer excused himself, went over to the door and closed it. 'Cigarette?' he asked as he returned to Demchak.

'No thank you, sir.'

Bauer took a cigarette from his cigarette case, lit it and inhaled. No wonder Demchak had wanted to speak with him in private. 'You're not mistaken?' he said. 'He didn't bump you by accident?'

'Sir, he put his hand on my thigh and was reaching for my dick.'

'And how did you react?'

Demchak looked incensed. 'I knocked his hand off and got out of there. How else would I respond?'

'Settle down, Private. I'm only trying to understand.'

'I can't work with him any more. I won't. I refuse.' Bauer hadn't seen him so animated since his denunciation of Bolshevism on their way to Malevka. He wanted to disbelieve the accusation but found that difficult. An athletic build, snowy blond hair and, despite the cleft-lip scar, a handsome face: it was easy to see how a man inclined in that direction might find Yuri Demchak attractive. Apart from anything else, Demchak had no motive to lie; in fact, he was creating problems for himself. Indeed, as a Ukrainian making allegations against a German officer he was putting his life at risk.

'Why were you alone in the sauna with him anyway?' Bauer asked.

'I wasn't, not at first. When he arrived there were several of us. Straight away we went to go, even though it was him who wasn't meant to be there, not us. He told us to stay, but after a while the others left anyway.'

'But not you?'

'He wasn't meant to be there! I didn't see why I should have to go. How was I to know he was a pansy?'

'All right, all right, there's no need to speak like that.'

'Why not? It's the truth.'

'Look, just leave this with me. I'll speak with him and work out what's going on.'

'He's a pervert, that's what's going on.'

'Just leave it with me.'

'Sir, I can't work with him,' Demchak said, his voice rising again. 'I *won't* work with him. Not today, not ever.'

'You *will* work with him today. I'll need time to sort this out. You've made a grave accusation. If you're disbelieved, things could go badly for you.'

'I'm not making it up.'

'Just work with the lieutenant as normal today, and this evening I'll sort it out. You haven't mentioned this to anyone else, have you?'

'No, not yet,' he said sullenly, making it sound like a threat.

'Good. Then keep it that way.'

★   ★   ★

In surgery that day Hirsch and Demchak said even less than usual and nothing at all to each other. Still recuperating from his illness, Bauer felt weak and distracted, a tussle of hope and apprehension in his gut – about Katerina; how soon he would

326

see her again; and, increasingly, infuriatingly, about the need to question Hirsch. What a fool the man had been! If Demchak had placed himself in danger then so too had Hirsch, and in another unit either man might have found himself facing a firing squad.

Surgically speaking the shift was routine until, early in the evening, he opened up a grenadier with a suspected case of appendicitis and discovered, instead of an inflamed appendix, the livid, rubbery mass of a colon tumour. Further exploration revealed more tumours in the stomach lining, the pancreas and on the liver. Even to his operating assistants it was clear what was wrong. Bauer set about excising as much of the cancer as he could – to remove all of it was impossible – and then closed the incision. The grenadier was thirty-nine. Later Bauer would have to give him the news he was dying, a dismal duty to add to the annoying one concerning Hirsch.

He meant to speak with the lieutenant when their shift was over, but before he could ask him to stay behind Hirsch was out of his scrubs and away. Bauer strode after him into the entrance hall, and there came face to face with Katerina. 'Look at you,' she said, 'all splashed with Aryan blood.'

For all his thinking about her, the suddenness of the reunion caught him by surprise, and at first he couldn't speak. He looked down at his scrubs, the bloodied midriff like a child's experiment with paint. 'I'm sorry,' he said, and gestured at Hirsch, already in his greatcoat and heading through the vestibule. 'I wanted a word with my anaesthetist.'

She followed his gaze then looked back again. 'In that case, you'd better run.'

'It can wait,' he said firmly.

'Good,' she replied. 'Because I'm here to see you.'

'You do know that the lieutenant colonel wants you to liaise only with him now?' he asked, aching for her to stay.

'I do, yes.'

He nodded. 'Then let me clean up.'

He returned to the operating room, removed his scrubs and washed his hands and face. It occurred to him that she might be here about poor Pyotr Kirov, his missing eye, in which case he was about to be lambasted, though for the incorrect reason.

'Is here all right?' he asked when he got back to the entrance hall.

'I think not. Is that dental room empty again?'

'My anaesthetist is also the dentist, so yes.'

He went ahead of her up the steps, frowning to mask a sudden sense of trepidation and to ward off the stares of several corpsmen who were watching.

In the dental room he closed the door behind them, switched on the overhead bulb and was debating whether they needed the examination lamp when he became conscious of Katerina staring at him, her stance unnaturally still. Her eyes were unnerving, wet and bright, and instinctively he too went motionless, blood tunnelling in his fingertips, his throat. Then she advanced on him, so abruptly and with such purity of intent that he knew he would either be kissed or killed, and even raised an arm to fend her off, so strong was his instinct that she might have a knife. Her momentum drove him back against the wall and, yes, she was kissing him – no reconnoitring of his lips, just her invading tongue, then her fingers on his teeth, opening and claiming him; and he let her, counter-kissed and adored her, lifted and whirled her and placed her back down, and their hands opened gaps in their clothes.

★ ★ ★

They lay on the floor, panting, still mostly clothed but warmly and wetly joined, he on his back, she slumped on his chest, her Amazonian strength expended. He smelled her hair, the particularity of her skin, and vowed to remember it – no, to always have it near. Then he held her and lay unmoving for a time, until Katerina raised her head and fixed him with her warm brown eyes.

'Well,' he said.

'Well,' she countered.

He was still firm in her. Between them, the savour of their scents. 'I thought I was in trouble,' he said.

'This isn't trouble?'

'A different sort of trouble.'

'Like?'

'Pyotr Kirov?' he said.

She shook her head, still smiling. 'You fool,' she said, calling him *du* for the first time – a jolt of intimacy as thrilling, or more so, than their coupling. 'You were the one who tried to save him.'

He felt himself go soft. 'It was me who shot him,' he replied. Katerina frowned, made to speak but didn't, and abruptly rolled off him, letting in the cold. Bauer cursed himself. Katerina propped up her head on one elbow and, in a voice that was suddenly forensic and cool, asked him what had happened. He'd presumed too much, he thought, been foolishly greedy – not for absolution, exactly (that was too much to ask), but for unrestricted communion. Resigning himself to the worst he described the morning of the failed offensive: the bombardment, the confusion at the dressing station, seeing Pyotr Kirov running by and shouting at him to stop. The boy's reaction. Gunning him down.

When he was finished Katerina was quiet for a time. The greed he felt now was to keep gazing at her, or with his fingertips to trace the lines on her face as year by year they deepened and branched. She said, 'I take it you've killed in surgery? Inadvertently, I mean. Done something that caused or hastened a patient's death?'

'Yes, probably,' he said. 'In fact, certainly. Though that's hardly the same, is it?'

'It's similar,' she declared. 'You didn't plan to shoot the boy. Any sane person would have acted as you did. I would have, in your position. And I *have* been in your position, or something like it.'

He doubted he deserved this forgiveness, but the allure of it was strong, her leniency a sweet benediction. He thanked her, and she hooked a thigh across his hips. Drew him closer, warming him where their bodies met. And there again were her eyes, her irises, filigreed brown, which if not for the curfew he could have studied for hours. Furtively he glanced past her shoulder at his watch, a movement she sensed and immediately deciphered. 'How long do we have?'

'About forty-five minutes,' he replied.

'Not enough,' she said. 'Could you hide me somewhere?'

'My God, if only,' he said, both frustrated and elated.

'You've managed it poorly, this business of being German,' she said.

'True,' he said. 'Though if I wasn't German I wouldn't be here,' he pointed out.

'I know, and I hate you for it,' she said, running a hand across his chest.

He told her then of the dire conditions he'd witnessed at the front, his countrymen's low morale and his newfound certainty that Germany would lose the war.

'That's what I've been telling you,' she said.

'And I should have believed you. Anyway, now I've seen for myself.'

She would be unaware, he realised, of the Japanese attack at Pearl Harbor, and so he told her what little about it he knew.

'Hell's bells,' she said, 'the Americans won't like that.'

'No, I don't suppose they will.'

'Now you'll *definitely* lose the war. Is that a fascist quirk: attacking nations more populous than your own?'

'I don't speak for fascists,' he replied.

She prodded the eagle and swastika embroidered above the pocket of his tunic. 'Just dress like them.'

'A necessary ruse,' he said.

'Your camouflage.'

He drew her still closer and they said nothing for a time, Bauer nuzzling her hair until she lifted her chin and they kissed again, gently this time, less urgently than before. With his lips he mapped her throat, her ears. He kissed her forehead and both her eyelids in turn. For a long time he luxuriated in not needing to speak, until, growing conscious of time passing, he pulled away from her a little. 'Why now?' he asked her.

She met his eyes again and smiled. 'Because I missed you,' she said. 'When you were gone I missed you. I tried not to but the feeling got worse.'

'Better, surely?'

'Worse,' she said firmly, 'because look at me now.'

'I am looking.'

'My arms around a man I'm going to lose.'

Was there a word for what he was feeling, he wondered, this polarity of exhilaration and despair? If there was he didn't know it. He thought of asking Katerina, an expert, but that would waste what little time remained, and so instead he leaned closer and feathered his lips against hers, wanting everything: the soft, the steely, the pain, the joy – the alpha and omega of her body, heart and mind. He checked his watch and groaned. 'You have to go!'

'How soon?'

'Too soon for me.'

'Oh, my poor darling,' she said and, with deftness and force, manoeuvred herself beneath him. 'Then you'll have to hurry. I'm not finished with you yet.'

TWENTY-ONE

They parted at the entrance gates under an almost full moon. *Joy*, he thought, his heart volcanic, pained, *this is joy*. He wanted to bound after her but there were sentries watching, and this alone explained the pain, he realised. He and Katerina weren't parting, they were *being* parted – meaning by circumstances, by forces that were hostile or, at best, indifferent to their fates.

The sky was clear and mercifully still, the stars like specks of ice. Katerina was clearly visible in the silvery light, a booted, quilted and hatted silhouette walking away towards the village. Both sentries were casting glances at him, a madman voluntarily lingering out of doors, and because he couldn't bear yet to turn away he brought out a cigarette and started smoking in a ruminative style, as if he were reflecting on the glories of the stars and the moon and not of the woman disappearing down the road.

When he could no longer see her he flicked away what was left of his cigarette, nodded to the sentries, turned and trudged back along the driveway in the dark. The artillery fire around Tula was muffled, intermittent, a giant murmuring in sleep.

Back at the house Zöllner told him Hirsch had gone to bed, for which Bauer was greatly relieved. Tonight was not the night to be grappling with a problem of that kind. Instead he prepared for bed himself, his heart brimming with Katerina, determined for now not to think of whatever lay ahead. Reluctantly he washed his hands and face. For a change he fell quickly asleep.

In the morning he woke still thinking of Katerina, though alongside his happiness there was a sense of unease, a recognition that having a new stake in life also meant having something to lose. It was foolish, he supposed, to let this thought mar his mood, but years of dread and sorrow about Clara's illness had taken their toll, and the best things in life now came with a quota of fear.

As he and Molineux were getting dressed, Hirsch appeared in the corridor outside their room. 'Well, look who's here,' Molineux said, 'the scourge of wit. What do you want?'

'I asked him to drop by,' Bauer said.

'For what?'

'To decide the fate of Europe.'

'Nothing important then. I'll leave you to it. But remember, Hirsch, I've got my eye on you.'

'Don't mind him,' Bauer said when Molineux was gone. 'He's trying to cope, like the rest of us.'

'By being nasty?'

'By being provocative. But I agree it's uncalled for.'

'Hans said you wanted to see me, sir.'

'That's right. Take a seat,' he said, gestured at Molineux's bed and sat down on his own. 'There's no easy way of raising this, Volker, so I'll just begin. I've had a complaint about you.'

'A complaint?'

'From Private Demchak.'

'*Yuri?* About what?'

'You can't guess?'

'I have no idea.'

'He says you tried to touch him. Touch him sexually. This was in the sauna, he says.'

Hirsch looked, or pretended to be, amazed. 'But that's ... crazy. I can't believe ... that is, why would he say that?'

'Are you denying it?'

'Yes!'

'Then why do you think he's come to me?'

'I don't know. I can't explain it. He's made a mistake. Or ...'

'Or?'

'Someone has put him up to it.'

'Why would anyone do that?'

'Because they hate me.'

'They?'

'They all hate me.'

'Now, now, that's not true,' Bauer replied, a little uncertainly, taken aback by the force of Hirsch's loneliness.

'Ehrlich, for one. He hates me.'

'What makes you say that?'

'He always lurking around,' Hirsch said. 'Poking through my stuff. He's got it in for me.'

'He's your orderly,' Bauer said, 'it's his job to tidy up your gear.' The fact that Bauer also distrusted Ehrlich made it no easier, somehow, to take Hirsch's accusation seriously.

'Or Captain Molineux.'

'Now I know Molineux is rough on you, but I don't think —'

'Or Drexel. Even Metz.'

Bauer breathed in deeply and exhaled. 'Even if all these people hated you – and I don't believe they do – it seems frankly incredible to me that Ehrlich or anyone else would want to land you in such serious trouble. Or that Demchak would agree to make a false accusation.'

'Why wouldn't he? He's their subordinate. They must have pressured him somehow.'

Bauer paused. They were getting nowhere. 'Could you have done anything that Yuri might have misinterpreted? Touched him in some other way?'

Hirsch looked downwards, and his forehead flexed. 'I suppose it's possible I could have touched him accidentally,' he said, and raised his head again. 'We were sitting quite close. I wasn't paying much attention.'

'All right, but then the question arises – sorry, I need to understand what's gone on here – why were you sitting so close to him in the first place? There was no one else there. For that matter, can you explain what you were doing in the sauna at a time set aside for the men?'

'That was a mistake, I see that now.'

'You didn't know the roster?' Bauer asked, guiltily recalling that not long ago he had also ignored the roster and intruded on Sepp Winkel's time alone in the sauna. Not that anyone else would learn of that now.

'I didn't think it mattered very much. Obviously I was wrong about that.'

'And sitting so close?'

'When I went in it was crowded, and Yuri – Private Demchak – made room for me on the bench. Then the others

336

gradually went away and it was just the two of us. I didn't think of moving. It would have seemed rude.'

Bauer glanced about, suddenly fed up with having to play the interrogator. He turned back to Hirsch again. 'However it came about, it's placed you – it's placed both of us – in a difficult position. You do know, don't you, what the official penalty is? I mean, for homosexual conduct?'

'I've never looked into it.'

'Well, I'm sure you can guess. Not that there's any question of it coming to that. I only mention it to point out how carefully this has to be managed.'

'I'm not a homosexual.'

'Very well. But regardless of what you say you are or are not, Private Demchak is refusing to work with you again.'

'He says *that*?'

'He does.'

'That's ... unbelievable. We're comrades.'

'Not in his view. Not any more.'

Hirsch looked miserable, more distraught, apparently, at the thought of Demchak's antipathy than at the prospect of being shot.

Bauer stood up, anxious to bring the conversation to an end. 'Look, I'll try to speak with him again. Explain to him there must have been a misunderstanding of some kind, that you're terribly sorry and that nothing like it will ever happen again. All right?' Hirsch was staring at the floor, lost in misery. 'All right?' Bauer repeated more sharply.

'Yes, sir. A misunderstanding.'

337

My God, there was something so deeply dubious about Hirsch. It was nothing malignant, nothing bad, but it did emphasise the need to shield Hirsch from formal proceedings of any kind.

'I'll do my best,' Bauer said. 'In the meantime don't do or say anything to Yuri that he might misconstrue. Not now, not ever.'

★   ★   ★

By chance it was Metz's turn to operate, which gave Bauer an opportunity to placate Demchak before he next worked with Hirsch. Bauer's first duty, though, was in the post-operative ward, where he had to break the bad news to the grenadier with cancer. The man took it well, or seemed to, and even chuckled, if only for a moment, at the absurdity of dying of natural causes. Would he be able to go home and see his children? Bauer told him he would, and this seemed to cheer him. Presumably the reality of the diagnosis was yet to sink in, but Bauer hoped that if he were ever confronted with his own impending death he would be able to behave with equal composure.

He spoke with Demchak in the hospital vestibule, lowering his voice whenever another corpsman went by. Demchak heard him out in silence. When he was finished he replied, 'Sir, that isn't good enough.'

'Oh?' Bauer said, disguising his annoyance. 'And what would you prefer?'

'He should go up on charges.'

'For a misunderstanding?'

'It was no misunderstanding.'

'Hirsch says it was.'

'The lieutenant is a pervert. If I have to, I'll say so to the lieutenant colonel himself.'

Bauer narrowed his eyes at him. 'You want Hirsch to go before a firing squad?'

'If that's the penalty, yes.'

'You hate him that much?'

'I don't hate him at all.'

'And yet you want him dead?'

'They're your laws, sir.'

There was a debate to be had here about politics and jurisprudence, but now was not the right time. 'Have you thought about the damage you'd be doing to the battalion?'

'What damage?'

'Lieutenant Hirsch's service is invaluable,' he said. 'Not only in surgery but as a dental officer. I thought you wanted to beat the Bolsheviks.'

'I do. That's why justice should be done.'

'You'll have to explain your thinking there, because I'm certainly not following it.'

'All right,' Demchak said, his tone insultingly patient. 'Ask yourself what we're fighting for.'

'Why don't you tell me.'

'We're fighting to defeat Bolshevism. But what is Bolshevism? First and foremost it's the Jews. Marx was a Jew. Intellectuals are usually Jews.'

'But Volker Hirsch isn't Jewish. Or intellectual, come to that.'

'He's a homosexual, and that puts him on the side of the Jews. Homosexuals, Jews, the intelligentsia – they band together in cities, and what do they do there? They hatch ideas like Marxism – ideas they then force onto others, however many they have to kill to do it. The point is we have to be morally superior to the enemy. If we aren't, what are we doing? We want a better world, and Hirsch and his ilk don't belong in it.'

Bauer regarded him for a moment then said, 'I see you've thought about this. In fact, it seems to me you're on the way to becoming something of an intellectual yourself.' Demchak's eyebrows rose at this but quickly resettled. 'I'm a surgeon, not an intellectual,' Bauer continued, 'but like you I used to be a farmer, and like most farmers I have a practical side. You come to me with a problem, a problem that needs a practical solution. You're not satisfied with the lieutenant's explanation, so tell me, what would you be satisfied with? What if he went to another unit?'

'And did the same thing there?'

'Or if we transferred you. You said you wanted to go to a fighting unit. Maybe it's time we looked into it. See if I can pull some strings. Your good German should help. And the blond hair won't hurt. As you said, we need committed men at the front.'

Demchak hesitated, clearly considering the offer, only for his face to harden again. 'Not at the cost of sweeping this under the carpet.'

Bauer contemplated him, this blond crusader, this Teutonic Knight, bent on purification by the sword. That he was ethnically Slavic was an oddity, a paradox that might explain some of his fanaticism, with the nightmare of his adolescent years accounting for the rest. Arguing with him was probably futile, Bauer realised, but he would give it one last go, both to save Demchak from his own zealotry and himself from a great deal of paperwork.

'Remind me how old you are,' he said, though he knew the answer already.

'I'm twenty-two,' Demchak said warily.

'Me, I'm forty-one,' he said, and paused, preparing his argument. 'From the vantage point of forty-one, twenty-two seems …' Ignorant? Simplistic? 'Admirable,' he said. 'Twenty-two seems admirable in ways that make forty-one seem – *feel* – weary, unimaginative and in some ways confusing. In you I see clarity of purpose, the sort of clarity essential to winning the war.'

'That's just what I'm saying —'

'But which will just as surely lose it if older, wearier men don't also have their say.' He thought of Bagration and Kutuzov in *War and Peace*, unflashy generals whose recognition of the limitations of command paradoxically made them more formidable. Demchak was looking guardedly at him. Bauer went on. 'I'm not trying to convince you you're wrong. I wouldn't succeed. But I am asking you to accept that we all bring something different to the war effort. Let me deal with Hirsch. You're clever, you're energetic, and by age and temperament, yes, you're probably better suited to combat than to standing beside an instruments tray and handing me forceps or gauze. So let's find a way to get you under arms.'

'In return for me saying nothing?'

'Yes.'

Demchak shook his head, apparently not even tempted this time. 'Sorry, sir, but I won't bargain away my principles.'

'Rather proving my point about your youth, don't you think? An older man might be readier to bargain.'

'Will you have Hirsch charged?'

'No, I won't.'

'Because you're homosexual yourself?'

Bauer felt the full venom of this, and the threat. 'Perhaps because Lieutenant Hirsch is a fellow German,' he said. 'You've been clear with me and so I'll be clear with you. If you take this over my head I will tell Metz you're lying, that you have something against Hirsch and that you want to bring him down.'

'You think I'm lying?'

'What I think is of no importance. You've made that quite clear. What I'm *saying* is that if you go to Metz I will make things as difficult for you as possible. I will deny having had this conversation. I will accuse you of making sexual advances on Hirsch and then lying about it to protect yourself.'

'So you are a homosexual.'

Ignoring this, Bauer said, 'Who do you think Metz will believe? A Ukrainian *Hilfswilliger* or a fellow officer and surgeon?' Demchak eyed him narrowly, and Bauer stared back with an appearance of calm. 'I'd call that stalemate, wouldn't you?'

★ ★ ★

'Right away,' Katerina said.

'Why, what's the problem?' Bauer said, his delight in seeing her instantly blighted by her tone.

'Daria Grigorievna went off with some of your enlisted men. Tikhon Vassilyvich saw them.'

'Off where?'

'To the Kusminsky Wing.'

He cursed. It was dark and getting close to curfew time; a benign explanation was unlikely. 'This was how long ago?'

'An hour at least. More.'

'All right. I'll get my coat.'

From his room Bauer fetched his greatcoat, gloves and cap and clattered back downstairs. Katerina was waiting for him in the vestibule. She opened the door and together they stepped out into the dark, passed the sentry on the porch and strode onto the snow. No wind. A heavy mist. Tooth-fracturing cold. The urge to hold her hand was great, but now was not the time; from the Kusminsky Wing came the noise of carousing.

'Was she distressed?' he asked. 'Did Tikhon say how she looked?'

'Your men had alcohol, so I'm sure she was pleased.'

Ahead of them the barracks loomed out of the mist, the cheering inside it increasingly loud. On the front steps the duty sentry greeted him with suspicious bonhomie; Bauer returned his salute then turned back to Katerina. 'Better wait here.'

She scowled. 'Better leave that decision to me.'

Together they went into the entrance hall and the noise of the revelry grew. Its source was the common room, whose entrance was crowded with corpsmen looking in, cigarette smoke rolling overhead. 'Follow me,' Bauer said to Katerina and muscled between them, entering a crush of men chanting and clapping in time as Daria Grigorievna, wearing only her drawers, danced drunkenly on a table at the centre of the room, boot polish smeared across her breasts. With no hope of making himself heard Bauer pushed deeper into the throng, followed closely by Katerina, men on either side of them quietening as they passed, though when they reached the table another half minute went by before the entire room came to attention.

'Show's over, gentlemen,' Bauer said, as Katerina helped Daria off the table.

'Why, where's the harm in it?' someone called – Norbert Ritter, Bauer realised, his grating voice slurred. Bauer sought out his face from the crowd, saw Ehrlich and Knoll and eventually made out Ritter, who hadn't come to attention but was instead holding a mug between boot-polished hands.

'No fraternising with enemy civilians,' Bauer said. 'Lieutenant Colonel's orders.'

'It's not fraternising,' Ritter said. He grinned and glanced around the room. 'It's *cabaret*.'

Widespread laughter, giving Bauer time to hope there was no afterlife from which Sepp was watching on.

'Where are her clothes?' Katerina called. No one answered her.

'Where are the lady's clothes?' Bauer repeated.

'The *lady*,' Ritter sneered. 'What's it to you anyway?' he asked, and waved his mug at Katerina. 'You've got pussy of your own.'

The laughter this time was less rowdy. 'Sergeant Major, you're drunk,' Bauer said, avoiding Katerina's eye. 'Get out of here and sober up.'

Ritter didn't move, and abruptly Bauer's greatcoat felt too hot, the fiction of his rank unpleasantly exposed; then Ritter

344

did move, looking theatrically scornful and disgusted, opening a path through the crowd to the door.

Bauer gazed about the room. 'The clothes,' he repeated. There were murmured consultations and then from somewhere on the floor the clothes appeared, Daria's dress partly ripped and with buttons missing. 'Now clear out of here, all of you,' Bauer said.

There was a general movement towards the door and with it more talk, mostly grievance, a low hubbub of complaint. By the table Katerina was supporting Daria by the arm; already she had boot polish on her jacket and face. Bauer asked if she needed help, and curtly she refused. He would be just outside, guarding the door, he told her.

Most of the men had dispersed, but about thirty, including Ritter and Ehrlich, had taken their drinks into the entrance hall and onto the stairs and were growing raucous again. Ritter wasn't the only one with blackened hands. From the common room came the sound of Daria and Katerina arguing, to which the men raised a mocking cheer. Bauer wondered if Daria's drunkenness ever took a violent turn; he guessed she weighed at least a third more than Katerina.

The women emerged a few minutes later, Daria dishevelled, one arm hooked around Katerina's shoulders. Both women's faces were streaked with polish, Katerina's even more than Daria's. Bauer went forward to help them just as Daria sagged, pulling Katerina down on top of her. In the hilarity that followed Bauer could make out Ehrlich's high and irritating laughter, like a terrier's bark. Did Ehrlich have a mother, Bauer wondered, who doted on that laugh, who always smiled when she heard it? Possibly, he supposed.

In a world-weary tone he called for quiet, then set about organising a sled to carry Daria to the estate's front gates, where according to Katerina the steward was waiting with a sleigh. Her manner was distant, her sentences short, the gap between them more than Bauer could bear.

When they stepped outside the cold was a slap in the face. *This* was the land they wanted to conquer? Jesus Christ, in winter was it even habitable? Two of the corpsmen whose aid he'd enlisted brought Daria out of the house on a stretcher and lashed it to the sled. They covered her with blankets, and seconds later were dragging the sled in the direction of the gates, Bauer trudging wordlessly alongside Katerina in the rear. The cold was stupefying, his head as empty as a bell.

As Katerina had promised, Tikhon Vassilyvich was waiting for them opposite the sentry post, snow in his beard and on a blanket-draped nag that pulled the sleigh. With the old man's help they loaded Daria in the back, and Katerina climbed in beside her.

'I'm so sorry about all this,' Bauer said.

'I should get her home,' Katerina replied.

'Will I see you tomorrow?' he asked her in a whisper.

'I don't know.'

Tikhon Vassilyvich geed up the horse, and Bauer gripped the side rail of the sleigh. 'Katerina, I love you,' he said, and at last her eyes met his.

'I know you do,' she said. 'I know.'

The sleigh jerked and Bauer's gloves slipped off the rail, then with a cry and a crack of the whip Tikhon Vassilyvich urged on his horse and the sleigh picked up speed and was gone.

TWENTY-TWO

He had just sat down at breakfast with a steaming hot bowl of oatmeal when Ehrlich arrived with a summons from Metz.

'Now?' Bauer asked him, and gazed down at the oatmeal, which his brain already had in his stomach.

'Immediately,' Ehrlich said. He looked pleased with himself, which put Bauer on guard and made him wonder again at the cause of Ehrlich's malice. It seemed too late to ask.

'Very well,' he said, got up, took his mess tin to Pabst to keep warm and then followed Ehrlich out of the mess. Possibly there was *nothing* behind the corporal's dislike for him, he thought – nothing specific, at least, nothing personal, his hostility more like a parasite that passes from one to another and pupates and squirms in its host.

Standing in the corridor outside Metz's study was Yuri Demchak, his expression calm. You idiot, Bauer thought, you bloody fool, but he said nothing and made his face inscrutable. Ehrlich ducked his head into the study and announced him, then ushered him into the study and withdrew.

Metz was at his desk, pen in hand, his head bent over some documents. 'Captain,' he said without looking up. 'Sit down, will you,' he added, annotating – or pretending to. He looked up. Cleared his throat. 'Your *Hilfswilliger* … no doubt you saw him in the hall?'

'I did.'

'What's his name again?'

'Demchak, sir. Yuri Demchak.'

'This Demchak has come to me with a repulsive tale. He says Lieutenant Hirsch has made certain advances towards him. Of an improper nature. Advances of a sexual kind. He also says you refused to do anything about it.'

Bauer hesitated. He'd told Demchak he would deny everything, but now couldn't bring himself to lie. 'Yes, sir, Private Demchak did mention this matter. But I acted on it straight away by confronting Lieutenant Hirsch with the claim.'

'And?'

'He denied it.'

'I'm glad to hear that. So this Demchak is a troublemaker?'

'I wouldn't put it like that, sir,' he said, not yet ready to abandon Demchak entirely.

'Then how would you put it? A foreigner impugning, in the foulest way, the honour of a German officer —'

'It was a misunderstanding, sir. Lieutenant Hirsch was where he shouldn't have been —'

'The delousing station, wasn't it? The sauna?'

'Correct. They were in the sauna, and what I believe occurred is that Lieutenant Hirsch touched the corpsman accidentally.'

'Is that likely?'

Bauer explained the sequence of events: Hirsch's arrival and the gradual departure of Demchak's comrades, leaving the two remaining men sitting close together.

Metz scowled. 'Sounds to me as if the Hiwi has a score to settle. Let's get him back in here.'

'Sir, this whole thing is a distraction. We have far better things to do.'

Metz looked at him sternly. 'I'll be the one who decides that, thank you. In fact, it was very wrong of you not to bring the matter to me straight away.'

'Because I thought it was trivial.'

'Unit morale, Captain, should be the leader's paramount consideration. There are two types of officer: those who make it their business to know what's going on in the ranks and those who don't. Now, let's have this Hiwi in again, shall we. *Ehrlich!*'

Ehrlich reappeared and Metz told him to bring Demchak back in. Demchak reappeared, marched to Metz's desk and came to attention.

Metz said, 'I've been speaking with Captain Bauer about the matter you raised. I think you're lying.' Demchak's normally rigid eyebrows twitched. 'The captain here merely thinks you're mistaken.'

'Sir, I'm not lying,' Demchak said. 'And I'm not mistaken.'

'So tell me, what *did* happen? The details. This is your chance to tell the truth.'

Demchak drew himself even more rigidly to attention and repeated his story, its facts unchanged from the version he'd told three days earlier but the phrasing somewhat different, a combination that to Bauer rather enhanced its credibility.

349

'And was the lieutenant aroused when this happened?' Metz asked.

Bauer looked at him sharply, unsure he'd heard correctly. Demchak, too, looked disconcerted. 'How do you mean, sir?'

'Good grief, man. Was he erect?'

'Well, no, sir, not really.'

'Not really?'

'He was, I would say, sir, semi-erect.'

'And were you? Erect, I mean?'

'No!' he said, shocked into raising his voice.

'And what else do you have to say for yourself?'

'Nothing, sir. That is, nothing apart from what I told the captain yesterday: that I have no axe to grind against the lieutenant, no reason to make any of this up. My only concern is with the moral health of the battalion.'

Metz harrumphed then said, 'We'll see about that. You can go back to your duties. On your way out tell Ehrlich to fetch Lieutenant Hirsch.'

'Yes, sir,' Demchak said, saluted and left the room.

'Forgive me, sir,' Bauer said, 'but this is all a waste of time. Private Demchak says one thing, Lieutenant Hirsch another. It's one man's word against another, and questioning Hirsch again is unlikely to get us closer to the truth.'

'There you go again with your counsel of despair: it can't be done, it's pointless, we shouldn't bother to try. Well, as it happens, I don't regard it as one man's word against another. Hirsch is a comrade. The Hiwi isn't. He'll have to go.'

'Go where?'

'A POW camp, I should think. Where else?'

'Sir, he's in German uniform, and even if we could find him a Soviet one he might be found out by his fellow prisoners and killed. Can I suggest another option?'

'Such as?'

'If the incident was an honest misunderstanding, it follows that sacrificing Demchak would be a mistake. He's an outstanding operating assistant. Let's not waste those skills. Let's separate these men by transferring one of them out of the unit. As you know I've been unhappy with Hirsch as my anaesthetist —'

'No, absolutely not,' Metz said. 'I won't have Hirsch suffer on account of the allegations of a Hiwi.'

'Even if we end up with a better anaesthetist?'

'That matter is closed. Apart from anything else I would need to find a new dentist.'

'Very well, then transfer Demchak, if not to a medical unit then to a fighting one. God knows it's time we put Hiwi volunteers under arms. Demchak in particular hates the Reds.'

There was a knock on the door, and Metz called out, inviting whoever it was to come inside. It was Ehrlich. 'Lieutenant Hirsch to see you, sir.'

'Send him in.'

Hirsch entered, looking nervous. Nothing unusual in that, and to set him at ease Bauer caught his eye and smiled. Unlike Demchak, who'd had to stand, Hirsch was offered a chair.

'Lieutenant,' Metz said, 'I've asked you here to discuss this nasty business with the Hiwi. I believe that Captain Bauer here has raised the matter with you?'

'He has, sir,' Hirsch said, and sent Bauer a look of reproach.

'It's an outrageous claim, of course,' Metz said, 'the kind of thing that could only come from a diseased imagination. You deny it, I take it.'

'Yes, I do, sir,' Hirsch said with impressive conviction, then rather spoiled it by adding another yes.

'Good,' Metz said. 'Any idea why he might have made something like that up? Does he hold a grudge against you?'

'Not that I'm aware of, sir.'

'Just malice, then. Stirring up trouble. I told you so, Bauer. So much for your dewy-eyed postulations. When the next POW column goes past, our Hiwi will be joining it. Till then I'll have Ritter put him under lock and key.'

'Sir, as I said, I believe you're making a mistake,' Bauer said.

'I bet Hirsch here doesn't see it that way. Do you, Lieutenant?'

Hirsch looked confused. 'POW column? You're sending him away?'

'He's lucky I'm not having him shot,' Metz said.

Hirsch's gaze darted from one to the other.

'What is it?' Metz said.

'It's just that I agree with the captain. You're making a mistake.'

'Oh? Why is that?'

Hirsch looked down and then up again. 'Because Yuri is telling the truth.'

'For Christ's *sake*,' Bauer said. 'Just shut up, Volker.'

'It's all right, sir,' Hirsch said, standing up. 'It doesn't matter any more.' Calmly he unbuttoned his holster, pulled out his pistol and held it to his head.

'Don't!' Bauer yelled, and leaped out of his chair. The shot punched Hirsch sideways, spraying matter from his head. Too late Bauer covered his ears.

'*Scheisse!*' Metz screamed. 'Shit and fuck it all to hell!'

Bauer squatted beside Hirsch's body. He was definitely dead. A chunk of his left skull had gone, and along with it much of his brain.

'Ehrlich!' Metz cried, but Ehrlich was already there, and when Metz spoke again his voice was changed, strangely calm. 'Clean it up, will you, Corporal.' From the corridor came the sound of men running; a sentry strode into the room, and in the doorway several others appeared, among them Drexel, Zöllner and Waldo Pabst. Ignoring their presence, Metz sat down, dragged his paperwork towards him, picked up his pen and started marking the pages.

'Sir?' Ehrlich said.

'Clean it up.'

'He's dead?'

'Of course he's dead. Get him out of here. And mop the damn floor.' He glanced up and saw the onlookers. 'Get out, the lot of you!' he yelled, suddenly furious again. 'To work, to work. What do you think this is, a *zoo*?' The men in the doorway backed away, but slowly, some hesitating in the corridor. 'The lot of you! You too, Captain, *out*,' he shouted, and Bauer made for the door. To the sentry Metz shrieked, 'Not you, damn it! Give the corporal a hand.'

Bauer reached the doorway and looked back inside just as Ehrlich and the sentry raised the body by its armpits and ankles, causing more bone and brain tissue to tumble to the floor. Where the head had lain, a Rorschach puddle of blood.

TWENTY-THREE

Stanford, California
3 January 1969

Dear Paul,
How tenacious you are! It's becoming clearer to me how
you survived the Gulag. No, I don't believe anyone would
want to publish my novels in translation. Why would they?
Forty-five years on, and despite your kind comments about
them, their main value is not literary but sociological and
historical, and anyone with those interests can read them
in Russian. Oh, and by the way, when I say that your
comments were 'kind' I also mean they were mentally
deranged. You think *Europa, 1975* is reminiscent of Kafka?
In the same way, I suppose, that Walt Disney's *Bambi* is
reminiscent of ... I don't know, *Battleship Potemkin*? Good
God, Paul, in a single sentence you have shattered my faith
in your critical faculties.

  Anyway, who really cares about novels any more?
Outside of the Soviet Union and its vassal states, I mean,

where the authorities have done wonders for the prestige
of good writing by banning it. In contrast, the more time
I spend in the West the more I realise that the visual media
are destined (and not only in the West) to eclipse the novel
as the premier method of telling stories. This isn't only a
matter of technology but also of talent. A generation ago
an ambitious and reasonably gifted man like my son would
have gone into publishing rather than television; and what
is true of an ancillary worker like Marlen is also true of the
primary producers. If a Tolstoy were born today, would he
choose to become a writer? Of course not. Tolstoy aimed
for cultural pre-eminence, and any writer seeking that
today would turn to film. Actually, Tolstoy's ego was so
gargantuan that even the global fame he got from writing
wasn't enough for him, which is why in later life he had
to establish himself as a latter-day Buddha. His thinking
had an enormous effect on Gandhi, you know, and even
now there are Tolstoyan communities dotted about,
naturally enough including here in California (where I am
participating in the first of a series of events that will take
place around the world this year to celebrate the centenary
of *War and Peace*).

To be clear, I'm not saying that the novel as a form will
disappear, any more than poetry has disappeared since it
lost its status as the most prestigious branch of literature.
But its importance will fade. Everything fades, I suppose,
certainly everything made by human hands, and yet I can't
help feeling bereft to witness this diminution of the novel,
which for all its inadequacies has trained us to see the world

from others' points of view. To borrow a Stalinist idiom, the novel is a machine, a noisy, violent thing whose product, oddly enough, is often human understanding, perhaps even a kind of love. I daresay some might look at the last one hundred years and say, 'Nonsense, what love?', but if so they are naive because the terrifying truth is that *it could have been worse*. Hitler could have won. Kennedy and Khrushchev could have blown us all to hell. And who knows what other horrors we've evaded because someone, or someone's teacher, or someone's mother or grandfather, once put down a novel and thought, 'My God, I am like that stranger' or 'That stranger is like me' or even 'That stranger is utterly different from me, and yet how understandable his hopes and longings are.' And in the future, as fewer and fewer people use these engines of empathy, what horrors will we not avoid?

Lately I've had warmer feelings towards Natasha Rostova. Your letter, you see, has sent me back to my work on Tolstoy's plotting, and in turn back to *War and Peace*, in which I believe I have discovered something new about Natasha's near elopement with the cad Kuragin – new to me, that is – making me think of her with more compassion. Natasha's archetypal element would of course be Air, since by nature she is sunny, spirited, light-hearted and, let's face it, at times more than a little empty-headed. Certainly I've always regarded her failure to wait a single year for Prince Andrei as a demonstration of her fundamental lack of seriousness, but in this recent reading I've noticed the severity of the lust she endures quite literally at Kuragin's hands. Her primary emotion during this episode is not passion but dread. The poor thing is twenty, has believed herself to be on the verge of marriage, and now here she is starved not so much of love but of sex. To put it another way, the airiness of her nature has been driven out, not by Fire – the fire of passion, the fire of love – but by Earth, the dank and pungent urges of fecundity, so closely related to the death imperative. And I like her much better this way, as a corporeal being, human not sprite. What's strange is that I didn't notice these urges in Natasha when I was a younger woman and had them myself. Was I unusually innocent, or was our generation not equipped to notice such things? Is it possible, after all, that I have discovered something new, something hidden to previous readers – possibly even to the author himself? Picture me at my desk now, smiling at my own presumption. I daresay there have been plenty of readers less innocent than I who noticed Natasha's lust, and that rogue Tolstoy certainly knew what he was up to – his grubby fingerprints are all over the affair.

Thank you for the information about the various fates of your wartime comrades. How pleasing that Hermann Molineux managed to evade the Red Army and all it threw at him and instead ate and drank himself to death; if ever there was a man unfit to die tragically it was he. Mind you, news of the tragic death of your Major Weidemann left me cold, I'm afraid – no doubt because this was the effect he had on me in life. As for Zöllner, I had to struggle to remember him. He was absurdly handsome, was he not,

in that slightly witless, Nordic way? (Blond eyebrows –
what on earth is the point of them?) To hear he had been
killed did affect me, however, if in a rather abstract way:
the beauty of youth cut down, et cetera, et cetera. Do I
sound unfeeling? If so, I apologise. It's just that so *many*
people died. Believe me, if I could I'd mourn them all, and
in the unlikely event that I see out the twentieth century
I will pause as the sun sets on its final day and think of its
myriad dead.

Now to the matter of you wanting to meet me in
person, which like your evaluation of my second novel
makes me wonder about your judgement, Paul, if not your
sanity. No, you simpleton, they wouldn't let us have dinner
alone together; your fantasy press conference would be
followed by some vulgar banquet attended by KGB agents
and minor Party dignitaries. And what could you hope to
gain from that? A further meeting? And then what? Are you
trying to woo me, Paul Bauer? If so, the odds are stacked
against you, I'm afraid – not only due to the geopolitics
but also because I've turned into a cantankerous old cow.
Haven't I conveyed that to you yet? Or are your motives
carnal, is that it? If you're thinking along those lines you
should know I'm now a wreck of a woman, and that if I
tried to ravish you as I did at Yasnaya Polyana you would
likely panic and defenestrate yourself.

Anyway, weren't you the one who pointed out in
your first letter that an unrequited love is better than a
consummated one? Wise words. You should heed them.
I should heed them, since now I have to admit that

against my better judgement I have asked Marlen what he thinks about you and I meeting with the approval of the authorities, since the idea has the potential to harm Marlen at least as much as me. Naturally he was surprised to learn of your existence, and because I censored my account of our time at Yasnaya Polyana he was also puzzled why I would consider endangering my career for some German I met in the war, even one who went on to become the Mayor of Nuremberg. Probably he was suspicious, his Oedipal ganglia all aquiver, as yours evidently were when your mother's former admirer came sniffing about; but like you, Marlen managed to remain calm and rational about it. His verdict? That we should wait for a thaw in East–West relations, when the Party is more likely to take kindly to the idea. Such a thaw is inevitable, he believes, as both sides will soon be forced to cut spending on weapons and on space – us because we didn't have any money to begin with, America because of the sums it is haemorrhaging in Vietnam.

So neither a yes nor a no but a maybe. Will that do for now? In the meantime you have my letters, and I yours. I am looking forward to the next of them very much.

Love,
Katerina

★　★　★

28 Jonah Strasse
Nuremberg
18 November 1969

Dear Katerina,
Looking over our letters (I've kept copies of mine) I see
that we tend to begin by discussing the past before moving
on to the present, leaving any talk of the future to the
end. Perhaps as the lesser writer I ought to hold with
this convention, but I have a question for you that's too
pressing to wait.
   Katerina, will you marry me?
   Since your last letter arrived I've had plenty of time to
contemplate this proposal, and plenty of time to imagine
your reaction. But just hear me out. The fact is that from
shortly after our first meeting I have loved you; and for all
that's happened to us since, and despite sometimes trying
to subdue it, I can't dislodge the feeling. Yes, yes, I know
I've claimed that unresolved love is the most precious of
all (a mistake which of course you pounced upon), but
allow me to formally say that I have changed my mind. The
platonic ideal, I've come to realise, is all very well, but our
letters have given me a renewed appetite for *involvement*,
not only with the joys of life but also with its untidiness,
imperfections, ambiguities and woes. Be assured I'm not
harbouring any strong illusions about you! When, for
instance, you say you've become a cantankerous old cow,
I say, nonsense: you were always cantankerous. At Yasnaya
Polyana you were a cantankerous cow in her prime, and

I expect you were cantankerous in your youth as well. And I love you for this. I *trust* you for it – trust that whatever you say is likely to be sound, forged and tempered in the furnace of your scepticism.

And what would you get from marrying me, I hear you ask? In my repeated attempts to draft this letter it is this paragraph that has given me the most trouble. Modesty is part of the problem, but the greater difficulty is reality. What am I, after all? A 68-year-old man who hasn't shared his life with a woman for over thirty years; a man, moreover, who is moderately ill with emphysema and therefore presumably unlikely to live into his eighties. What I keep asking myself, then, is: what's in it for Katerina? My answers strike even me as unconvincing, but mostly they relate to *soothing* you, and by soothing, helping to concentrate your strength – for instance, on that special book which I believe (despite your claims to the contrary) is still inside you awaiting release.

Even in its final form that damn paragraph dissatisfies me. What it leaves out is the texture of life, the trivial episodes I imagine sharing with you. I want to brew your morning coffee, for instance. (Do you drink coffee? Is coffee readily available in Moscow? Is that question insulting? I must admit there's a lot about your life I don't know.) I want to pass your reading glasses to you, or share your indignation at what's in the newspaper – *Süddeutsche Zeitung* or *Izvestia*, you decide (more of that below). I want to discover you asleep over a book and switch off your bedside light. I want to hear you snore! And I long to appear alongside you in public, though my motivations here are suspect, I'm afraid, as I've managed to track down a photograph of you at the conference at Stanford. When I saw it the words that came to mind were *elegant* and *chic* – those boots, that woollen skirt, that silver bob! It's time we stopped disparaging our appearances, wouldn't you say, since the truth is I'm more or less presentable and you remain as striking as ever.

The purpose of this letter is to ask rather than convince you to marry me, and I'm acutely aware that probably you've already made up your mind. If so, and if you've decided to say no, the rest of this letter can only deepen my embarrassment, but on the off chance that you're undecided, or – my God – persuaded, let me address some of the practicalities, as I'm all too aware I won't be able to write to you again for months. As I understand it, Soviet citizens are in principle allowed to marry foreigners, though naturally the bureaucratic obstacles are formidable. Of course if you wanted you could come and live in West Germany. I am assuming, though, that for reasons of work and family you would wish to stay in Moscow, and accordingly I want to assure you I am willing to move there to be with you and if necessary to take up Soviet citizenship. Yes, I know what I'm saying, know as well as any Westerner could what inconveniences and discomforts I would face as a result, not to mention the probable surveillance. Do bear in mind, though, that I have experienced far worse, and also that my Russian is quite serviceable – certainly good enough for daily conversation or for reading *Izvestia*. (Speaking of which, would I have to refrain from scoffing at *Izvestia* over breakfast, which is to say, would the KGB bug your apartment? Is your apartment even big enough for two? Could I live nearby, or are such Bohemian practices frowned upon? Naturally there would be a great many problems to sort out, but if I have learned one thing from the three years of my retirement it is that a problem-free life is insipid.)

Of course I can't hope to foresee every difficulty that might arise, or anticipate all your possible objections, but sex and death seem issues worth addressing, the first because you mentioned it yourself (how seriously I wasn't able to tell) and the second because in your position I would be worried about becoming my nurse one day. Regarding sex I am, to put it mildly, out of practice; not entirely without desire but sufficiently uninterested to do without it if that were to be your preference. My health, too, as far as I can judge, is in a state of equilibrium (or should that be 'precariousness'?); that is, neither excellent nor terrible. As I said, I don't expect to live to a great age, a fact that explains the directness of this letter, and for that matter makes it probable that one day you would get to resume your single life. As for the risk of you becoming my nurse, I should point out that I have no interest in a drawn-out death, which if necessary I could avoid by pharmacological means.

Is this the gloomiest marriage proposal ever made? In presenting it this way I have aimed above all for realism, partly because I sense you will prefer it this way but mostly because our ability to speak candidly to one another is (in my experience, at least) unique, and at the core of why I love you.

One more thing: I can cope with refusal. Confessing my full feelings for you has caused me some anxiety but also much relief; if you choose to say no I will undoubtedly feel sadness, but this will be easier to bear than the regret of not having spoken at all. Katerina, how I hope that you might be reckless again, that your last great folly will be me, but if not please know I will be all right, that I will adjust and go on loving you as I have done for years, grateful for the blessing of having known you at all.

Your loving Paul

TWENTY-FOUR

In snow that dithered on a changeable wind Metz officiated at Hirsch's funeral service, which took place beside a hole hacked from frozen ground in the Tolstoy burial glade. It was a brief affair. Metz kept to the official script and Bauer delivered a short eulogy, aware of how keen the mourners were to get indoors.

After dinner he normally liked to read, but that evening he made his way instead to the officers' common room, intending to somehow mark Hirsch's passing with his comrades. Drexel and Zöllner were there. Also Molineux and, facing him across a chessboard, Demchak. 'Nobody minds Yuri being here?' Molineux asked. 'I've been meaning for ages to tackle him at chess.'

Bauer did mind, but while everyone knew Hirsch had shot himself, only Bauer and Metz and Demchak knew why, and because Metz had ordered him to stay quiet about it Bauer was obliged to bite his tongue. It wasn't as if Demchak was solely responsible; Bauer himself felt culpable – for not doing enough, for not setting aside his exasperation with Hirsch long enough to see how badly he was faring. As always Molineux had schnapps to hand, and for once Bauer accepted a little. 'To Volker,' he said, raising his mug. To hell with Demchak; he would just have to live with what he'd done.

'To Volker,' agreed Zöllner, who unusually for him was also nursing a mug. 'I keep asking myself if I should've noticed something wrong, if I could've done more for him.'

Bauer said. 'Of all of us, you were the kindest towards him.'

'I don't know about that. Sharing a room with him … well, I just can't work it out. Why did he *do* it? It makes no sense, not that I can see.'

'Jesus Christ,' Molineux said, 'my rook! I go forward and this wunderkind attacks my flanks. And we've hardly started! It's like sorcery. *Is* sorcery,' he said, and took another slug of schnapps.

'What about Hirsch?' Bauer asked him. 'Anything to add?'

'What do you want me to say? Boo-hoo, I'm sad? I was sad about Dieter, I was sad about Sepp, I was sad about poor Pflieger. Now I've run out of sad. Men die in war. Half of us here will probably cop it and have no say in the timing, whereas Hirsch went and did it to himself. I have no sympathy for the man.'

'Christ Almighty, can't you at least pretend?'

'Bah. Why should I? You yourself said he was a danger in theatre.'

'He was twenty-four years old.'

'My point exactly. What sort of ingrate spits on the sacred gift of life?'

There was a long pause. Eventually Zöllner said, 'It is true that suicide is a sin.'

'And we have no idea of motive?' Drexel asked. 'Why do it in front of Metz, for instance?'

'For the attention,' Molineux said.

'Look who's talking,' muttered Bauer.

Molineux wheeled around and almost fell off his chair, looking angry and far drunker than Bauer had realised, though by the time he'd regained his balance there was a broad grin on his face. 'It's true,' he said, and guffawed. 'I've been upstaged! The poor sod's upstaged me, and that I can't forgive.'

Drexel said, 'It's my belief that the reason one man cracks and another doesn't is to be found not in the life but in the chemistry of the brain. Fix that and a man can endure anything. If Hirsch had come to me I might have saved him.'

'Check,' Demchak said to Molineux.

'What do you mean "check"? Don't lie to me, Yuri, I'm carrying a pistol.' Demchak tapped the threatening piece, a knight, making Molineux reverse into his chin. '*Outrageous*. Black magic. Fabian, hand me that bottle.'

'In fact,' Drexel said, handing him the schnapps, 'there's no reason in principle why a treatment of that kind couldn't be administered to the entire population, say in the water supply. Human misery could be abolished at a stroke.'

'Good God,' Molineux said, 'do that and there'll be no need for alcohol. Plus you'll drive a stake right through literature. Philosophy too. Painting. Sculpture.'

'What about misery that's justified?' Zöllner asked. 'Someone who's dying, say, or – I don't know – who's lost a limb or an eye.'

'Same principle: it's all in the brain,' Drexel said, for emphasis tapping his own squarish head. 'The day will come

367

when pharmacological interventions will make even the worst misfortunes endurable.'

'Not my queen!' Molinuex cried. 'Damn and blast it, Yuri. Dominate the centre, that's my strategy, and dictate terms, but you're cutting me to shreds. But I persevere, my word, I do. Down with your bishop – *voilà*. Death or glory, that's my motto.'

Behind them the door opened and Metz strode in, bringing all of them to attention. Metz spotted Demchak and frowned. 'What's an enlisted man doing here?'

'I invited him over to play chess, sir,' Molineux said.

'This is an *officers'* common room.'

'Yes, but Private Demchak is a phenomenon, sir, you've no idea. I'm a fairly good player – not a grandmaster, understand, but not bad, and —'

'You,' Metz said, pointing a finger at Demchak, 'back to barracks. Now.'

'Yes, sir,' Demchak said, then turned about and left the room.

Metz swung around. 'From now on I want no fraternisation between officers and enlisted men. None! Do I make myself clear?'

'But, sir —'

'Captain, quiet! You're under the drink. Shamefully so. Where did you get it from, anyway?'

'It's a gift from my wife, sir.'

'Well, she ought to know better.'

'I'll make sure she doesn't do it again.'

'Anyway, I haven't come here to discuss Captain Molineux's domestic arrangements,' Metz said, addressing the whole room. 'I'm here to announce news of true historical importance.

Of *immense* historical importance. I am here to report that, not three hours ago, Reich Foreign Minister Joachim von Ribbentrop summoned to our Foreign Office the American *chargé d'affaires*, and there informed him that in reaction to a series of intolerable breaches of neutrality, the Greater German Reich has declared war on the United States of America.'

For several seconds there was absolute silence in the room, then Molineux flopped back onto his chair. 'Come again?'

★ ★ ★

Though shunted for hours between and through two sets of lungs, the air in the room stayed cold, and Bauer, having woken in the early hours, couldn't get back to sleep. Quietly then, so as not to wake Molineux, he lit the lamp beside his bed and opened *War and Peace*, manoeuvring to keep his arms beneath the blankets. He had arrived at the novel's climax, the capture and burning of Moscow, though 'culmination' was perhaps a better term for the protracted havoc being wrought in the characters' lives.

About three-quarters of an hour later Molineux turned in his bed and groaned. He sat up, 'Sweet mother of God. This is intolerable.'

Bauer apologised. 'I didn't think you'd wake. I'll turn off the lamp.'

'It's not you, it's the cold,' Molineux said. 'Shine the lamp in my eyes for all I care: it might warm up my eyeballs. I swear, even my farts are cold. If I went to the lavatory now I'd shit ice cubes. We could chill champagne.'

'I'll try to remember to ask Ritter for a bottle.'

'And here was I thinking it's the *idea* of death that's chilling. Ye gods, killed by a metaphor. Bauer, will you promise me something?'

'Probably not.'

'If I don't make it through the night, will you tell my wife …' Here he paused, searching for a suitable phrase.

'That you loved her?'

'That she should've sent more socks.'

When they went down for breakfast the mess room was freezing, the windowpanes crazed with frost. Apart from Pabst and a helper only Drexel was there, his already stocky frame bulked out by his greatcoat and a blanket, but then shortly afterwards Zöllner arrived, looking if anything even cheerier than normal. Seeing Molineux, he said, 'Sir, have you checked the temperature yet?'

'Do I look as if I give a damn?' Molineux said. Zöllner chuckled at this, making Molineux bristle. 'You think that's funny?'

'It's just that Frau Kälter was right.'

'How so?'

'It's too cold for you.'

In Bauer's chest a riot at the sound of her name.

'My God,' said Molineux, brightening, 'the woman's a seer.'

'Or a witch,' Drexel said.

'That's true,' Molineux said, 'a witch.'

'Don't say that to Metz,' Bauer said. 'He'll have her burned at the stake.'

'God, I hope so,' Molineux said. 'In fact, if this cold keeps up I'll shove her off the fire and clamber onto it myself.'

'Aren't Frau Kälter and Metz best friends now?' Drexel asked.

'Metz likes to *think* they're friends,' Molineux said. 'In reality it's me she's closest to.'

'Has anyone seen her in the last couple of days?' Bauer asked, attempting nonchalance. Four days had passed since he and Katerina had made love, only two since he had seen her off in Tikhon Vassilyvich's sleigh, but it felt to Bauer as if both events had happened long ago.

'Not me,' Zöllner said.

'Nor me,' added Drexel. 'Or any of her staff, come to that.'

'You see,' Molineux said. 'That's how you know it's cold: even the Russians are scared to go outside.'

'I don't blame them.' They all turned and saw Weidemann in the doorway, his epaulettes flecked with snow. 'It's minus forty-one degrees out there.'

★ ★ ★

Later that morning a convoy of casualties arrived, most of them frostbite cases. To Bauer one of the medics described conditions at the front. Men's gloves freezing to rifles. Firing mechanisms icing up. Lorries and tanks immobilised. Corpses stripped naked for their clothes. For every man killed in combat, up to eight succumbing to the cold.

Around midday came news by radio that the Soviets had launched a big counter-offensive around Moscow, and although nobody knew the details it was clear the Wehrmacht was falling back. Among corpsmen and patients alike an unsettled mood

371

spread over the wards, a mix of sombreness and irritability, but also defiant insouciance, bombast and madcap humour. Some, such as Molineux, cycled through all of these states. At 16:00 hours Metz issued an order forbidding discussion of events at the front, though this had little effect. Molineux told Bauer that Knoll had told him that the pilot of a patient-evacuation plane, a ski-equipped Fieseler Storch, had told one of Knoll's men that Army Group Centre was retreating in such disorder from the outskirts of Moscow that it was leaving behind weapons, vehicles and even the fallen, not just the dead but also in some cases the wounded.

'For Christ's sake,' Bauer said, 'don't mention that last detail to anyone around here.'

Molineux looked hurt. 'Of course not. What do you take me for?'

'An incurable gossip.'

'You make it sound terminal,' Molineux said.

'If only. What bothers me is the risk of contagion.'

He thought repeatedly of Katerina and burned to know how she was, what was in her mind, in her heart. He longed to discuss with her what was happening at the front and what it meant for them, even knowing that for Katerina a German withdrawal would be a cause for celebration.

At dinner – pressed meat pimped with pickles, complained Molineux – Metz was tetchy and monosyllabic, and because the subject on everyone's minds was forbidden, the conversation around the table was scant.

After dinner the mood was less subdued. 'Cards!' Molineux cried, wielding a pair of bottles like alpenstocks as he strode along the upstairs corridor, trailing Zöllner and Drexel and Ehrlich. 'Come, come,' he said, hooking Bauer by the arm.

'More gambling?' Bauer asked.

'Life's a gamble. Gambling is life.'

'I'd prefer to read.'

'Don't be such a philistine, Bauer. *Carpe noctem!* as the Romans used to say. We won't see its like again, you know.'

Bauer disentangled his arm. 'We saw it last night, and the night before that.' Molineux handed over one of his bottles to Ehrlich and, with a stub of chalk, emblazoned the word *Kasino* on the common room door.

'Katerina Dmitrievna won't like that,' Bauer said.

'Fuck her,' Molineux said, then stopped and turned around. 'If you haven't already, that is.'

'Hermann, don't be ridiculous.'

'Well, that's a crying shame,' Molineux said, and pushed open the door, 'a copper-bottomed tragedy. If ever there were two people who were meant to be together, it's you and Katerina Dmitrievna. And Ehrlich, don't even *think* of invoking the race laws – the bond between the captain and Katerina Dmitrievna transcends race, it transcends law.'

'You've been drinking already, I take it?' Bauer said.

'Not at all. Sober and sincere is what I am. And don't tell me you haven't thought about romancing Katerina.'

'No point.' Bauer said. 'Pretty soon we'll be gone.'

'Listen to yourself!' Molineux said. 'I mean it. *Listen*. Get out your stethoscope, put it over your heart and tell me you're not in love with her.' He uncorked one of the bottles. 'Sure you won't join us for a drink?'

'Thank you, but no. Not tonight.'

Molineux shrugged. 'Then damn you to hell.'

'Likewise,' Bauer said, and made his way to their room, took off his boots and lay down in bed with *War and Peace*, hoping to distract himself from thoughts of Katerina. Pierre Bezukhov had just narrowly avoided being executed by the French and, as their prisoner, was now being forced to retreat with them from Moscow through the snow. The similarity between these events and what was unfolding three hundred kilometres to the north wasn't lost on Bauer, and though magical explanations held no attraction for him – how surprising was it, really, that an army should be forced to retreat? – the historical parallels sharpened his sense that there was something unrepeatable about his reading of the book, something orchestrated, or at least made possible, by Katerina. God, how he missed her. If she didn't appear by the following morning he would slip out somehow, he decided, on foot if necessary, and search for her in the village.

Around midnight Molineux made his way drunkenly to bed and instantly fell asleep, and though Bauer knew he should try to do the same he kept reading, borne along, as he often was towards the end of a novel, by the gathering momentum of the plot. A long time later he heard a faraway bombardment commence, looked at his watch and cursed. Four o'clock. He had to get to sleep straight away, but before that he needed to urinate. He got out of bed and padded down the corridor towards the lavatory, only to be brought up short by the sight through a window of flashes on the horizon, not to the north around Tula but to the east, a sector that until now had been quiet. The barrage sounded broad, its accent unmistakably foreign.

TWENTY-FIVE

'Our forces around Tula are straightening the front,' Metz said.

'Meaning falling back?' Weidemann asked.

'Meaning concentrating their strength,' Metz replied. He looked unwell, Bauer thought, like a man who hadn't slept for days. 'B Company is redeploying along with the rest.' He tapped a divisional dispatch edgewise on his desk, asked if there were any further questions, and without waiting for a response began to stand.

'Sir, I have a question,' Zöllner said.

Metz paused halfway between sitting and standing, then slumped back onto his chair. 'What?'

'Is there any question of us having to retreat? I only ask because the men will want to know. The patients too. They can hear the artillery.'

'Of course there isn't.'

'So what do we tell them?'

'What I've just told you: that the front is being straightened prior to our next attack.'

'Jesus, Joseph and Mary,' said Molineux under his breath.

'You have something to say, Captain? If so, kindly have the courtesy to share it with the rest of us.'

'It's nothing, sir. I was just wondering if, when they've finished straightening the front, someone could get to work on my back — my bed is killing me.'

Metz stood up, tucked the dispatch beneath one arm and rounded his desk. 'I know how that feels,' he said, and left the room.

They all looked at one another. Metz had never left a briefing without announcing it was over. 'Was that sympathy or a joke?' Molineux asked, turning at random to Drexel, who was gulping saliva and could only respond with a shrug.

'I think we should go,' Weidemann said.

They all rose, put on their caps and scarves and coats and made their way in a loose column to the hospital. The weather was relatively kind: overcast, minus fourteen degrees. If it stayed that way until evening, Bauer thought, there would be no better time to go looking for Katerina. From the north and east came the kettle drumming of Soviet guns. Tchaikovsky, *1812*.

At the hospital they learned that more casualties were due at any time. Worse, a report had come in that one of C Company's ambulances had been ambushed by partisans en route to Yasnaya Polyana from Chern, leaving both the driver and his offsider dead, the supplies they had been carrying ransacked and the vehicle destroyed. From a coldly rational perspective, the loss of an ambulance was at least as bad as the deaths; certainly Metz saw it this way, and his already brittle mood worsened. When the casualties arrived he was thus ill prepared for wounds

376

of a type none of them had ever seen before: in one case an ugly but non life-threatening slash across the face, in the other a laceration that had penetrated the abdomen through the back.

'*Sabres?*' Metz shrieked when a corpsman told him the cause. The rapidly filling reception room quietened, with only the grossly wounded not focused on Metz. If here a surgeon was a god, this was a troubling deity: pale, shivering, neurasthenic, wild. 'Sabres?' he repeated, his voice only slightly less hysterical.

'Cossack attack,' the corpsman replied. 'I didn't see it myself, sir, but someone who was there told me about it. They were mounted troops. On horseback,' he added helpfully when Metz kept staring at him. 'Rode out of nowhere, laid about them, killed several, wounded these two lads and disappeared.'

Metz was still staring – not quite at the corpsman but past him. Lightly Bauer touched his hand and calmly asked his opinion about the order of triage. Metz shivered a little but answered nonetheless, not as firmly as usual but at least cogently, setting the room in motion again. For the next several hours he and Metz operated as normal, though due to Hirsch's death Bauer had got his way at last and had an enlisted man performing anaesthesia – Yuri Demchak, in fact, whose technical judgement and presence of mind Bauer continued to trust, even as his dislike for him had risen. Metz barely seemed to notice the Hiwi's changed role, much less care about it.

Early in the afternoon the second dispatch of the day arrived from divisional headquarters. Metz read it, asked Ehrlich to fetch Weidemann and announced the suspension of surgery. Ten minutes later he dismissed the operating assistants, leaving only officers present. 'We're going,' he said.

There was a pause while they took this in. The first to speak was Weidemann. 'How long do we have?'

'Until tomorrow. It can't be done, of course.'

Weidemann looked thoughtful. 'I agree it will be hard.'

'Impossible,' Metz said.

'But we have to try.'

In a trance Bauer heard them debate the viability of moving an entire field hospital and two hundred patients in less than twenty-four hours. He had waited too long, Bauer thought, would never see her again.

'The X-ray machine?' Metz was saying. 'The generator? The laundry? Beds? Impossible! The kitchens? The incinerator?'

'We've moved before,' Weidemann said. 'We all know what to do.'

'In two *days*, not twelve hours.'

'Sixteen hours. Maybe more. If equipment has to be left behind, so be it.'

'A fantasy,' Metz said.

A fantasy, a fever, Bauer thought – was this what Yasnaya Polyana was to be for him? Including time spent at the front he had been here barely six weeks.

Weidemann was growing impatient. 'Sir, if we don't start right away we certainly won't make it.'

'Very well,' Metz said, 'but we'll have to prioritise. I will draw up a plan.' He walked over to his operating notes and, incredibly, tore out a page. Taking up a pencil he started to write.

'While the lieutenant colonel is working on that,' Weidemann said, 'let's make a start. Zöllner, liaise with Bauer about getting the most serious cases to Chern. The rest of you, you know what to do.'

'I'm finished,' Metz called. They all stared at him. He got up and came over, waving his torn-out page. 'Here,' he said, passing it to Weidemann, who put on his glasses and examined the list, which Bauer could see consisted of only five or six lines.

'All right,' Weidemann said guardedly. 'In a worst case, yes.' He tapped the topmost line. 'But "Leo Tolstoy"? What do you mean by that?'

'Exhuming him. That comes before everything else.'

'I'm not sure …' Weidemann said.

'Don't worry, Major, I'll handle it myself. I'll need a work party of course. Four men ought to do. Of course the ground is frozen, so it might take a while.'

'What I meant to say is I don't know why you'd want to exhume him.'

'Major, I'm disappointed in you. Isn't it obvious?'

'Tell me.'

'I'm taking him hostage.'

Molineux tittered. 'That'll show him.'

'Exactly,' Metz said. 'Thank you, Hermann. We thought we could beat the Soviets in months. We were wrong. This is destined to be a drawn-out conflict, and we have to think strategically. By seizing Tolstoy we retain the initiative, our spiritual ascendency over the enemy.'

'I see,' Weidemann said.

'Hermann understands. And Drexel here will also back me up – in fact he deserves some of the credit for the idea. Weeks ago it was he who raised the idea of establishing, in Berlin, a Museum of Superseded Cultures – an ethnographic cabinet of curiosities, if you like. What finer item to put in it than the bones of Leo Tolstoy?'

Nodding gravely, Weidemann said. 'I see your point, sir. Brilliant. Quite brilliant. You too, Drexel – well done.' In response Drexel nodded and gulped.

Metz looked pleased. 'Splendid. Then I'll go straight away.'

'Forgive me, sir,' Weidemann said, 'but why not leave the digging to others? It's just a labouring job. You're needed elsewhere.'

'Such as?'

'In Chern. Or even Oryol. We don't know yet how far we'll have to pull back, but wherever it is your leadership will be crucial.'

'I don't know,' Metz said. 'I feel my place is here.'

'You've always led from the front, sir, and we're going to Chern.'

'I don't know. I'd prefer to escort Tolstoy's remains in person.'

'There are only two more hours of daylight,' Weidemann said, 'and we've seen what can happen on that road in the dark. Take your limousine and you'll get there by dusk. Leave the digging to us.'

Metz pondered this then said, 'I suppose that's logical enough.'

Bauer stared at him, amazed he couldn't recognise such a blatant untruth. No one wanted to meet his neighbour's eye.

'I'll order Ehrlich to fetch your kit from the main house,' Weidemann said. 'Drexel?'

'Yes, sir?'

'Medical crates. I'm sure the lieutenant colonel won't object to transporting a few. Put Ritter onto it.'

'Right away, sir.'

Swiftly they dispersed, each to his allotted task, though Bauer's attention was bifurcated: half of it on triage, half on ways of getting a message to Katerina. He had little time to work on either problem, however, before being called away with the other officers, this time to the hospital vestibule. There Metz was waiting with his helmet on, evidently ready to go, Egon Ehrlich at his side. Parked directly outside was the ZIS.

'Farewell, gentlemen, and good luck,' Metz said when all of them had assembled. 'Remember, on the road keep your helmets on and ensure that the men do the same.' To Weidemann, he said, 'The Tolstoy matter? It's in hand?'

Weidemann nodded and said yes – a soothing, minimal reply.

'Good. Then I'll take my leave. Courage, gentlemen, we'll be back. *Sieg heil.*' He turned around, went though the doors and out to the car, closely trailed by Ehrlich. It struck Bauer that by rights Katerina should have been there to see Metz off with some stinging remark, but that was not to be.

'So much for our gallant commander,' Molineux said.

Weidemann turned to him. 'If the lieutenant colonel isn't at his finest right now it's not for want of courage, Captain. Or a lack of heart, for that matter. Rather the reverse, I'd say.'

'Amen,' said Zöllner earnestly.

Weidemann dismissed them and the group broke up.

'Happy now?' Bauer asked Drexel as they walked away, a childish question but one he couldn't resist.

'You mean, do I regret giving the lieutenant colonel some pharmacological help? No, I don't.'

'What, what, what?' Molineux asked, stopping and waiting for them.

'I'll tell you later,' Bauer said.

'Any great endeavour involves a quotient of risk,' Drexel said.

'There's a quotient of risk in surgery, but we don't do it needlessly or for self-glorification.'

'You're critical, I know that,' Drexel said. 'But actually I don't concede I'm responsible for the lieutenant colonel's state of mind. Not at all. In fact, without me his condition might be a lot worse.'

'Without you?' Molineux asked.

Ignoring him Bauer said, 'But you'll stop now, yes?'

'Now that *would* be irresponsible,' Drexel said. 'Not wise at all. No, for the lieutenant colonel's sake you'd better hope I make it alive to Chern.'

★ ★ ★

For the rest of the afternoon, the evening and throughout the night Bauer worked furiously, as they all did, to get ready to leave, spurred on by the noise of artillery and, towards morning, distant bursts of machine-gun fire. Two-way radio reports gave a confused impression of the fighting, though it was clear enough that the Soviets were advancing, and fast.

382

Searching for Katerina was out of the question, and the only way to keep anguish at bay was to launch himself at each task in turn.

The evacuation was to start at dawn, and in the hospital's forecourt ambulances and lorries were assembling, though too few to move the patients in a single convoy. As if by osmosis, the men lined up on stretchers in the entrance hall and corridors were reaching the same conclusion, making an already anxious mood fearful. As Zöllner had pointed out, they could all hear the guns. In an emptying ward a patient in traction seized Bauer by the sleeve and begged not to be left behind. 'Swear,' he said, 'swear on all you hold sacred.' What Bauer thought of was Katerina. He assured the man he had nothing to fear.

Around 05:30 hours the generator was disconnected, forcing work to go on by the light of lamps and electric torches. Half an hour later Weidemann called for the officers and NCOs to assemble in what had been the reception room. In the strangely emptied-out space their torch beams duelled, an annoyance that Corporal Knoll ended by placing a single lamp on the floor, though this made the faces of the gathered men ghoulish.

'Well, well,' Molineux said as Drexel entered the room, 'if it isn't Fabian, our pharmaceutical Svengali. I've a bone to pick with you.' Drexel gave him the look of a man too tired to care. 'What I want to know,' Molineux went on, 'is why you haven't tried your dark arts on me. I'm as perfectible as the next man.'

Before Drexel could respond, Weidemann brought the gathering to order. Metz had reached Chern safely, he reported, but was continuing on to Oryol. In the meantime, Major-General Oeding had appointed him, Weidemann, battalion acting commander. A round of subdued congratulations followed.

Exit Metz, Bauer thought. It was hard to imagine the battalion without him, but there was no time to reflect on their eighteen months of service together. Patients and personnel, announced Weidemann, would withdraw to Chern in two stages, using the same vehicles twice. Most of the patients, half the men and any essential equipment would leave in the first convoy. The second would evacuate whoever and whatever else remained. He asked if there were questions.

Drexel raised a hand. 'Will the convoy have time to come back, sir? Even heading south there'll be delays. Coming back against the traffic … well, that won't be easy.'

Bauer looked at Weidemann, who ran the hospital in a rule-bound if unobtrusive way and had never commanded the battalion, let alone in a crisis.

'It's a journey of eighty-five kilometres,' Weidemann said. 'Of the three legs, only one will be against the flow of traffic. But you're right: the Soviets could get here before our vehicles return, and for that reason I propose to remain until the evacuation is complete.'

There was a pause then Zöllner said, 'Sir, let me stay instead. You'll be needed in Chern.'

'A gallant suggestion, Lieutenant, but I can't leave our most junior officer in charge.'

'Then leave me in charge, sir,' Bauer said. 'Lieutenant Zöllner can act as my second in command.' Weidemann looked searchingly at him, and Bauer went on, 'As our ranking officer, you shouldn't risk capture.'

'I could say the same of our only fit surgeon.'

'No one doubts your courage, sir, but I'm twenty years younger than you – if necessary, I could lead an evacuation on foot.'

Weidemann hesitated for a moment. 'Well, I can't fault your logic. Very well then, Bauer, I accept your offer. I'll lead the first convoy, you the second.'

Bauer wondered if he had just got himself killed for love – if Katerina failed to appear, the mere idea of love – because however sound his arguments for volunteering to stay, he couldn't hide from himself his true motives. How selfish these were became clear moments later when Weidemann specified who else was to stay: Bauer's men, Zöllner's likewise, as well as Ritter and his security detail. Dying for love might be romantic; getting others killed for it was not.

The briefing ended and the loading of patients began. It was still dark outside and very cold, and those not engaged as stretcher bearers gathered in the entrance hall. Low conversation. The clatter on floorboards of webbing, weapons and kit.

'I can't say I envy you,' Molineux said when Bauer went over to wish him luck. 'In fact, I think you're insane.'

Truth seemed to be called for. 'I'm hoping to see Katerina Dmitrievna.'

Molineux clapped his hands together. 'I knew it!'

'Keep your voice down, for Christ's sake.'

'Is it … *love*?'

'On my side, yes,' Bauer said.

'On hers, not?'

'I don't know,' he admitted.

'But you've tupped her?'

Bauer squinted at him, and Molineux held up his palms. 'All right, all right. I take that as a no, or you wouldn't be risking your life to stay.'

'I haven't seen her for three and a half days.'

'Do you know where she's living?'

'Not exactly.'

'Daybreak's coming. How about I stop at the village and make some enquiries? Find out where she lives. Let her know you're still here.'

'Thanks but no,' he replied. 'It would look bad for her.'

'Then you'll just have to leave it to fate,' Molineux said.

'In other words, forget about it.'

'You know, sometimes I think Metz is right about you: you're a lugubrious soul. But buck up. Tonight in Chern we'll drown our sorrows together. By tomorrow morning Katerina Dmitrievna will be just a hazy memory.'

'Thank you, Hermann, I'm touched by your concern.'

The last patient carried out was the man who'd been in traction. Bauer met his eye and nodded as he passed. Then a sergeant came in and barked the order to leave, and the men who were due to depart hefted their kits and made for the door. Weidemann came over, shook Bauer by the hand, wished him luck and promised to stay in radio contact. Bauer thanked him. Weidemann went outside and the convoy got underway. Despite himself, Bauer felt a pang of abandonment.

Spread about the ill-lit hall were the fifty-three patients who remained in his care, including twenty-two who could walk (two of whom had been blinded) and thirty-one stretcher cases. To care for them he had forty-four corpsmen and NCOs, plus one fellow officer in Zöllner.

From the direction of the storeroom, Ritter arrived with his security detail and several of the other men under his command, all of them heavily armed. Bauer asked him where they were going, and Ritter replied they were taking up defensive positions. Bauer wondered if the sergeant major was high enough on Drexel's dope to believe that he could hold off the entire Soviet advance, and carefully he ordered him to send most of his men to flag down passing vehicles, including wagons, which had space on board for the wounded. 'Commandeer them if you have to. Tell anyone who's fit they'll have to walk.'

Ritter looked displeased by this but saluted and took his men away. When they were gone Bauer had Zöllner draw up an order of evacuation, and in case not enough vehicles were forthcoming he sent several men to gather all the available sleds. This left him free to concentrate on the patients, since some were at risk of deteriorating, and all were in pain.

In the hour after daybreak Ritter's men brought in a lorry and two wagons, permitting the evacuation of eighteen of the thirty-one stretcher cases, nine of the walking wounded and six nursing attendants. There was still no clear information about how close the Soviets were, but at 09:33 hours the radio operator reported that the main convoy had arrived at Chern and that several of the lorries were already heading back to

Yasnaya Polyana. The journey to Chern had taken almost two hours, and Bauer calculated that, travelling contrariwise, the vehicles wouldn't reach Yasnaya Polyana much before midday, and possibly later.

Half an hour later a second commandeered lorry arrived, its driver a visibly shaken Waldo Pabst. There had been an incident, Pabst explained, a confrontation between Ritter and a sergeant who had been driving the lorry, who had refused to get out. Words had been exchanged, then bullets, and the sergeant had been killed.

'Ritter *shot* him?' Bauer asked.

Pabst nodded, looking miserable. He plucked at a dark patch on the seat of his trousers. 'His blood.'

There had been passengers in the lorry, Pabst went on, men of the Grossdeutschland division who, though armed, had been in no condition to retaliate for the killing of one of their own. The Soviets were less than five kilometres away, they'd said, and immediately made off on foot. 'We should go as well, sir, don't you think?'

'Yes, and it's being organised. But first I want you to go back to the road and tell Ritter to report to me immediately.'

'I can't, sir. He left.'

'Left where?'

'I didn't see. He sort of slipped away.'

Good riddance, Bauer wanted to say. If Ritter showed himself again there would be consequences, but now there were more pressing concerns. Quickly he summoned Zöllner and the remaining NCOs and ordered them to get ready to leave straight away. The lorry that Ritter had killed for was being loaded with patients, leaving only five stretcher cases to be moved by sled, plus a total of thirteen walking wounded and a platoon's worth of corpsmen to help with stretchers or to carry and sled equipment and food. Personal belongings would have to be left behind. With a pang Bauer thought of his copy of *War and Peace*, which he had come within seventy pages of completing.

Then in walked Katerina.

My God, he thought, my God, the need to keep his composure in front of patients and corpsmen at odds with a berserk inner joy. Alongside her was one of the sentries Ritter had posted outside; Bauer dismissed him and turned back to Katerina. She looked solemn, though at the edges of her eyes other emotions were at play.

'Katerina,' he said.

'Paul.'

She had on the same heavy skirt and quilted jacket she'd had on the night they'd first met, as well as a humble headscarf he'd never seen her wearing before. Her cheeks were reddened with cold.

He said, 'I didn't think I'd see you.'

'Or me you. We noticed your lorries going by.'

'A first convoy. They're coming back.'

She said, 'We're here to stand guard, my staff and I.'

'Then tell them to take care. There could be stragglers.'

'Isn't that what you are?'

'Regular troops, I mean. They'll be tired. Maybe scared. Likely dangerous.'

'I'm going now to the main house,' she said, and held his gaze.

'Then I'll come with you.'

'You have time?'

'Just,' he replied, unsure if this was true.

'Good,' she said simply, then in Russian went on, 'Just don't get yourself captured. My countrymen won't be kind.'

He fetched his helmet, buckled it to his belt and rejoined Katerina in the entrance hall. From there they passed though the vestibule for what Bauer guessed was for him the final time. On the doorstep he crossed paths with Zöllner. 'I have to go to the main house,' he told him. 'While I'm gone, take command. Get the men and the patients together and leave right away.'

Zöllner looked alarmed. 'What about you?'

'I'll catch up.'

Zöllner made to speak again but Bauer cut him off, promised he'd be quick and strode outside. On the frozen forecourt were gathered about fifty corpsmen and patients, the stretcher cases heaped with blankets and secured to sleds. A short distance away stood Katerina's staff; Bauer spotted Daria Grigorievna and also her sister. Tikhon Vassilyvich, too. However triumphant they were feeling they had the sense to disguise it. Katerina went over to them and spoke in a Russian too quick for Bauer to follow, then the group broke in pairs and made off in different directions. To Bauer's dismay Katerina was joined by Tikhon Vassilyvich. 'He insisted,' Katerina said curtly in German. 'For all I know he guesses there's something afoot. But he means well. He's worried for me. God knows, he's probably right to be.'

The three of them set out for the main house. The air was icy and still, the noise of combat unnervingly clear, a crackle of small-arms punctuated by machine-gun fire.

'Are you sure about this?' Katerina asked him in German.

'No. But I couldn't stand leaving without seeing you.'

'I'm glad,' she said, 'but hurry.'

'What about Tikhon?' Bauer asked. Already the old man was lagging.

'He knows where we're going.'

In fact the house was already coming into view. 'I still love you,' he said. Just the essentials now.

'And I still know it,' Katerina answered, her voice so warm it hardly mattered she hadn't used the same phrase, which in any case was unworthy of a writer.

'After the war I'll come back for you,' he said. 'If I survive it.'

'Try to,' she said. 'Find me. Or I'll come looking for you.' She asked for his address, and he gave it to her. No, she didn't need it written down.

The front door of the main house was flung open, and when they crossed the threshold he dashed his helmet away from where it was hanging on his thigh and they kissed – their mouths hot and sealed against the cold. A universe he could dwell in forever.

It was Katerina who broke away first. 'You had to do something? Get something?'

'*War and Peace*,' he said. 'You were right: I couldn't finish it in time.'

'You're here for *that*?'

'I'm here for you,' he said.

Taking two steps at a time they went up to what had been his room. His and Molineux's gear was untouched since the previous morning. Bauer shoved *War and Peace* into his kit bag and, with Katerina looking on, added some of Molineux's gear to his own. He was already wearing most of his clothes. From downstairs came the sound of Tikhon coming inside. Bauer shouldered the bag and took a step towards Katerina, meaning only to embrace her but instead falling into one more kiss. As in dreams of flying he tried to make the moment last, to stay aloft in an instant he knew must die, just as downstairs a machine-pistol opened fire, jolting them apart. Katerina's eyes were wide with fright, the first time he'd ever seen her afraid. 'Stay here,' he ordered, and went for the door.

'No, stop!'

'It's one of ours,' he said grimly. An MP 40. Involuntarily he had come to learn the language of guns.

In the entrance hall he found Norbert Ritter setting fire to the stairs, behind him Tikhon Vassilyvich's bullet-bitten body.

'Put it out,' Bauer said from the uppermost step, drawing his pistol and waving it, first at Ritter then the fire, which so far was smoky and small.

'Captain,' Ritter said, 'I didn't know you were here. Or her, for that matter,' he added, nodding at Katerina. Bauer descended the stairs, keeping his pistol trained on Ritter, whose own weapon was on a strap and dangling at his hip. He seemed neither surprised nor aggrieved to have a pistol pointed at him.

At the bottom of the stairs Bauer held out one hand. 'Your weapon.'

'The old fucker tried to kill me,' Ritter said, jerking his head at the corpse. 'What was I expected to do?'

'Intercept lorries,' Bauer said.

'And I did that!'

Katerina hurried down the stairs, darted to the fire and kicked it apart before smothering the embers with her jacket. She dropped to one knee next to Tikhon Vassilyvich's body.

'You told me to stop lorries,' Ritter said. 'I stopped them.'

'Hand me the gun,' Bauer said. 'And, yes, that's an order.'

'More of a threat, sir, isn't it?'

'Do it,' Bauer said, and jabbed his pistol at him.

'All right, all right,' Ritter said, unslinging his weapon.

'Slowly,' Bauer warned. 'By its strap.' With exaggerated slowness Ritter passed him the machine pistol. Bauer gripped it and was about to strap it across his shoulder when Katerina held out her hand.

'To me. The gun. I want the gun.'

Ritter turned to Bauer. 'What the fuck's going on here? Since when has that slut been giving the orders?'

'Shut up,' Bauer said, 'or I'll do as she asks. Get out of here and rejoin the men. We're leaving. I'll deal with you later.'

Ritter gave both of them a look of contempt, turned about and, stepping over Tikhon Vassilyvich's body, stalked out through the vestibule.

Bauer turned back to face Katerina. 'I'm sorry,' he said. 'So sorry.'

'Tell that to Tikhon's wife, to his grandchildren.'

'Sorry about all of it.'

'As you have been from the start. For goodness' sake, just *leave*. Scram! Get out of here or else.'

'Or else, what? Be captured? Isn't that what I deserve?'

'Or else I'll cry, you dolt.'

He smiled crookedly at her. 'Now I'll *have* to stay.'

'Don't be an idiot – you'd be killed or die in a camp. So go. Just go,' she said, and seized him by both arms.

Strangely it was her grip that freed him, her touch the closing of a circuit of good sense. Of course he had to leave – it was his only chance of seeing her again.

'All right,' he said, and in response she let him go. For several seconds they gazed into one another's eyes, then he turned and strode into the vestibule, passed through the doorway, crossed the forecourt and, still holding Ritter's gun, began jogging down the main drive, kit bag thwacking at his back and helmet bouncing on his thigh. A minute later the estate's front entrance came into view, a Napoleonic tableau of grey sky, bare trees and snowy ground, trudging over it the hunched, coated figures of medical corpsmen, some with kitbags and weapons, others hauling the wounded on sleds. He was panting, exhaling great vaporous clouds, but with the column now in sight he slowed to a walk and slung the machine pistol over his chest. When he reached Yasnaya Polyana's ornamental gates he unhooked his helmet from his belt and shoved it onto his head, then he looked back and saw Katerina at other end of the drive, standing alone in the snow. Neither of them waved. It was not his head that needed protection, he understood, but his heart.

TWENTY-SIX

The heat is violent, the sun sharp, when on an afternoon in August 1975 Katerina steps out of her son's Zhiguli into the carpark opposite the Tolstoy estate. From the passenger footwell she retrieves her handbag and a broad-brimmed hat, shoulders the bag – which is probably too heavy, she thinks – puts on her hat and sets out with Marlen across a tarmac oozing and blistering in the heat. In Moscow that morning she had refused her son's offer to call ahead and arrange to park within the grounds; she was not so infirm that she required special treatment, she told him, and besides she meant to spend the day wallowing in nostalgia, a state of mind best achieved in anonymity.

Neither of which had been lies, she reflects, as they skirt a crowd of Young Pioneers emerging from a bus and making their way across the road to the gates. No, she hasn't lied to Marlen, only neglected to mention (and what business is it of his, after all?) that as well as sentiment she has a practical objective today.

At the ticket booth the queue is long, and for a moment she questions the wisdom of her plan. The heat really is ferocious and she feels a little dizzy, but before she can even mention this to Marlen he guides her by the elbow to a shaded bench by the wall. With his usual foresight he has brought a vacuum flask of water, and after a couple of mouthfuls she begins to feel better. Good God, the Russian summer! Small wonder, she thinks, that this land of extremes should have produced a people of such intemperate passions.

Once inside the gates Marlen asks her where she would like to go. The Volkonsky House, she says. 'We'll save the main house till last.'

'You won't be too tired to enjoy it?'

'What are you? My parent? Have I become your child? I'm perfectly fine, my dear.'

'Yes, now I've given you some water,' he says, smiling down at her exactly like a father to a child.

'Don't be impertinent,' she says. 'I just needed a rest, that's all.'

They set off along the main drive, its avenue of beech a tunnel of shade.

'How does it feel to be back home?' Marlen asks.

'A little strange,' she says, 'but, you know, I've never considered this as home. To me Yasnaya Polyana is, was and always will be Lev Nikolaevich's.'

'Well, as far as I'm concerned it's yours,' Marlen says. 'Your tenancy postdates his.'

'How very biased of you. I'm touched. Though of course Yasnaya Polyana belongs to the Soviet people.'

'Of course,' he replies, echoing her mock-pious tone. Could it be that in his late middle age her son is finally loosening up a little?

They stroll on to the driveway that leads to the Volkonsky House, and as if to confirm how little personal claim she has on

396

the place, a group of the Young Pioneers troops past, chatting and laughing and, liberated from their bus, practically bouncing with adolescent vigour. In no time at all they are well ahead, their red neckerchiefs and white shirts or blouses seeming to flare in the sunlit gaps between the trees.

At the front of the Volkonsky House she and Marlen join the end of a short queue. How much of her life has she spent in queues? Less than the amount spent sleeping and eating, or reading and writing, she presumes. Less than she has dedicated to teaching, too, though measured across her whole lifetime it might be a close-run thing.

'Excuse me,' says one of the Young Pioneers, a tallish girl about sixteen years old who has stepped out of the queue and is now standing before her, hands respectfully clasped. 'Are you by any chance the writer Katerina Trubetzkaya?'

'Well, yes, I am,' Katerina says.

'I knew it!'

'And what's your name?'

'Oh, I'm nobody,' says the girl, 'but I've read your book, and I just want to say —'

'Come, come, you must have a name.'

'That's true,' says the girl. 'It's Natalya. Natalya Kirillovna Rudova.'

'Pleased to meet you, Natalya Kirillovna,' Katerina says. She shakes Natalya's hand, introduces Marlen then asks the girl where she is from. Saratov, Natalya replies; she and her fellow Pioneers are on an excursion.

'All the way from Saratov?'

'We left yesterday morning.'

'Good grief. And this is your first visit to Yasnaya Polyana?'

'That's right.'

'Well, enjoy yourself. It's a special place.'

'I'm very excited,' the girl says, 'I've read all his books. Well, not all, exactly. But the main ones: *Anna Karenina, War and Peace, The Death of Ivan Ilyich, Resurrection*.'

'Wonderful,' Katerina says, meaning it, always moved and somehow surprised to meet a young person who loves literature as she did at that age, though logically she knows that culture is precisely this: a baton passed from one generation to the next.

'The fact is, though, *your* novel means more to me than any of his,' Natalya Kirillovna says.

'My goodness, what an exorbitant compliment,' Katerina replies, resisting the mischievous urge to ask which of her novels she means. 'Take care that Tolstoy doesn't hear you,' she adds, gazing about them.

The girl smiles. 'You think he might?'

'Of course. You can't feel his presence?'

'Not yet. Maybe later at his grave.'

'Maybe there, yes,' Katerina says.

'My mother is performing for you,' Marlen says to the girl. 'In reality she's an arch rationalist – aren't you, Mama?'

'I don't believe I'm an arch anything. Not any more. I just watch. I listen.'

The girl brightens. 'That's what I love about *A Life on Earth* – one of many things, I mean – the lovely details, the textures, the scents. The impression of being there, of seeing through the heroine's eyes, of being in her skin.'

'That's most kind of you,' Katerina says, hoping by a hint of formality to cut this panegyric short.

'What else do you like about it?' Marlen asks.

Katerina swats his arm. 'Don't be wicked. He's trying to embarrass me,' she explains.

'But it's not embarrassing,' the girl says. 'It really is a brilliant book. I love its integrity – the sense you get from that accumulation of detail that you are reading a true account of a woman's life, and by extension a true account of her society, what it was like to be alive in a particular place, at a particular time.'

'You make it sound as if I'm already dead,' Katerina says, laughing to show she hasn't taken offence. 'But you know, I will be if we don't get out of this sun.'

The girl looks around. 'Oh, sorry.' The queue has dissipated; all her friends have gone ahead. 'Shall we go inside?'

'Let's do that,' Katerina replies.

The grand entrance hall seems almost dark after the brightness outside, but rapidly her eyes adjust. The air is blessedly cooler. Natalya Kirillovna hesitates, apparently not ready yet to rejoin her friends. 'Oh, I wish I had my copy of *A Life on Earth* with me now. I could ask you to sign it. How you've lived, Katerina Dmitrievna!'

'Thank you, but you mustn't go assuming that everything in *A Life on Earth* is true. Tatyana isn't me. Details of her life that might seem autobiographical are made up. And vice-versa. Writers are slippery creatures. In fact, just about the slipperiest of them of all was Tolstoy,' she says, hoping to redirect the conversation.

The girl smiles. 'I'd love to know which parts of *A Life on Earth* are true.' Her eyes light up. 'May I make a request?'

'Go ahead.'

'Might I interview you? I have a sort of column, you see, in my school magazine. It's not much, but ...'

'I'd be delighted.'

'You would?' exclaims the girl, rising on her toes and doing a little half-pirouette, before remembering herself and growing serious again. 'Would now be a convenient time?'

'Perhaps not *now*,' Katerina replies, and the girl's face immediately falls. 'I'm a bit hot, you see. A little tired.'

'You told me you were fine,' Marlen says good-naturedly.

Katerina stares sternly at him then turns to Natalya Kirillovna in mock exasperation. 'You see what I have to put up with? The insolence of youth.'

The girl peers doubtfully at Marlen, at his weathered face and grey, thinning hair.

'Here, let me give you my address,' Katerina says. 'You can mail me your questions. That way I'll be able to sound wiser than I really am.' From her handbag she unearths a pencil and a scrap of paper, scribbles her address and hands it to the girl, who thanks her profusely. They shake hands and say goodbye. The girl thanks her again then hurries off to find her friends.

'That was kind of you,' Marlen says.

'Not in the least. I'm just terrified of snubbing the next Tolstoy. Or worse, the country's next great literary critic. It pays to remember that some of the young will be our betters, or at the very least our peers.'

'Maybe. But it was also kind.'

They take a turn about the Volkonsky House, never her favourite of the estate's buildings, the scale of it more reminiscent of an institution than a home.

'You know,' says Marlen, 'you're too diffident about your work, about yourself. Here you are, author of one the most highly regarded novels of the decade, and yet you're worried about being outstripped by a schoolgirl.'

'Not worried, just realistic.'

'That you'll be surpassed by Natalya Kirillovna?'

'If not by her then by someone else. *A Life on Earth* isn't a particularly important book, you know.' He makes an impatient gesture and she adds, 'I'm not saying it's *bad*, my dear, only that it isn't important, because on a fundamental level it isn't true.'

'True to what? To your life? As you said to that girl, all writers are slippery.'

'There's a difference between a slippery writer and a slippery book. I'm not talking about literal truth here, the evocation of facts; I'm talking about a deeper veracity, a fidelity to what life is really like.'

'But you heard what that critic of the future said: your book has integrity!'

'What would she know?' Katerina says. 'She's barely lived. The book leaves so much out, you've no idea. The pith of life.'

'Like what?' Marlen says.

'Politics, for a start.'

'But that's not true. "A powerful condemnation of Stalinism" – that's what *Izvestia* said.'

'But not of politics as it is today.'

'Because if you'd done that you wouldn't have been published at all.'

'Precisely. My pact with the Devil.'

'The Devil here being the State?' Marlen asks in a lower voice, affecting casualness but instead conveying unease.

'If you like, though even in the West I daresay authors make similar bargains: worldly success in return for sanitising the truth.'

'My God,' Marlen says, throwing up his hands. 'Who needs critics when the author herself does the hatchet job? You'll end up convincing others, and what if you're wrong? A male writer wouldn't disparage his own work the way you do. This obsessive self-criticism – is it because you're a woman? Have you thought about that?'

She goes quiet, wondering if her son could be right about this. Certainly the truths she's talking about, the ones left out of *A Life on Earth*, are for the most part a woman's truths – abortions, her lusts, her low opinion of men as a class, her high regard for a foreign invader. 'I don't know,' she admits at last. 'I'll have to think about it.' By now they have returned to the entrance hall. 'Where next?' she asks. 'Shall we go to the grave?'

Marlen grins. 'If we must.'

They set out for the grave, toiling again through the heat. Now that she has invited him into her mind, Paul Bauer is busy making himself at home there. This is the same route, she realises, that the two of them followed all those years ago when she took him to Tolstoy's grave, though the weather conditions, she recalls, could not have been more different:

402

snow and ice on that day, the trees leafless and thrashing; today those same trees nodding heavily in green.

Tolstoy's burial glade, if not exactly thronged, is certainly busy with tourists. Predictably enough, one of them is Natalya Kirillovna, now reunited with some of her fellow Pioneers. Natalya smiles at her but doesn't press for more contact, allowing Katerina to detach herself from her son and go over to the burial mound. As usual she is struck by the steepness of its sides, an unnaturalness at odds with the covering of grass – a note of discord that she supposes is entirely in keeping with the perverse, indispensable man who lies below.

Of the Wehrmacht graves that thirty-four years ago laid siege to the mound there is not a single trace. Who was right, she wonders, her or Paul? Has Tolstoy triumphed or is his memory indelibly stained? Presumably for the likes of Natalya and her friends the incident of the graves, if they learn of it at all, will be no more than that: an incident, a footnote of minor interest and no lasting importance.

She meets Marlen's eye. 'The main house?'

'I'm at your command.'

As they leave she nods in the direction of the great man's grave – like some peasant departing a church, she thinks, a little cross with herself. Then they set off down the hill, and again she is reminded of her long-ago walk here with Paul Bauer, his nose blanched by the cold, his touching willingness to obey her commands. How much she misses him – no longer acutely but abidingly, his death a sadness that accompanies her everywhere these days, even in her moments of joy. Which are frequent enough, she supposes; she can't complain. But Paul, Paul.

Not that her grief is unalloyed. During their week together five years ago in Moscow, much of it spent under the gaze of their minders, she said yes – yes, she would marry him, whatever the bureaucratic obstacles might be. They would tear red tape into confetti, she told him, even as privately she worried she was making a mistake. And when two months later she learned of his death – by stroke, a week shy of his seventieth birthday – she was conscious of a small, shameful flicker of relief, if only at not having to force such a tender love through the grinder of marriage. Oh, but she grieved! Still does grieve, daily. She misses him. His visit to Moscow, though an open one, cost her her job, which in turn allowed her to write *A Life on Earth*. He had revived her writing, then, though not as he'd expected. Sad to say, even his dying helped.

She and Marlen arrive at the bottom of the slope and take the path towards the main house, where she is looking forward to getting out of the sun. Old age, she has read somewhere, should be treated as a gift, an opportunity for reflection and repose, a view that in her opinion skates too glibly over the physical trials, and which in any case strikes her as logically flawed, since as she gets older she tends to like herself less, making self-reflection unconducive to repose.

They reach the main house, go in by the front entrance and almost immediately encounter Irina Petrovna at the bottom of the stairs. A noisy exchange of greetings follows, in which Irina reproaches them for not having told her they were coming. Katerina and Marlen then congratulate her on her promotion, and although Irina hears them out with a dignity befitting her new station, Katerina can tell she is pleased. 'Of course, without you proving that a woman could do the job, I would never have got it,' she says.

'Nonsense, I was just a stopgap. And that was years ago. You're the real thing.'

'Well, that remains to be seen.'

'You certainly look the part,' Marlen tells her, nodding admiringly at her outfit, a dark blue cotton jacket with broad lapels, plus, rather daringly, matching slacks and a pair of equally elegant sandals.

'Please excuse my son,' Katerina says to Irina, 'he's traditional, you see, and doesn't comprehend that a woman might want to be praised for her abilities rather than her clothes.'

'Oh, that's all right,' Irina says. 'At my age I'll take any compliment I can get.'

The fact is, thinks Katerina, Irina *does* look the part: a poised, self-confident middle-aged woman. As an adolescent, she recalls, Marlen was rather sweet on Irina, though unluckily for him she hardly noticed, being two years his senior.

'Anyway, it's lucky we've met,' Katerina says, 'or I would have had to come looking for you.' From her handbag she removes a large book with a green cloth cover. 'From the library.'

'What is it?' Irina asks.

'*Krieg und Frieden* – *War and Peace*, the first German edition.'

'You had *that* in there?' Marlen asks. 'I could have carried it for you.'

'I suppose I felt it was my responsibility,' she replies – a foundation of truth for the story she's devised. 'During the occupation I hid it – their lieutenant colonel wanted it destroyed. Then it got swept up with my own books and, what with one thing or another, I accidentally moved with it to Moscow. I only noticed it on my shelves the other day.'

'Well, thank you,' Irina says. 'That's quite a lengthy loan.'

'I know. I'm embarrassed. And then there's the matter of these,' she says, then opens the book and shows Irina the annotations. 'They're Tolstoy's.'

'Intriguing,' Irina says. 'Anything interesting? My German isn't what it ought to be.'

'Nothing seismic,' Katerina replies. 'Just authorial grumbling. If you like I could write a summary for the catalogue.'

'Do that,' Irina says. 'Will you need to keep the book?'

'I've taken notes, so no.'

'Shall we put it back on the shelves?'

In the library Katerina locates the German collection and then identifies the book's correct position: between Schopenhauer's *Die Welt als Wille und Vorstellung* and Tolstoy's own *Der Tod des Iwan Iljitsch*. As she weighs the volume in her hands for a final time her sense of communion with Paul is so powerful that she has to shield her face from Marlen and Irina. Of course they both know about Paul, who in Moscow told much of his story to the press; but neither they nor anyone else (not even Simon Fleet) know the entire truth. Silence enshrines what was special between her and Paul Bauer, their sweet collusion, and Katerina likes it that way. As she slides the book home she feels a sense of spatial satisfaction, as if finishing a puzzle.

Before she and Marlen return to the carpark, Irina insists on detouring to her office in the Volkonsky House, where a secretary brings them glasses and a jug of chilled, mint-infused water. For half an hour they talk about Irina's plans for the estate, then about the success of *A Life on Earth*, until Katerina is forced to admit to feeling tired. Marlen offers to fetch the car, but she tells him no, a short walk will do her good. She rises from her seat, and from one of her knees comes a crack like a rifle shot. Marlen and Irina look at her in alarm and she laughs. 'It's nothing. Incipient rigor mortis, that's all. Nature's way of telling me to slow down.'

The sun is lower and the air decisively cooler when she and Marlen leave the house and set out towards the gates, a change having arrived in the short time they were inside. The shady laneway makes her shiver. 'This country!' she exclaims. 'You know, I think I'm actually cold.'

'Do you have anything warm to put on?' Marlen asks.

'Only a scarf. I brought it for the sun.'

'If I were you I'd put it on.'

'Once we've walked a little I'll be all right,' she says. 'The thing is to keep moving.'

'Then you'd better go on ahead. My shoelace,' he explains, and squats down to tie it up. 'I'll catch you up soon enough.'

'You're sure?'

'I'm certain.'

'All right then,' she says and, still shivering a little, walks on alone down the tunnel of shade.

ACKNOWLEDGEMENTS

The Tolstoy Estate is the love child of War and Peace and a much less well-known book: Journey Among Warriors (1943) by Ève Curie – an account of Curie's journey through several theatres of the Second World War, including a visit to Yasnaya Polyana in January 1942, just three weeks after its liberation from the Germans. In particular, I was inspired by Curie's discovery that during the six-week occupation, many of those present – Soviets and Germans alike – had been acutely conscious of the site's cultural, ideological and even metaphysical significance as the former home of the author of Russia's great national epic of resistance to a foreign invader.

For the surgical scenes in the book I relied on The German Army Medical Corps in World War II (1999), edited by Alex Buchner, and two identically titled memoirs by British military surgeons: Surgeon at War (1955) by J.C. Watts and Surgeon at War (1979) by Stanley Aylett. In Deadly Combat (2000) by Gottlob Herbert Bidermann provided brutal accounts not only of warfare on the eastern front but also of Bidermann's captivity in the Soviet Union after the war. For insights into

Soviet cultural and political life in the interwar years I drew on Nadezhda Mandelstam's memoir *Hope Against Hope* (1970). Katerina's early writing career is modelled on that of the revolutionary author Alexandra Kollontai, as described by Gregory Carleton in *Sexual Revolution in Bolshevik Russia* (2004). The excerpt from *War and Peace* on page 78 is from the translation by Richard Pevear and Larissa Volokhonsky (2007). The sculpture that Katerina describes on page 286 is Giuseppe Sanmartino's 'Cristo Velato' (1753), which can be found in the Chapel of Sansevero in Naples. For the sake of clarity, I have somewhat simplified the unit structure and system of ranks used by the German army late in 1941.

During my research for the book, several people generously donated their expertise, including Dr Tess Abbott (emergency caesarean section), Dr Paul Goggin (anaesthesia), Anne and August Tischlinger (German), Anna Kouznetsova (Russian), Bernardo Foth (Franconian tongue-twisters), and historian Jack Radley (Russian mud). James Greentree catapulted Norbert Ritter from a place of obscurity in my first novel to a bona fide character in this one.

I am also indebted to my test readers: Brad Clingin, Brigid Foard, Max Kelly, Lucy Marshall and my mother, Rosemary Thomas. Susan Gray has been a dear friend and shrewd editorial advisor throughout. Julia Stiles and Madeleine James were wise editors at the end, and Scott Forbes a sharp-eyed proofreader. HarperCollins' commissioning editor Catherine Milne took an early punt on the book and cheered it all the way to the finishing line.

Thanks is also due to the Australia Council for the Arts for their funding of *The Tolstoy Estate* in the form of an Arts Development grant. The financial support was useful; the vote of confidence precious.

Lastly, I'd like to thank Jackie Bowe, who supported me financially and emotionally throughout the writing of this book and whose faith in it never flagged. In fair weather and foul, she was and indeed remains an irreplaceable friend.